SHARPSHOOTER

a novel

by David L. Hoof

Quiller Press

An Imprint of Panther Press

Denver, Colorado

Printed in the United States of America

Respectfully Dedicated To

Senator Ben Nighthorse Campbell

Brave, patriot, veteran,

warrior, legislator, chosen bipartisan representative

of the American people

and member of the

Tribal Council of the Northern Cheyenne People

Three quarters of the royalties and revenues from this novel
or any derivative form, foreign or domestic,
will be distributed to the
Tribal Council of the Northern Cheyenne
for any use or cause that they may choose.

2002

HIM

Against a Montana sky too blue for words, a solitary buzzard rises and turns. Under its keen eyes, Jeb Holloway appears with the indifference of God to a heretic's prayer. The white Suburban's suspension cries as it crashes down the dusty, rutted draw. Just ahead, gilded pale by autumn sun, the narrow sibilant river dimples with light. Entry splashes gurgle into wheel wells, trailing a distant frothy wake visible along a long octagonal rifle barrel. An ancient slotted Creedmore sight tracks Jeb's head, till the vehicle halts on a pebbled shore. The air goes silent. Nearly a thousand yards from the rifle's steady muzzle, Jeb Holloway cocks his wrist to check a black-faced Rolex watch. The second his wrist comes down, the buffalo gun's lethal round web-holes the driver's window. Across tinted glass inside the cab, fractal blood perfects death's art. In the sniper's hide, a smudge of black powder hangs on the air as the killshot's report echoes off the naked river bank, drawing the buzzard in for a closer look.

ONE DEAD

Leaving the murder scene, Deputy Redfawn Kravitz splashes across Big Muddy in his vintage Ford pickup, finds blacktop at Fergus County 73 and climbs a shallow grade edged in pin grass. Like most natives, Kravitz has only his thoughts for company, and those thoughts echo history with the slug that killed Jeb Holloway. At .50 caliber with long reach, it could have come from a Sharps buffalo rifle. To the buffalo, it was the most lethal killing machine in the west, brought straight to their grazing grounds on the great plains by trains disgorging dudes to test their marksmanship. A fast breech loader, it let a good shooter get off up to ten shots a minute using a cartridge as big as a man's finger. Unevolved to meet the new danger, the bison toppled while their kind watched and kept chewing. The most famous buffalo hunter claimed five thousand kills. Together the hunters left so many critters to rot that it seemed that soon they would exist only on the nickle, a flip away from Thomas Jefferson, who started it all with the Louisiana Purchase in 1803 by dispatching Lewis and Clark to map the unexplored west two years later.

The buffalo gun's favorite target took the western American Indian tribes as a collateral casualty. They used those animals for food, clothing, harvested by bows and arrows. Perceived as savages obstructing Manifest Destiny, every Indian resisting resettlement earned the right to be hunted down and killed like the buffalo, sometimes by the same gun. Born in 1874 from predecessors used by Union sharpshooters during the Civil War, Christian Sharps' civilian issue was offered to tourist hunters and snapped up by the thousands. In the hands of an expert, it could down any target within a thousand yards, about the distance separating the most recent victim from the nearest concealed roost at Poker's Bluff.

To Kravitz, Jeb Holloway's murder is as ironic as it is clueless. The gun that Holloway's great grandfather provided General George Armstrong Custer was only two years old when the United States Army met the coalition Indian forces under the Lakota chief Sitting Bull in 1876. Custer's victory that day was intended to put him in the White House. His slaughter by redskins outraged whites and incited the reprisals of General Phil Sheridan, who vowed to America that the only good Indian was a dead Indian. One hundred and twenty-five years later, even a half-breed like Kravitz doesn't stand half a chance of doing much better. The best he can do is hold down the half-time job of a pro-forma Deputy Sheriff in a half-dying town headed the way of the buffalo. With Jeb Holloway dead, now nothing stands between the future and that fate.

The battered Ford pick-up pitches through a rut, returning Kravitz's mind to the road.

Three hundred feet ahead the blinking tail lights of a blood red Lambourghini Diablo cross a faded center line, then veer back. Kravitz ignites his dash bubble. A quarter mile off, from a transom on two posts, swings the Circle A, a hollow plus an A: for Holloway. To the left stands a small gatehouse. Resisting a temptation to gun it, the driver brakes to a halt on the shoulder.

The deputy pulls over and gets out. Raindrops drumroll on the Diablo's hot-wax finish. Kravitz saunters up and raps the driver's window. The car's door pops open along hinges in the roof, gaping like a shark's mouth. Out of a haze of Opium and brandy comes her words, "What's your problem, Tonto?"

Kravitz answers by removing her keys from the ignition. "Mrs. Holloway, it would be a singular honor if you would allow me to drive you home." Far off, a bush of lightning blossoms, then withers to darkness. He offers her his hand, pushing the door down and shut after she steps out. Assisted by Kravitz's strong arm, she makes a wobbly dash and leaps into his pick-up. When they reach the gatehouse, a heavy Chicano shoulders into a slanting rain. Kravitz gives him the keys. "Maybe you should bring Mrs. Holloway's car up ¿Comprendes?"

Reaching the spacious ranch house, Kravitz pulls under a broad gently sloping roof. Throwing her door open, she slides off the bench seat and lurches for the house. Framed by an open door, backlight reveals a svelte figure in a tight miniskirt and a white silk top dangling from spaghetti straps. Kravitz follows her through rainwater coursing off the sloped roof. As he steps inside the house, Mona Holloway yells, "María! We have a guest!" Inside, the maid takes his dripping hat and damp trail duster, then hangs them on a peg behind the door.

The deputy takes a few seconds to absorb the place.

Cedar and redwood, mixed with oak. The colors are warm, light, glowing, but the effect is raw power tamed by brute force, right up to the rough-hewn roofing timbers. Broad windows, an expansive floor admitting a dining area beside the kitchen, a balcony that lets down a gleaming-funneled fireplace between fieldstone walls. On the wall to the right hangs a portrait of Jeb Holloway, topped by a white JB with a Montana crease, draped with a doeskin coat, his long legs well heeled in Lucchese black gators.

Opposite Jeb, far across the room hangs a haunting portrait of a pregnant woman, her eyes mirrors of mystery. As Kravitz studies it, Mona explains, "It's by Gustav Klimt, an Austrian Successionist. Very popular around the time the Vienna Academy rejected Adolf Hitler. Hitler hated Klimt. He and Jeb have that in common. Neither liked Klimt very much. What's your take, Deputy?"

"Kind of grabs hold of you and won't let go," he says.

"My sentiments exactly." She crosses slender, elegant arms and smiles.

His eyes fix on a long yellowing bruise slanting from her right shoulder down across her chest, then continue scanning the layout.

"There's more," she says, shaking diamonds of mist from her dark hair. "We're just starting to redecorate. Your friend Bear has his place going up at Pine Ridge, so he comes by to get ideas. That's the thing about new structures. There's plenty of opportunity..."

She slips a Cohiba from an inlaid humidor, offers one.

He defers with a raised palm.

She lights up with a sculpted Georg Jensen of Mercury bearing a torch.

"Mrs. Holloway..."

"Please: Call me Mona. It's an election year." She sashays past, turning just enough to brush a breast on his shoulder, then sinks into a sprawling Chesterfield sofa. Releasing her next thought in smoke, she asks, "Would you like to take your clothes off?"

His head snaps her way.

"You're all wet, deputy. María can wash, dry and iron everything in about half an hour. Wash takes eight minutes; drying another ten. Machines by Krupp, the folks that made guns for the Nazis." She draws and blows smoke, marbling the air. "If you're shy you could borrow one of Jeb's robes."

"That's a true fact. Because he won't be needing it tonight."

She brings her eyes up, lets out a thin line of smoke, then sheds the ash into a silver-rimmed Wedgwood tray. "Goddamn I told him he couldn't go around crowing family virtues and then go down nightly on Doris's bastard daughter, Moonglow..."

"Moonlight," he corrects.

"Whatever." She gets up, draws a lungful of Cuban smoke and blows new questions into it. "What's happened? God, don't tell me. She said 'no,' and he, what?, beat the shit out of her?" Mona's trembling hand covers her own bruise, the ash from the tip of the smoldering Cohiba shedding like snow onto the naked floorboards. "God, you're here to tell me he..." Her pupils widen. "...killed her?"

"No, Mona. I don't know anything about – "

"You're not very bright, are you, Kravitz?"

"I hope that's not true, Mona. Because I'm responsible for finding out who killed your husband," he says, dealing her the cards straight, fanned out and face up.

Mona Holloway lets out a sharp, smokey bark, a sound that rises to a mocking laugh then dies in full understanding. "When?" she asks.

"Forensic team is working that out."

"Where?" Softer, but still low in pitch.

"About a thousand yards east of Poker Bluff."

"How?"

"He was shot."

"Who did it?"

"I don't know."

She looks up, rubs each forearm with the opposite hand. "Who found him?"

"B.S. Walsh," he says.

Trembling hands cover her face.

"Mrs. Holloway..." He stares at the silk spaghetti strap, follows its line down the bruised flesh, stops at the nipples crowning darkly through the fabric. "...I'll be wanting to know where you were once we determine when your husband was killed."

"I didn't kill him," she whispers with the harsh scrabble of a chain smoker.

"That's exactly what B.S. Walsh said when he called it in."

Her eyes are dry and clear, her mind seems running off the hangover with a rush of thoughts, each tracked with a flutter of lashes as it passes. She abandons her cigar in the Wedgwood ashtray. "Would you like to sit down, deputy?"

He does, pauses, then probes the awkward silence, "How, exactly, would you describe the relationship between you and your husband, Mrs. Holloway?"

She looks up, laughs, then heaves toward retching. He pulls her up and rushes her into the kitchen. María dodges just in time to avoid Mona's vomit. The new widow heaves once, twice, then fights between breathing and puking, emerging red-faced.

"Plain water's best just now," the detective tells María. The maid goes to the SubZero, retrieves a liter of Evian and fills a faceted crystal goblet. The lady of the house gasps hard, then sips. Once upright again, she braces both hands on the gleaming stainless steel sink. "I'm not a suspect?"

He dodges the question. "I need to find out who Jeb was meeting today."

Both women stiffen. Slight but definite, like the first movement of an aspen leaf before a luff of air becomes a breeze.

"Let's start when your husband got up," Kravitz continues.

Mona sips more water. "You'd have to ask María. She fixes his breakfast."

"The mister he leave," María shrugs. "Mas o menos nueve."

"Nine, then. And when did you wake up?" he asks Mona.

Her eyelids remain motionless, "Eleven, maybe noon," she whispers, then turns it around. "So what are you going to do now?"

"Get back to The Elk. Talk to a couple of people."

She stiffens. "Like who?"

"B.S. Walsh."

"He must have told you he didn't do it," she says.

"So do most killers."

"Walsh didn't kill my husband," Mona Holloway says. She draws a hard breath and turns, resting her back against the sink. "But he isn't innocent any more than I am. We're both guilty of adultery. I woke up with him this morning. He didn't leave me until he hopped onto that stupid little dirt bike of his and headed off. Then tonight at The Elk, I thought he was nervous, maybe, that Jeb had found out." She shrugs. "You know. Black man breaks unwritten laws and the NeoNazis come after him with a rope. I mean, Jesus," she barks a hard laugh, then draws a long breath. "The Holloways were the first to throw in with Granville Stuart and the Stranglers over a hundred years ago. I think you can appreciate the kind of fear that puts in a man, can't you?"

"I'm the law here, Mrs. Holloway. No man in my custody is going to get lynched."

She blinks at him. "You're not even packing a gun."

"Your husband had one today. He's dead; I'm not."

Refolded arms bulge her breasts from a scoop neck. "Maybe you just don't know enough to need killing yet, Kravitz."

ONE TOO MANY

Hunkered down in the lee of a rotting butte, The Elk Tavern emerges from the storm like a family secret, too ugly to ignore, too insignificant to matter. Through lifting rain and wind-churned skift, sepia glows crystallize into windows.

In a gravel parking lot, Red Kravitz parks his powder blue pickup beside an old rust-eaten Caprice and gets out. Inside, the bar faces vinyl-seated stools leading straight down twelve yards to a vintage Rockola. From worn 45s, the older patrons fetch memories from fading dreams. Fronting shelved bottles, and muscled like a Frank Frazetta fantasy, six-foot six inch Standing Bear Hatcher plays DJ with a remote, shooting in a new tune just as Red enters.

Above the lulled chatter of ranch hands, the selector plucks a vinyl disk out as Kravitz eases in next to Noisy Noyes. Worn like ancient granite, the skinny drunk smells of hard living and slow dying. Ignoring him, Bear towels his hands dry and sidles over to Red. With an unsmiling face, he asks, "Who tried to drown you?"

"God, if you believe in him."

The Rockola's needle scratches out

"Please Mr. Custer, I don't want to go."

Forward, Ho!'

"Listen, Mr. Custer, please don't make me go."

Noisy's toothless mouth lets out a blast of rank air. "Our bardog thinks is funny!" The drunk thrashes for the remote, but Bear snaps it back with every lunge. Finally he lets the controller pass to Noisy and shifts his attention on the only black man in a hundred miles, B.S. Walsh, going high lonesome with Jack Daniels in the corner booth. The deputy asks his friend. "What time did Mona get here?"

"About six-fifteen. Thanks to you, my only waiter, Walsh, was still at the scene and I was here hustling munchie baskets." A bottle of slivovitz slides across the bar, tips into a shot glass, followed by, "You're the only Jewish asshole who drinks this shit."

Red knocks it back. "What time did she leave?"

Bear pours another and whispers, "You're not thinking she was the shooter?"

"The slug was big. The kick could have whacked her shoulder. She was wearing that low-cut white silk top. You see the bruise?"

"Yep. But if a black man bruises, you wouldn't notice." Bear jerks his chin up. Trying to lose himself in a thin crowd, B.S. Walsh slinks toward the exit. Red rises and follows, catching him by the shoulder. "Buy you a drink?"

Walsh raises his red-rimmed eyes. "Already had too many. Bad fuckin' day, man."

"For Jeb Holloway it was." Kravitz eases him back to the booth, slides in across from him. Behind them the Rockola throws a backbeat of Indian drums and

"Runnin' Bear...loved Little White Dove
With a Love that wouldn't die..."

"Look, Kravitz. Like I already told you and am tellin' you again, I did not fucking do it!"

Red plays a finger through the condensate from Walsh's drink. "When I left the widow not too long ago, I reckon she was thinking about heading down to those new timeshares to engage in the magic snake dance with a suspect in her husband's murder."

"Man, Red. She's just one of those broads likes a lot of cock."

"You say. But she's got a big bruise on her chest. She can claim that you beat her, raped her, tied her up, went out and shot her husband, came back but didn't tell her, then cut her lose. Stunned and in shock, she drove down to The Elk to drink up the courage to tell this wonderful husband of hers, this candidate for the U.S. Senate. You starting to get the picture, or do I need to sharpen the focus a bit?"

Walsh leans closer. "Red. I didn't have to kill the old man to bang his wife. She came on to me. Man, think about it."

Kravitz slides from the booth. "Here's the deal. If it turns out that you couldn't have been there when Jeb bought it, you won't even appear in the official file."

Walsh seems unsure.

Red reaches out to squeeze the black man's hand. "In the meantime, stay away from Mona. Drop in and see me tomorrow. Three sharp."

Resting his head on both arms Walsh mutters, "Where you going now?"

"Not to a warm bed and an eager woman, that's for sure," Kravitz says, buttoning up the damp trail duster.

* * *

Buzzing with slivovitz, Red Kravitz coaxes the ancient Ford pickup west, along Rocky Ridge Road, then off the cracked asphalt into a shallow gulch still slick with runoff. Balding tires rumble across wet dirt road before plunging downhill through shallow crumbling ruts.

Here the road banks right fenced by deer brush and sierra juniper, Red coasting on momentum, slaloming through a boscage of mesa oak, encino, lodgepole and loblolly. The last copse forces a hard left where headlights illuminate a daub-and-log cabin with a shingled roof.

Getting out, Red is met by the high-pitched scream of a lathe cutting metal, then mucks across flat yellow pin grass, up five half-bole risers to the porch. He finds the door open and eases in.

The broad back of Ivan Konev greets him. The big man is sixty, his head huge and globular, crowned by an aura of snow-white hair. Like many man sized for this country, he carries three hundred and fifty pounds on a six foot-seven inch frame and keeps mostly to himself.

This is a family trait, the love of solitude. The first to reach Montana arrived seven years before the Sharps buffalo rifle was born. He was Ivan's great-grandfather, Sergei, who came south when Alaska passed from the Russian Czar to become a United States territory. Seeking riches, the first

American Konev trapped beaver, then marten and fox, sold to the American Fur Company, which worked fine for someone who had to learn English at the age of forty-three. A pelt was a pelt, a dollar was a dollar, and a deal was a deal. After 1874 he carried a Big Tom, as the Sharps was called, for protection against the occasional Grizzly.

Inside Ivan's cabin, above the lintel of the door hangs a Hawkins 0.53-214, family owned and operated. Above the mantle of an unlit fire stretches a Le Mat over-and-under, vintage and nearly priceless. In the far corner, resting on its butt stands a .44-40 Model 1873 Winchester lever-action yellowbelly. That one makes Red smile, because it was the weapon that doomed Custer's 7th. But the host's family pride occupies the opposite corner: a dreaded Konev fuke, offering a one-volley rejoinder that had ended many heated discussions.

Red shuffles in, but Ivan's stare remains pinned to the computer monitor as the lathe repositions the barrel of an emerging rifle. His huge fingers dance over the keys, then seize the mouse resting beside the screen. "I already got a call from Micky and Mo."

"Shit," Red muttered. "I wish they'd wait..."

"Don't be too hard on the Tweedles. They knew you'd be up to see me."

Ivan picks up his calumet, scores the skulls from the bowl with a Green River knife and unlaces a doeskin poke. From that he overpacks a bed of Durham Bull with a head of kinnik-kinnik, lights up and begins to puff. Turning in his swivel chair, he rests his massive palms on bowed knees and says, "Quick and dirty? Your killer's a keener, damn good shot. Or damn lucky. Bullet: .50 caliber. Vintage: If I had to guess I'd say about 1882."

Red gets suddenly dizzy. But Ivan nods. "Can't say nothin' about the casing, 'cause nobody's found it. Not yet anyways. But this damn slug's a museum piece. These days they leave out the arsenic because of disposal problems."

"Propellant?" Red asks.

"Du pont black. But that don't mean diddly. They're loading black powder for competition shooting. Everybody trying to out-Dixon Billy Dixon."

The legend of Billy Dixon's famous killshot during the Battle of Adobe Walls in 1874 had been elevated from wild west legend to fact when Army ballistic tests proved that the .50-90 slug from a Sharps buffalo rifle could do what the story claimed: knock a brave from his saddle at 1538 yards, nearly a mile away.

Ivan ssquints. "Mo's computer trajectory program – downloaded from the FBI – puts the shooter in a roost near the Hickok knoll." Then he gets up, checks the bore and rechocks the lathe with a grooving bit. "I got better empirical data on drops and windage, plus I made a call to a guy at GM who does laminate fracture testing, asking him what the lower velocity limit is on a fifty caliber slug for a through-and-through chassis puncture on a Suburban. Which they have because the Secret Service uses Suburbans. Plug that number into the terminal velocity and adjust for down angle makes the shooter a bit closer, just outside the Bluffs, aiming down about seven degrees, figurin' the drop dead perfect."

"So you reckon the man shot from Poker Bluff?"

"Or woman," Ivan counters. "Mona can shoot. And Jeb has guns."

"You're talking about a four foot rifle that weighs sixteen pounds, carried around by a woman just five-three, who weighs maybe a hundred and five pounds."

Ivan shrugged. "Want a bigger gal? Try Caldera Cunningham."

Caldera Cunningham owns property next to Jeb's, a spread he was pestering her to sell. They both know Caldera to be a lethal shot. Maybe she reached a point where she'd had enough of Jeb.

"And the bluffs is just north of where Crazy Daisy squats," Red adds.

Ivan's focus came back. "You're right as Reagan. She's got a Sharps, too."

"But Daisy's..." The deputy twirls a finger near his temple.

"A little crazy, sure. But that's not your biggest problem. We've got five companies selling Sharps clones at a thousand bucks each and they're back ordered two years. You see what I'm sayin'?"

Kravitz nods, then ambles to the door. "I'll be back, Ivan." Outside, the storm is blowing south. In its wake, the heavens open on the gleaming tangle of the Milky Way.

Sheltered by the cabin's porch, Kravitz buttons up the duster against a wind-honed edge of chill. But as he shoulders toward the pickup, it cuts through him like a knife, hard and brutal and deep.

* * *

Back in the town of Sanctuary, Red Kravitz parks behind a two story wood frame structure rebuilt on an 1880 foundation eighty years later.

What passes for home is a walk-up, braced against long winters by a single kettle-bellied wood-burner known hereabouts as an estula. The apartment has spaces to cook and eat, a front room with a sofa and stand-up lamp with a frilled shade and two bedrooms with pictures of his mother and father on the walls. A floor below lies Kravitz's Trading Post, which his father took over as a failing business. No businessman, Red leaves that end of things to his receptionist Doris's daughter Moonlight, who has a knack for it.

Turning in the gelid dark, he pulls the door shut behind him. The latch clicks like an flintstock trigger as it drops. Snoring rumbles from the sofa, then stops.

"Who's here?" Red asks.

B.S. Walsh yawns, then mutters. "Bear say I can stay."

Kravitz peels off his shirt. "You sleeping okay?"

"Bad dreams," he shivers.

In the shadows, Kravitz can hear the black man's teeth click. "What you doin' on the couch when there's a spare bunk."

"Didn't know which one was yours."

"Cold?"

"Been warmer."

"I'll get you a sougan. You hungry?"

"Do not even mention food. I drank too fuckin' much. And, hey, sorry, I barfed in your toilet, man."

"You have a shower, clean up?"

"Bear only say I can sleep over, not shower."

Kravitz hoists his guest by the closest arm. Together they head down a hallway. In passing the deputy ignites an overhead bulb. Walsh shields his eyes from the glare while Red tells him, "You know, if I put a sign on this door saying 'White's Only,' then I'd never get to crap in my own house. Do I look that stupid?"

Walsh sputters a feeble laugh, chased off by a rattling shiver. "Okay, man. And hey. I'll clean up my puke, too."

"White of you," Kravitz says. "Take a long, hot shower. Hear?"

"Hey, man. You think your killer fucked Mona, you best check a list of who's been fuckin' her."

Kravitz points at a rack beside a small mirror. "Towels and wash rags there. Soap and shampoo in the dish. Anything else you need, give a shout."

"Do you hear what I'm sayin'?" A few inches shorter than Red, Walsh's skin is too dark to reveal the kick of a Sharps buffalo rifle into his shoulder. After staring too long, Red asks his guest, "Did you call Mona?"

"You said not to fuck her tonight. You didn't say don't call."

"I hope you didn't tell her where you were staying tonight."

"Hey, man. She's all torn up and scared. I had to calm her down, so..."

Kravitz holds up a single palm. "We need to keep thinkin' about how things were in the old west, Buffalo Soldier. You know why?"

The black man shakes his head, no.

"Because Montana still is the old west. Now take your shower. Wash Mona's perfume off." As he starts to close the door Walsh grabs the edge.

"Tell me no bullshit, Red. You think I did it?"

Kravitz shrugs. "What I think doesn't matter, amigo. Tonight my job's to keep you alive."

ONE SUSPECT

At sunup, a braided mist swirls on Kravitz's bootheels as he crosses Front Street in doeskin leggings and a denim work shirt. Covering his long black hair is a cattleman's hat in white beaver, crowned by a Montana crease, banded in crow feathers. Stopping at Doris's desk, he picks up the day's notices from the Montana state police, shuffles through and chucks them back.

Doris lights up a quirly and talks around it. "Caldera Cunningham phoned in a bitch about Jeb Holloway trespassing on her place.."

"Doris, this is a nonsmoking building."

"So what are you going to do, arrest me for smoking?" she laughs, crossing her legs slowly.

He smiles back. "You don't look a bit like Sharon Stone."

"Not lately. That angle I gave up a long time back to Moonlight. She's got the snatch for it. And more brains than ten of her johns."

Kravitz looks around. "Not too loud. The mayor may be in."

"No chance. He's still out cold from an all-night faro game at the Hollow-A bunkhouse night before last." Doris coughs twice and digs into a stack of notes. "This came for you. From Molly Mendelbaum. Says she knew you at Penn."

The deputy feels a rush of heat. "Probably after money." He wads up and arcs the note at a waste basket. Before it backboards off the wall and rattles in, Doris asks, "What's she need money for? She's the best paid talking head in the country."

"Forget it," he says. "We got business. Remember that brawl at The Elk couple years back? Some passing investor filed assault charges against Walsh? Pull the Buffalo Soldier's booking shot. Call. Slo Lehrner See if he's got a program can generate a drawing from it."

Doris's long sigh collapses into a hacking cough. Finally she rocks back, then blinks. "Jesus, you don't think..."

"And his prints. After you get this stuff together, scan a digital file and send it off to NCIC and VICAP. See if we can find a RAP sheet out there in cyberland." Kravitz swings around and heads for the door.

"Where you going?" she asks.

He tips his Resistol brim-up and turns back around. "If I don't show for my appointment with B.S. Walsh, have Bear come out to pick up my body from Crazy Daisy's."

* * *

Crazy Daisy's place lies twelve miles northwest of Sanctuary on benchland that peaks where Poker Bluff looks north across the Missouri River into Timberland Wildlife Preserve.

Red leaves his dusty blue Ford pickup behind a rocky berm spiced with twinkles of flecked mica and shattered fledspar. Then he crawls in on his elbows. Sentinels of loco weed crown the rise. A cautious peek over the rim shows a shallow bowl radiant with pixelated blooms: reds, yellows, violets and brash oranges, pushed up by last night's downpour. Every petaled grass, plant and scraggy bush that showed itself had names and uses that his mother could always extract from a memory longer than time.

He listens for them to come to him in her voice, but can hear only the dying whisper of wind. Reminding him that she really is dead, her knowledge buried with her, and making him doubt it will ever be resurrected, even as random weeds push up from her grave.

His eyes continue to scan until Daisy Ramirez pops out of her galvanized shebang. The crack of a Sharps echoes and the heavy slug whines by inches to his right. "I don't like folk creepin' 'round my spread!"

In fact, the land isn't Daisy's. Its ownership is still disputed by several parties in a long-running suit. But over uncounted years of nesting, Daisy has stockaded quite an arsenal. Among her several traditional firearms is a Big Fifty, long-barrel variation rifled inside the trademark heavy octagonal barrel with a six-groove one-in-forty-eight inch left twist. Other than the postal carrier and UPS drivers, she would fire on most anything that trespassed, 24/7.

Dead center on the oval sprawl she patrolled stood a rickety shack. It started out as nailed ripple sheets on a braced hardwood frame. In the far corner squats a promiscuous estula that low-stacks a smudgy grey spoor a mile downwind. A conical flue cap traps and kills rising embers. A good thing, because last summer was the driest in a hundred years, and Timberline Wildlife Preserve just across the river is ripe for a bonafide inferno.

"Who's there?" She punctuates her yell with another .50 caliber slug.

"Red Kravitz!"

A third round explodes a blossom of shattered quartz three inches to his left. "Go away, deputy. I've broke no goddamn laws."

He feels another slug impact just opposite where he lies. Only four feet of packed dirt kept his head from looking like Jeb Holloway's.

"Just show me a little scalp, Crow, and I'll part that long black hair for you."

"Daisy," he shouts. "It's about your alimony check." This time there's no returning shot. "Luke Brody, your postman, asked me to bring it."

"Long as Luke sent you, why don't you mosey up here and have a drink."

Waving a white handkerchief from one hand, Red Kravitz rises up and approaches. One hundred yards away, Daisy lowers and props the Sharps against her shack. "Put your hands down. This look like Wounded Knee to you?"

Daisy wears an XXL Denver Bronco's home field jersey with the number thirteen below the name, BITCH. Over that hangs tattered coveralls. Her hair is as white as the tattered cloud streaking the sky, her skin like the soil, dun-brown and etched with wrinkles. Her eyes, set in pockets narrowed and parched by weather, are wild and bright blue, her teeth yellow and generously gapped. To say she's a big woman doesn't quite do it. She goes two hundred and forty-seven pounds on a six feet and six inch frame.

After exchanging smiles, she says, "Welcome to my hacienda."

He tips his hat.

She returns a faux curtsy and pushes back the flap. "What you drinkin' these days, deputy?" she asks, running her fingers along a row of bottles. Next to a half-mason jar of home-brewed pulque and some evil-looking red-eye stand a few bottles of white wine and a dust-choked six-pack of Chief Oshkosh beer.

"What's the house special, Daisy?"

From an unseen spot behind the red-eye she pulls up a dusty bottle of Hennessy VSP and reads, "Very special piss, deputy. This'll put hair on your balls." She sweeps a huge arm across a gritty clapboard shelf, pulls down a shot glass, blows the grit out and tops it with cognac.

"You're not drinkin'?" he asks, sipping at his.

"Too early." She takes off delicate wire-framed glasses to clean them on her Denver Bronco's jersey. "Besides, I take rookus juice anymore, it funnies the way I see." She blinks. "Focus going. Old age I guess," she smiles. "Can't believe Ramon is dead."

Ramon had run off at fifty with a woman young enough to be his granddaughter. Ramon Ramirez was the love of her life and she never forgave him for that. Nor was she going to risk feeling that way with another man again. Instead, she had just hunkered down in this little trinchera and drove off everything in range with a withering fusillade.

Down deep, Kravitz senses she still likes men. He sorely hoped that he was one of them. Because as Jeb Holloway may have recently discovered, Daisy could shoot the eyes out of a spooked locust at two hundred yards.

"To freedom," Kravitz proposes, raising his glass.

"Hear, hear," Daisy says, sitting down with an audible crackle from her knees. "What really brings you out here, Red?"

"Got some complaints, Daisy. About your..." he seeks a word, settling for, "...shooting at everything that moves. That..." he searches again before deciding on, "...unsettles a lot of folks, I guess."

"I usually hit what I'm aiming at."

"No doubt. Were you aiming at anything yesterday?"

She laughs, slaps her knee. "Took bead on an eagle."

"Jesus, Daisy. You can't shoot an eagle. It's against the law."

"Federal law don't count. Besides, he was after a ground squirrel. Or squinch owl. Or prairie dog. All them critters's about the same size. I couldn't tell, but if I don't get my quota of meat for appalos, my brain goes funny on me."

"Can't have that," Kravitz says. Appalos is a way plains Indians had of eating buffalo, by skewering pieces of lean meat next to fat on a sharpened stick and roasting over a slow fire with potatoes and vegetables, a native American kabob. For which Daisy has her own personal recipe. "Myself I use tipsinah, camas, squaw cabbage. After, you wind some tasajo 'round soopollalie and it makes a good follow. Since I started with it, haven't had mal de vanche once."

Kravtiz stares at his glass. "You bring down this eagle?"

"No. Damn. It was just a feather shot, in and out. But he took off and didn't come back. He didn't get any of my varmints either. Very good, is varmint."

"I've had it," Kravitz admits.

"How about taxel? Meatier than varmint. You can long-cook it in clay under coals."

"Can't say I've had the pleasure." To Red there are a few more entrees he'd like to try before he got around to eating ground-baked badger.

She removes her glasses again. Tears moisten her eyes but she doesn't sniff. "Pitty about Ramon. He had a big one and knew how to use it."

"I think Ramon's still alive. At least Luke Brody has another check for you."

"Then what did you..." she looks puzzled. "Why did you come all this way out here to..."

"Just to talk. You holding up okay?"

"Yeah," comes as a whisper, followed by a nod.

"Anything you need? I can have Luke bring it up from the store with your mail."

Daisy seems to think about the question, then, like a little girl, purses her lips and sniffles. "I think I'll be alright."

Kravitz gets up. "Nobody came up here to see you yesterday?"

She pauses, then snaps her fingers. "About the time I winged the eagle, there was another crack. At first I thought it was an echo. Then I was sure it was too soon and too loud. But things get strange and I didn't want to think about it."

"Yeah?" He senses there's more.

"Because sometimes it's hard to know what's real and not, Red. I mean, not so much now, although, sometimes, in the mirages, I think I see Ramon waving, coming back, and smiling, not a year older. And that cute little blond bitch is not with him. But usually everything is…just like you see it now. But at night there are dreams and voices and I wake to see shadows, and the shadows have faces and eyes that glow…" She looks up, terrified. "Red, you don't think I'm going crazy out here, do you?"

"No more than the rest of us," he says.

There's nothing here but a looney old woman, and for a prickly instant he feels stupid for making the trip. But maybe it's just him, maybe he isn't asking the right questions. "During that same time, did you see anything unusual?"

A shiver rattles her. It takes no Ivy League diploma to tell that Crazy Daisy is afraid. Until he could get past her fear, he'd never reach the truth.

So he starts there.

"When I was a kid," he confesses softly. "I used to love this place. There were no words for it. Not Indian words, not white man's words. It was just the sense of being powerless in the face of it. And usually, though I was sure of the beauty and at peace with it, I knew there was a darker side to it. It was what I felt, but I couldn't tell anyone. My secret. And it made me afraid and lonely. Because I couldn't share and no one could exactly ever connect with me. You ever get that feeling, Daisy?"

She nods. "Some. More lately. Things…" Then shakes her head. "Strange things. Maybe I am just going crazy."

Red lets gentle silence mellow into trust.

Apparently certain that he is now open and listening, she says, "Do you believe in ghosts?"

No less than half honest, he says, "Yeah, in fact, a part of me deeply believes in a spirit world. Why?"

"Do you believe the dead come back? Ancient Indians to claim tribal lands?"

"It is possible. Medicine men see spirits." And still do on the res', all that was left for the pure Indian, the kind that see ghosts dancing, the kind that hear tribal music that's been silent for a hundred years.

She rolls herself a joint, licking the paper from the prayer book and pouring out the dried marijuana and peyote. After she lights up and takes a deep draw, he feels her relax. "Yesterday with dawn still behind him, I saw a dead man, a shadow ghost, or ghost rider..."

She finishes another draw and hold it, then lets out the smoke and closes her eyes, perhaps conjuring the remnants of what she had seen. "At a slow trot, moving like a broomie or fuzztail, comes a spotted horse. Big one, Appaloosa or Colorado Ranger. At first I'm thinking a maverick, but I see it moving like it's been broke. And it's a beauty, this horse, sliding along, so easy. Not a gallop. More like a saunter. In no hurry, but headed in a definite way. And then I see, just a hint of the rider, down the other side of the horse, so that you can't see more than the fingers of a hand combed deep in the mane, the rider hiding from me."

Daisy lets her next thought out in a long burst of smoke. "But you can tell by the way the horse's feet move sidestep for balance that this rider is tall, like you, more than twice vara and then some. He's not a rider really but part of the horse, moving together, like one animal. So the Appaloosa and rider just slip by..."

Daisy is known to see things, but this seems somehow different.

"Headed where?" he asks.

She raises her chin in the direction, but he wants to be sure. "Where would he end up when he came to the drop-off?"

"Some'eres near Poker Bluff, I reckon. Why?"

He raises a palm and lies to her. "Just wanted to try and figure out if this ghost-brave you saw might be heading for Indian burial ground."

"I don't know. He didn't come back this way." Her eyes come up as her old, palsied hand touched his arm. "You do believe me, don't you?"

"Yes. I do."

Meaning he believes that she believed she had seen this apparition. To her it was real. Sometimes, when it's the only thing left, you leave a person with the dignity of their self-deceptions. What's the point in tearing them down?

For a long and uncomfortable moment he locks eyes with her, allowing her terror drain into relaxation. When her eyes close and her lungs rush to empty, he gets up, knocks the dust off his hat and asks, "Can Luke bring you anything?" he shrugs, "News magazines?"

She stares down toward a wooden packing crate.

Inside is a thirteen-inch Sony television with a twist dial and rabbit ears. Leaning down, she clicks the power switch, then hammers on the chassis with one hand. "Don't get all the channels. I think it's interference. UFOs, I believe. Like that fence-lifter last night. The UFOs come in over Bearpaw Mountain, drift west, then south, recharging their batteries. That's all lightning is, UFOs recharging their batteries. Then when they have full charge, they take off, the clouds break up and it just gets beautiful."

"You ever seen a UFO?" Red asks.

She shakes her head. "They're real shrewd about staying just above and inside the anvil heads. And that's the real conspiracy, Red. Why the FAA won't let jet pilots fly through anvilheads. They're full of UFOs recharging their batteries."

"I'm sure you're right," Red says, then tips his hat good day, thanks her for the cognac and begins to saunter off.

Each step taken is a silent prayer that she wouldn't pick up the Sharps and imagine Ramon walking out of her life, thirty years ago. He closes his eyes and whispers a little prayer, then risks another: if Daisy doesn't lay him out plain dead for trespass, he prayed that he would discover a Sharps cartridge laying at the stony feet of Wild Bill Hickok and his partners at Poker Bluff.

* * *

Red sits behind his official desk in Sanctuary luckless. Sans cartridge, trace, or tracks. The clock on his office wall shows ten minutes past three when Kravitz finishes reading the fax from the Detroit Metro Police Department. After he returns the file to its manila folder, his hand is reaching for the phone when B.S. Walsh appears at the door. Seconds later, Doris eases Walsh aside long enough to announce, "Molly Mendelbaum called again. Is there something between you two?"

"Doris, could Mr. Walsh and I have some privacy here?"

"Oh, so sorry, your majesty." She shuts the door and departs.

"Wha's up?" Walsh says. And while the deputy's eyes work over him, he adds, "Got any suspects yet?"

A shrug comes and goes, but Red's eyes pin the black man like a bug on an exhibit board. "We have a problem, Mr. Walsh. There's a guy with your face wanted under a Michigan fugitive warrant following flight from Detroit."

"You talkin' Seven-Eleven, right? Son of a bitch Koh-ree-han had hisself a fucking Uzi under the counter, man. Wasn't me that shot first. No, suh. Was another brother wit me and it was pure self-defense, Red. And I didn't even kill the chink." Another page in the dossier turns in the deputy's lap. His eyes come up. "Suspected as an accessory after the fact in the murder of..."

Walsh snaps his fingers. "That was my sister's boss, and man, he wouldn't leave the bitch alone. He come over to her place, I mean push the door in, start wailin' on the bitch and what's she do? Instead of screamin' like a normal woman, she shoots the motherfucker. Then she call me. Me. Why me? 'Cause she thinks jus' like everybody else, that her brother's mix up with..."

"Wally...," Kravitz begins. "Waldo, Wals. Black Sampson... where'd you get that handle, Mr. Walter Stanley Addison?"

"I used to shave my head and had me a bitch named Delilah."

"Look, I don't care what they called you, but you were runnin' a game on us."

"I didn't kill Jeb Holloway."

"But you wanted to," Kravitz says.

"Shit, Red, most every swingin' dick who knew Jeb wanted two things: to kill the guy and to fuck his wife."

"And you got both wishes," Kravitz sums it up.

"Bang the bitch. You bet. She goes after you, you do the same."

Red drills a stare through Walsh until he breaks.

"You wonder why I split? Look at them Dee-Troit RAP sheets. You think they care if it's me or some other nigger? All the same to them. Jus' kill all them blacks until there's only whites and redskins left to hold up Seven-Elevens."

Red tosses the manila folder onto the desk. "What made you leave Mona's tender embrace and jolt your sorry black ass over river cobbles to the very spot where the victim died?"

B.S. Walsh squirms. "Hey, Red, you don't like my story? Fuck you. I want a lawyer."

"Give me a good reason and I'll let you go," Kravitz says.

"No bullshit?"

"Honest Injun."

He leans in to whisper, "Night before I was at The Elk..." True so far. "...and Noisy is a little more than usual drunk..." True but irrelevant, like saying snow is frozen "...and he's got me alone, and it's near last call, and he looks around, like there's nobody else he can trust, and he says that he was up by Crazy Daisy, prospectin'...and Daisy lets on that she's seen some glitter down around Sidewinder Twist. Now Daisy can't get around owin' to her asthma and bad knees and stuff, so she asks Noisy if he go down, check it out..." The rest is coming, as predictably as any northster. Kravitz fights an impulse to lip-synch the ending that Walsh now whispers. "Red, it was gold.

Noisy said there's gold up there."

"And that's why you ended up where you ended up."

"Yes, man. Look, I swear. And you know, bein' as how he was after to buy up property and such, maybe, like, Jeb Holloway knew that, too. And that's why somebody popped him, man."

Kravitz plays the straight man. "Probably Noisy."

"Noisy, maybe. But maybe Len Jarnow. I mean, if there's gold, he's the one been fightin' Holloway for the right to the land, right? If Holloway's dead, then one of the litigants ain't no longer around, if you see what I mean, to keep the other claimant, if that's a word..."

"It is," confirms Kravitz. After four years at Penn he could recognize a lot of white man's words he didn't know before, and, if absolutely necessary, could even spell them.

Breathless and whispering, the fugitive who had re-invented himself B.S. Walsh extends wringing hands to plead. "Man, why else would I go out there with all them snakes and scorpions and wolves, flash floods and Crazy Daisy with that Sharps of hers..."

"You ever fired a Sharps?"

The man passing as B.S. Walsh sits back in the second chair, pushes until two legs lift from the floorboards, and leans against the paneled wall. His only answer is a long exhale, then silence.

"I'm keepin' you overnight."

"Hey, man. Who's gonna be swamper at The Elk?"

Kravitz gets up and leads his prisoner by the elbow. "That's the least of your worries."

"Hey, man. You don't need to put me here. I'll stick around. I swear it."

"Like you did in Detroit?"

"That was different. It was some real serious shit back there."

Kravitz turns the key in the old plate lock and says, "Here, too."

"I told you I didn't do it."

Kravitz coils powerful fists around the old rolled-iron bars and leans forward. "Maybe. But you're the best suspect I've got."

"What happened to my one phone call, Red?"

The deputy releases his grip on the bars and backs away, double-thumbing the oval buckle on his belt. "Well, let's just say we have a different sense of time out here. It moves a little slower and you have longer to think before you open your mouth. But if you want, you can make your call right now."

"Bet your redskin ass I want to make my fuckin' call."

"Well, maybe that's good, B.S. Because I've got a call to make, too."

A dull glow kindles in the wells of Walter Stanley Addison's eyes. "Oh, yeah?"

"Yeah. We got so wrapped up talkin' about that scaly highbinder Jeb Holloway, I forgot to tell the Detroit police to start extradition papers on Walter Stanley Addison."

"Now just wait a second, Red...I got to think about this a bit."

"You do that."

Fear and confusion wrestle for a lock on Walsh's expression, neither triumphing, the battle for control played out in terror and panic that flickers with each bat of the eyelids.

As the deputy heads for the exit, he looks in on Doris as she puffs out the words, "I know, I know. It's a no smoking area."

Red snaps his fingers. "Shit. I forgot to have the prisoner empty his pockets and put his doofunnies in a property satchel. Could you cover that for me?"

"What if he refuses?"

"Mind the store."

Doris smiles. "The store got an order from Molly Mendelbaum. She wants you to call her back, pronto. Getting to sound a little pissed off."

Kravitz grabs his hat off a peg. "Tell Bear that Walsh won't be working tonight."

Doris stubs out her cigarette. "Moonlight can stand in."

In the back Walsh screams, "This is a fucking nonsmoking jail. I'm gonna sue your redskin ass, Kravitz. You givin' me cancer in here, man! You hear?"

Karvitz whispers to Doris. "I'm going to have a chat with suspect number two."

"Goin' to see Mona, huh?"

He shakes his head. "Mona is suspect number three."

SUSPECT NUMBER TWO

As dusk snaps into night, Kravitz reaches the Mountainview Shooters Gallery south of Helena. Floodlights have already popped on, illuminating downrange targets. After casting glances around like a fly fisherman's line, he spots Leonard Jarnow shooting prone with a Sharps buffalo rifle, its muzzle braced on a fancy tripod. One eyelid shut, Jarnow sights with a caliper on a traditional Creedmore vernier. Shaped like a guillotine, it is snapped vertical from the metal butt plate behind the breech, aligning with a cylindrical tube front sight. Facing him downrange is an iron bison that rings like a mission bell when hit. Kravitz watches him take a bead on the silhouette, then place a round just below the ear.

When the deputy starts to advance, a big man in a pricey black suit lowers an arm, drop-gate style. "And you are?"

Red produces his badge. "I need to talk to Mr. Jarnow about Jeb Holloway."

"You wait here," a voice behind him says. The first man catches Jarnow before a reload, points back toward Red and takes a single nod from his boss. The massive bodyguard gets as far as, "He say's he'll..." before Red sweeps past him as he finishes, "...see you now," punctuated by an ear-ringing explosion of black powder.

From the prone position, Leonard Jarnow looks up at the deputy. Even stretched out on the ground, it's easy to tell that the surviving Republican candidate for U.S. Senator is tall, a raw-boned man as lean and harsh as a Montana winter. His face is a moonscape of pockmark valleys separated by sharp ridges, the salt-and-pepper hair drawn straight back from his forehead and slicked in glossy sheets separated by grooves. Odds are none of his advisers has dared to tell him that he looks like an old raven after a good soak.

Luckily the effect isn't total. Light blue eyes in deep seem to glow. Beneath wide thin lips, big teeth thrust into a massive overbite. Stroking the long barrel of the Sharps, Jarnow says, "Gun that won the west," then rolls into a sitting position and rests the long tom across his lap. "More than nine thousand buffalo rifles were made by Christian Sharps by the late 1870's. Add another ten thousand replicas sold worldwide. Some guns lost, stolen, unclaimed in estate sales, resting in dusty attics... where do you start looking for your assassin?"

Red squints out at the distant silhouette. "That's what I came about, Mr. Jarnow. To let you know that we're on the case."

Wincing with back pain, Jarnow comes upright. From the standing position, he scores another hit on the metal bison, leaving a sting of black powder floating in the air. The spent cartridge clatters to the deck. Downrange, the resulting gong reverberates on darkening air. Like a father-gunsmith, he cradles the polished walnut buttstock in one arm. "Enough," he says. "I've got a press conference. Maybe you'd like to attend."

"Appreciate the concern, Mr. Jarnow, but I've got a murder to solve."

"Well, you best solve it tonight, because tomorrow the FBI is taking over."

"Based on what?"

Jarnow struts along, passing the Sharps to an assistant. "Clean and oil it up," he commands, tugging off this shooting gloves, then returning to Kravitz. "Jeb Holloway was killed on Federal land. Timerberline Wildlife Preserve. Technically that falls under the National Park Service, but I doubt they're qualified to pursue a murder of this..." he searches for the right word, settles for, "...complexity."

Kravitz has another take. "Oh, it's not that complex. Somebody wanted to kill Jeb Holloway so now he's dead. It's just a matter of finding out who set up the ambush, and was a good enough aim to kill him with one shot."

"Any witnesses?"

"One," says Kravitz.

"One who actually saw the killing?"

"Nope. One who saw the killer."

"Any physical evidence?"

"No shell casings. And there was a hard rain last night, it washed off any tracks. Plus the shot was made from a sandstone roost, not the best place to pick up trace."

"Seems to me there's still a lot you don't know, deputy. And that suggests that you could use some serious professional help."

Kravitz sticks an arm out, lightly. "Could I have a minute?"

The candidate checks his timepiece, a Seiko diving watch with more dials than all the TV sets in Sanctuary. Kravitz eases into, "Mr. Jarnow, this is Montana. The last time a federal task force tried to catch a killer in Montana it took them over fifteen years and if his brother hadn't turned him in, Ted Kaczinski might still be making bombs in his cabin. My second point is that once the feds settle on a plan, they never stop to figure how something like Ruby Ridge is going to trickle down at the local political level. Now my guess, Mr. Jarnow..."

Jarnow scowls. "Deputy, how many murders have there been since you've been deputy in Sanctuary?"

Ignoring the town's darkest secret, Red insists, "I think we can handle this one, Mr. Jarnow. If the FBI wants to provide support, I could use the help."

Jarnow's big aide leans in to whisper, "They're waiting, Mr. Jarnow."

Strutting toward a small conference room, Len Jarnow half-turns to ask, "By the way, deputy. I was wondering, have you ever fired a Sharps?"

Red shakes his head.

"Really. That surprises me. Because Jeb Holloway has... or had...a very fine historical gun. And I know that you were out to see the widow right after the killing..."

They keep walking, the deputy half a step behind the candidate, led by men in black. Ahead, silhouetted by the hard light of the conference room, stands Molly Mendelbaum. And reflexively, in a hard burning arc that jump-started memories too hot to die, he suddenly cares far less about who had killed Jeb Holloway, and begins revisiting what might have been.

* * *

Red loses Molly to a rush of questions. Len Jarnow swaggers along in a checked flannel shirt beneath a shooting vest, then slides to the lectern. Into the mike he declares, "Here in Montana, nearly everyone owns a gun and we have the lowest per capita murder rate in the country." After smattering of applause from his shills, he rolls on. "Jeb Holloway will be missed. We disagreed, but I respected him. And justice will be done. Tomorrow the Director of the FBI will commit the modern crime fighting technologies that the people of Montana deserve in pursuing this killer." Applause starts to build, but the speaker lowers his head and closes those huge hooded eyelids. "Mona Holloway, you have my deepest condolences." He looks up. "And now I'll take questions."

Molly Mendelbaum blurts, "Mr. Jarnow. You're very good with the kind of gun that supposedly killed your opponent. Aren't you a suspect?"

"I was with my campaign manager, Sue Slade, during the time when Jeb Holloway was shot, yes. Next question."

A middle-aged man with a gaunt face and liver-spotted hands clears his throat. "A piece of land near where Jeb Holloway was killed is now being contested between you and Mr. Holloway. Couldn't that be a motive for murder?"

"I've already got a whole lot more than the piece under litigation, so the land in question is not worth killing over."

"What kind of man do you think this killer is?" Molly Mendelbaum asks.

"Why don't I ask Deputy Red Kravitz to take that question?"

Jarnow turns and gestures for Red to come forward. With a shuffle and a rustle of denim and doeskin, the Deputy Sheriff of Sanctuary leans toward the mike. "The state forensic team is studying the evidence right now. When they report we'll know a little more about the killer."

"Do you have any suspects, Deputy Kravitz?" Molly asks.

"Yes," Red answers. "But no one indicted."

A swell of excitement rattles like sheet thunder. "Can you give us the name of this suspect?" Molly shouts to be heard.

"I'm not in the position to discuss a crime that is still under investigation." True. But he had already said more than he wanted to. Molly always had that effect on him. So he steps down and Jarnow escorts him back to Moonlight's supercharged Cavalier, instructing his goons, "Wait here," while he hangs a thin-boned arm on the deputy's shoulder. "Nice ride," he says.

"Not mine."

Len still smiles. "I think it's a good idea to keep you involved in this thing. You make good copy, Kravitz. And if you cooperate, it could change your life. I'm looking for senior staff to take to Washington and — "

"Mr. Jarnow, you'll excuse me. I've got a long drive back. In the dark. And the road ahead has a lot of blind spots."

"We'll be talking," Jarnow says, clapping him on the back. As Jarnow's entourage melts into the night, Kravitz keys open Moonlight's car and sits inside. Before he can shut the door, a familiar woman's voice lights up the darkness. "Do you remember that night in the visitors's locker room at Franklin Field?"

He takes his hand off the ignition key as Molly Mendelbaum crystallizes out of the cool shadows. Then answers, "Hard to forget, a night like that. At least for me."

"Me, too." She tosses a spray of auburn hair off her face. Her lavender eyes seem too much the same, hot and eager, full of mystery and magic and wonder. Or maybe the dream of that night has never ended. "You look real good, Molly," is what he can't prevent being said.

"You, too." She saunters in, leaning against the hood.

This close again, only silence separates them. But his mind tells him it's more, and his lips say, "I've got a long drive back."

"Mind if I drop in tomorrow, do some location shots of the town, the murder scene? You know, just background?"

He watches the wind blow her hair into loose banners, the strands letting on to the stars in the night behind her. And even here, three feet away, he can feel her heat and taste the memory of her sweat. So he buckles. "If you shoot as a backdrop, and not approach Holloway's Suburban, I'd say, 'why not?'"

* * *

After fetching a search warrant from his father's old buddy, Judge Paul Weigen, Red Kravitz pushes the Cavalier hard, more concerned about unfenced heifers than Winnebagos from Indiana. The parched center line blurs as the supercharged ragtop blows down the shoulder of a steep ridge, heading east through patchy autumn grassland.

Driving alone at night across Montana's sprawl, along lonely stretches of two-lane asphalt dulled grey by pitiless sun, with the twinkling grandeur of stars staring down and an edgy wind to keep you awake, you will find yourself, like Red Kravitz, dwelling on the land, its past, its people, its history, and its future. Half redskin, Kravitz was gene-deep partial to the land as the Indians had known it. In that time the Buffalo blackened the prairie, living off the endless waves of grass, packed in thundering stampedes that shook the earth to its bedrock. For those tribes, including Red's Crow and Bear's Northern Cheyenne, the land provided for them and restored itself. Killing happened, yes, but rarely wholesale slaughter. Small tribes died out for lack of warriors, who were needed less often to fight than to feed their families.

Then came the whites, in numbers without limit, infecting by diseases like smallpox and measles, carrying repeating rifles like the Winchester and long-range killers like the Sharps. Civil War veterans inured to killing found fertile ground for slaughter here, where the gun was law and unwitnessed opportunity often became recreational destiny. With the railroad came dude adventurers, offloaded on grasses stops to aim the mighty Sharps at majestic creatures who could not imagine an opportunity to run with the herd without a fair chance to get away, without many surviving. For mere sport hundreds of thousands of buffalo were killed and left to rot in the sun. As more recently at Poker Bluff, only the flies, wolves and vultures won.

Travelers looking to outrun the horror of the Civil War fled straight across Montana. Despite its breathtaking splendor, most found the place too dry, too sparse, too lawless and too lightly settled for their ambitions. Those staying in places like Sanctuary were mostly those who couldn't or wouldn't go on. A rig driver who buried his wife here and then lost all of children to fever seemed to have nothing left, and slowly died in place with them, over many numbing, empty years. As in so many fledgling towns, eligible women arriving in Sanctuary took one look at the place through a stagecoach window and kept traveling.

The male folk they witnessed in passing glances didn't justify serious interest. Working unproductive land aged these men quickly, and it showed. In their faces, the stoops in their backs, their dead-slow foot-dragging of simply pushing on, one foot after the other. None promised opportunity, longevity or prosperity. Outlaws too old for the game and too distant from a warrant drifted out of the Missouri Breaks, looking for a good bed and steady job. Finding here and there a few places like Sanctuary, which gathered still others. Men so close to God that nobody else could understand them ended up standing on muddy street corners beneath painted signs, or carrying rough-cut crosses, railing about the Second Coming. Gaggles of disciples gone crazy for want of real hope could be found sitting in the mud beside them shouting Amen, their only congregation. Con-men, snake-oil salesmen and grifters, bad men with worse goods, blew into and out of town with the wind, never to return. Men vowed to staking their futures on gaming tables arrived with a pack of cards, a stack of chips and a six gun, looking for a spare crate to throw a sprawl of felt across. Men wanting only the next shot of whiskey would sweep out floors and hawk players for them. Men wanting to be kings arriving from Chicago with a small fortune and big ideas, having by an arrangement of convenience adopted a baker's dozen teenage girls, orphans, half-bloods, chinks, spics or niggers, cast-off Mormon wives, to serve the men's needs. Good, bad and ugly, men without an idea of why life had gathered them into its misery, tried to impose it on others. Fools chasing gold and finding too little to matter, or too much to hide, died of others's greed when their claims got jumped and their bodies dumped. Malignantly growing lesions or unmoderated ambition, Sanctuary and other places like it denuded forested slopes into mud slides and threw timbered towns up as fast as they sent timbered shafts into the earth, and called it development. Wretched, miserable and often terminally ill with tuberculosis or syphilis, the townsmen frequented saloons, player-piano whore houses or dead-silent opium dens to forget their woes and fantasize their part of a rosy future.

In Abe Lincoln's dream society all men could hope to be more. There was plenty of back-breaking scut work for emancipated blacks, who now got paid for what they used to do for free. Then Chinamen imported to drive rail spikes traded in opium, taking the first step toward the American dream of endless prosperity. In a land of limitless opportunity, only one group was excluded: the ones who lived here for thousands of years before a single white landed near Plymouth Rock:

The Indians, being ignorant savages and understanding nothing of white superiority, and unwilling, in their damned Godless heathen souls, to see the majesty of Jesus and His selection of the European white race as His exclusive representative on Earth. At first by the year and eventually by the day the good Indians became the dead ones, fulfilling Civil War hero Phil Sheridan's prophecy. Despite protective treaties signed in Washington by the Indian chiefs and the Great White Father, when the Civil War ended in epidemic unemployment, waves of desperation, greed, fear and hysteria drew whites west. The method of resettlement extermination, the justification Manifest Destiny, and the survivors's administrative inconveniences. Four years before the Battle of Little Bighorn, the United States government formally annexed the land of the Northern Cheyenne to form the first National Park, Yellowstone. When Custer and his Seventh Cavalry were annihilated at Little Bighorn, Washington screamed to eliminate these godless heathens and dispatched a surge of additional troops to hunt them down like wild animals.

If the Indians were pacified, with their passing came an sustained orgy of exploitation that has left modern Montana a land dying with ugly sores of abandoned open pit mines, caustic runoff, tainted groundwater, deforested slopes, diseased trees and infertile prairies, a land already dry and moonlike becoming more lifeless. Enforcing this relentless progress every step of the journey were guns like the Sharps buffalo rifle. For settlers heading west after 1880, Indians were less often a problem than bushwhackers. With Sharps, two men could leave a little whistle stop like Sanctuary and ride out to a perch like Poker Bluff and wait. Soon, two or three trusting families would rumble by. One by one the teamsters would be blown from their benches. Then as their wives and children screamed and fled, they, too, would be cut down in dreadful splatters of gore. Finally, into the lifeless silence, the ambushers would descend, almost casually, and check for life. If they found any, it would soon end. Then they would transfer valuables into their saddle bags or pack mules, fire the wagons and skedaddle back to town to report a terrible Indian ambush, three families dead. In the sky, circling vultures would lead you to the massacre, many hours behind the wolves and flies. And so the townsmen, outraged at the butchery, would mount up in numbers and hunt down the savage heathen butchers. And so, joining that tradition, Jeb Holloway had just joined a long line of victims felled by a famous rifle, but not likely shot by an Indian. If the Indians were not all dead, on the res', or standing wooden on some trading post porch, they were pacified, Christianized, selling their mineral rights for handfuls of beads, or holding respectable civilized positions like, for example Deputy Sheriff.

Reconnecting with that eternal Indian moment that is always the present, Red's mind dissolves from reflection and focuses on a ribbon of asphalt that slowly reels in the speeding ragtop. High beams groping at the darkness. Far ahead, an eerie shape in fringed buckskin and yoking a long rifle across his shoulders begins to cross the road. The form keeps striding, ignoring headlights that paint him bright as a target at Mountainview's shooting gallery. Letting up on the gas, Kravitz allows the car to rumble onto the graveled shoulder.

By then the trudging figure has left the road. Running after him, Kravitz cups his hands and shouts, "Hey!" And finds himself staring down the octagonal barrel of a Sharps. Beyond the clearly focused muzzle is darkness. Out of it comes a voice, "Nearest town's ten 'r more miles."

"Dooley?" Kravitz asks.

"Red? What you doin' out here this hour?"

"Been over to Helena."

"Goin' into politics?"

"Nope. Official business." Although he couldn't see Dave Dooley, he could smell a stench that almost made his eyes water. "Goin' early this year," Kravitz guesses, trying to make sense of the coincidence.

"Late," he disputes. "You see signs. Other day saw me a snow bunting gone cold-molted. So it's time." A long sigh. "Got to get walkin', Red."

"You okay?" Kravitz asks.

Dave Dooley steps forward, cradling the Sharps in one arm and revealing his cartridge belts. They hang over the straps on his possibles sack, cross-shoulder in an X shape, heavy with .50 caliber ammo. Looking straight at Kravitz he says, "Ivan's got me all set." Then comes the smile, half-tooth, half-gum. "I'll drop game in one shot. Rest's for wolves, rouge bears. They'll come for my food, then I'll add 'em to the larder. You ever et wolf, Red?"

"No," he says.

"A little stringy but funny how what you shoot gets to seem real tasty the hungrier you be. Even et me bear, one time." One stiff blast of cold air reminds Dooley of the trek ahead. In a quick fluid motion, he yokes the Long Tom across his shoulders again and grunts, "When the coteau thaws, then."

From the unblinking look in the mountain man's eyes, it's easy to imagine Dave Dooley killing Jeb Holloway. A lot easier than imagining B.S. Walsh squeezing the trigger. He recalls Mona Holloway's almost flirtatious pride, the hope to shock and intrigue with admission of an affair with a black man. With all that implied. The pillow talk, Walsh's macho bravado, tales of crime, violence, maybe even murder in faraway Detroit. And Mona Holloway's mind turning and turning, like a lone buzzard rising on a thermal, imagining herself way above the scene, looking down as B.S. steadied the Sharps on Poker Bluff, lined up the sights, set the double trigger and eased back the hammer.

Kravitz stands in darkness as the sounds and spoor that defined the unseen figure of Dave Dooley dissolve in a rising wind. Red clutches the curled brim of his hat and squints up at the stars. They burn in the blackness like his unanswered questions, none more than a spark of speculation in a mind clouded by confusion.

* * *

At The Elk's bar, Ivan Konev claims the red leather bar stool next to Noisy Noyes. Wrapped in a dirty apron, Standing Bear Hatcher polishes a tumbler that vanishes in the fold of his huge hands. All eyes rise to greet Red as he enters, then fall away as the Rockola saws off a violin concerto by Tchaikovsky, Ivan's choice.

Red scans the empty front booths, then turns to Bear, who shrugs. "Out of respect for Jeb, maybe." Who always sat there, when he was still breathing.

Noisy pipes in, "Down New Orleans, when somebody die, they have a big party in the street. Ev'ybody's blowin' brass, singin', dancin.'" But the only music here is Tchaikovsky.

In a democracy of mongrels, every dog has his own howl. Like a council elder at a pow-wow, Bear made patrons feel at home, unless they get unruly. Off the back corridor stands a stuffed silver-tip Grizzly, upright and snarling, to remind them that this was the dreaded pro wrestler Standing Bear, formerly a legendary All-Pro outside linebacker for the Dallas Cowboys.

In that phase of his life, a role model he was not, nor tried to be. But when it was time to move on, he never looked back. The illustrations hanging on The Elk's walls are for the customers, not Bear. When he thinks about it at all, he recalls the whole NFL trip as a mock re-run of Little Bighorn, where he could whoop and scream and do all the hellacious damage the rules allowed. When the ancient spirits flooded into him, Bear could break from his post at linebacker, charge in low, grabbing opposing linemen like ragdolls, lift them off their feet and sprint this juggernaut of destruction into quarterbacks who had already begun to go fetal.

Commentator Frank Gifford once said, "When he's got the whole left side of the offensive line wrapped up, that's nearly eight hundred pounds uplifted and he's still running a five-second forty. At his best Dick Butkus was never a force like this."

Actually, Bear has a lot a admiration for Chicago's legend. The stuffed Grizzly is nicknamed Butkus, because he is, after all, a Bear. And those glittering dead-black glass eyes dominate the back passage like a feral skookum looking to drag lost souls into hell.

Once when headed back to the storeroom Bear had stopped, turned and asked Red, "Now why the hell couldn't you draft a Grizzly like Butkus here? If I was Chicago, he'd be my first three draft choices." Bear closed his eyes and looked almost serene. "Just let your Indian dream-mind open to a nine hundred pound middle linebacker rearing up, his growl sayin', 'don't even think 'run.'" Then Bear laughed until he howled.

There was a ferocity in the sound like a wild man, too untamed for this century and its preoccupation with politically correct image. After one unconfirmed transgression against an under-age white girl, the image-conscious Dallas Cowboys couldn't find a place on next year's roster for an All-Pro Native American. "Even before my release, my agent tried to cut a deal with the Redskins," Bear once said. "But they didn't want me. Then he tried the Chiefs. They didn't want me either. Pro wrestling, on the other hand, ate it up."

Bear found a path to reflection that avoided the morass of bitterness, which is as bad a definition of retirement as any. Like all real Indians, who have only a sense of the present, he cherishes the eternal moment providing a traditionally valued community service to consenting adults. "Grab a stool, officer," he says. "We were just talking about you."

Red plants himself next to Ivan. "Coming back I just about road-killed Dave Dooley. Got out to check. Since by then he was pointing a Sharps at my chest, I didn't have the heart to tell him it was illegal to hunt Grizzlies."

Eyes shut, rapture flooding his expression, Ivan stops humming Tchaikovsky long enough to whisper, "Dave reckons Grizzlies eat their own young. So every male he kills is a way of saving the species."

Red re-aims the conversation where he wants it. "A hundred years ago, men were killing from a thousand yards and got admired for it. These days it's called murder."

Noisy's drunken eyes roll to attention. "Now why'd Dave want to blow out Jeb's lamp?"

"Maybe for target practice. That's where I found Len Jarnow tonight in Helena." He scans the bar for a snack basket.

Bear says, "I got some trail mix and munchies, but Moonlight's up to the jail feedin' the prisoner." He pours Red a slivovitz. "You think the grieving widow promised to make Walsh the first black cattle baron in Montana?"

The deputy slowly turns the glass in his hands, blows out exhaustion and shakes his head.

"Forget the law," Noisy says. "In your bones. You reckon Walsh did it?"

"No." The first sip of slivovitz sends a rush of fire down his throat. He lets his guts cook in it before he adding, "If a black man went up the table near the tongue, Crazy Daisy would've seen him quicker 'n a fly on milk."

"She didn't?" Bear asks.

Red shakes his head. "Of all the men I've met, Walsh knows how dangerous a witness can be."

"Not my read of the man," Noisy says.

Kravitz is intrigued. "You on close terms with B.S, Noisy?"

A shrug turns defensive, "I mean, I know him. Hell, everybody knows him." He raps his knuckles on the bar to punctuate his point. "I mean, you got to trust the guy who slops your grub, right?"

Kravitz returns the old man's shrug. "What can you say about some guy who turns up in a little watering hole in the middle of nowhere and kills the biggest man in town, and still the local lawman has no idea who it is?"

"Maybe we need a new lawman," Noisy slurs.

"Election's two weeks off. You up for running, feel free," Red says.

Ivan Konev stops humming Tchaikovsky but keeps his eyes closed. "Everybody talks about the Billy Dixon shot. But now lots of people can make the same shot. Even back in Billy Dixon's time, lots of great shooters started on a Sharps. Even one who's now froze in stone up at Poker Bluff."

"Wild Bill Hickok," Kravitz says."And Pat Garrett, who shot Billy the Kid."

"But not with a damn Sharps," insists Noisy.

His back turned to recap a bottle, Bear checks the mirror and adds, "Don't forget Geronimo and Captain Jack of the Modoc."

"Indians knew a good gun," Red admits. "But they didn't have the numbers, in guns or braves."

"Except for Little Bighorn," Bear smiles, flexing his massive bicep.

Noisy again: "Buffalo Soldiers. Blacks in cavalry. His kin were..."

Kravitz corrects, "His kin are in Detroit. His story is B.S. He's a short-timer on a long run from warrants in the Motor City."

A moment of silence absorbs this new information in traded glances.

"You think he did it?" Bear wants to know.

"It's an election year. You have any other nominees?"

Bear rolls his massive shoulders. "Hey, I just work here. At least that's what Mona always tells me."

"Who always says and does whatever she wants," Kravitz responds.

Bear wipes Noisy's slopped drink from the bar. "I just know she pays her bills."

"B.S. and Mona..." Kravitz starts. But Bear interrupts. "Now, Red. You just said Walsh is a liar. And he's your witness against Mona?"

"You seem pretty eager to stand up for the widow," Kravitz says, eying his friend hard.

Bear returns the glare. "Hey, I'm just saying, don't jump to conclusions. You got a nigger con from Detroit and you've got a wildass drunk woman from the lone prairie. Which one's more likely to be a trigger man?"

Ivan volunteers, "A Sharps does not discriminate by gender, my friend. Annie Oakley Butler was a crack shot with a Sharps, from the saddle, while riding."

Bear laughs. "Now she's stupid enough to kill her husband without an alibi?"

"She's got an alibi," Kravitz says. "But I've still got to check it out."

"Why?" the three men ask at once.

He tells them, "Because if it doesn't hold up, the press makes me look like a donkey seen end-on. Now I may not catch this killer, but I won't bungle the investigation."

Bear shows his palms. "Hey, deputy, you got my vote."

His eyes run over the men, one by one. "Okay, what's going on?"

"We're just all sayin'," Noisy screeches, "That you ought to give Mrs. Holloway the benefit of the fucking doubt is all." Then the old guy studies his empty tumbler.

Kravitz narrows his eyes at his best friend.

Bear looks around at the other men, who nod, one at a time. Noisy is last to fall in line, mumbling, "Well it doesn't have anything to do with..." before Bear cuts him off. "Red. It was in the works before Holloway went off to the last round-up, okay? It was him, Mona and Jarnow all in on the Bearpaw ski resort thing."

"Don't I know it," Red says.

The green lobby was bulldozed by overcompensated legislators eager to redefine the word development as a thirty trail mountain with tiers of time-share condominiums, a competition-scale ice rink hosting an expansion NHL team, and a year-round staff of support and service personnel. From one side of the state to another it is heralded as a seed for growth in central Montana. But to Kravitz it feels like a runaway fungus, living off the decay of more vital wilderness, killing the substructure that gave it life. And yet, for as long as it lasted, the white man's money would always play king of the mountain with traditional Indian land.

Kravitz looks around The Elk, examines the vacant booths and smiles. "She's offered you jobs."

Bear admits, "She said she wanted an old western celebrity bar tender, for something like the Million Dollar Cowboy Bar in Jackson Hole. But bigger, better, more. I mean it would only be a winter gig. She says the kind of glitz they'll have up there, these people will stuff hundreds in your tip snifter." Bear shrugs. "Hell, with global warming and all, it's just for a couple of months."

Kravitz turns to Ivan. "What about you, my Ruskie friend?"

Ivan fumbles into, "Mrs. Holloway plans an indoor shooting range.

The guns and ammo's already in inventory. And the foundation's already set. Roof's going up. She asked me to cover maintenance and safety. This would be..."

Kravitz laughs. "... dude target shooting?"

"Something like that," he says. "But no live buffalos this century."

"So Len Jarnow can bring in his friends from Washington and have a little fun, peddle a little influence, get a little drunk, maybe a little laid. No, wait." The deputy holds up both hands, "Let me guess. Moonlight will work as a receptionist, shift on as a biscuit-shooter, then roll into the graveyard shift as part-time hooker." He turns to Noisy. "What's Mona got for you, old timer?"

"Well, nothin', really. Except indirect. Sometimes I could snowmobile around... Bear lets me practice a bit already... so as I could scout the trails for hobbled drunks before sundown..."

Kravitz barks a sharp laugh. "Hey, men! What? You didn't suggest that Deputy Kravitz could be in charge of security at Bearpaw? Or maybe I'd make more panning for gold down by Poker Bluff." He stares at Noisy.

Noisy guesses, "You found out from Walsh when you was twistin' his nuts down the hoosegow." The deputy's stare forces the old timer on. "Shit, Red. After I show him the nuggets in my poke, he starts comin' by on the dirt bike. Him and me kept fishin' ejected brass near Sidewinder Twist, Walsh gettin' all pissed off, me tellin' him we can still sell the used ones back to Dave Dooley for reloads. In fact, it weren't Davey what killed him, 'cause he was wit' me when Jeb were shot."

Kravitz's eyes grapple the drunk. "How'd you know when he was shot?"

"There was two shots, real close. Davey and me we heard 'em," Noisy says.

"When?" Red asks, none too hopeful.

"Morning. Wouldn't know the time exactly. Don't carry no watch. Davey neither." He punctuates his claim with a resonant fart.

The beer clock over the door bubbles and hums in the ensuing silence until Moonlight bursts in, blanched and breathless. "B.S. Walsh is going nuts about the busted toilet."

"I'll be back," Kravitz promises.

* * *

Approaching town hall, Kravitz passes his vintage pickup. From its load bed he snatches a sawed-off ax haft, drawn in by the Buffalo Soldier's vile curses. Following them, he sneaks down the side of the brick building and hears what sounds like an off-balance washer walking across a floor. When he turns the rear corner, two black hands are rattling the grate of window bars.

Then the rattling stops and he watches Walsh gouge the rotten mortar with an all-in-one tool. After blowing away the crumbled grout, B.S. re-grips the grid of bars and resumes abusing them. Indianing-up in silence, Kravitz takes careful aim and blurs the bobbed haft across the prisoner's knuckles.

Impact produces a sharp scream followed by, "Who's fuckin' with my fuckin' hands!" A hiss of pain bleeds into a loud, "Damn!"

Still melted in shadows Kravitz whispers, "Just me and the finger stick."

"What's a finger stick?" The suspect's forehead presses against the bars before the deputy whacks again, the clang of steel reverberating through Walsh's skull.

Red tells him, "Now it's a head stick."

He smacks the iron again. "Now it's a bar stick. You want to show your famous dick I can make it a prick stick."

Red finally makes himself visible. "You tryin' to join the wind, Walsh?"

"Fuck you, you motherfucking beluga half-kike, half-redskin no good bastard country-ass Uncle Tomahawk!" Walsh shouts.

"Now is that any way to start a plea bargain?"

"I tole you I din't kill Jeb Holloway, man! You got to believe me!"

"Of course, I believe you, Walsh. So why don't I just scare up a White Bronco while you finish breaking out of your cell, then you can pack up your golf clubs, drive off into the sunset and swing happily ever after?"

From effort or pain, Walsh pants like a ruptured bellows.

Kravitz leans in and rests his forehead on the bars until Walsh lunges for his throat with both hands. The deputy steps back and arcs the haft with a blurring whoosh across Walsh's forearm.

The prisoner yowls and retreats, then comes back to snarl. "You got the gun, huh? Got my fingerprints on it? You got a witness? Got the guilty cartridge, White Cloud? Hell, asswipe, you ain't got shit! And how I'm gonna get a fair trial out here with all these country-ass nigger-hating Righteous Aryan Bundsmen? Man, they gonna have to try me so far out of state the closest Indian's gonna be in New Delhi!" Walsh starts to laugh, a good solid belly-roller.

Kravitz lets the laughter die. "Okay. Tell you what, Walter. I'll go along. We send you back to Wayne County, Michigan. That's Detroit, right? And we get you an all-black jury, and you walk. But then you're bonded over for trial on the charges and maybe you beat them. But you're gonna do time on interstate flight. And maybe you run into some of your old friends. Maybe you find out they're not so friendly anymore."

"What you want from me, man?"

"Be nice if you could tell me who shot Jeb Holloway."

"I don't know, man. But it was not me."

"I hope for your sake it wasn't. Because let me clue you in, Walsh, you're not acting like an innocent man." Kravitz backs away, into the darkness.

"Hey, where you goin'?" Walsh yells.

Before the prisoner can make another sound, Kravitz reappears inside with an armful of blankets. "I'll trade these for the tool." Walsh slides it across the floor, then steps back. The deputy kneels down and picks it up. "Empty your pockets," Red says.

Walsh turns them into rabbit ears.

Kravitz pushes the blankets into the cell. "Stick a wrist through the bars. Your choice which." Walsh gave him the left and a share of his concern. "You not 'fraid they come for me wit a rope?"

Red shackles the prisoner, steps back, and hooks his thumbs over his belt. "Not really, Walsh. If Mona's gonna send some boys down here to play black jack with you, they won't be able to get you out of the building."

"They can always shoot me through them bars," Walsh says.

"They won't. Around here they like to see their niggers beg and cry before they gag and kick." Red snaps off the lights, locks up and leaves.

* * *

Bear is sitting on the bar when Kravitz passes under the humming beer clock and sniffs the air. With a sharp laugh, the owner says, "Noisy puked in the crapper. I had him write out a sign."

Red's eyes turn left, where the old man's shaky handwriting reads: Out of Oder. Then he looks back at Bear, who says, "Walsh is my swamper, but you've got 'im."

"Why didn't you ask Moonlight to..."

The big Cheyenne stops the question with a hard smile. "Moonlight's with Augie. I can't match her hourly on that."

"Where's Noisy?"

"Crawling back to his hole," Bear says.

"You sure he's okay for that?"

"I ain't his squaw, Red."

"Goin' crimpy tonight."

Rolling his shoulders, Bear says, "We all die. Just a matter of when."

"And where and how," Kravitz says, thinking of Jeb Holloway. Then coming back to the moment. "Man, it's really vile in here."

"What do I care? I'm out to Pine Ridge to siwash and listen to spirits. But if you cut Walsh loose he can clean up."

They trade a hard stare before the deputy responds, "You're serious."

Bear hops off the bar. "Why not? He can sleep in back."

"What if he high tails it?"

"Hey, if I vouch, nobody's gonna make bad on me. Not white or black or Indian. Come on, Red. Let's put the nigger to work."

* * *

When Kravitz uncuffs Walsh from the jail door, the prisoner crabs back to the far corner of the cell. "I go, then what? You say the niggah was tryin' to excape..."

"Walsh," Bear growls, stepping inside the cell. "Shut up and find your feet. Or I'll push you out through the window."

Walsh looks up. "Window's got bars on it, man."

"You're beginning to get it."

"Constitution of the United States guarantees against cruel and unusual punishment. So why I got to clean up Noisy's puke?"

"We're leaving the cell open," Bear says. "You can stay or go. But if you go, it's down The Elk. You go to The Elk, clean the restrooms. And stay till I get back."

"Where you guys goin'?"

Kravitz ducks into his office, picks up his case file and tucks it under an arm. Re-emerging, he raises his free hand and salutes his prisoner, "Adios, amigo. May God help your sorry ass if you take off."

* * *

Across Front Street, Kravitz stops at Doris's two-story clapboard house. Before he can knock a small dog inside breaks into high-pitched yapping. Into a dark crack between the jamb and door appears the squinting eyes of his receptionist. Without a word, he pushes the case notes through the door. "Going' crimpy I figure. You might think about a fire."

"You're sure?" she yawns.

"Good night, Doe. I need to see Augie tomorrow early."

"That's not his routine," Doris rattles, then coughs until she turns red.

"You should see somebody about that."

"I know." She begins to close the door, but he slips his hand in. "Stay warm," he says.

"I got the message." She squints through the dark toward the sound of the pickup's running motor. "Tell me that's not Mona Holloway out there."

"Doris, you worry too much."

"That woman's poison."

Kravitz wants to tell Doris that Mona Holloway is just a pathetic lonely drunk a bit behind her best game. But he couldn't. Men will always be drawn to her, and he wonders if that isn't why her husband's dead.

* * *

At the crime scene, Red Kravitz gets out. Standing Bear hesitates, then asks, "You sure this is alright, me being along?"

"I'm making you an Assistant Deputy. Now get out here and assist."

On huge boots, what remained of the All Pro linebacker steps onto the yielding mat of wet sand, silt and smoothed dornicks, switches on a MagLite and washes the beam across Jeb Holloway's wounded white Suburban.

A sudden scampering disturbs the river's steady gurgle, drawing Bear's hand across Kravitz's chest. As the two stand frozen, a coyote streaks off into the night. Bear tracks it with the beam. "He smelled the blood."

Sanctuary's lone policeman clicks on his own flashlight and moves toward the vehicle. The wizards of forensic science, Micky and Mo Morris, have already determined that no one forced the cab locks, nor left any footprints or tire-marks to indicate that anyone other than B.S. Walsh had approached the site after Holloway was shot.

"What're you after?" Bear asks.

"I don't know exactly," Kravitz answers, piercing the flashlight beam through the window above the Suburban's broad tail gate. The intruding beam finds a naked king-sized mattress stretched out in the bay.

Kravitz paces to the side of the vehicle, illuminating the dashboard controls with a circle of light. By scanning he can see the ranch ignition, the darkened gauges. "Bear, you want to nose my Ford up to Jeb's?"

When their front bumpers meet, Red fishes out nine-foot jumper cables. "Pop the hoods, Bear." That done, Red bites the jaw clamps onto the battery terminals.

After firming the connections, Red says, "I figure that Jeb was waiting for someone, his engine idling. Next he gets killed. His engine idles till it runs out of gas. Then everything else is running on battery, till the battery dies."

"So what does all this prove?"

"We know how far it is from the ranch, so we can subtract the gas needed for that mileage — Micky and Mo have figures — and then figure how long it takes an idle to run the tank dry. We know from Maria when he left the ranch. So we can put an inside limit on when he got here and an outside limit on when his vehicle ran out of gas. From that..." he turns and looks at Bear "...we can determine the time interval when Jeb Holloway was murdered better than the M.E."

Kravitz checks the Suburban's console gauges. Gas, zero. Battery dead. No lights or flashers on. So Jeb wasn't signaling anyone. Whoever was supposed to meet him was well hunkered down at Poker Bluff.

Bear stares up as he paces. "Man, I'm not sure this is a good idea. Not at all."

Kravitz leans across the bench seat and checks the glove compartment. Micky and Mo have already removed the victim's .357 magnum Colt Python, but Kravitz works his fingernails along the inside seams, more a prayer than a hope. And so the deputy is unsurprised to find nothing. No hidden notes, no easy clues.

"That's all," Kravitz says. "Unclamp." He looks over to see Bear gazing up, past the descending moon, at the stars. Then Red stares up himself and watches a curtain of cool green light quiver the night sky.

Aurora Borealis.

"Early this year," Bear observes. "When I was a kid, the people said it was the ghosts of warriors past, dancing by campfires in the sky, and if you listened hard with your spirit, you could hear the drums, and the warriors chanting."

Kravitz still feels Indian enough to stop and listen. But only hears the sibilant splash of river water snagged on rotten willows and broken cottonwood trees, gurgling water roiled by humped and crested bancos, or split into a frothing bow wakes by settled boulders. "Why'd you want to come here tonight, Bear?"

"It's Sanctuary, Montana. What else is there to do?" A beat later he adds, "And why'd you come here tonight, Red?"

"To eliminate suspects. Anyone who's got an alibi gets scratched off the list."

"You got a list?"

"I got bupkis," says Kravitz.

"What?"

"It's a Yiddish word," he stares, then laughs, knocking himself on the forehead with the heel of his hand. "I'm really fucked up, Bear. When I'm with an Indian, I think like a Jew. But when I'm with a Jew, I think like an Indian. How'm I 'sposed to make connections? I'm both things and neither." A pause, then, "When we were kids, we used to play human beings versus the palefaces. But I'm a white, too. I mean, you never made much of it, because so many of us are breeds, but the other kids would say..."

"Jindian or Indijew. I remember. They were assholes."

"If we killed every white man because he was an asshole..." Red starts.

"We'd have enough human beings to take the land back, like it should be..."

"Aux aliments du pays? The way Dave Dooley lives it?"

"You're thinkin' Dooley dealt Holloway aces and eights?"

Kravitz wonders. "I don't know who's dealin' and who's holding the cards, but the game is braced. Somehow the last hand's gonna leave somebody with all the chips."

"And that's what's got you down here?"

As if jump-started himself, Kravitz scans the surrounding darkness. He hisses at Bear, "Headlights. Off. Now." His friend douses the beams. "Down," Red tells him, going to his knees behind the Suburban.

Bear kneels, one hand knuckled through fine oval pebbles. "What?"

Eyes wide with fear, Kravitz rushes to explain. "They think that some killers revisit the crime scene..."

"We were all lit up down here, so he could've shot us," Bear rasps.

Kravitz comes up off his knees, dusts his doeskins, then shakes his head. "Unless he got us lined up, he'd only get one of us."

"I can't believe... if what you said.... What were you thinking about, brother?"

"Relax," he says, watching Bear's hurried breathing whiten the chilly air. "Nobody knew we were coming. And what? He's going to sit up at Poker Bluff? If he's a local, you don't think folks would miss him?"

Bear points out, "Some kinds of people nobody misses because they don't want to be missed."

"You're talking about Dave Dooley."

Bear nods. "Or Crazy Daisy."

Kravitz couldn't disagree. Because Crazy Daisy isn't always crazy. Sometimes, when she talks about UFOs refueling in anvilheads and Ramon walking out of the shimmer of mirages, she's pure bonkers. Other times she can look at a clear sky and say, "Snow this weekend," and it does. So with Daisy, you can never tell for sure which channels her rabbit ears are picking up.

Into the silence Bear guesses, "You're thinkin' she saw the shooter?"

Another long wait works through a sigh into, "Maybe. But I was able to work around her place, keep out of her bead. So if somebody was really sneaky enough to set up Jeb Holloway, why leave a witness that could identify you?"

"Good point," Bear agrees. "So where are we on this?"

Nowhere. And Kravitz knows it . He has dragged his best friend along because he wanted someone to break the solitude and share the fear. Or maybe, as the town's bar-dog, because the huge Cheyenne knew more secrets than anybody. So he has to check. "Bear?"

"Still here, brother."

His pupils have finally accommodated the weakly moonlit dark, and hold the bartender's eyes as he answers. "Walsh believed Noisy about the gold. But our Detroit con's never panned a stream." Kravitz comes right to it. "Problem is that Noisy says he saw the 'gold' the day before Walsh came down to look for himself. And if that glitter was really a Sharps cartridge, it was in the river before Jeb Holloway was shot."

Bear says, "Why not? If you're not sure you can make a shot, what do you do?"

"Practice," he says, thinking of Leonard Jarnow. "Go to a range."

"I'm talking about a down-angle shot with local swirl winds, a shot you have to hit because if you don't, your target's going to haul-ass away. Even if you're Billy Dixon it's harder to lead a driver inside a Suburban than a rider on a horse."

"Meaning the shell from the killshot might still be in the river."

Bear looks downstream. "You'd have to work the whole bed half way to Fort Peck. And you still might not find it. You say it glitters, like gold. And an old drunk like Noisy's sure it is gold. You think some fly fisherman or kid ditching school won't spot it and pull it out?"

"You're not being helpful here."

"Sure I am," Bear smiles. "FBI tries to horn in, just tell 'em. 'Long as they're out here combing the riverbed for the discarded brass, you can run your own show."

TOO MUCH HISTORY

Without a scrap of new evidence, the Ford pickup clatters into The Elk's lot. Bear throws his door open. After it slams shut, Kravitz asks, "You think Walsh is still in there?"

Bear tips back his hat. "He takes off, I'll catch him and kill him."

That much is like to be true. Bear has killed before. His victim's death came both live and in multiple replay on Monday Night Football. Dallas vs. Pittsburgh. The Steeler's tight end had something to say while untangling from the pile-up. On the next down, the receiver slanted into a crossing pattern. Bear fell back, then looped around toward the offending player. The hurried quarterback threw high, so the target was stretched out when Bear hit him, lashing the receiver's head back with a loud crack. The man dropped like a sack of grain and never got up.

On the sad rainy night Red's mother died of cirrhosis in a Bozeman hospital, Bear had asked him, "Anything I can do to help?" and Red had only wanted to know, "Yeah, just tell me what he said to you, that Steeler, before you knocked him out of this world?"

Bear had laughed and said, "I just answered his question, is all," and went back to polishing gritty fingerprints off smudged tumblers.

Kravitz pushed his luck. "What was the question?"

The All-Pro linebacker had turned, rested both palms on the bar and said, "He asked, 'Is that all the harder you can hit, you pussy-ass homo redskin drunk?'" Then Bear shrugged. "Sometimes a nonverbal response has more impact."

Red thought about that before forming another question. "I thought pros said stuff like that all the time."

"I gave you the short version."

"I've got time. Tell me the rest."

Putting down the bar towel, he braced himself on those massive, corded muscles and cocked his head, as if talking to the beer clock. "The long story is the guy's name was Bubba Pound. Out of Oklahoma State."

"The Cowboys," Red muttered.

Bear smiled at the beer clock. He never liked Cowboys, even though he played for them. Then came the real reason. "I already told you what he said coming out of that pile up. But it was the untangle before that got him killed."

"The one where he said..." Red prompted.

Bear brought his eyes down from the beer clock. "The one where he said, 'I like titty purses. Kind they made from squaw.' Then he said how much he'd like to stuff his re-signing bonus into one made from my mamma.'"

"If I was as big as you, I'd've done the same thing myself."

Charges were never brought because autopsy revealed a weak artery in the victim's brain. Bear's hit just triggered an aneurism. Or that was the call of the Dallas coroner, who didn't want the embarrassment of another scandal on America's Team.

Back in the ongoing moment, Bear walks to the door to The Elk.

The lights are on, but Kravitz still says, "Tell Walsh to stick around."

Bear half turns to ask. "You're not doing anything stupid tomorrow, are you?"

"Stupid? Me, an Ivy League graduate?"

"Stupid, like Little Bighorn."

Kravitz stares at the darkened neon sign over the bar, understanding how things all hang together, in both Indian and Jewish lives. Sometimes the connections are so real that you can feel the dead kibitzing beneath the tunes throbbing out of the old Rockola. A single heritage like that would be too much, but two of them are paralyzing. Good thing the bar was closed.

"I thought you were going to siwash up at Pine Ridge tonight," Red says.

"After I check on Walsh. Make sure he's cleaned up Noisy's puke. If not, I'll clean it up with his fuzzhead." He barks a laugh before stepping back. "Tomorrow."

"If we both make it," Kravitz responds, then pulls the truck around.

* * *

At the top of the exposed landing Kravitz turns the key in the tumbler. The only other sound comes from the gentle rustle from stunted sage, naked mesquite and scrub pine. He turns the doorknob and enters. Beneath the fading tang of pine sap is a subtle scent, sweet but not saccharin, evocative but shy of bold, catchy but not preoccupying.

Inside, the scent sharpens and a cool spike of adrenaline goes through him like a Comanche war lance. Out of the shadows a woman's voice whispers, "Welcome home, Deputy."

He switches on an electric sconce. It flickers like a dying dream before settling into the dull glow of fires too old for warmth. Which reveals Molly Mendelbaum, arms embracing her knees, in an ice-blue peignoir.

"Who let you in?" he asks.

"Your friend Doris. She said there wasn't a room for rent in all of Sanctuary."

Red hangs up his hat, slips off his coat. "In a month motels will open up like wildflowers after a goose drown'der."

"Because of Jeb Holloway?"

"He was key to the Bearpaw ski resort."

"You think that might've got him killed?"

Red shakes his head. "Mostly you don't shoot big employers in a small town. Most you do is shoot off your mouth at The Elk."

"You're saying that Jeb Holloway was not a loved man."

"If you want gossip, try Doris."

Treacly light twinkles Molly's lavender eyes. "Doris thought I could twist your arm."

"I don't know why somebody kills somebody else." His mind flashes back to images of Bear knocking the life out of Bubba Pound, then admits,

"But usually it's personal."

"And this is your chance to beat the FBI to the killer, am I wrong?"

He gives the question enough time to settle, to see what might be lurking around in the media mud near the bottom. Then answers, "Somehow, I get the feeling you'd rather be in Philadelphia."

She laughs and shakes her head. "No really. It's good to see you." Biting a lower lip, then adding with a nod, "You're still looking very good."

"It's been a long time, Molly, since — "

She lets her knees fall to one side, hangs one arm over the back of the sofa and shivers, "Cold in here."

"I can pitch some fat pine into the estula," he begins, but she holds up one hand. Her eyes comb the images, settle on the burned-down Jahrzeit candle, then come back to ask, "Your father?"

"Cancer."

"I'm sorry."

"Me, too. He tried to be proud of me."

"That was so hard?"

"For some people their sun rises and sets on expectations. For them, it's hard to escape disappointment."

She shivers again.

"I'll put some heat in the kettle-belly." He drifts to a brass cradle of split logs.

She stops him. "We'll be going to bed soon."

"I've got an early start tomorrow."

"Me, too."

"Look, Molly. I can't take you along. It's an official investigation."

"But you promised."

"I'm not going to the crime scene."

"Who is she?" Molly asks.

"Who?" he asks back.

If he hadn't known her so well, he wouldn't have recognized that she was being honestly coy in saying, "Whoever kept you out this late."

He rubs the chill off his face. "I've already been back to the scene," he admits, before realizing this is just what she had wants. So he tries to cut it off with a simple, "I had to re-check a few details."

She lets her glance drop, as if she were examining that thought to see how it would line up in tomorrow evening's news. Finally she lifts her breasts with folded arms, her eyes glowing with a sad smile. "I always figured you for Wharton. Or was it law school? I seem to remember law school."

"Yale. But if you aren't sure how things will go, always plan your exit."

"I would have said 'entrance,' not 'exit.' For a guy like you, I mean."

"I guess you were wrong," he says.

"Maybe we were both wrong," she says back.

"I've got to get some sleep. There's a guest bedroom back there. Guaranteed free of cinch-bugs."

"I want to sleep with you tonight." The conviction in her voice makes him want to believe that some things don't change. But at the same time it makes him wonder which other things do. Because you just don't pick up and carry one after fifteen years without a single word.

He closes his eyes. "Molly..." But before he can think another word, her hands are on his chest, her breath, sweet and gentle and warm invades his nose and brain until he can't think straight anymore.

She whispers, "I've wanted to sleep with you ever since we... ever since I've known you as a woman... that part of me was always like a magnet, drawing me to wherever you were. And maybe it was just fate that brought us back from worlds so different..."

He takes both her arms at the wrist and holds them. "Molly. Understand this. The big news is we're about to invade Iraq again, okay? Once that happens, everything else slides into insignificance. You need some perspective. I am just a small-time deputy in a town that will drain out of tomorrow's news like meltwater down the Missouri."

"But you said you had a suspect." There it is, finally. On the table.

He lets his hands fall away from her. "Get some sleep."

"So you don't want to be with me tonight?"

"We're both tired. Let's talk more in the morning." And so after she plants a too passionate kiss on him, they settle into separate beds.

For two hours he sleeps like his dead ancestors. Then comes the dream. And he is seeing down the long octagonally faceted barrel of a Sharps, over the raised Creedmore sight, aligned over the muzzle on a man's back, a back draped in denim. The target turns as the hammer comes back, and Kravitz sees that he is the man in the rifle's sight.

As the hammer begins to fall, he wakes up screaming, "No!," panting hard, the sheets soaked in sweat.

Before he can tell himself it was only a dream, her voice makes the same thought into soft, comforting words, her hands stroking his slick, black hair, pushing him down as she lifts the cover and slides in beside him, whispering, "I'm here."

*   *   *

The next day Kravitz arrives at the Hollow-A Ranch to find Mona out back, shouldering a Sharps' and saddled on a horse, a hybrid of the rugged yakimas of the plains with the more powerful Arabians raised on Kentucky racing farms, with a little roan thrown in for extra spirit. Kravitz knows this from the muscles, the relative shapes of the legs, the angles of bone around the big dark eye, from the flow of the mane, from the way the mount snorts and tosses his head, the way that the tail falls and blows in light gusts, carrying a scent that confirms everything else.

Even to a half-Indian, different breeds of horses smell different. In that way, they're like women. Molly with her particular scent, Mona with hers. It's piquant and subtle all at once. It comes off her like nectar from a blossom and breathes with her heat when she moves.

Which now she barely does at all. Every motion disciplined, she lines up a heavy iron silhouette eight hundred yards off. After setting the double trigger, she eases the firing finger down and pulls back. The detonating black powder expels a puff of smoke. A steady northerly catches and sweeps it off. Far from the muzzle, a massive slug clangs the target, which lurches on a stiff-spring hinge, recovering its position before the first echo returns.

Kravitz squints downrange and sees the fresh ding just above the metal Indian's eyebrow. Turning in her saddle, Mona cradles the vintage weapon. "Care for a shot, Deputy?"

"You have a different silhouette?"

She aims the muzzle toward the damaged target. "That's a Blackfoot. I didn't think a Crow would object to bagging a Blackfoot."

"Our great Crow warrior, Eelapaush, killed twenty Blackfoot before they got him. Since we're ahead on body count, I think I'll pass."

"Sounds like the tribes were doing a pretty good job killing each other off. If the whites had waited thirty more years, all the Indians left would have been dead."

"If the whites hadn't pushed the eastern tribes west, there would have been land enough," he stares at the rifle, "and buffalo enough, for all."

She swings the muzzle onto Kravitz's chest. "You've come for this."

"And whatever other rifles like it you have," he says, keeping his eyes on hers.

"People out here don't like having their guns taken," she says, moving the bead over the deputy's heart. "It would be unfortunate if you just burst in here yelling, startled me, I turned and, well, with a woman's protective instincts...accidents happen."

"You forgot to reload. But that was quite a shot just now. I sure as hell wouldn't want to be on the receiving end of it."

She hands him the Big Fifty, pushes her hair back with both hands and stares at the horizon. "You know, the Crow were always very savvy. They rode with Custer as scouts."

"And paid the price, Mrs. Holloway."

"Mona," she insists sweetly. But the look on her face is the way he imagined a snake would appear, if it could smile.

He shoulders the Sharps. "Mrs. Holloway, Len Jarnow expressed some very peculiar ideas to me about someone you thought looked a lot like me who was here, night before last, in an official capacity to inform you of your husband's death."

"Yes, I remember something about that." She looks down to María. "Don't you remember something about that, María?"

"Sí," is all María can manage before looking down.

Kravitz turns back to the widow. "When people have a bit too much to drink, they tend not to remember things clearly."

"And who knows what you said to me?"

"I do. And so do you. But that doesn't matter." He holds up the rifle. "What does matter is that I have a search warrant." One-handing the stock of the Sharps, he digs it out and passes it across. "Duly signed and presented. And I'm going to take my time looking around."

She passes it back without reading a word. "María will show you around. I'm going for a ride."

* * *

Scared because she's likely illegal, María fumbles the keys into custom-made deadbolts. When both are unlocked, she shoulders the door open. Inside, each wall presents an arsenal of weapons, double-racked. Each rack tracks on slots in the ceiling so the front ones pull away to access those behind.

Red reckons maybe four hundred shotguns, rifles and skeet guns, varmint guns and small-bore target rifles, antiques, both historical pieces and working replicas. If all these pieces have ammo, Jeb Holloway's private army was braced for a standoff longer and more violent than Waco.

Passing the ranch on county roads you see his hired hands, tall in their rigs, outlined against a sky curdling with storm, their rifles snug in leather boots. The rifles are for troublesome critters. They could be coyotes, wolves, badgers, bear, anything that moves in a way Jeb didn't take to. And that would certainly include his wife's lover. It's this thought that always circles back, like a lazy buzzard on a thermal, to the man they'd all come to know as B. S. Walsh.

From the arsenal, Red picks out a single-shot 1873 Remington carbine and works the action, ensuring that the breech is clear before replacing it. His eyes trace the racks, stop on a second Sharps. Examining it closely reveals a carbine of Civil War vintage in .45 caliber with a short barrel. Not what killed Jeb Holloway.

He turns to María. "Did Mr. Holloway have a private office?"

She keeps her eyes down while answering, "Sí. Esta aquí."

The adjoining room is secured with a retinal scanner and PIN pad. Maria brings her eye up, pushes in 62742, an easy pneumonic for M-A-R-I-A. Turning to him, she explains, "Este dice a quien entre, por la tiempo exactamente."

"Okay," he says. For whatever reason, Jeb Holloway had trusted more people with his guns than whatever he cached in here. A wood-paneled door opens onto a sumptuous office. A gleaming redwood desk sits to the right, supporting a laptop computer. Across from it is a large-scale architect's model of Sanctuary region, centered on the ski complex nearing completion at Bearpaw Mountain. Stepping up, he studies it, sees a number of plots marked Future Development. One is the plateau Crazy Daisy calls home.

He puts the Sharps aside and sits down. Looping endlessly across the laptop's screen is a view taken from the helmet camera of a downhill skier attacking a double black diamond run called Aces and Eights. He clicks the mouse. The screen saver defaults to a two-line security gate: authorized user name on the top line, access PIN on the bottom. María is looking over his shoulder when his eyes met hers, but she just shakes her head. Not an authorized user.

So what now? Maria's PIN for admission to the room is her given name converted to the corresponding numbers on a touch-tone pad. Maybe the sometimes drunken Mona Holloway would want something painlessly easy to remember. Using the keys, he tries:

Authorized User Name: MONA

PIN: 6662

And waits.

Large red letters flash ACCESS DENIED. In desperation Red hits the escape key. But the words keep flashing. Backspace works no better. Delete is a complete bust. Having nothing to lose, Red tries the only other trick he knows, an ancient DOS command for exit: the F7 key.

The command entrance sequence and blinking cursor return. Red rubs the temples of his aching head and plays a game. Suppose you're Jeb

Holloway. It's your computer. There's something you don't want your wife to see. So you don't delete her name. Instead you change her PIN. But to what?

Knowing Maria used the keypad equivalents, Red seeks a word that would have delighted Jeb to enter. Daisy Ramirez's Denver Bronco's jersey gives him a crazy idea: BITCH. So he checks the keypad of the touch-tone phone and copies the number below each corresponding letter: B = 2; I = 4; T = 8; C = 2; H = 4

And tries again

Authorized User Name: MONA

PIN: 24824

Across the laptop screen the instruction WAIT... comes on, while the ellipsis pulses dots, followed by a window capped by a tool bar. He clicks on file. At the top is a CALENDAR tab. He clicks it. A window pops open. The last entry is on the day Jeb was killed. October 7, at 0930. Meaning 9:30 A.M. And Jeb was going to see... the line runs across to a single designator: HIM. The meeting place is no longer a secret. The agenda that morning, and who HIM is, are still unknown.

Checking the penultimate date for meetings, September 28, he found TELECON: 2030 (8:30 P.M.) LJ re: BP. Leonard Jarnow regarding Bearpaw? So Jeb and Jarnow had talked. If the next meeting was slated for HIM. Could that mean Jarnow?

Kravitz clicks on the e mail tab and is prompted for a user name and PIN. He tried JEBHO with the corresponding key-pad numbers: 53246. It brought back ACCESS DENIED. "María," he says. "Any ideas?"

Still avoids his eyes, she shakes her head. "Is for the mister."

Dead end?

Kravitz can't believe that two guys as rich as Holloway and Jarnow would piss away their time over a patch of wasteland. Not unless the mineral rights amount to something big.

Tapping the F7 key again produces the view of a skier glissading near the end of a snowclad trail. Red gets up, reclaiming and cradling the Sharps that Mona had surrendered. If not the one that put Jeb away, at least the same caliber. He will leave the rest to Micky and Mo. After exiting the office, María relocks the door and turns to Red.

He guesses, "'The mister' might keep a rifle in his bedroom. Let's have a look."

TOO MUCH TOO FAST

Red pushes the door open, looks back and asks María, "This is the mister's bedroom?"

Remaining behind him, she swallows and clutches her hands together.

The victim is dead and gone, but the tang of a macho aftershave survives. Recently soaped leather blends with that scent. Ungraced by a woman's touch, the room feels cold and utilitarian, a place for a man to collapse and sleep, then rise and conquer the world. Any women who got this far would be conquered, too.

He looks back through the open door at María, and signals her down the stairs. Then steps to the oiled walnut armoire, big enough to conceal another Sharps. When both doors swing open, he sets the Sharps against the nearest wall and begins to slide the clothes aside.

Behind him, the space changes. Indians can tell. It may be the way that sounds reflect, or odors dilute. Or the way unseen movement creates a subtle web of light and shadow. But whenever he gets the feeling, it makes him ease around.

Through the rush of hot mist from the adjoining bathroom, Mona Holloway emerges with a cushy teal-colored towel knotted above her breasts, ending just below her crotch. Except for the glowing eyes, she looks almost Indian. Or Jewish. Or both. At some level deeper and more ancient than the womb, this is what Red Kravitz most fears and wants in a woman, and why he freezes.

She sits down on the bed and slaps both thighs with the palms of her hands. "Well, your warrant didn't say you could look for this!"

"I look where I'm let in."

"Will any judge believe that you would be looking for guns among the most private personal and business files in my husband's private office just one day after conspiring secretly in a parking lot with his arch-rival, Leonard Jarnow?"

"If the computer contained lists or directions or inventories of rifles, then I am well within my rights — "

Mona flips a dismissive hand. "You were fishing," she says, playing at her wet hair and asking herself, "Where's my other towel?"

He advances just one step to protest when she pulls the towel free and starts drying her hair with it, explaining as if to a child, "Now will any judge believe after you admit that you were in the victim's bedroom with his naked widow that you don't have an incurable conflict of interest in continuing the investigation of Jeb's murder?"

He wants to stop looking but can't. And she knows it. Her breasts dance as she dries her hair. "And then you show up here with this huge gun and order me to get undressed..." She ties the towel around her head and lets her hands fall to her thighs, staring at him.

"I'm through with my search," he says, turning around, snatching up the Sharps and marching for the door. But she steps in to block him, whispering, "You can have what you've always wanted. So why not here and now?"

He tries to push past her, but she presses her body against him, leaving the wet tracks of her breasts on his shirt. Opium slams up his nostrils and puts starch in his business. She grabs between his legs and hisses, "This is where you live."

With monumental will, he pushes her hand away. It goes straight to the Sharps and pulls. He pulls back but she joins one hand to the other and holds on. "Any judge I know in this state will rule that this was acquired during an illegal search. So you can just leave it here."

* * *

When Red rolls into Sanctuary, the hot hue has drained from his face, the rush of sexual sweat evaporated. The trip back has taken him via the crime scene, where he recorded the mileage traveled from the Hollow-A ranch. Passing a corkboard directory in the unlit lobby, he veers right, down a creaky run of risers to a dim landing, then down another run to the basement. The bottom riser leaves him looking at Doris, parked at her desk attacking a twist of beef jerky. She looks up, working the words in around bites. "Get whatever you're after up there?"

He avoids her eyes. "Give the Tweedles a call. Ask them to find out how much gas a Chevy Suburban uses to travel eight point four miles off road, then how long, after it's stopped and idling, it takes for what's left in a full tank to run out."

Doris tears into a ribbon of beef jerky. "Caldera Cunningham called. Wanted to know what you were doing about her complaint on Jeb Holloway."

"Tell her she won't be bothered again."

"Last item: your woman's back there," she tips her head toward Red's office. Doris's nose goes to work, sniffing like a hound. "Come to think of it, you might want to wash up first.."

He shakes a finger at her and opens his mouth.

Doris looks toward the office. "Tell her, not me."

He hangs his hat on a peg, shambles back and posts himself against the jamb. Molly sits with outstretched legs resting on his desk, hands spidered together. Her nostrils draw at the air, then she says, "It's Mona Holloway, isn't it?"

"Look. Nothing happened. Okay?"

Her eyes radiate disbelief. "Where is it?"

"Where is what?"

"The rifle you think killed Jeb Holloway, the one Mona Holloway fucked you into leaving behind."

"Nobody fucked Mona Holloway, okay?" he says, louder than he wanted to.

"That's not what Doris says. She says that Mona Holloway fucks anyone she wants, any time she wants, anywhere she wants. So why not you, Deputy Kravitz?"

"She doesn't like Indians," he mutters, crossing his arms.

"I don't think Mona cares what tribe a man comes from, as long as he's good and willing."

"When I got out there, she was shooting a target of a Blackfoot in full war dress."

"Did she hit him?" she asks.

"She can shoot," is the only answer he gives.

As if a switch has been hit, Molly transforms to crisply cool newswoman. "Do you think she killed her husband?"

"I honestly don't know who shot Jeb Holloway."

She swings her legs down off his desk, flashing him enough thigh to get his full attention. Then stops and lets her eyes settle on Kravitz. "Why did you desert me?" She crosses her arms and squints anger. "You know, we had a very sweet thing going at Penn. When you left, I was a basket case."

"You're well recovered," he says.

"I threw myself into my work and tried to forget. Maybe I wanted you to have to turn on your TV every night and see what you missed out on..."

"Don't watch much TV."

She ignores him. "... but no matter how hard or far I ran, once I reached full speed I was going to smack right into those memories again. And after last night I knew I was still on fire for you. And that you were still on fire for me." She picks up a slag paperweight and hurls it at him. He ducks and it bounces off a brick wall. "Then you go out and have to piss the case away because you can't keep your schlong in its scabbard."

He unbuttons his shirt, peels it off, feels her eyes run over his chest. Then he bunches it up, smells it and nods. "I was searching her husband's bedroom and she came out of the bathroom with a towel around her. She dropped it off and pressed herself up against me. That's what's on the shirt."

"And that's all? That's all the... farther... it went?"

"That's all the farther it went. I may be the only man she wanted that she couldn't have. And that means that if Mona Holloway can help solve this crime, now she won't."

"Okay," she says, sounding half convinced. "You never were a very good liar."

His naked back is turned when he hears the whir of a video camera, and a harsh cackle of a man's voice. "Oh, this is spicy. Hey, Mol, I'll sell this back to you for a thousand bucks." Kravitz spins, feels his hand stab out, cover the lens and yank the camera down.

"Hey, what..." the bearded guy begins. Before he can produce another word, Red's powerful hand collars him and shoves him toward the unoccupied cell. "Hey!" finally gets out.

Kravitz rips the gridded door open, hurls the man in and slams the bars shut. Then he fishes the key ring off the wall peg, locks up and turns away, opening the camera, prying out and cracking the disk like a dry saltine.

"Kravitz?" Molly says. "What's..." Before she can finish, he whirls on the new prisoner and says, "Don't you ever threaten this lady's character in any way, do you hear? Because if you do, the world isn't big enough for you to hide in."

The prisoner turns to Molly. "Is this guy fucking crazy?"

"Sometimes," she says. "Just don't provoke him and It'll pass."

"Provoke him? Fuck him! What about me? What's the charge, man?"

Kravitz snaps back. "If anyone asks: unauthorized trespass on public property, interference with a lawman during the investigation of a felony, resisting arrest..."

"Anything else?" the man screams, his clenched hands white on the bars. "Any little fucking thing else in this pisspot scumbag of a town!"

"Yeah. Aiming a camera at a Native American."

"If I ever fucking get out of here..."

"Try the window bars," Molly suggests. "They look loose."

"Don't I get one phone call or something?"

"Our one and only phone is broken," Kravitz informs him.

"Hey, this commode's broke, too. Somebody took a..."

"Doris," Red yells. "You want to see if you can bring a bucket and plunger for our prisoner. He's volunteered to clean up the cell."

"Hey!" the captive whines. "How long till the phone's fixed?"

Kravitz lets his eyes study an old crack in the ceiling. "Out here in this pisspot scumbag town, gee, it could take a week or more. You've got to learn to relax."

"Mol! Are you gonna let him — "

Molly closes her eyes and shakes her head. "Al, smarten up, buddy. Redfawn Kravitz is the law here." Then she loops an arm around Kravitz's waist and presses her face against his bare skin, then licks it. He looks down at her and she stares back up. "I always liked the way you tasted."

"You, too," he says, risking a smile.

"Let's go home, take a long hot shower and get Mona's scent washed off you."

* * *

Kravitz rebuttons his shirt while Molly leads him up the stairs. Hypnotized by the slow pendulum of her hips, he follows the beat of her steps across the upstairs lobby then yells, "Hey! What are you doing for Yom Kippur tomorrow?"

Without responding, she steps toward the light, her shape dissolving around the edges in the fierce glare. On leaving she swivels past a man with a creased Palo Alto hat and a serious eastern suit. To show what smart kind of an Indijew the arrival is dealing with, Red opens, "What can I do for you, Special Agent?"

The man tips his big hat at Molly, then advances with cadenced steps across the old floorboards. His genes take him in the direction of Aryan purity: blonde hair, blue eyes, clean shaven and salon-tanned. Slipping off his sunglasses, he studies the place. "You have electricity?"

"Enough to get by," Kravitz says. "If you're not planning to refine aluminum."

The FBI man takes one creaky step down the first run of stairs, continuing his assessment, knocking on the paneled wood. "Washington tried giving you a 'head's up,' about my arrival," he says, offering a steady hand. Red returns the pressure each time the agent ups the ante. Until the newcomer releases and pulls back, saying, "So we wonder if you had phone service out here."

"Sometimes."

"Computers?"

"We keep an old Wang rechipped, star-seventy the link, because we've only got one line in here."

Finally he says, "I'm Pete Rollins, out of the Great Falls Office, FBI." The special agent has the chiseled good looks of a film star, skin stretching in hard ridges around bone, framing sad eyes. Red notes that the left ring finger is unbanded. He also checks out the slicker's duds, tips his hat and says, "I'm Red Kravitz, Deputy Sheriff of Sanctuary. What can I do for you, Agent Rollins?"

"Pete," he insisted.

Kravitz crosses his arms, blocking Rollins advance. "What are you orders?"

"I'm to set up a one-man temporary field office to coordinate an interagency task force to identify and apprehend the person responsible for the murder of Jeb Holloway."

"What does this mean for my investigation?"

Rollins advances another step. "You are to surrender all evidence and file notes to me immediately. And I am to take over pre-emptive coordination of all your activities as they relate to this case. Which means that you are to consult with me before pursuing any initiative, and not to make any moves, conduct any interviews or enter any crime scenes related to the murder before first getting prior approval from me. Are we clear on this?"

"Hold your horses, Agent Rollins." A palm comes up, blocking his way. "I can't just surrender evidence on an investigation in progress."

"You're refusing a federal court order?"

Red Kravitz shrugs. "I'm not refusing. The way our charter in Sanctuary is set up, I don't have the authority. To give you those things, you're going to need mayoral approval."

"Let's get me set up here," Rollins says. "Then see the mayor."

Kravitz jerks his head and leads Rollins to the basement. In passing Doris, she looks up and twirls a stalk of beef jerky, staring through the newcomer as she says, "How long you gonna be in town, cowboy?"

When they get passed her, Rollins whispers, "Who is that?"

"Secretary," he says. "Be nice. She's got a very special daughter."

Drifting down the narrow hallway, Rollins finds himself walking and turning, studying details. As they pass the holding cell, Molly's cameraman Al stabs both arms between the bars to grapple Rollins by pinstriped lapels. "This maniac Indian is holding me illegally!"

"I'm FBI. Yours is a local matter." Rollins encircles the man's hands at the wrists, twists hard and releases himself. But Al insists, "Abridgement of freedom of speech."

"You seem to talk just fine," ventures Kravitz.

"Illegal search and seizure..."

Rollins gives Kravitz a puzzled look, which evokes the response. "This asshole used his camera to assault a law officer. I relieved him of it using nonlethal means."

The FBI agent shrugs at the prisoner.

Prompting Al to shriek, "You've got to get me out of here! I'm claustrophobic! The toilet won't flush!"

Kravitz turns away from Al and passes his office.

Rollins nods, "This'll do fine."

"That's mine," he says. "Here's yours"

Turning to his right, he opens a closet bearing the hand-painted words: Other Stuff. Inside a narrow entrance a rust-stained set tub is catching rhythmic drops from a failing faucet. Overhead a forty-watt bulb ignites by a beaded string. On flanking walls stands a mildewed inventory of brooms, mops, buckets, sponges, scrub brushes, squeegees, a fifteen gallon drum of Solvent Nine Plus.

Rollins blinks. "You're fucking kidding."

"Kidding is not in the budget this year. This year it's all fucking serious."

"Why can't I use the mayor's office?"

"Then where's the mayor going to sit?"

"Look..."

"No, you look," Kravitz says. "Jeb Holloway is dead. Now unless you know somebody who was out to kill him, I think we're a lot better able to find out which people might have wanted to."

Special Agent Rollins hangs an arm around the deputy. Whispering low, he asks, "Can we talk?" then checks back to where Al, sans videocam, is all eyes. "Somewhere else?"

Kravitz re-shuts the closet and signals the Fed to follow. As they pass the cell, the cameraman screams, "What about me?" This freezes Rollins freezes, who turns to ask the deputy, "Can he be released on my recognizance?"

"If you sign for him, it sure would simplify my life."

"All right!" says the prisoner, pounding out a fast riff on the old bars.

Silencing the celebration, Rollins holds up one hand, tanned, slim and strong. "I've never had a prisoner run on me. If you get on a plane back to Atlanta, that's interstate flight to avoid prosecution. Are we communicating?" The eyes boring through the prisoner are hard and grey and terrible. And so all that Al can do is whine, "Oh, man!"

Turning to Kravitz, Rollins says, "Now I don't want to communicate to the prisoner that he is able to violate the local ordinances with impunity. So I wonder, Deputy Kravitz, if we could agree that the prisoner might do some community service, simply to indicate that he's aware of the seriousness of the charges against him."

"That works for me," says Red.

"Good," agrees Rollins, then comes back to negotiate. "Why don't we say that he plunges out the toilet, cleans up the cell, paints the walls — a pale blue would be nice, don't you think?"

"Soothing," nods Kravitz.

"And runs some new extension cords in here, maybe a phone jack, too?"

"These assholes got no phone," says the cameraman, seconds before Doris's starts to ring. Kravitz looks that way, then shrugs. "We do now. Run a line for Special Agent Rollins."

As the two lawmen head for The Elk their prisoner shouts, "This is bullshit! You're violating the Sixteenth Amendment to the Constitution, against slavery! Do you hear me!"

They reach Doris, who has submerged the phone's receiver between her pillowy breasts. Looking up with affected innocence, she tells Kravitz, "It's Micky and Mo. Shall I have them call back later?"

Kravitz says, "No, I'll take it." The receiver goes to his ear and all he gives up is, "Yeah... yeah...yeah. Okay. No. That's fine. Sure." before handing up.

Rollins extends a hand. "Who are Micky and Mo?"

"Poker buddies. Follow me, Rollins. We'll... what's the expression in Washington?... do lunch."

* * *

Special Agent Rollins studies the menu. Kravitz has already introduced Bear, while B.S. Walsh skulks around in violation of the Sixteenth Amendment. Rollins looks up to ask, "The Reuben. It's good?"

Kravitz checks. "Bear, this sandwich killed anybody lately?"

"Not on the premises," he answers, then to Rollins, "You want one?"

"Yeah. I'm hungry."

"Walsh!" the owner yells. "Reuben and..." he turns to Rollins.

"Perrier?" he asks.

"Water!" he shouts back. "And polish the silver."

The FBI man checks around. "It usually this busy?"

Bear shrugs. "When the Bearpaw resort starts up it'll jump to three thousand a week. No room for that many in the new lodges or time-shares. I reckon we'll pick up the slack."

Rollins looks at Kravitz, then back at Bear. "Fill me in," he says.

Bear plants both elbows on the bar and leans forward, checking both sides as if folks would overhear. Then he confides, "Up the ranch they've already dropped in a few modulars for the winter crew. Now the time-share he's buildin' is done, Holloway was going to spruce up the bunkhouses, save skiers two hundred a night over what they'd pay at the mountain. They'd throw in a shuttle van to take them to and fro, rake in more."

"I guess that won't happen with Jeb Holloway dead," Rollins says.

Bear says, "Mister, you've got a lot to learn about people with money."

In the hard silence that follows, B.S. Walsh blows through the swinging kitchen door with the Reuben, sets it down with a glass of water and flatware, then says, "French fries come with it."

Rollins directs his question to the plate. "How'm I gonna lose ten when I'm eating all these fries?"

Walsh shrugs. "You need anything else?"

"Yeah, if you could bring out the guy who killed Jeb Holloway, that would make my day."

Walsh goes a shade paler. "You see him on the menu?"

Rollins smiles. "Let me guess. You took a wrong turn west on Seven Mile outside Detroit and kept going until you blew out a tire, and now here you are."

"I ain't never even been to Dee-troit," B.S. insists.

Rollins laughs, stroking a fry through a lake of poured ketchup. "I did a tour in the Bureau's Detroit office. So I recognize the accent. I mean, if you're trying to make the lie work, don't say Dee-troit, stepping on the first syllable and picking up speed as you go through the word. It's a give-away."

"I got a job here to do," Walsh says, turning for the kitchen.

"Yeah, I bet you got time to do, anyone catches up with you," the agent says back. When he turns to Kravitz, the question is: "What do you know about that guy?"

"That he stays in line, doesn't do anything a lot of other guys don't do. Why?"

"Bad vibes is all," Rollins whispers, tearing into his Reuben.

Bear stops observing long enough to backstop the deputy. "Oh, the Buffalo Solider is a real good nigger. We put the rawhide to his back when he isn't, to let him know his place."

"How's the food?" Kravitz asks.

Pete Rollins burps. "Good. You're not eating."

"Not hungry." Kravitz waits out a couple of hums of the bubbling beer clock behind them before asking, "Look, you mind if I drop you back at town hall while I check with the mayor about this jurisdictional matter."

"You want me to come along? I mean, I don't want it to look like I've sent you scampering over there..."

"Red don't scamper," Bear says. "The style don't much suit."

"Well, I'd like to meet the mayor anyway," Rollins presses the issue.

Kravitz senses a climber. So he just says, "Well, strange as it may seem for a politician, the mayor can be a very private man. Sometimes it's best not to spring things on him."

TWO TO TANGLE

Red finds Augie Suder in the loft at Doris's place. Sanctuary's mayor is crowned by a flared topper, 20XX in black beaver with matching eye mask, but otherwise nude, as is Moonlight. Both are tucked in a large bolster bed enclosed by burning incense and scented candles. After closing the door behind him, Red doffs his Resistol and waits for Augie to ask, "Three guesses who I am?"

The deputy tries, "Looks to me like the Long Ranger."

"Shit, Red. Maybe you'll catch this killer yet."

Doris's daughter greets him, "Hi, Red. Wanna join the fun?"

"Official business, Moonlight."

The mayor lifts his mask. "Any news?"

"Augie, an FBI type just crawled into town. Jeb Holloway was killed on federal land. So they want to take over the case."

"Well, we might as well want tits on a bull! FBI takes over and like that..." he snaps his fingers, "we're the next Waco!" Augie turns florid. "Can you keep 'em from getting my town burnt down or blowed-up?"

"I can try, Augie."

"You do that, Red. Because we got all those outlet stores due on Front Street after Bearpaw opens up. But unless you grab hold of the jerk line real quick, these retailers'll get cold feet quicker 'n a newborn mole rat at the north pole." Augie rails on. "Every town has a murder now and again. And I don't want a bunch of eyeballers tryin' to horn in or let any journalist snoop around. Promise me that's not going to happen, Red."

"That's like asking for a winter without snow, Augie. Truth? I think we'll see a wave of media crest through here before it breaks off chasing the next story."

"Can't you scoot 'em off to chase the build-up to the war?"

"Maybe we'll just get the B Team, Augie, rookies and rejects, plus folks not wantin' their heads blown off by friendly fire in Iraq."

"I won't have to do a stand-up, will I, Red?"

"So far nobody's asked, Augie, but I can't make promises."

Watching Augie stew was at least a very peculiar experience for the only fully dressed person in this loft, and Red had to marvel at the mayor's ability to discourse on public matters while remaining at full mast without Moonlight's encouragement.

Clearly unready for a media storm, Augie fretted. "If I'd liked press conferences, I'd've gone into public life in Helena, like Jarnow. But you ever try to get a word in edgewise with Lenny Jarnow?"

"Not my place, Augie."

"Well, just stay wide clear of him is my advice."

"I'll take that to heart."

"Anything you need, just ask."

Redfawn Kravitz releases a long sigh. "Well, Your Honor, our visitor is a bachelor, so I was wondering if Moonlight could make his stay more enjoyable."

"Moonlight?" Augie solicits.

The titter again. "Is he good looking?"

"He's trying to lose ten pounds."

"What's his name?"

"Pete Rollins."

"Where's he staying?" The mayor asks.

"That's between you and him," Red answers, figuring that Augie Suder is a real estate man. He knows every wickiup, garret and crawl space in the region, from the top of grain elevators to the bottom of abandoned mines.

"Leave it to me," Augie says. "Now earn your salary and catch me this killer, deputy."

* * *

The sky glows violet as the earth goes cold. Not with the edge of chill that cuts away the last trace of autumn, but still crimpy enough for snow. Red raises his sheepskin collar and swaggers toward what Sanctuary makes do for town hall. On the steps stands Molly and her cameraman Al, along with Pete Rollins. Leaning against the cool brick wall, the G-man takes Molly's question: "Do you know why Jeb Holloway was killed?"

Rollins doesn't shrug. Shrugging on camera reflects genuine puzzlement, a condition forbidden to the FBI by act of Congress. Instead he gives

Molly the pained look of a man fighting outrage with vigilance. "We're still studying the evidence."

"And why...?"

Rollins holds up one hand. "That's all I have for now. The only other thing I can tell you is that we will get whoever did this."

"Thank you, Special Agent Rollins." Molly turns with her mike and faces the video camera, seeing Kravitz but continuing, "And so the mystery in Montana continues, why U.S. Senate candidate Jeb Holloway was killed by a single shot from a deadly sniper as he sat alone in his Chevy Surburban, parked on the pebbly shore of the Timberline Wildlife Preserve. This is Molly Mendelbaum, CNN News, Sanctuary, Montana."

Pete Rollins stands in the shadows while Molly smiles at the local lawman.

"You look great," Kravitz says, a conviction that passing years hasn't changed.

She hops down the ancient, worn risers and squeezes his arm. "Would you like a spot? As the hardass squint-eyed gunslinger who's stepped out of the American imagination looking for showdown with the heinous killer?"

"Molly, nobody steps into a showdown 'gainst a Sharps buffalo gun."

"See if I offer to put you on national television again."

"Safer not to," he says. "When do you get off work?"

"Never," she says. "How about you?"

"Same," he returns. "How about six-thirty?"

"That's a long way off. I'm grabbing some lunch," she says.

"It's Yom Kippur. Aren't you supposed to be fasting?"

"I never fast when I'm hungry. I just turn into a bitch." She ambles away.

He turns to watch Rollins watch Molly make for The Elk. "She's hot. I've thought so since the first time I saw her on TV." Turning to Kravitz, "Something between you two?"

Ignoring the question, Red reports, "I talked with the mayor. He doesn't want Sanctuary to be the next Waco. So we need to know your plans."

"What about leaks?" Rollins crosses his arms and stares down the street at Molly. "We don't want to telegraph our next move to a suspect."

"It gets no farther than me."

Rollins half-nods. "It's okay by me, but I'll have to run it up the ladder."

"Until I hear otherwise, then," Kravitz says, "That's the deal."

"Why don't we split things up right now?" We have resources, manpower, authority, and expertise. During the investigation, we've got staff and consultants on call 24/7. All of this we bring to bear. Equipment is being flown in. When an indictment is made, you'll be the proud owner of state-of-the-art telecommunications and jump from the nineteenth to the twenty-first century in one day."

The deputy folds his arms, nineteenth-century style. "Well, you know, Rollins, I don't come from a culture that sees Santa Claus a whole lot, so I never believed the gifts under my tree are free. What's the catch?"

Rollins lowers both chin and voice. "Well it's an election year...and the President would like the killer caught without attention to the issue of guns. That's the spin we'd like put on it."

"I'm putting no spin on it at all, Agent Rollins. But you should check with the media about what spin they're using to sell it."

"If there's no leaks..." Rollins fiddles with his tie, one of those Red silk jobs the President likes to wear.

With a toss of the shoulders the deputy confesses, "Well, right now they wouldn't get much because I don't know anything."

"The law gives me the right to look at your case notes," Rollins reminds him.

"Then you'll have to twist my head off and look inside, because I don't write anything down. Not until I'm sure. And I'm a long way from sure," Kravitz says. "We don't keep files on citizens out here, Rollins. That's not what a bacheeitche does?"

"A what?" Rollins asks, trying hard to figure where he stands.

Red told him. "In Crow the word comes nearest to meaning 'good man.' It's the basis for all authority in the tribe."

"You're an elected official," Rollins reminds him. "If you withhold evidence, we could place you under arrest and..."

"What evidence?"

"Kravitz, you're up for re-election..."

"Well, I may withdraw from the ballot. Then you could deal with the new man."

"Whoever is deputy of Sanctuary," Rollins counters, "We'll solve this case. With the computers and programs downstairs, I bet they even create a suspect list."

"Then why do you need me?"

Rollins slowly shakes his head. "Because every murder is site-specific and victim-specific. But you know that. Your file says you've done the course at Quantico."

"It wasn't trout season," Red admits.

"Well, why don't you take a crack at a victim profile. Tell me who Jeb Holloway was, other than a Republican candidate for the U.S. senate."

The truth is that Red Kravitz doesn't know all that much about Holloway. And, traditional in at least one respect, Red has no interest in developing fat dossiers on private citizens. People settle in Montana because everyone minds his own business. There is no better proof of that than the man who had called himself Buffalo Soldier Walsh, a born-again back-door man for Mona Holloway and, so far, the best suspect in Jeb Holloway's murder. Unless it's Mona herself, who can shoot from a saddle like Annie Oakley Butler and ride like the wind. Nor did she have any trouble getting around unseen. She knew every crest, rill, wash, gully, arroyo and draw on and around her property, and frequently took private rides for hours at a time.

But thinking back on the pitch Rollins just made, it reoccurs to Red that maybe more than personal animosity was involved.

Enter suspect Leonard Jarnow, Jeb's opponent in the upcoming runoff primary. Also his opponent in a court case over property perhaps containing a rich vein of gold, and strangely his partner in the new Bearpaw ski resort. Whoever killed Jeb, the victim's demise is a win/win/win situation for Jarnow. And if Jarnow was waiting at Poker Bluff, from several previous visits he would have known the property, down to the way the soil would imprint on departure. So maybe Rollins is right.

Local matters in local hands makes good sense, and lately few had shaken as many local hands as Senate hopeful Jeb Holloway. Like many big names in this big state, he had family money and land. Lots of both. But his private life was secret and his public life was a facade of dazzlingly choreographed rhetoric. He told the voters what they wanted to hear, vilified his opponents as if they were devils incarnate, and cut a figure larger than life at the same time. Maybe that's what got him killed.

But only maybe. What Kravitz really needs to clear the brush is a network of interlinking conditions that trims that long line of suspects to a short list. Because right now only one thing is certain. Anyone with a Sharps and a steady hand could have popped Jeb Holloway from Poker Bluff. Or at least anyone who knew he was coming. Anyone who corresponded to HIM on Jeb Holloway's computer calendar.

Who is HIM?

If he knew that now, he could skip the victim profile and make the arrest tomorrow. But whoever HIM is, he has to be: (1) personally known to Jeb Holloway; (2) trusted or bribable; (3) reliable, because Jeb Holloway wouldn't wait long if the other party was late.

Of the victim Kravitz had already learned a few things, including that his wife believed that she could lie, seduce, manipulate and bully her way out of trouble. Maybe that has something to do with this, too. It comes neatly back to the whispered rumor that Mona Holloway had recently come to be in a family way, if perhaps not entirely in the family line. Turning suspicion like a descending buzzard toward B.S. Walsh again.

Kravitz's focus sharpens inside his own thoughts until Rollins brings him back by snapping his fingers. "What can I expect from you by tomorrow?"

"Tomorrow's a religious holiday. Yom Kippur."

Rollins draws a long sigh, lets his eyes roam down the street again. "I'm not Jewish. I'm not fasting. I'm going down to The Elk."

"Mazel Tov," says Kravitz.

Rollins turns. "Sure there's not something between you and Molly Mendelbaum?"

Kravitz watches the only woman he ever wanted sashay down the street. Without taking his eyes off her, he answers, "Ask her."

* * *

Molly sits next to Red on the bumpy ride to Slo Lehrner's place, a kind of nondescript bungalo-cum-cabin that escapes being prefab by the clever modifications of an engineer's mind. Because that's how Slo used to make his living at Idaho National Engineering Laboratory, an isolated top-secret place dating back fifty years to the birth of the nuclear Navy.

Although Slo has never said much about the accident that took the thumb off his left hand, last Yom Kippur after slivovitz and red wine, he opened up. "It was stupid, really. I was telling a tech, 'Never initiate a start-up test without activating the force-deflection arrest switch.' Now I was pointing to the thing directly under the shear, when an experimental capacitor failed. Then, bye-bye thumb." Slo had taken another hit of Beaujolais while Red asked, "They didn't try to reattach?"

Slo had actually laughed. "When the machine failed it went it to an ultra fast mode and the severed thumb kept jumping under the thing as it got battered and smashed. I was holding my left hand with my right, in shock, but it stopped the bleeding. Still, when the machine quit, my former thumb was just pulped." He shrugged. "There was nothing to reattach. Now you're going to ask what I learned from this, and the answer is: It's amazing the things a man can learn to do with just one thumb."

At which point Red told him, "No sweat. You're lucky to be in cattle country. Folks'll just assume you're a dally man."

And Slo had laughed harder. A dally man was a cow poke who lost his thumb because he failed to loop his rope around his saddle horn before he braked his mount to bring a steer down. Dally men, too, learned to get by like Slo and to do the many things required by the rest of us.

Like prepare Yom Kippur dinner for three while the feast is being stalked by two cats, one black one, the good guy, named Mensch, and his nasty counterpart, the white one, called Mamzer. After preliminaries, Molly is ushered to her seat by Slo, and can't wait for water to be poured before asking, "Why 'Slo?'"

He first explains that Slo was short for S-ha-LO-m. But then admits, "And it fit. But it was embarrassing to be one of the chosen few who is dumber. Or slower, rather. My father would never let me believe that I wasn't smart enough. I could always work the problem, just not as fast as everybody else. That's what cost me the thumb. I was slow. But the machine was very fast."

"Oh," is all Molly says, recovering to add, "The linens and settings are beautiful."

"Naomi's," he says. "She left them behind when she took off with the two girls and the Elvis impersonator from Las Vegas."

Molly wonders how to follow that, giving Kravitz a look that screams, 'help,' then asking, "Can I lend a hand?"

He raises both before saying, "Already got two. Only one thumb but two hands."

Insisting, she says, "I'll pour the wine." Praying, no doubt, that her cultivated New York thirst wasn't about to be quenched by Mogen David.

Slo gets the food out and places it in dishes, then sits down across from Red. Both men serve themselves, then begin to eat.

"No ritual? No blessing?" asks Molly.

Slo tells her. "If you want, knock yourself out. We're pretty informal in the western diaspora."

She mutters something more perfunctory than reverent, then digs in, asking between swallows, "What is it you do out here?"

Kravitz answers, "Slo works twice a week. On computers. Down in Billings. At the State Archives. Sorting, classifying and loading things on-line."

Their host smiles. "Slow work. Not a lot of people these days interested in dusty old documents. But it's interesting stuff sometimes." He chews, swallows and says, "Did you know that Wyatt Earp's wife was Jewish?"

"No way," Molly says, shaking her head.

"Way. Her name was Josephine Sarah Marcus and she was a dead ringer for you, Molly," he says. "But there's lots of other connections that tie things together, let them make sense. That's why history is relevant." He holds up a fork skewered a still steaming piece of brisket, "The French have a saying: The more things change, the more they stay the same."

"Delicious," is Molly's nonsequitur to take Slo's mind off brooding. But solitude gives you that: lots of time to brood. Pushing farther out of the dim cobwebbed shelves of the Billings Archives and closer to the moment, the reporter in Molly can't resist asking, "So who do you think shot Jeb Holloway, Slo?"

"Somebody with a Big Fifty and attitude. You want any potatoes?"

She defers. "Murder on the waistline."

"That's an unfounded myth. A few potatoes are fine if you skip the butter and sour cream." He sucks his one thumb and Mamzer starts mewing, getting a sharp, "Shut up!" from Slo, who tells Molly, "He's really a bad example for Mensch."

"Oh, he's so cute," she says, reaching one hand down to pet.

"No, he's not, really. He's a vicious little bastard and will bite right through the hand that feeds him, thumbless or no. Now Mensch, he's the sweet one." He looks up and asks, "Is my language offending you?"

"Oh, no," she says, laughing. "Why do you ask?"

Slo stares at his plate. "Well, the last thing Naomi said before taking off with Elvis the Goniff was that she refused to allow her children to be raised in a place where foul language was so prevalent."

"So she took them to Las Vegas?"

"Go figure." Slo turns to Red. "So who shot Jeb Holloway, deputy?"

"Ask out intrepid FBI man, Pete Rollins." He turns to Molly. "He catch up with you down at The Elk?"

She stops her fork halfway to her mouth to admit, "Yeah. He just said that it would be better if the media kept it nonsensational."

"And?" Slo encourages her.

"And I said I was just one reporter. Then he says, 'But you're the first one on the scene, so maybe we could work an exclusive insider deal after the arrest.'"

"And..." both men say.

"And I said a newswoman couldn't be compromised by deals."

"Any other compromises he offer," Red says. "As an alternative?"

"In a roundabout way, he fumbled to find out it we were an item."

"And?" Slo asks, eager for the answer.

"And I said that was a story in the writing." She checks for their reaction. Which is for both men to lean back in their chairs and relax. Until she continues, "He did want to know if I was available for dinner, and the obvious answer was, 'I have a previous engagement,' and then he mentioned that he needed a place to stay, and asked if I had found one. And I said 'yes.' And he said would it be possible if my innkeeper could put him up. And I said I would ask. So Red, is it possible that we could rent the bed in the other room to Special Agent Rollins tonight?"

Kravitz chokes, gasping for air. After it's clear he doesn't need Heimliching, he assures Molly, "The mayor promised to look after him." But Slo isn't slowed up a bit and quickly asks, "Where's Augie gonna stuff this Fed?"

Getting from Red an honest answer: "Moonlight's place, I think."

"Who's Moonlight?" Molly asks.

Kravitz looks at Slo, then back, saying, "Doris's grown daughter."

"This is okay with the mayor?" Slo wants to know.

Kravitz heaves his shoulders up and lets them drop. "It's election time and this... federal presence...in Sanctuary is of great concern to him."

"What's that supposed to mean?" Molly says.

"Nothing, "says the deputy, going back to his meal.

"Okay, okay. I'll find out on my own who Moonlight is," she says.

Slo is too quick to volunteer, "She works odd jobs. Sometimes pitches in down at The Elk, at Red's family store, or at town hall. Sometimes helps out up at the Holloway-A." Into a silence that tightens like a trip-wire, Slo rushes to add, "But everyone does odd jobs for Jeb. Me it was computers. Just format reprogramming and system security, but the man likes..." he stops and corrects, "...liked things his own way."

The diversion doesn't work. Two swallows later, Molly turns to Kravitz. "Is she a good-looking woman?"

"She, who?" they both say at once.

"She, Moonlight. Who else?"

The guys look at one another, then admit. "Well, yeah."

"And she's — let me guess — young?"

"Well...yeah," Red concedes.

"So what you're saying is that this good-looking young woman worked for Jeb Holloway, if I'm getting this, under the nose of another beautiful, if somewhat older, mistress of the house. Now does this seem like an explosive mixture, or what?"

"Not Moonlight," Kravitz says. "You've got to learn to read people."

"And situations, too," she says back. "So can she shoot a Sharps buffalo rifle, this Moonlight?"

Red answers honestly, "I really don't know, Molly. She doesn't seem the type who would..." Before he could qualify or backtrack, Molly's instincts cut in hard. "How often has an older man told a younger woman that he would leave his wife for her? But that it was an election year and for her to wait until he made it to Washington, so the messy divorce wouldn't affect the voters' choice? And how often has that story served the man so well that he really didn't have to make a choice, because he..."

When Kravitz guesses, "This sounds like the voice of experience to me," she gets up, turns away, and goes quiet as a stone. Gently he rises, touches her shoulders, and feels them stiffen. To Slo he says, "We've got to go. Thanks for the yarmulke. I'll call you tomorrow."

"Why don't I wrap some stuff up for you. Surprising how good something is when you reheat it later."

Molly goes red, and Slo asks, "Did I say something wrong?"

Kravitz said, "No. Everything was great. Later." He pats Slo on the back.

"Button up," he tells them both. "It's colder than death out there."

TOGETHER AGAIN

Atop the landing, Molly turns her back on a razory wind. Red twists a knob and shoulders the door open.

She rushes, throwing off a shiver like a wet dog. He shuts the wind out, then kneels and ignites a tangle of shredded birch bark and squaw wood nested beneath a grid of fat pine. Yellow light and hissing snaps reach into the room as flames devour the tinder. Seconds later he banks the damper and tunes the air feed. Minutes after that, the old kettle-bellied iron stove starts shedding heat.

Then he comes up off his knees to announce, "I'll be back."

But she grabs his wrist. "You're not going to see Mona Holloway again, are you?"

"Molly," he dips his chin. "It's a Jewish holiday. Give me a Jewish break."

"So why aren't you taking it off, Kravitz, this Jewish holiday?"

"I'm only half Jewish, so I only get half a day off."

"Maybe you should get more in touch with your Jewish half."

* * *

The next morning Kravitz awakens to dawn's first blush and Molly's hand gently cupping his pride. In the lingering shade of night, an indulgent smile seems drawn on her lips, as if this is exactly what she wants. And for Molly, that doesn't surprise him.

She has drive and tenacity. He had never felt the same urges. Maybe it was the Indian in him. Philadelphia's skyline never stood up to the soar of the Rockies; Chopin lacked the magic of a rushing stream, nor did the promise of riches tug on him like the lure of a good fly caster.

And that's where he is when the sun clears the high crest of the battlefield. Water lapping at his waders, a wicker creel slung cross-shouldered, about fifteen feet from Standing Bear, in the Little Bighorn River.

The two braves move quietly, at one with the water, not even minding if the fish bit, really. To Bear, if you believe that the fish will come to you, you will not go hungry. To Kravitz, that's a bit too Indian.

On the rising slope to the east, melting snow still glimmers on the blades of pin grass where Yellow Hair had fallen amidst his own soldiers. Running along the foot of the hill, the river goes bone-numbing cold. Any self-respecting trout should be wrapped in PolarTec on the bottom.

But Bear's patience tells you otherwise. He is pure quill Indian, all right. A vanishing species, a man of too great faith and too much passion to survive a place like Philadelphia.

Back there, they'd stuff him in a display case. In the only part of the white man's world open to him, they had already done much the same thing, first in a Dallas Cowboy's uniform, then the wrestling ring to the jeers and hoots of a frenzied morons. Finally he came home. Red Kravitz hadn't heard him complain since.

Out here like this, as things were one hundred and fifty years ago, spoken words are just noises that trouble the peace of the spirits. Every rock and tree and animal has a spirit, and in using them or hunting them, you are paying homage to the whole of nature.

At moments like this it isn't possible for Kravitz to synthesize the faiths of his mother and father. The Crows's creation story puts humans and animals at the same level, where the Bible puts man a day behind and above it all. Red couldn't see how it was maybe a little bit of both. For him it is and always had been a matter of slipping into the view that fits the moment best.

Along the battlefield's backlit ridge the markers of fallen bluecoats erupt like rotten teeth in Noisy's snoring mouth. But more than a century later, the battleground holds a cold silence that transcends mere air, a feeling that old spirits are still moving.

Bear keeps teasing monofilament. And watching and waiting as if undeparted spirits still inhabit this land. As if those spirits have voices that whisper so that only a tuned mind can hear. Like the feeling Libbie Custer had as she watched her husband's troops depart to their regimental battle song, Garry Owen. When its last strains had melted with the rearguard column into a consuming mist, she knew they would never return. Or like the dream that Sitting Bull had the night before the battle, blue-coated cavalrymen falling upside-down into a camp of tepees. Feelings and visions of prophecy, common premonitions to people living in fear.

Kravitz wonders if Jeb Holloway had anything like that, the tickle of the distant muzzle of the Sharps buffalo gun lining up its erect Creedmore sight on his temple, adjusting for the refraction of the image passing through the Suburban's tinted window glass, holding that spot, then...

But there is no indication that Jeb Holloway knew anything except the expectation that HIM would soon arrive.

None at all.

Out of that deep thought a splashing and slapping turns his head to Standing Bear, who plays the reel, bringing in the thrashing fish, then smiles and turns, still silent, to Kravitz. Not until they are sitting on the dornicked bank does he make words with his hands. I told you we'd catch one.

Probably the last one, conjured by Indian trickery, Red's signing hands respond.

Bear answers in kind. Sometimes I think Indian trickery is all we got left.

The eerie morning silence admits only the song of rushing water. Sitting close, the two trade Plains sign language. Kravitz follows the story his friend's hands are forming:

When I was a boy my mother brought me to this place. She said it was full of spirits. But she was a superstitious squaw. And I was going to be a great brave and savior of our people, free them from the reservation and the whites. But she made me sit and watch the sun rise over the ridge where the long knives fell. And in the way of all boys, I sat and squirmed and pouted, and felt foolish.

His hands move with a fluid rhythm of beauty in motion and power in conviction, as if sounds could not bear such truth. I sat for very long. Too long for a young boy. It was getting hot and I had to pee. It was a sky of bright light and no coolness. Above all things I wanted to leave and go, to not look like a foolish squaw-boy.

The big man's eyes turn and look up the hill, as his hands limn memory into images that Kravitz can share: Then I heard a horse. Far away. Beyond the crest of the hill. Maybe a wild pony, I thought. But behind me my mother drew near, as if the rider was long overdue. In her silence, I got up and shielded my eyes from a fierce sun. Backlit and hard in shadow came the rider, a Northern Cheyenne chief in full war dress and feathered bonnet. He rose on his mount, the silhouette of an old Winchester in one arm. With the sun behind him I could not see his eyes. But I could feel them. And they held me there, staked out like a bison hide in the sun. Then as the rider stood there came another man behind him, on foot. At first I thought it was a white man, because it wore a white man's uniform. A war uniform, except that on the helmet a single feather hung from the IV strap. But the way he walked was Indian, and the way he slung his M-16 was the way the rider was cradling his Winchester, and there was the same shape and feel and spirit to the two figures.

They stood there and looked down at me, Red. And in a few minutes they turned together and went back over the hill. I never saw them again. When we were alone and no one else could hear, I asked my mother who these men were.

And she told me, Red, that the rider was my great great grandfather, Elk That Drinks, who was killed at Little Bighorn. And that the Indian in white man's uniform was my uncle, Tom Whitefeather, who volunteered for the white man's army, was assigned to the 7th Cavalry in Vietnam, ambushed by the natives at Ia Drang and killed.

A long moment passes in silence before he signs again.

Their bones are both buried up there. One at the battlefield, the other at the national cemetery. Lesson: you fight the white man, you lose; you join the white man, you lose.

Kravitz signs back. So what's to do?

Beat the white man, Bear gestures.

Kravitz makes light of it. Crazy Daisy says the ghost dancers and messiah are coming in a UFO on the next thunderstorm.

But Bear does not laugh. Good fish, magical fish. We go now, eat later.

They are on Indian land now, filled still with Indian spirits, forces as unprovable to a white man's mind as they are undeniable to an Indian's. It is a cruel irony, it seems, that Indian reservations owned by the Northern Cheyenne and Crow now peacefully encircle the cemetery when the plains Indians had encircled and destroyed Custer's 7th Cavalry one hundred and twenty-six years earlier. And it was not the chilly water that sends shivers through Kravitz, but the realization that when he goes quiet, very quiet, soul-deep quiet, he can hear – faintly but distinctly – the violent sounds of that ancient conflict, like voices from a distant radio station about to drown in static.

With this, Kravitz feels red enough to mention, Speaking of visions, Crazy Daisy claims to have seen Jeb Holloway's killer riding Indian-style, heading for Poker Bluff.

Bear's hands and fingers tell him, Dave Dooley has been riding Indian-style since I taught him, same as Ivan taught him how to live aux aliments du pays.

Kravitz still doesn't know where this will lead him. But somewhere in his white and Jewish mind a woven thread holds cause and effect together on the same line of reasoning. So he keeps playing on that thread like monofilament, hoping something would grab on and pull back.

* * *

Kravitz's apartment door stands ajar, just a crack.

His boot eases it open.

At the kitchenette table Molly has made herself at home with her cameraman, Al. Into Red's phone Molly is making promises that sound desperate. Hanging up hard, she demands, "Did you run over to Mona after I fell asleep?"

"No." He posts the fishing rod in a corner and drifts to the sink. Drawing water, he charges a coffee pot.

"You want me to believe you went fishing with snow on the ground?"

"When the sun rose it all melted."

"Did you catch any fish?"

Red holds up a finger. "One. Bear actually caught it."

Molly posts hands on her gorgeous hips. "You don't care who killed Jeb Holloway?"

"I don't know who killed Jeb Holloway," Red tells Molly. "He wasn't the most popular guy around. But tomorrow's the funeral," he looks at Molly, then Al. "And I need a favor. I want you to video everyone who shows."

Al confesses, "Special Agent Rollins already asked us. Besides, I didn't know if you would, you know," Al stammers. "Want to see the pictures of people because, like, maybe you thought I was stealing their souls."

"Oh, no," Kravitz says. "The folks at Holloway's funeral sold their souls long ago." Al half-smiles back, not knowing if his host is serious, then offers, "But I'll dupe you a copy."

Making Red Kravitz grin. "Great. I'll be duped by the network and dubbed over by the reporter. My God, by the time you slickers are though with me I'll be a genuine nationally famous dime-store Indian."

Molly stands up, jerks her head and Al, the good soldier, falls in behind. Before closing the door, she turns back. "I'm not finished with you, whether your fish story pans out or not."

He doesn't correct her.

You don't pan for fish. You pan for gold. Maybe Noisy skimmed some up downstream of Poker Bluff. But that can be run down later. Right now he has to check on his prisoners.

* * *

First comes Special Agent Pete Rollins. Getting to him takes Red past Doris, who is smoking a long roll that smells to Red's Indian nose like cannabis, kinnik-kinnik, raiz diabolica, shongsasha and prayer book as fixins. "Put out that smoke," he says. "Or I'll lock you up."

"Cell's already in use," she counters.

Red follows the corridor back.

Pete Rollins is humming, of all things, Deutschland Uber Alles. The cell floor writhes with cables and power cords. A new chair faces the old hinged bunk, now sagging with computer gadgets. Without looking up, the FBI man taps the monitor and says, "Have a look at this."

Red stares down. The image staring back is an aerial photograph. The contours are familiar, but the display is rendered in false color: reds, purples, oranges, greens and yellows. "What is it?"

Rollins pinstriped suit jacket is off, the tie loosened and sweat crescenting his armpits. Beaming like a kid, the agent announces, "This is your crime scene, Deputy. Downloaded by satellite. Check it out."

Kravitz does, and guides the Fed through it. "Here's a hut. That's where a local lady we call Crazy Daisy lives. What you see," he points around the shack, "is just her footprints. She just sort of patrols her turf and shoots at anything that moves."

Rollins mouses the tool bar and clicks the magnifying icon five times. A boxed area comes into focus. Faint curved bands of color edge some marks. They move north-by-northwest toward Poker Bluff. He alters the color coding for better contrast and says, "Now I'm no expert tracker, Deputy. In fact, I expect somebody with Indian blood in him would do a lot better, but to me this look a bit like..."

"Hoofprints," he says. "What's the span?"

Rollins superimposes a scale in inches.

Red studies the images. "How come I didn't see them before?"

Rollins explains, "Without this technology, not even the best tracker in the world would pick up these prints. The rainwater on flats seeps down. So it doesn't erase features, just lifts silt and redeposits it, leaving an impression under the surface."

"How can you tell the hoofprints's age?" Red presses.

"We ran that by a Smithsonian fluviologist, an expert in how things flow. Doesn't matter what: water, air, volcanic ash, lava, mud, dirt, dust, even glass. Anything that moves faster than bedrock. She said that unless the prints petrify, the most recent tracks are clearest. In quartz sand and mica, the average duration of an imprint this time of year is about five days. Shorter if there's wind and rain. And we just had wind and rain. That's why, except for Daisy's footprints, most everything else got washed away; so these tracks are all we see."

In the prints, Red notices that the horse's shoe is atypical. Meaning it isn't from a mustang or res' horse. The horse that made it belongs to a white person.

"By the way," Rollins asks. "Does Mona Holloway ride?"

"Maybe you should have a talk with her, Pete."

Rollins gives up a quick nod. "Why don't you get to work on that victim profile?"

"Let's smoke the peace pipe, Rollins. Tomorrow I'll tell you what I found out about Jeb Holloway. You get me the dimensions of those hoofprints. They'll fit only one horse exactly. But there are some people around here who couldn't shoot a Sharps."

"Such as?" Rollins presses.

"Noisy, down at The Elk is too drunk to hold a Sharps steady, too poor to own one, not smart enough to steal one. While he's invisible in that nobody pays too much attention to his coming or goings, he literally doesn't have the guts for this kind of thing. That leaves your suspect list one shorter than it is now."

"Anything else?" Rollins asks.

"The killer went out and back on horseback. Maybe someone saw the rider leave, noticed they were missing from their jobs, or saw them return. Maybe they even saw the Sharps booted under the saddle or riding blanket. But it's Montana, after all. There are too few people around, a lot of them alone, none of them guilty. So that gets you nowhere."

"Nothing you've said gets me anywhere. I got that far while you were out fishing."

Red stops to measure his tone just right before asking, "How'd you know I was fishing?"

"I walked to The Elk and found a sign: Gone Fishin'. On the way back I bumped into Molly Mendelbaum. She's doing surveillance for me at the funeral tomorrow."

"She said. By the way, Pete. Did Moonlight get you settled in okay?"

Crimson tops Rollins' buttoned-down collar but he keeps his poker voice. "Yeah. The arrangements are fine."

"Super." Once outside the converted cell's bars Kravitz turns back and says, "Oh, you might want to check my store for a change of outfit. Moonlight's got keys and knows the inventory. That suit you've got is too cold, too clean and too obvious."

"You're right," he says, losing his blush. "Do you take government vouchers"

The question, asked in just those words, informs Red how far out of touch this man is. For most of the time that the white man has been in the west, the word 'voucher' meant an Indian scalp recently removed from its owner.

So the Indian in him has to count to twenty, then consider a native American riposte like "More beads?" But the Jewish half persuades him to respond, "Whatever."

TONIGHT'S NEWS

At Red Kravitz's place Molly sits on the bed in a silk slip, blurring an emery board over her nails. Peering up through lashes long, thick and natural, she pauses long enough to ask, "What do you hear from Pete Rollins?"

He shrugs off his sheepskin coat. "Going cold soon. So he's coming by downstairs to get outfitted. I don't want him standing out on some ridge like some gung-ho platoon leader at LZ Albany."

"Where?" Molly demands, looking totally lost.

"Landing Zone Albany in Vietnam. North of the Ia Drang valley. About this time thirty-six years ago. Bear's uncle Tom Whitefeather came up on the lead Huey on day two, trekked up from LZ x-ray. A couple of companies from the second battalion of the 7th Cavalry walked in on four battalions of NVA regulars. The men who lived through it call it Little Bighorn II. Tom Whitefeather was not among them. What the AK-47s left of him came back in a body bag."

"Jesus," Molly whispers. "How old was Bear?"

"Not quite two."

"So he doesn't remember."

Red shrugs. "Experts say we don't remember until we're three. But Bear can tell you things about Tom that make you think he's standing in the next room. Bear's saved a wall of the house he's building up at Pine Ridge for the only photograph he'll have in the whole place. All that's left of his favorite uncle is a silver star, purple heart, and unit combat citation. Metal, paper and silver halide."

She shivers. "Seems suddenly colder."

"Join Rollins downstairs. Go with a sheepskin. Or upgrade to doeskin. Got a couple of nice ones in from Santa Fe. Even Robert Redford has one."

She slinks toward him. "Robert Redford has one of everything. Now come on, Red. If you're off the case, why don't you just give me a little inside skinny on what's jumping?" Her hand rests on his chest, her breath, sweet and hot and light, pulses on his neck. Her scent du jour, Forbidden Pleasure, grabs him where he lives. She jiggles his collar tabs, melting her breasts against him. "Come on, Kravitz. Help a girl out, will ya?"

He breaks away to perk another pot of java. While it's brewing he says, "Molly, on obstruction of justice for divulging inside information during the investigation of a federal murder case, I end up at Fort Leavenworth, a lawman on the inside of a maximum security facility. And there's nothing shorter than the lifespan of a cop in max."

"Where does it go from here?" Always the newswoman.

He raises and lowers his shoulders. "Rollins will send the shots from the funeral to Washington, run IDs on all the mourners: backgrounds, connections to Jeb Holloway, basic cop stuff, looking in detail at everything because he's got nothing."

"What else?" she presses.

"That's up to Rollins. But a common trick is to stake out the grave site for about a week. Sometimes the killer pays a visit. To stand in triumph over the vanquished. To apologize. To cry, laugh. Sometimes to urinate or defecate."

"So you think I should stake out Jeb's grave with a camera crew?" she says.

"You're living too fast, Molly. If you don't slow down, it'll all be over and you won't even have a tag line for your own life."

* * *

Red cuts through chilly air, headed for The Elk. Despite her clunky city-slicker shoes, Molly has no trouble catching up. But by the time she does, he's parked on a barstool across from Bear, clutching a vintage tumbler of slivovitz. Molly grabs the stool beside him, puts on a smile, tosses the hair off her face and breathes, "Hey, Bear. Can a girl get a BLT around here?"

Bear half-turns and yells, "Walsh!"

Without prompting, the Rockola bursts into

Hah, hah, hah...

Hey, hey, hey...

Before the song reaches its third stanza Bear vaults the bar and whacks the machine with a powerful palm. Noisy wakes up long enough to shout, "Don't break the damn thing!"

Bear shouts back, "It is broke. And I hate that song."

Dropping the thought like a quarterback after a hard sack, Bear saunters back to the bar and bellows, "Walsh! We got a lady out here wants a BLT."

"Mona?" Walsh pokes his head through the kitchen service slot and looks out.

Molly apologizes. "Just me."

He says, "Sorry, Miss. I'll get it for you."

Bear turns with a smile and re-vaults the bar, wiping his hands on a towel. "We know how to keep our help in line."

She asks, "You think that was Jeb Holloway's problem?"

Bear tries to put her straight. "You work up at the Hollow-A, you take the man's money, you do things the man's way. You don't like it, you can still come down here, drop into a bottle, punch up the other rousters, get thrown out and crawl back."

"Any other ideas?" Molly probes.

From the back comes the sizzle and sharp scent of frying bacon. Walsh adds a melodic rendition of something soulful by Smokey Robinson.

Red drums a knuckle on the bar. "Be hard for it not to be somebody local," he says. "For somebody to come in, shoot him and get out just doesn't work. A little thing like a blown tire could leave a trace. In time, that trace gets run down and he gets caught."

"So you're sure it's a 'he'?" she asks.

Bear provides the answer. "Far less women than men out here. We got just Doris, Moonlight, Mona..." he hesitates and scowls, then goes on, "...Daisy..." then remembers, "Caldera Cunningham. Five. Now there's six with you, Molly, but you don't look like the killer type. Besides, you didn't blow in till Jeb was blown up. Not counting lost tourists, that's about it for females. Now I'm not with Red in saying it can't happen, especially if you're the wife of a son-of-a-bitch like Jeb Holloway."

"You think Mona did it?" she asks.

In the back B.S. Walsh goes falsetto to croon, "Never met a girl who made the feel the way that you do..." before Red answers, "I don't think so."

"Why?" she wants to know.

"Because she's the kind of woman who likes hogtying men in Gordian knots. Then they sit there wondering how they're going to disentangle until some other guy with a big sword comes in and starts hacking away at them."

"Ah, the man who would kill for love," Molly sighs.

Red looks her way. "You think the one who killed Jeb got Mona's love?"

"If so, jealousy could be a motive," she speculates.

"Anything could be a motive at this point," Bear says.

"Even a BLT," Red whispers with a smile. They laugh before Molly starts up again. "But you're convinced it's a local guy and have not an inkling?"

Still in back B.S. Walsh tries to get it Smokey's way with, "Take a good look at my face, oh, yeah..." as the bacon stops sizzling.

Red doesn't answer. There are things she knows and things she didn't know. She knows that Jeb Holloway was shot through the side of the head. She knows the weapon. She doesn't know about the satellite images of hoofprints supporting Crazy Daisy's story of a rider passing by. She doesn't know that Jeb's computer calendar made HIM due for a nine-thirty appointment. She doesn't know that the prior entry in the same calendar was a teleconference with Len Jarnow. Nor does she know that Jeb kept a .357 magnum Colt Python revolver in the glove compartment of his Suburban.

In all, she knows not enough to worry the killer. Which is Kravitz's real concern. And not just for Molly. Despite the media frenzy over the coming invasion of Iraq, overnight other major networks had wheeled in a trailer village west of town. Neither they nor Molly know about Noisy's putative gold. Maybe they would guess who might benefit from Jeb Holloway's death. But the word 'benefit' covers a lot of territory. It isn't necessarily limited to material gains. And if the murder were politically or romantically motivated, the most likely suspects remained concealed behind unbreakable alibis.

Kravitz keeps drumming the bar with a knuckle. "Someone needs to look into the summer ranch hands before they head south. By the time Rollins figures this out, they'll be gone."

"That's a big job," she says. "Need some help?"

One big story puts Molly Mendelbaum behind a news desk in New York. She's on the way up. Deputy Red Kravitz is just on his way through. Finishing his drink, he answers, "Ask Pete Rollins. He's in charge."

"Here's your BLT," B.S. Walsh yells, holding the plate out. Bear takes it and busses it over.

Red slides off his barstool.

Bear looks up to ask, "What time we leaving for Great Falls tomorrow?"

"Early. So we get there before the gliterati arrive."

"Molly," Bear says. "Why not join us tonight for cutthroat trout. Pure and healthy and natural. Right from the sacred waters of the Little Bighorn on the Northern Cheyenne reservation."

"Actually," Red corrects, "The river is on Crow land." Sees Bear taking exception and modifies, "Sort of."

She looks at Bear, then Red. "Will there be enough of this poached trout to go around?"

* * *

Molly pokes at the sliver of trout with her fork before looking up at Bear with a pathetic smile. "This is it?"

"Three way split," he says. "Try it, you'll like it."

She samples it and says, "Um," then, "I'm not going to choke on a bone am I?"

Kravitz offers, "I know how to Heimlich."

"Thanks," she says, "I'll skip the broken ribs and be careful."

"Trout used to be bigger, more of them before the white men came. But there's more food coming," Bear promises, and gets up, yelling back into the kitchen, "Hey, Walsh, you want to bring out the sides now?"

Pans rattle in the kitchen before they get the response, "Hey, Uncle Tomahawk! You know what? You can take your jive-ass raggedy-redneck town and shove it up your..." Before he can finish, Bear is glaring into the kitchen, his voice low, calm and final. "Walsh, do what I say. You hear?"

In less than ten seconds, B.S. Walsh airlifts the potatoes, greens, butter and sour cream to the table, smiles nicely and says, "Y'all let me know when you're ready for dessert, hear?" Then disappears through the swinging door to the kitchen.

"He looks ready to kill you," Molly notes.

Her dinner companions lock stares.

"What?" she asks. "What did I say?"

"Nothing," Kravitz tells her. "Bon appetite."

* * *

The next morning they rise before dawn. The sun catches up with them on the road, rising quickly as they reach the graveyard. Behind a crush of mourners, Kravitz stands next to Bear, both men wearing hands clasped into codpieces. A pallid sky is ulcered by a shrunken sun when the service ends. In strained silence, mourners await the interment. A screaming winch lowers Jeb Halloway's casket, then sticks, requiring assistance. Ignoring the difficulty, a hired pastor raises beatific hands, unleashing a rousing summons of peace that passeth all understanding, then steps back while the widow sprinkles crumbling earth onto the stalled coffin. Len Jarnow steps forward, clamps Mona's hands in his and waits out the photographers's clicking shutters. Then he pats the widow gently on the back and steps aside for the Vice President, looking grim and a bit constipated.

Layers of others follow Len Jarnow's lead, wrinkling into a zigzagged reception line. With rehearsed dignity, Mona touches flesh, returns faint smiles for assurances that things will work out for her. Certain of little else, Red Kravitz is sure of that much. He peers around and sees Molly finishing up a take. Avoiding her, he asks Bear, "Wanna go?"

"You think Mona noticed us?"

"I think she's seen who she wants to."

* * *

Bear brakes Moonlight's supercharged Cavalier at town hall and lets Kravitz out. Leaning down, he tips his hat back and asks, "You'll be at The Elk?"

"We'll open early, close late. Drinks on me. Memory of Jeb."

"Generosity costs, Bear."

He shakes his head. "It's good business. They'll all come back."

The deputy wonders for how long.

For a century and a half, Sanctuary was never more than a watering hole on the way west. Back then, Burlington Northern's main line passed no closer than seventy miles. Even now, the nearest interstate is thirty miles west. But after red warriors closed the Bozeman Trail, the relentless stream of pioneers diverted north, creating a place with a suitable name for safe sheltering while breaking the journey. Long past anything resembling viability, the remaining denizens of Sanctuary prayed privately for the Bearpaw ski resort. They had no other choice. The last church here closed its doors in 1918, when half the congregation died in the Great War. The returning half brought influenza, joined the casualty list and went to rest in boot hill. More former citizens were buried up there than now lived within the city limits, even including the Holloway ranch. Somewhere in a stretch of collective imagination matching the sprawl of the land, an ominous bell was tolling the eleventh hour. Without the ski resort, the town that map quest forgot would crumble to dust and blow off with the wind.

"Later," Kravitz tells Bear. He slaps the chassis of Moonlight's car like the flanks of a horse. The Elk's bardog turns the steering wheel with one big hand, eases the gas pedal down and rumbles away.

Red saunters up the cracked, worn steps of town hall. Before coming in off the porch, he sniffs at the air.

Definitely colder tonight. Downright crimpy.

* * *

Doris's hand is waving through lingering smoke as Kravitz clambers down the wheezing risers.

Tipping his hat, he says, "'Day, Doris."

She starts coughing, then stops, hammering a fist on her chest. Then shakes her head until the lavender blotches begin to fade. Finally she rasps, pointing back to the cell area. "He wants to see you."

Red loosens his tie, pops the button on his collar. Trampoosing in, Kravitz announces, "You owe me a printout of those hoofprints."

With the mechanical efficiency of a man who is always prepped, Pete Rollins flips him a sealed manila envelope. Red catches it in one hand and rips the gummed seal open. Ignoring him, Rollins watches data fly across a monitor as he whispers, "We caught a break."

Red studies the hoofprints, throwing back an equally casual, "Oh?"

Rollins hammers the keys and switches to the mouse like some kind of hacker-ninja. For seconds only the agent's eyes flick his way. "You've been holding out on me, Kravitz."

A hard sheet of cold freezes him inside. Hadn't Rollins caught Walsh in a lie about Detroit down at The Elk? And wouldn't that be the first place an agent with time in the Detroit office of the FBI would look? All these thoughts fire through the deputy's head at once, but all he can think to say back is, "Oh?"

"But you were right," Rollins says.

"How so?" Play dumb.

Giving Red his full attention, Rollins admits, "Your theory about the killer being local. This guy should have been obvious."

Kravitz tucks the satellite photo under one arm. "Who are we talking about?"

"You know a David Corinth Dooley?"

"Sure. Almost ran him over coming back from seeing Len Jarnow in Helena."

"Where was he going?" Rollins asks.

"To the mountains. To winter over, the way they did a hundred and fifty years ago."

Rollins gets up to roll his neck. "Say David Corinth Dooley carries a Sharps buffalo rifle and left town, just after Jeb Holloway had been killed by the same weapon."

"Same kind of weapon, Rollins. There's lots of Sharps around. And if you want a better suspect closer to home, get yourself a warrant and go up to the Hollow-A."

Rollins lets his chin drop. "David Corinth Dooley is a member of the Montana Militia..."

"Was a member," Red corrects. "He was a kid looking for acceptance, not such an uncommon feeling. Sure he was up there one summer, but that was all."

Rollins rolls through Kravitz's interjection. "...spent a summer up there soaking up hate literature, the usual stuff about Aryan supremacy, killing off all the Jews and Indians and blacks..." Interruption is futile. The man has made up his mind. "...but Jeb Holloway admitted only that in urban environments, certain elements should not be allowed to carry handguns if they had criminal records. And the Montana Militia cited the Constitutional right to bear arms in order to maintain a standing militia, then made a threat that Jeb Holloway should change his position or they would see that he never made it to Washington..."

"This is crazy," Red mutters.

"Does Dooley ride a horse?"

"When I saw Davey, he was walking."

Rollins brushes it off. "So he picked up a horse somewhere..."

"Dave Dooley doesn't have the money to buy his next meal, let alone a horse."

"Then he steals one."

"The days of horse thieving are a lot longer dead than Jeb Holloway."

"Then how did Dooley..."

Kravitz explains, "Dave is a project of Ivan Konev, whose great grandfather was one of the early mountain men. Ivan throws Davey a bone whenever the going gets tough, because he doesn't want to see those particular old ways die out. And there's a lot of that out here, deep-rooted nostalgia, orneriness, people who make choices and do things their own way because that's the only damn thing they have left."

"That's a very sentimental defense, deputy. But it doesn't rule out the very distinct possibility that the Montana Militia knew that Dave Dooley would be invisible in Sanctuary, and that he would be leaving because of weather after he killed Jeb Holloway."

"Jeb Holloway wouldn't sit out at Timberland waiting for Dave Dooley."

Rollins barks a laugh. "You need a year or two in Washington, Kravitz. You'd learn that in an election year, politicians will do anything to pick up five thousand votes."

"Five thousand votes? We were just talking about Dave Dooley."

"The Montana Militia votes as a block. There are five thousand of them registered state-wide, including the ones compounded at Foster Forks. Given the fracas in Florida in the last election, you don't think Jeb Holloway would have thought at least twice about a ten thousand vote swing?'"

"Pete..."

Rollins's hands come up. "Okay, would you just hear me out? I'm not asking you to agree or disagree. Just see how this hangs together."

"Okay," he says, but that's not what he thinks.

Rollins rolls on. "Fact: Dave Dooley was or is a member of the Montana Militia. Fact: Dave Dooley owns a Sharps buffalo rifle, provided by Ivan Konev. Fact: Dave Dooley can shoot that rifle well. Fact: Dave Dooley will not be missed if he moves on because he always leaves this time of year. Fact: The mountains are to the Northwest, which, fact, is the direction of the Foster Forks compound. Now if he left here three days ago..." Rollins hits the space bar, revealing a stack of multi-tasked programs on the monitor. Clicking on one window brings up a map of central Montana. Clicking once on Sanctuary and again on Foster Forks a line appears. Hitting the enter key posts a number in a box straddling the line. It reads: 107 MILES. "Well, well, well. What do you think about that?"

Red has better than a slam-dunk rebuttal. Dave Dooley was panning gold at Sidewinder Twist with Noisy when both men heard the killshot. But if Noisy were put on the stand to alibi, some lawyer a lot smarter than Pete Rollins would shred his credibility. Town drunks get a bit confused, more than a bit riled and become less than entirely convincing. So Red can only say, "This is a mistake."

Rollins stops. "If you've got a better suspect, I'd like to know who it is."

"Rollins, we have no good suspects. It can only hurt the case to make one up."

"You want to come along?" Rollins asks.

"Not my collar," he returns.

"Coverage can enlarge your exposure..."

"Pete?"

"Yeah?"

"If you're going up to Foster Forks, bring three things: one: legal warrant, and stick to it; two: a small army of federal agents; three: a flak jacket. Because they have an arsenal of weapons up there you don't want to know about. And you won't find Dave Dooley there," Red warns.

Rollins slips into his suit jacket and flicks a speck of dandruff off his lapel. Then he whispers, "Dave Dooley is under the legal limit for this kind of operation. We've got other fish to fry, and we're not talking about late-season trout."

* * *

After seeing Rollins out, Red phones the Tweedles, Mickey and Mo. "I've got a white Chevy Suburban found by a black man sometime around four-thirty. I've got Holloway's maid saying her boss left about nine that morning. And I've got the victim planning to meet someone at nine-thirty. I've driven the Hollow-A ranch house to the meet site, know how long it takes. Being Jeb Holloway, he will wait not so long for any man."

"That was his style," Mo admits.

"He gets there around, say, nine-thirty, keeps the engine idling. My bet is he was shot soon after that," Red reasons.

* * *

At The Elk the only cost of hard drinking today is a hangover tomorrow. Bear is setting them up for the hands at the Hollow-A ranch. The fellahs wear chaps and leather vests over checked shirts and go by names that Red has known for years: Jake Laney, Head Hanley, Mel Keppert, Zack Farnes, Bass Sanders, Lou Andrews, Pak Randal, Mangey Fuller, Kyle Halloran, Amos Crag, Whitefeather Carpenter, Sam Bates, Shamus O'Leary,

Bill Smathers. Half the regulars. Missing are Otis Puller, Marty Boczar, Pete DeLorca, Slim Duncan, Doug Fornier, Paco Gonzales, Chuck Grunwald, Ben Inman, Sandy Jasper, Jimmy Mote, Hugh Marston and Ian Bently, the kid from reform school who made work-release and dodged hard time at Deer Lodge state prison. The illegals, probably María's kin, usually never show in town, and favor drinking mescal at the bunkhouse. With Pete Rollins creating a federal presence, you can wager these folks, mostly Mex but some Guatemalans and Hondurans, will dry up like the washes around Poker Bluff.

Not counting them it comes to twenty-six men present and accounted for. All of them good with a horse and rifle. The ones crowding the bar raise their first glass to Jeb, warming to the hope that nothing would change for the core crew. Through the winter they will ride range, tractor out baled hay in blizzards, herd half-frozen cattle to barns and wind shelters, mend snow-snapped fences, patrol for anything with sharp teeth and fast legs sizing up a side of beef. Then they'll trot their bushed mounts back to groom, feed, stable and thaw. After that, sit down to muckamuck and tumble a bunk, too exhausted even to dream, too stoic to dream of anything else.

On weekends, half got Friday night off, the other half Saturday. The whole crew less Latinos will come on Sunday, but are curfewed to midnight. In shifts less predictable but still steady, crews from the Lazy Z to the south will head in for drinks that put old cowboys in bone yards long before the first Holloways arrived. For men whose only break from thirty-and-found brings insatiable thirst, Sanctuary is The Elk.

Red pulls the door away from the wind and shuts it as Head Hanley hoists his fourth Jack Black and proposes, "To the bardog!" The place goes quiet as men knock their drinks back. The glasses come down in a single thump. Bear endures a volley of burps as he refills glasses, watches the spark in the wells of his customer's eyes kindle, then uncorks a bottle of the good stuff.

Surrounded by familiar rousters but totally by himself, Red holds down the end of the bar next to the Rockolla.

Bear drifts over and says, "Slivovitz?"

A shake of Kravitz's head answers before he jerks his chin up at the TV. "You got it fixed."

Bear corrects him. "Brand new. Even got me a dish."

"What's the occasion?"

"For the customers coming into town from Bearpaw this winter. I'm fixin' to knock up some prefabs out back for skiers. And if things really take off on the mountain, maybe I'll turn my place at Pine Ridge into a B&B."

Red's eyes flood with doubt.

The big Indian leans in close. "Create a bottom-end rental and Bearpaw sells more lift tickets. Gasoline being high, lots of folks can't afford to stay at the mountain. I can charge fifteen percent more 'n the mortgage, depreciate the property, deduct the expenses and come away with thirty percent profit the first year."

"You're serious about getting rich, that's for sure."

Bear looks puzzled. "How'd you figure?"

Red recollects economics from Penn. "Smart investors never use their own money; they leverage borrowed cash and make the lender carry the risk. That way they can cash out before the crash, surrender their rights to their partners and walk away if the thing goes belly up."

Bear seems skeptical. "Now you have as much money as, say, Jeb Holloway, why'd you want some lender taking a percent and messing around in your deal? And why the hell would the lender underwrite the risk?"

Red gives him the textbook answer. "First of all, the lender won't, not unless he likes the way the numbers run out. Second, the lender takes the risk because Jeb is connected enough to run interference at the statehouse, make sure the environmental groups are neutralized, permits expedited, voters aware of the employment bonus. A guy like Jeb's financially solid, so there's no downside if they have to go after him. Plus if he walks away and they want to remain invisible, they can step in and save the project. If not, they just bootstrap the real estate market, break up the land into lots and sell off at profit. Or if the market goes bear, at a loss, declare a deduction from their taxes and still come away even."

Bear whispers, "You sayin' that Jeb and Jarnow was just figureheads?"

Red shakes his head. "I don't know. All I know is the rich never go into their own pockets. Some shadow partner's always covering the ante. As long as Bearpaw's in the black, nobody knows. Sure as hell I don't. But Jeb Holloway's not going to subtract as long as he can add."

Bear wears a mean smile. "And you don't need a goddamn Ivy League degree to add, brother. Even the dumbest Northern Cheyenne can work all this stuff out on a spreadsheet, plug-and-chug fashion."

"You're gonna need a manager down here," Red cautions, "while you're up at Bearpaw making pousse-cafes for fags."

"I'll bet the buffalo soldier would consider it."

Red wonders. So he gets up, works through the rowdy crowd and latches onto Walsh with a "Howdy."

Walsh tries to shoulder by. "I got drinks to run, man."

"Like I tried to tell you before. We go a little slower out here. Look, Bear is thinkin' maybe you'd like to handle things this winter at The Elk."

Walsh's eyes catch fire and flick at Bear, who is laughing with Mangey Fuller about something. "He ain't give me a redskin cent since Jeb got blowed away."

"You plannin' on raisin' dust?"

Walsh swallows hard. "I just want this thing over."

"You know Mona's pregnant?" Red springs it on him.

"I already said I did not kill the muthafucker. When you gonna believe me?"

"Only thing I can tell you is that Rollins agrees it was someone local, someone motivated. Sooner or later the FBI is going to stumble across some guy with a record."

"Let me talk to Rollins. I put him straight."

Before Red can respond, Mona Holloway pushes into the bar, raking a fall of short dark hair from her eyes. She wears tight black denim slacks, a black silk shirt and matching knee-high patent leather boots.

The room goes quiet and the men turn.

"Won't anyone here buy a lady a drink?" she says. Like parched leaves, four men scatter from their table when she whisks a wrist. Then she sits down and folds her hands together.

Bear tells her. "Drinks on the house."

"Will these men be able to work tomorrow?" she demands.

Jake Laney shuffles on the scratchy soles of his Justins. "We was all figurin' a day of mourning... a matter of respect is all..."

"How respectful of the man who paid your wages is it to lie in bed while gray wolves from Timberline come after the cattle?"

Laney responds, "There's not a salty dog here who can't drink his fill one day and be up to work the next. I'll see the crews are out as usual."

Walsh wipes hands on his apron and manages, "What'd you like, Mrs. Holloway?"

"Would you stop the Mrs. Holloway crap? The man's dead and buried. You know what I like, B.S., don't you? So why don't you just put it straight up and uncapped on the table."

Tension tightens like a garrote.

With carefully measured intent, Mona relieves it with a sigh, saying, "Could we have some damn music here? The funeral was over hours ago."

Bear fires the remote at Rockola.

Seconds later The Byrds break through the guitar riff, "I'll probably feel a whole lot better when you're gone... when you're gone... when you're gone."

Mona strangles the bottleneck and glugs three swallows before coming up for air. "Isn't this supposed to be a bar?"

Her crew raises glasses, Bass Sanders stammering into, "Tuh...tuh... to Muh...muh...muh..Mr. Huh...Hollo...whu...whu...way."

Mona raises the bottle and laughs. "Why not?"

Red Kravitz sidles in, pulls a chair up to her table and asks, "You okay?"

"Me? Fine and dandy, Deputy. How about yourself?"

He doesn't answer, telling her, "When you're through, why don't you get Bear to give me a call. I'll give you a ride back when you're ready."

She pats the back of his hand and whispers. "I was ready the other day. But you know what they say." The bottle goes up and then down. "When opportunity knocks, you better be ready to grab on and hold for all you're worth. Because you never can tell when another chance like that will come your way."

"I'll remember that." He tips his hat, gets up and elbows through the staggering crush of ranch hands. "Bear," he says.

The big man slides in close.

"When Mona's through, don't let her drive back."

Bear looks over at Mona, then back to Kravitz. "She's mighty willful, brother."

"You know, Bear. In Montana a bartender who sells a drink to a customer seen to be intoxicated can be charged if she has an auto accident."

Before the exchange can escalate, Molly Mendelbaum is chased through the door by a rush of cold air and powdered snow. Throwing off a quick shudder, she joins Red at the bar. Bear fetches Napoleon brandy, half-fills a snifter and eases it in front of her. "On the house," he says. "In memory of Jeb."

She picks up the balloon glass and peers over her shoulder. "The grieving widow looks like a whore at a rodeo convention," Molly whispers.

Overhearing this, Sam Bates is about to take exception when Bear glares him down. The man goes back to his wormwood willy. Against the wall, the Rockola shuts down The Byrds. Checking the time, Bear aims the TV remote and gets CNN news. "And now, this report..."

All eyes go to the set, including Mona's. When Bear sees her, he raises the remote again to turn it off, but the widow shakes her head. Like her men, Mona's glazed, cynical eyes track the replayed funeral as she listens to Molly's voice-over.

"Today in Great Falls, Montana, Jeb Holloway, the murdered candidate for the U.S. Senate, was buried in a ceremony attended by family, friends, acquaintances and admirers. Holloway, who was killed by a high-powered rifle, was mourned not only by his widow, Mona, but by his opponent in the Republican run-off election, Leonard Jarnow. As part of the ceremony, the Vice President of the United States offered a brief eulogy. Avoiding the issue of gun-control in a strongly pro-gun state, the Vice President nevertheless promised a relentless search for the killer. This is Molly Mendelbaum, CNN news."

At her table, Mona Holloway begins slow metronomic clapping. The television rolls into a promise of fast relief from migraine headaches. Ignoring Mona, Molly turns to Red. "Did I look okay?"

Red turns to Bear. "I'm prejudiced. What'd you think?"

Bear tells her. "Looked fine to me. I like the sheepskin coat. Whose idea was that?"

She elbows Red. "Aren't there any secrets in this town?"

He answers, "At least one: who killed Jeb Holloway."

"Maybe I can help," she says.

* * *

Together they review the video of the funeral, Molly scanning images of people Red doesn't recognize, giving them all names.

"How do you do it?" he asks.

"Part of the job. Most of these people you have to meet. Not exactly bottom feeders, just names in your first Rolodex. The first ones to get chucked when you move up. Staffers, strap hangers, bag men and gophers. Most of them weren't invited, but hoped to get into an out-take with the widow hovering over the coffin," she says. "Do you mind if I smoke?"

"Try breathing, Molly. Up here the air's still clear and fresh. Do you good."

"I'll take it outside later," she says.

"Careful. It's been real dry this season. Make sure your butt is out."

"That's the problem. My butt is way out on this one and we're nowhere."

"Any face you don't recognize?" he asks, replaying at one-quarter speed.

She studies the passing frames. "I don't know the pastor, the ushers, the grave diggers, the guys trying to fix the broken winch, the funeral director." She closes her eyes and sighs. "There are a couple of faces, like the foreman — ranny, rather — at Hollow-A..." she snaps her fingers. "God, what's his name. I just saw him at The Elk?"

"Jake Laney."

"That's him. God, he looks like a barroom brawl itching to happen. And he's standing right behind Mona." The frame zooms in on Mona, in black with a simple pillbox hat and veil. Molly reverses it, then restarts. Mona steps to the grave. "Look! She's doing the Jackie Kennedy thing. You know, from the JFK funeral. Invoking the image. Wait, don't tell me!" Both of Molly's palms go up. "She's going to run against Len Jarnow in her husband's place."

"Might," Red admits, certain of nothing at this point.

Her expression clouds. She reaches in and runs the tape back again, then stops just before Mona kneels down. "Who's this?" She taps the spot and sharpens the image, whispering, "This woman in the ratfur coat or whatever?"

The deputy tells her. "Local religious fanatic named Caldera Cunningham."

"What's she doing at Jeb Holloway's funeral?"

"Don't know," he says. Before an idea can form, Molly checks her watch.

"We late for something?" he asks.

"Let's get back to The Elk," she says. "I've got a surprise for you."

* * *

Red looks back from the bar at a big table full of new faces and asks, "The strangers?"

Molly tells him. "Media. ABC, CBS, NBC, Fox. I'm going over to press flesh." She winks at Red. "Never can tell where your next job is going to be."

He watches her do the circuit, laughing, tossing the hair off her face. Then he comes around, checks and asks Bear, "Where's Mona?"

"She wasn't up for a press conference, so took off with Laney." Bear looks over at Molly, then back to Red. "You two just pirooting, or is this a serious plew-chew?"

He ignores the question. "You know if Dave Dooley's got himself a horse?"

"Not as I can say. Why?" Bear asks.

"Just thinking. When it goes cold so many folk mosey on. Hollow-A's summer crew. Dave Dooley. Anybody else not nailed down or too stiff to move. Sanctuary gets to be a ghost town."

"Long as global warming don't kill the snow, Bearpaw's going to change all that."

Molly returns with a sly smile, checks the beer clock and prompts Bear, "It's time." The TV jumps from the Idaho-Montana State football game to CNN as the anchor announces, "Now a special report, from CNN's Molly Mendelbaum."

"CNN loops 24/7. We've seen this before," Red insists.

But this bit is new. Not the funeral, but Molly, in her warm sheepskin coat, standing in the sniper's nest and confiding, "The locals in Sanctuary, Montana, call this place Poker Bluff. Over thousands of years, ice and wind and rain have carved out figures of men, including an effigy of the famous Wild Bill Hickok, hunkered down behind me studying the famous aces and eights he was holding the day he was shot dead. Looking down from here..."

the camera pans onto the crime scene "... you can see where senate candidate Jeb Holloway was sitting in his vehicle when an assailant pulled the trigger of a Sharps buffalo gun. The fifty caliber bullet flew a thousand yards before penetrating the window and crashing through the side of the victim's head." The camera comes back to Molly, who continues, "The body was found by a local man, B.S. Walsh..."

Stopping behind them, five empty glasses pinched together by fingers, Walsh says, "Hey, man. That's me!" His reflexive happiness turns to woe, then, "Hey, Red, man. I gotta talk at you, man."

"Shush!" Molly says, holding onto Kravitz arm, whispering, "Here it comes."

"...who reported the crime to town's Deputy, Redfawn Kravitz. Since that moment Kravitz has been working with the FBI to bring the killer to justice. Although officials remain noncommittal, this reporter believes that the search is now focused on one man. If so, an arrest can't be far away. Molly Mendelbaum, CNN news, outside Sanctuary, Montana."

Kravitz lets his face fall into his hands and shakes his head. "Molly, Molly, Molly."

"Hey!" She jabs him with an elbow. "I just made you a household word, Kravitz. And this is what I get for thanks?"

Bear laughs. He half-fills a balloon glass with slivovitz, does the same for Molly.

"Against the cold." Red raises it.

"You've got me against the cold," Molly says, grabbing Red's hand and dragging him off. Outside the first big flakes of snow are floating through still air, like flower petals shaken from a meadow of dark gray clouds.

* * *

After they take each other beyond feelings that want for words, Red lies on his back and wonders what a man is supposed to do in this situation. For a woman it is always easier, because in her script the scene would play out all the way to morning and melt away in the bliss of chatting intimacy over a shared breakfast. But 21st century whites were still bullying Native Americans. There is nothing to do but hope she'll understand.

Instead of understanding he gets the same old Molly, plus fifteen years, more reasoned and less emotional. "Red, why are you busting your balls when Super Pete Rollins is leading the cavalry? He's got jurisdiction and you've got bupkis."

A taut silence admits to his stubborn pride. Which so infuriates her that she rolls out of bed and paces, waving her hands like a mourner at a New Orleans wake. "Okay, give me just one reason why you should go, one really good reason and I'll be yours as long as you want me."

Red draws hard at the air before confessing, "Rollins thinks a kid named Dave Dooley killed Jeb Holloway."

She goes too quiet before saying, "But you think not."

"Feels wrong. But Slo Lehrner might be able to turn something up. So I'm going up to see him," he says, getting out of bed. She pulls near, presses herself against him. "Your body feels right next to mine. You know that, don't you?"

"It goes both ways, Molly."

"You coming right back after Slo?"

"Nope," he says, adding, "I'm going to talk to Ivan Konev. See you when I get back," is all he manages. But when he turns his collar up in the deepening cold, he misses her more with each step he takes.

* * *

"Mensch was prowling and jumping, and Mamzer's still hiding, so I knew somebody was coming." Slo Lehrner shuts the door on the blow and stands in nubbed gray long johns that look a hundred years old. He shuffles over and restokes the estula. Wedges of fat pine kick a spray of sparks from smoldering embers.

"The FBI guy wants a victim profile on Jeb Holloway," Red opens.

"This for pay, or just a 'thank you' at the end?"

"Tell you what, Slo. I'll send a nice Chanukah present."

"I was kind of hoping you'd ride down that other son-of-a-bitch, Vegas Elvis Weinstein, shoot him in the nuts and bring back my family."

"If I did it way out in nowhere, with no witnesses, I might just get away with it."

"So I guess you're plumb out of suspects is what you're telling me?"

Red admits, "Plumb out of good suspects," shambling for the door.

Slo opens it. Outside the wind is chasing poudrerie across a patchy skin of big wet flakes. "You head straight back, you just might make it."

* * *

When the door opens, Ivan Konev's eyes blink with the sting of sweat. Red unbuttons his sheepskin coat and snaps the fine dry snow off his hat. A peg reaches out from the wall and takes it. "Gone hot in here," he says.

"It's an upgrade: the Ilnivosik Stove. Survivor of the Nazi seige of Leningrad."

Red looks it over. "Antique is it?"

"Even got a testimonial from an old guy who survived the Wehrmacht blockade. Back then when another family starved or froze to death, the communist party consigned their house to firewood."

"I guess winter that year was springtime for undertakers," Red says.

"You guess wrong. The dead got left where they fell. Who had the energy to dig up a six foot slot in frozen soil? By the time you dumped the last spadeful of permafrost into the hole, you'd drop right in yourself."

"You're in a cheerful mood," Red tells him.

"Got orders to fill and I'm running behind. At my age, after slowing down comes stopping altogether. I get a little nervous thinking about that." Ivan sits at the computer and keys in commands: bore size, twist count and barrel length, then sets the lathe's yoke whirling. As metal curls gather in the catch tray, Ivan shouts, "This has to do with guns?"

"Partly," he says. "Dave Dooley has a Sharps, right?"

At the end of the lathe run, Ivan switches off the machine. "Please tell me this isn't about tryin' to put somebody's Sharps together with Jeb Holloway's brains?"

"Keep this between us."

"Sure," he says. "You're not gonna drive home in that mess out there."

Red grabs and hand-blocks his hat. "Got a woman waiting to warm up."

"So I heard. You be careful about that, Red."

* * *

When Kravitz reaches his place, snow has gone to sleet, encrusting the nightworld in a slick patina. The narrow steps to the landing sag with the weight of glazed ice. At the top, the jamb is frozen to the door. He bangs on the edges to crack the seal, then shoulders his way in and lets the glow of the dying fire thaw the numbness from his face.

Breathing hard from effort, he glances toward the bedroom. Except for the dull ebb of reflected porchlight, every daylight shape is melted in shadows.

"Molly!" he shouts. And gets no answer. Again, "Molly, hey! It's me!"

Nothing.

Rushing to the bedroom, he finds the sougan and flannel sheets thrown back, a trace of her perfume haunting the cold air. He reaches back and flicks on the light. On the top sheet, tucked beneath a pillow, is a note in paper so white it blends in:

"Gone fishin', Red.
I know it's too cold
But you never can tell what you'll catch."

- Molly

TODAY'S NEWS

In the dream, Molly Mendelbaum stands outside the Montana Militia compound at Foster Forks. Dave Dooley is shown in a four-year old photo, a man with a nervous look bracketed by a flex of grim neo-Nazis. As the FBI's Tactical Enforcement Unit stretches prone on snow-capped berms, Molly's lips keep forming unheard words. At the end, he can make out the shape of her tag line, "Molly Mendelbaum..." as a militiaman on a tower raises his rifle, takes aim and... Kravitz tries to scream, "Get down, Molly!" but she keeps that unblinking focus as a shot cracks into a reverberating echo and Molly's face explodes.

With a sharp gasp he wakes up to a dim glow eking through rimed windows. Beneath a gunmetal sky, a dull sheen of ice stretches forever in ghostly silence. Groping and cursing in half-darkness, he gathers and yanks his clothes on. Through stinging cold, Kravitz charges to The Elk, bursts in yelling, "Bear!"

Bear rambles out in long johns, yawns and shakes off the sleep with a jerk of his chin. Red explains the situation, then Bear says, "I've just yesterday got me a new Jeep Cherokee out back. For Bearpaw." He ducks into the corridor, then back out to growl "Fire up the java machine."

While the Bunn-O-Matic is dripping, Red aims the remote at the new panel TV over the bar and thumbs in CNN. The redhead anchor in Atlanta eases into, "And this report just in from Foster Forks, Montana."

The clip reveals Molly by night, hunkered down in a copse of pines, silhouetted by spotlights from distant watchtowers. "CNN has learned that suspicion in Jeb Holloway's murder has fallen on a latter-day mountain man named David Corinth Dooley, who was in Sanctuary at the time of the killing. The FBI has linked him to the Montana Militia, whose stockade-style compound you see behind me..."

He clicks it off. Bear shuffles in behind him, fully dressed. Red insists, "I've got to straighten Rollins out before he gets his ass shot off."

A picture of pure concern, B.S. Walsh appears, pours himself a cup of fresh java and says, "Tell Rollins B.S. Walsh wants to see him. You hear, Red?"

*   *   *

Outside Foster Forks, a sentry for the FBI's Tactical Enforcement Unit holds them up to check credentials. Clad in flack vest and riot helmet he tells Red, "Rollins is over there."

Kravitz looks toward a shallow ridge fenced by pines and spots him, dressed like the others in camo-black. Against the snow they stand out like blackbirds on a beach. Huffing hard after a quick sprint, Red reaches the ridge, crabs in and leans his back against a thin pine.

Rollins's binoculars scan, sizing up the defenses. "You want to stay low, deputy? They've got a couple of snipers on the front towers looking to pin your ears back."

"Headquarters actually blessed your little siege?"

Rollins rests against the tree's bole and smiles. "Blessed it? My office director liked it so much that in ten minutes it became her idea. I'm just here to assist."

"Well, Pete, at this range a Sharps slug would corehole that tree and still blow the lungs clean out of your chest."

Rollins slides down the trunk and slithers through the snow like a river otter. Once hunkered well below the ridge, he continues. "Other than concern for my personal safety, what brings you up?"

"That fancy satellite that gave the hoofprints near Poker Bluff. Did you check yesterday before it snowed to see if there were any prints connecting Sanctuary with Foster Forks?"

"Tell me something truly, Deputy. In Dooley's beloved old west, wasn't it true that hunted men were expert at dragging blind trail?"

Red answers in kind. "And isn't it true that satellites are expert at revealing latent prints in blind trails?" Leaving Rollins without a rejoinder.

So Red keeps hammering. "Look, if Dooley did kill Jeb, why does he run to the only place you're sure to check when Canada's just as close?"

This time Rollins has, if not an answer, at least a rationale. "Most disorganized criminals tend to panic, run anywhere."

"Someone who'd set Jeb up for a single killshot and reclaim his brass seems organized enough to escape afterwards," Kravitz counters.

Rollins disagrees. "If he's that organized, why wouldn't he seek help afterwards?"

"Given all the other problems he has with domestic wiretapping and such, my guess is that the Director of the FBI won't be handing out promotions for an election-year bloodbath of card-carrying NRA members."

In a long silence, Rollins ponders before asking, "What've you got in mind?"

* * *

Nadine Quigley is Rollins' boss. Her features erupt in sharp ridges, yet her eyes are vivid, flirtatious and canopied by long natural lashes. Her nose is almost Roman, her chin square and prominent, like a battering ram. Which is what she plans on rolling out for the Montana Militia. "You want it short and sweet? This operation is by Federal warrant. And you're not a Federal agent, Kravitz."

"But I am," Rollins says. "I'll go too."

Nadine Quigley scowls. "Stripped down to your long johns?"

Red argues, "Either they let in two men in their underwear, or face a hundred in APCs with automatic weapons. Which way would you swing on that, Ms. Quigley?"

She tips her head toward the compound. "If this goes like Waco, you'll be the first one killed. You know that."

"If they kill me, it's just the start. My sense is that they don't want to start."

"Rollins, you really want to do this?" Nadine Quigley says, a question within a question that has answers within answers.

"Unless you do, boss," is the one she gets.

* * *

It must irk Nadine Quigley that Dave Dooley isn't found. So two men, one local lawman, half-Jew and half-Indian, and one FBI special agent shivered through snow in their long johns to end up empty handed. No suspects, no Sharps buffalo guns.

Tented in a PolarTec blanket, Rollins sits in an official van and surrenders a bleak smile. "...so where do you think Dave Dooley really is?"

"No idea," Kravitz says. "But a guy back in Sanctuary may. He seems real anxious to talk with you."

* * *

Rollins wanders off to debrief Nadine Quigley before Molly ventures near Kravitz. "Red...We've got to talk." She lays a hand on his arm.

He turns around. "Molly, folks are watching. Don't make a scene. Let's just pretend we're old lovers rekindling a flame. People might actually believe it."

She pulls a manila envelope from her parka and waves it at him. "But I had proof. Satellite photos of Dave Dooley's horse, or the hoofprints — "

He looks around before quickly slipping her envelope into his sheepskin coat. "Molly, this is Federal evidence. Somebody finds you lifted this, you're facing ten hard."

"You going to turn me in?"

She knows too much. And she knows too little. So she makes up the missing part. All that Red can do is shake his head. "Rollins and company have unfinished business with the Montana Militia. But the guys inside the fort smell a set-up. They know how Waco and Ruby Ridge turned out. They figure, here it comes."

"Nobody died," she says simply.

"Too bad for ratings. Sorry I didn't start a small war out here. If that happened, you don't think you'd suddenly become bulletproof, do you?"

"Occupational hazard," she responds.

"What is it, Molly? You figure if you can't get the anchor desk you'd rather end up in some splatter footage in the CNN archives? I don't get you."

She closes in and loops an arm through his, tugging. "Yeah you do. You're the only one who ever got me. And I'm hurt that you think I'd betray you. I really am. I'm..."

"Now let's not get started on this dance. I've heard the music, remember the lyrics and know the steps. But I can never keep up," he says.

Yawning from lost sleep, Bear wanders in. "You two okay?"

"Let's get back," he says. "I've got a killer to catch."

* * *

By mid-afternoon the clouds peel back like eyelids, so the sun glares down on the land. In its fickle warmth, snow hisses wisps of vapor. Front Street is acned with bootprints as Kravitz marches to town hall. Inside he passes Doris, saunters back and leans on the cell door. "Special Agent Rollins. I'm a bit surprised to see you."

"How's that?"

"With all the exposure and nothing to show for it, I'd figure Washington would want some kind of scape goat."

"That's the irony. Nadine Quigley stole my idea, so it was her head they went hunting. She claimed the real fault lay with the guy who tipped CNN."

"You sure it's a guy?"

Rollins tells him, "For some time we suspected our leak was a guy in DC. So we put a sweep-proof tap on his phone. Turns out he's the one."

"Oh?"

"Yeah. But not the first one. The call he got came from Mendelbaum. Said she had a tip and wanted him to deny it, if it was bad. He didn't."

"Maybe Mendelbaum got it from Jarnow."

Rollins's pupils shoot open.

"Why not? He's the one who called you guys in. He's the winner when voters see him as a connected, can-do guy."

"But can we put those two together?"

"Guess where I reconnected with her to begin all this? Jarnow's press conference in Helena."

Rollins tents his fingers. "I've got a career to think about. I definitely do not want to buck Montana's next U.S. Senator." He checks the deputy. "Give me something solid, based on a victim profile of Jeb Holloway."

"I'm workin' on it. But right now B.S. Walsh is real anxious to chat with you."

*   *   *

Atop a heavy drum of Sudso All Purpose Cleaner, B.S. Walsh sits, rubbing sweaty palms together in the store room. The room is flanked on one side by the kitchen, another by a sixteen-seater back room and out back by the crested butte that shelters The Elk from the worst northers.

Arms folded, Kravitz leans on the rear wall next to the fire escape. Opposite him and facing the buffalo solider, Pete Rollins sits on an unopened crate of Jack Daniels, clasping his hands together. "Walsh, I've got a killer to catch. How can you help?"

"How can I help?" B.S. Walsh repeats. Then, more softly, "How can I help?" Finally erupting, "What I got to know, Eliot Ness, is ain't nobody given you a little jinga-dinga ling on your cell-phone thing? No die-rectives from headquarters in DC?"

Rollins combs fingers through his hair and blows out fatigue. "Man, I've been standing against automatic weapons in cold so deep my balls turned blue. Now I am very tired and a little impatient, so you will tell me what the hell is going on or I'm leaving."

Walsh whispers. "Here's what I wanna know, bro. How come when Glenn Vandrey put me in witness protection they give me a new name, new identity and promise everything's gonna be just fine. Then some..."

Bear pokes his head in to interrupt, "How long till I get my help back?"

Rollins holds up a hand. "Ten minutes."

Bear leaves and closes the door.

"... I was saying..." Walsh whispers lower, "some stupid sheepbanger pops Jeb and next thing I know Molly Mendelbaum puts my picture on national Tee-Vee!"

"Calm down," Rollins says, raising the imperial hand again.

"Now that you don't have Dave Dooley, you gonna do a lot more lookin'. Well, Mr. FBI, I did not do it. And so I want my black ass out of here before somebody in the Mow-Tah City notices there's a nigger here and it's me. Am I communicating at you?"

Rollins signals time-out, frees his wireless and speed-dials. In response to an unheard request he responds, "Rollins, Peter. IDO/VP. 55754321. Jango, get me a Glenn Vandrey in moving and storage ... I'll hold." He looks up, places a hand over the mouthpiece to say, "They're transferring." Taking his hand away he opens, "Vandrey. Pete Rollins here. Got a man says you're the top-down on an M&S... B.S. Walsh... Okay. Can I tell him? Okay. When?" His eyes shift to Walsh. "He's a little antsy. Any reason he should be? Okay. Will do. I'll look for the go-ahead." Then he hangs up.

Walsh keeps rubbing his palms together. "What did my man say, Rollins?"

"Said they had you cold on a murder during a bank robbery, and let that slide, so now we know you're a killer."

"Hey," Walsh says. "What about Dave Dooley, man? He's got the fucking gun!"

Rollins remains unmoved. "But a deal is a deal. You're getting shipped out. Still, I'd like to know where you were when Jeb Holloway was killed."

"This is bullshit, man!" Walsh looks to Red. "Tell this guy I'm innocent!"

"Huh?" Red says, catching his boot tip on a trap door's lift ring. Wedged in the shadows of the frame lies a twisted run of shiny metallic ribbon. It looks like tinsel, but when he kneels and pulls, finds it thicker and stronger, like narrow gauge wire.

"I said tell this guy... Red?"

Kravitz stares back. "What's down here?"

"How should I know? You have to ask Bear."

But Bear has other problems to solve. "Ten minutes, guys. Can I have my nigger back now?"

Red asks, "Any way Walsh could've stowed a Sharps down here?"

Bear says, "Try it."

Red does. The trap door doesn't budge. And Kravitz has no intention of letting his best suspect plea-bargain with Rollins while the yokum local deputy is poking around in dusty corners for incriminating evidence.

Maybe Walsh isn't the shooter, but without him, the case runs out of suspects. So now they need someone else with a strong and credible motive for murder.

TOMORROW'S WOES

Kravitz walks Rollins to town hall, finding Doris gone. As usual, Sanctuary's government had closed at sundown. Before Jeb Holloway's murder, the town was just a curiosity, famed only for its wrestling-football hero, Standing Bear Hatcher. Some additional distinction accrued from the Charley Russell paintings and historic kitsch posted on The Elk's walls. Otherwise it just confused lost tourists into asking, "I wonder what this place used to be?"

Prodded by curiosity or boredom, they might trek up a mild crumbling incline south of town, stop at the rim and snap a few photos of tilted and dust-scoured gravestones. Whenever he needs perspective, Red visits boot hill and reads names. Of the true Anglos: English, Scots, Welsh, the Europeans: Germans, Squareheads, Irish, Italians, Poles, Russian.

B.S. Walsh might be surprised to find a few blacks. Blacks and Indians and Jews. Whores and thieves and murderers lying side-by-side with their customers and victims. Here under hardscrabble and harder winds lies America's one true democracy.

Back in an era freer of government intervention, the select few planted their kin in private plots. Including the Holloways. Most of Jeb's ancestors now sleep under pin grass in the lee of a rugged cliff that lords over the family plot. Those graves, fenced by iron spears, now seem part of the landscape.

Viewed from the top floor of the big house, phallic obelisks stare back, ghostly whispers masquerading as dust devils bearing lessons from the underworld to the living. Remember who you are. Forget what we did to get this land.

Today those years seem as remote and unrecoverable as the lamented epoch of Elk That Drinks, who fell at Little Bighorn. When Red's parents came out here, idealistic young hippies looking for fresh air to breathe, they never asked where the Hollow-A ranch had come from.

By that time, it had always been there. Back then Jeb was just the latest crown prince in a long dynasty. Now the king was dead, with no heir apparent, unless you counted the bastard growing inside Mona. Pete Rollins knew none of this, or he wouldn't have to ask, "So basically what do you know about Jeb Holloway?"

"Basically, in some other place he'd be the same kind of guy. Like Dick Cheney that way. Enough attitude, enough money, enough connections and you can usually get away with anything."

Rollins sits in the old jail cell, turns one hand upside down to place a silver dollar between the ring and little fingers. Then he moves his fingers up and down like pistons, so the coin turns over and over, tumbling as it travels. Rollins keeps his eyes on Red while the coin stops and reverses, a hypnotic effect. "But if somebody wanted him out of the way to win an election, they'd sooner turn up a scandal. Hypothetically."

"Hypothetically, maybe. But you've got to watch the way the wind blows when you start slinging mud. Word has it that the happily married, born-again Len Jarnow was banging campaign manager Sue Slade when the Sharps that killed Holloway was doing its own banging."

"So says Jarnow," Rollins admits. "But guess what our cybergeeks just found?" He doesn't wait for Red's response before rolling on. "Picture of Len Jarnow with Obergruppenfuhrer Garrett Naylor. At a shooting range, along with some regional panjandrum of the NRA. Everybody's smiling. Especially Jarnow. He just got an endorsement and donation from the Montana Militia. The funds were sanitized by a kind of pureed PAC called Citizens for Personal Freedom."

"It's an election year. You pat backs, smile, make promises you can't keep and take money you never give back. If you arrested politicians who did that, you'd empty every legislature in the country."

Rollins keeps the coin moving, never looking at it. "There's more. Jarnow's nephew is one of the frozen few at Foster Forks. He marches goosestep-to-goosestep with Naylor himself, as Deputy Untergruppenfuhrer for political action and defense. Turns out this nephew is a crack shot. And a buddy of Dave Dooley." The coin stops moving to punctuate the bottom line: "What do you think?"

Kravitz barks a scoffing sound. "Here's your problem, Pete. The photo you gave me, of the hoofprint near Poker Bluff..."

"I know. You think we can't put Dooley on the horse. Let us worry about that."

"It's more than that. The horseshoe in the print is what we call a slipper. Real popular around the time the whites started rushing west, because iron was scarce." Red frees the manila envelope recovered from Molly, opens it and points out the details. "See how smooth it is. No calks. Not a grain of extra metal. Historical preference but modern curiosity. As the local trading post operator, I did a little scratching around. You can't even get them commercially."

Rollins scribbles this down. "Washington thinks Holloway's killing was political. It's planned, deliberate and almost professional. They want this son of a bitch pronto."

"Me, too. But in Holloway's Suburban our forensic team found a copy of the Bozeman Daily Chronicle splattered with the victim's blood. The front page reported Jarnow ahead by eleven points. If I had Jeb's ego, that might make me shoot myself. But your conspiracy line has all kinds of kinks in it. I don't think it'll run very far without fouling."

Rollins offers a peace-maker's smile. "Maybe you're right. But if not Jarnow, who?"

"I vote for B.S. Walsh."

"Why?"

"My guess? Mona's carrying his child. Jeb found out, offered Walsh money if he just cleared out. But Jeb had other plans. In the Suburban was a .357 magnum Colt Python. One through the head would put Walsh away. A mattress in the back was to soak up the blood while he took the body off to be buried somewhere on the Hollow-A."

Rollins flips the coin in the air, catches it with a snap and stuffs it in a pocket. "So here's the question: Jeb is sitting in the Suburban, ready for Walsh. And Walsh doesn't figure forensic technology would link him to the killing?"

"Walsh is what we call a mover, a man who can't settle down long enough to put down roots. Suppose Jeb gets rid of the body. Walsh turns up missing. Bear bitches. I'm told. But without a complaint against him, the man's free to go. In the unlikely event that Glenn Vandrey learns of his disappearance, you Feds aren't going to destroy the mythology of safety within witness protection by conceding that somebody from Detroit found Walter Stanley Addison and dealt with him. Holloway was probably betting that nobody would find Walsh's body. Ever. As for evidence at the scene, Jeb knew it would rain that night."

"But how could he know it was going to rain when he set up the meet?"

"If it didn't, he didn't have to show. What's Walsh going to do, call up and say, 'Hey, Jeb, how many times a guy have to bang your wife to get his bonus?'"

"That's the last problem: How was Jeb going to deal with Mona?"

Red remembers the bruises on her shoulder, then pushes down an older and deeper memory of a pregnant woman battered, bleeding from her face. Bracing a hand and fighting off a surge of dizziness, he manages to answer, "Get her an abortion, I guess. Send her to AA. Straighten her out."

Rollins speculates, "You really think Jeb Holloway was the kind of guy who could kill somebody and get away with it?"

"Yeah."

"You don't think Mona knew that?"

Red guesses, "She had to have it figured both ways. One angle if Walsh walked away, another one if Jeb came home."

"Right," Rollins says. "Now follow me on this one. Here are two reasonably bright law enforcement types asking who killed Jeb Holloway. Lo and behold, we come up with... tah-dah!... B.S Walsh. And why? He's the poster child for urban crime! He's just too perfect."

Rollins is right. But that doesn't explain why the FBI went after Dave Dooley when they knew that B.S. Walsh was really Walter Stanley Addison of Detroit. And that oversight bothers Red enough to mention, "Walsh is so perfect that I was able to get a ping on a guy whose records were supposed to be deep-sixed with his relocation. Did you check with Glenn Vandrey on that?"

"I did," Rollins admits. "You ask how did it happen?" He shrugs. "Walsh got stupid. His records were already pulled and shredded by Detroit Metro. But before the move, Walsh reverted to form. He took a short road trip to Ann Arbor, spotted some white co-ed snatch, then moved on it. A big white guy with her raised an objection that got him two bullets. Michigan's starting linebacker. You remember the story?"

"Vaguely," Red says, honestly for a guy who doesn't watch TV except in bits down at The Elk. Rollins completes Red's fragmented memory. "Walsh drove off with the coed, gun to her head, then raped her. What Walsh doesn't know at the time is that this sexy little coed is a PI's daughter. Behind the scene, this PI, a former Detroit cop, asks around inside the force. Turns out a sly capitalistic captain has stashed away dupes of Walsh's file, betting the bad guy can't stay good too long..." Rollins blows out exhaustion. "That's how it happened. No way we could do damage control."

"You think Mona knew?"

Rollins barks a laugh. "The real answer: it doesn't matter. This doesn't get prosecuted. Even if Walsh did it."

"Wait. Why? What are you..." he is baffled, but it slowly comes to him just as Rollins puts it into words. "The Federal government put Walsh in witness protection. He's ours forever. If there's a problem, it's our problem."

Red looks through the bars, feeling the prickle of the cold air. "Snow's coming. Give me one day. If I feel in my Indian bones the man didn't do it, I'll stand aside."

Pete Rollins pushes off both thighs and gets up. "You've got your day. The only thing bureaucrats are good at is delay. Besides, Moonlight wants to show me some of the countryside."

"You and Moonlight enjoy. Leave your friend Walsh to me."

* * *

Red moseys down Front Street. Overhead stars flash like trout in a bottomless stream. His boots crunch freezing snow as his breath whitens to mist. Shaking off the chill, he enters The Elk, saunters to the Rockola and picks The Drifters' This Magic Moment. As strings sweep into the lyrics, Red joins the others. Walsh is making his case to Bear. "I'm just saying I got to get me some."

"Try Moonlight," Bear tells him.

Red leans on the bar to advise, "Moonlight's not around."

"Where she at?" Walsh wants to know.

"Taken off with Agent Rollins."

Now Walsh is looking a little concerned. "When's my man Glenn Vandrey sending in the calvary to rex-cue the buffalo soldier?"

"What's the rush?" Red asks.

"You never had no gang of badasses after you, right?"

Bear corrects him. "We had a world of badasses after us, Walsh. That's why I'm behind a bar and not looking down an unfenced hill on a run of bison."

"Well, shit. That was a long time ago, anyway. I'm talking about here and now."

One-handed, Bear seizes a keg of beer, drops it in an ice tub and looks at Red. His eyes say, 'Tell this shithead what's what.' But Red just says, "Looks like you got a couple of days till you leave our fair town. Maybe you could help us figure out this Jeb Holloway thing."

Walsh raps on the counter, asks, "Hey, can I have a drink?"

"No," Bear says. "You work tonight."

"When I get paid?"

"After the holiday weekend," Bear says.

"What holiday?"

Red informs him. "Columbus Day, Walsh. It celebrates this white guy who sailed across the ocean, saw all these Indians and declared there wasn't another human being on the biggest landmass in the western hemisphere. It's a federal holiday but not a state holiday. So Rollins gets off, but

I'm stuck on the job."

"The Buffalo Soldier need to pow-wow wiff Glenn Vandrey."

Bear reminds him, "It's a holiday for Vandrey, too. Don't expect he'll be waiting around for your call."

"This is bullshit. After work, I'm going to Mona's. Get me some."

"Tie your apron on," Bear growls. To Kravitz he says, "You want something to eat, brother?"

Red defers. "Thanks, but I've got to check on Molly."

*　　*　　*

Outside, a whistling wind pries at the clapboards. Inside Kravitz sits in bed, one knee propped up, arms folded. From there he watches snowflakes click against the window, and to the right, behind a brass footing, Molly stands like a prisoner in the dock, eyes turned down. "Nobody was killed."

He raises his hands, claps three times, then lights into her. "Molly, you were walking around with evidence in a Federal murder case."

Molly insists, "Unless you told Rollins, who knows? They indict, you deny."

"You said it yourself, Molly. I never was a very good liar. That's why you jumped on the story and took off like a whore to a lecher's convention. The only reason you made that call to Washington was to keep someone between me and Rollins."

"And you're not glad I did?"

"I'm understandably relieved, but you're ecstatic."

"Me?" She stabs a finger between her breasts and feigns anger.

Above a bitter smile, Red's eyebrows arch, punctuating his certainty. "You. Because your primary source is still uncompromised and still talking to you. Not that Rollins doesn't suspect. He played around with the idea that since your phone call came from Sanctuary, your source had to be here, too. Where do you think he was headed on that one?"

"So how did you put the intrepid Pete Rollins off the truth?"

"I suggested it might be Jarnow, since that's where I hooked up with you recently."

"Oh, Jesus, you didn't," she says, losing her color.

"At the time it seemed like a shrewder response than mea culpa. Especially to the guy who joined me walking across an open field of snow in his undies."

"That was stupid what you did, Red. I was scared to death."

"You were scared?" She uses emotion to veer him, but now he wants to stay on course. So he reins in his argument and returns to the point. "How would you have felt if somebody had gotten killed?"

"If somebody got killed, it would have been you first. Do you need to ask?"

In a soft voice he says, "Answering a question with a question, Molly, is a fine rhetorical device, but it only tells me how I'd think you'd feel if I was killed. Now since I didn't think you'd misuse the information I gave you, I really don't know how you'd feel if I got killed. In fact, as I walked toward those rifles, I was wondering which of those NeoNazis would claim his fifteen minutes of shame by killing an Indian and Jew with the same bullet."

"Wait. You did this because..."

He admits, "Because if I was responsible for somebody getting shot before they could enter negotiations, then I ought to be the first one to be shot. That way at least the FBI could say that these guys were shooting unarmed lawmen who arrived with legal authority to conduct a search..." His voice rises and his fist hammers on the mattress. With each thump she flinches a bit. When he stops, she pushes a hand back through her hair and whispers, "I'm sorry you see it that way..."

"How else could I see it, except as your stepping stone to a nightly anchor spot?"

"That's not fair." she objects. "Don't you see that without the militia being tipped the thing could have... could have looked like a surprise raid and...and blown up?"

"Did CNN's legal staff stimulate your thinking?"

"They were a bit preoccupied by the run-up to the war when I ran it by them. But they didn't say 'no.'" She sits down beside him. On the windows snow is beginning to stick, the old panes rattling with the slap of wind, cold seeping through uncaulked cracks. Her voice still low, she says, "What happens with Dave Dooley now?"

"I swore to Rollins's boss Nadine Quigley that Dooley had no contact with the militia in four years. That pretty much poked a hole in their conspiracy theory."

"Who then?" she asks. "And why?"

"Good questions. If I get any good answers, I won't waste them on pillow talk."

She draws back as if struck, grabbing a breath. "You know, you can really be cruel for a man who expects a woman to spend the night with him."

He corrects her. "I've been screwed by you about as much as I care to be."

"Red?" The way she says the word, the sound of her voice, plus her lingering scent, begins to cool his molten rage.

After drawing a long breath he crosses his arms and whispers, "What?"

"I want to help you."

"I've had about as much of your kind of help as I can endure, Molly. Walking in on that compound today, I felt the spirit world. Now that may sound strange to a full blooded Jew, but to a half-breed Indian it means your dead ancestors are calling for you."

"What if you weren't..." she starts "...going to stay in Sanctuary after all this? What if it changed your view of things?"

"Already has," he says, letting the sting settle in.

"Don't say no," she begs. "At least not to everything."

"It's getting late..."

She shivers again, touches his arm. "I don't want to sleep alone to-night."

"Why not tell B.S. Walsh. He seems real anxious for company."

Before he can react, she slaps him hard across the face. "You bastard!" she hisses. "How could you even think something like that?"

"Look," he tries to explain his anger, but she is teary. Not crying, maybe not even real tears. But they do the trick.

"I'm thinking of the way people end up in this world and wonder why?" she says, sniffling and wiping her nose with the back of one hand, then holding that hand out imploringly. "When I was up shooting that last piece on Poker Bluff, there was an old woman with a rifle."

"She shoot at you?"

Molly shakes her head. "Our eyes met and there was some... connection. It was weird. But she came over, asked if I was with TV. I said yes. Then she asked I could fix her TV set. I said I'd have a techie look at it. She's got this thing in a shack without power or water, eating what she shoots and cooks on a fire... and claims that her set gets some programs but not all of them..."

"Crazy Daisy," Red whispers.

"And I'm looking at this and not believing it. That somebody lives like that and nobody does anything about it. What kind of people are we that..."

Red tells her. "It's all about freedom out here. That's the way she wants it. Until a court or state agency says she can't be there or somebody wins the legal squabble over who owns it, she has every right to squat."

Molly rubs her arms for warmth. "And she's up there now? In this storm?"

"She'll fire up her estula, slip into an Arctic mummy bag. Daisy's a tough old bird."

Molly shivers hard. And Red tells her, "Get in here before you freeze off that beautiful ass of yours." Cuddled together beneath a down comforter, ticking snowflakes and shrieking wind keep the silence between them from deepening.

TWO DEAD

Sunrise reveals Sanctuary encircled by corrugated snow. The wind howls like a rabid banshee, rattling building frames and casting white lines of blow-off as thin as monofilament. Red gets up, throws on his sheepskin and hat, then soldiers down Front Street to The Elk. Bear lets him in. Lowering a shoulder into the door, Red shuts the storm out as Bear vanishes into the kitchen. Bacon, eggs and hash browns scent the air.

"Walsh still sleeping?" the deputy asks, sitting at a table.

For a few seconds the only answer is the sizzle of eggs flipping over, until Bear shouts back, "I think he went up to Mona's."

"You let him go?"

Bear appears with two plates, sits down and digs in. Then chews an answer around the victuals. "Last night I took the Ski Doo up to Pine Ridge, to hang vinyl, keep the snow out. I get back, he's gone. So what? Without a snowmobile Walsh goes not so far, maybe freezes to death. Java?"

"Yeah," he says, watching Bear add cream.

Red imagines how the hand might play out. Mona can claim Walsh made unwanted advances, so had to be shot. And since shooting a bristly guest-turned-highbinder is an honored Montana tradition, no grand jury would return an indictment against the grieving widow. Not for a black ex-con spirited away to Montana without citizen consent.

On the wall next to the Charley Russell painting, the house dial-phone starts ringing. Bear walks over and picks up. His face goes sour as he says, "Yeah... yeah, he's here..." a long silence, listening, then, "...when... how again?...not an animal? You're sure?"

More silence passes as Bear looks at Red, then drops his glance to return to the caller. "Okay, I'll tell him. No. Don't touch anything."

Bear hangs up, leans a forearm on the wall and presses his forehead into it. "That was Luke Brody. He just found Daisy. Somebody cut her throat."

* * *

Bear's Jeep Grand Cherokee struggles in the soft snow, lit blinding white by a cyclops sun. "Careful," Kravitz warns, "Or we'll both be ice till the first chinook."

Just ahead lies the turn where he stopped Mona Holloway a few nights ago. Today there's no Lambourghini in sight. Just the big house, its main chimney flying a switching twist of smoke on a whistling breeze.

"How'd Walsh get up here?" Kravitz wants to know.

"I don't say he is. I'm just tellin' you he'd want to be." A silence so final it could stretch forever ends with "Seems a waste, Walsh killing Daisy. Hell, she was ready to go in her sleep."

"Maybe she was the only one who actually saw him kill Jeb Holloway."

That's what Red says, but suddenly – by instinct or desperation – his mind turns to the person who found the body, Luke Brody, the mailman. Luke Brody, Vietnam war vet, Section Eight, who regained his sanity in the peace and tranquility of Montana. Luke Brody, who like so many out here enjoyed his solitude, neither asked for or had many friends, and like so many others did pretty much what he wanted. And finally Luke Brody, whose daily journeys to Crazy Daisy made his all but invisible to her, and who knew her stomping ground better than anyone around. But as quickly as the idea flutters through his mind it's gone.

*　　*　　*

Mona swivels down the staircase, her long sculpted legs breaking through the splits of something longer, lacy and black, her high breasts bouncing behind the peak-a-boo pattern of roses and thorns. Turning toward her guests she smiles, tosses unbrushed hair off her face and purrs at Red. "Well, deputy, if this is an official visit, do you want to start by frisking me? See if I'm armed? Or do you need your official undies to conduct a legal search?"

"We were wondering if B.S. Walsh made it up here last night?" Kravitz asks.

She frowns at Bear before turning back to Red. "Well if you've already guessed he was here, whether he 'made it' is none of your official business. Unless you get better mannered, I'm likely to set the dogs on you."

"Is Walsh here now?" Kravitz presses.

Mona leans on a carved newel, pinching a crush of cleavage between her arms. "Pardon my inhospitality! Would you two heathen savages like a drink, or is that a politically incorrect question?"

"Coffee," is Red's request.

"He likes it with two spoonfuls of cream," Bear tells the maid, María. "Me, I'll do with some hot chocolate if you've got it."

Mona tells María, "And I'll have a glass of that nice New Zealand Sauvignon Blanc. New bottle. Takes the edge right off the morning hang-over and chases the throbbing from the skull. Sure you won't join me, the two of you?"

María comes back jiffy-quick with the hot drinks. Mona wasn't tipped to this visit, so Luke Brody must've let the maid know they'd be coming. "Gracías, María," Kravitz says.

"No hay de que," she whispers back.

Bear drinks his cocoa through a swirl of steam without wincing. María returns with the wine before retreating. Mona sips and swallows. "I hope you can appreciate how western hospitality forced me to offer shelter rather than sending him out in the cold."

"It was a hard night to survive," Red says. "That's proven."

"Did someone die?" Mona asks, playing the line for full shock.

Red tips his hat. "If you see Walsh, have him give me a call. And I'll be wanting to question your summer crew about their whereabouts when your husband was killed."

Mona's eyebrows arch up, followed by a big smile. "Most of them were playing faro in the bunkhouse. All night. Game broke up just before noon. Didn't Hizzoner Augie tell you?"

Red shakes his head. "Did you know about this game before we last talked?"

"Deputy, I make it my business to know everything that goes on at the Hollow-A. Otherwise, how's a girl to cope?"

Red is primed to leave but turns back to ask, "Oh, since you know about everything, are you stabling an Appaloosa on the Hollow-A?"

Mona switches to Bear before telling Kravitz, "Well, I'm not up on the complete inventory of horses. But Head Hanley could show you the herd."

"It's might crimpy today, Mrs. Holloway. But I'll be back." He tips his hat and turns to leave. Only then does he notice that the big portrait of Jeb Holloway has been removed from its former place on the wall. On a table below the vacancy lies a pile of today's mail.

* * *

Rolling into Sanctuary, Bear half-sleds his Jeep Cherokee down the road, blunting the harsh light with black sunglasses. Red reaches the Tweedles on his cell. "I've got another victim. Near Poker Bluff. You need to look at... No. Throat cut. Chopper in. When you're done, tell me whatever you can." He ends the call and stares at the keypad. Bear flicks him a glance and asks, "You want we drive up there, have us a look-see?"

Bear wants to be helpful. But Kravitz is thinking more clearly now. "We go, it just messes up whatever evidence there is. Other than Luke Brody's bootprints. Better we leave it to the experts." Bear keeps bulling through loose snow while Red punches in another number. "Slo, it's me. Where's your package?"

"The file was sent by e mail. Just click it up and download it to the printer." The signal begins to break up, but it's unneeded anyway.

"What's Slo sending in?" Bear wants to know.

"Complete history of Jeb Holloway. Our wunderkind FBI guest is sure that Jeb was killed for a reason."

*   *   *

Red leans his squeaky swivel chair leaning against the brick wall and opens the file on Jeb Holloway to a section labeled, "The Holloways Arrive in Montana." He doesn't finish the first sentence before Molly waltzes in, says Hi to Doris and rushes on back. Finding the door open, she raps on the jamb. "Your face is red as a highway flare. What's happened?"

He balks at telling her. But a beat later he realizes she'll know quick enough via the Sanctuary grapevine. So he says, "Daisy Ramirez died last night."

"That poor old woman! Somebody should have — "

"Somebody cut her throat."

"Jesus, no!" she says, collaring a hand on her larynx. Overhead the noisy clatter of rotors beats at the windows on Kravitz's office as the forensics chopper passes toward Poker Bluff. Cocking his head to indicate its direction, he says, "Micky and Mo are on their way up right now to look at the body."

"It's still there?" A sparkle percolates into her eyes.

"Luke Brody, the mail man, called it in. In Vietnam he worked as a Navy corpsman for the Marines in DaNang. If Luke says she's dead, I believe she's dead."

"Look, Red..."

He watches her restlessness grow and warns, "Don't get too close, Molly. Daisy was the only one who saw the killer."

* * *

Molly's monologue on Daisy and the cold had not been as much a premonition as a prediction. Someone who felt safer with all the witnesses dead had sent Daisy into the spirit world because she saw him riding an Appaloosa toward Poker Bluff just before Holloway was killed. And that certainty brought it back to B.S. Walsh.

Walsh had been spending a lot of time with Mona. Mona had a Sharps buffalo gun, one she had schemed to keep out of evidence. And Mona Holloway lied. In her call to Leonard Jarnow she told him that Red had tried to rape her.

Another connecting fact is that Mona also has a lot of horses and liked to ride. It seems probable that if B.S. Walsh was in the saddle with Mona he would want to follow the scent of Opium anywhere. To prove himself a man, he would need to be a genuine buckeroo, like Bill Picket, the legendary black bulldogger. If only to perfect his cover story. How could he be kin to a buffalo soldier if he kept falling off a mount? And Mona likes to teach men new tricks, maybe even riding Indian-style.

On the Hollow-A ranch, nobody told the mistress of the house what she could and couldn't do. Not even Jeb Holloway. And that may have taken the unhappy couple to the breaking point. Perhaps Jeb had Walsh's departure script all written in his head. After reading the family history once, Red could imagine Jeb in the Chevy Suburban, the .357 magnum Colt Python just an arms-length away, making the offer to Walsh, "I've got twenty thousand dollars. Go someplace I'll never see you again and it's all yours." Which would have set the stage for, "Walsh? Haven't seen him lately."

And no one would till the spring thaw. Detroit has street signs on every corner. So no matter how hard it blew in the Motor City, Walsh always knew where he was. But in last night's blizzard, he may have found Daisy before the storm found him. After that he would have become a man stumbling along in withering cold, confected with snow, his chilled teeth clicking so hard that their brittle edges broke, his eyelashes freezing together with futile tears. Then he would have screamed — maybe "Mona!" — before becoming a small bump in a vast unbroken white landscape.

Emerging from these thoughts, Red notices his ancient intercom button flashing, just as Doris appears, wheezing and red-faced. "I wish you'd get that damn ringer fixed. Or at least not fall asleep. I bet that little thing you've been schtupping has hardpacked your brains right down the barrel of your Hawken."

"I was just thinking," he says.

"Well think about this: B.S. Walsh just stumbled into The Elk."

* * *

A twisted warp of roiling skeins weaves the sky into an eerie gray tapestry. Across the featureless white below, wind shrieks at every corner that defies it. Kravitz turns up the sheepskin collar, pinches his hat down and lurches toward The Elk. After pressing its latch the door blows open, silhouetting him in the frame like an old western marshal. Bear stops polishing a glass and looks up. "If you don't shut that behind you, Walsh here's gonna die."

Red lowers a shoulder and pushes the door shut, takes off his ice-flecked hat and spins it onto a free peg. Then unbuttons his coat, catching his hips between thumbs and forefingers. "I was like to think the storm ate you for dinner, pardner."

Walsh's hands stay clamped on a hot cup of coffee. He shakes so hard that his words break apart as fast as they form."Whu...whu...what... duh...duh...do...yuh...you... you.care?" The man's eyes look dazed.

Red sits next to him. "We care about different things for different reasons. Me, I just want to talk to you."

"I...I...I...wuh...wuh...wuh...want...tuh...tuh..tuh...to talk...to my man."

Walsh would here be meaning the puppeteer in Washington who could yank the strings and make him disappear. But Red Kravitz is having none of that. "Walsh? Where's the blade you cut Daisy's throat with?"

"'Fuh...fuh...fuck you tuh..talkin' 'bout?"

Red looks up at Bear, then back at Walsh, whose eyes betray a flicker of awareness. Pure fear burns off his stutter. "Man, I was up the ranch last night, see. Bass Sanders come down, take me up. I wanted to talk with Mona about this whole thing..."

"So you go to the one guy on the crew who'd do anything for anybody anytime. Why didn't you scare up Bass Sanders for a ride back?" Bear asks.

Walsh fidgets. "Dude's not to be found. Hey, Bear, when you gonna refill this coffee, man?"

Drawing hot water, the Bunn-O-Matic sounds like Doris clearing her throat. Walsh blinks and races ahead, loud and fast. "I'm tellin' you she get up this morning and then you two show. I hide, man. I mean after I can't find Bass. Even when we go lookin'. And that's some time. Till afternoon. Then Mona has Jake Laney haul my ass into his truck, half-way back to town. The fucker stop there and I think he gonna shoot me. But he just open my door and kick me out. With his damn boot he kick me out. Then say, 'Here's the message, nigger. One way goes to Sanctuary. Other to the ranch. You go the right way you might just live.' Then he turn around, nearly run me over and drive back."

Red tells him, "Maybe. But so you don't wander off again, I'm gonna keep you in the calaboose till our friend Pete Rollins gets back. Now if in the meantime you chose to have a tantrum and wreck some computers, well, I'll get you on destruction of municipal property. And that'll hold you till Judge Jasper Cody rides the circuit this way."

Bear lets the Bunn-O-Matic finish gurgling, then ignores Walsh to pour Red a cup, cutting it with cream. Looking up he says, "Maybe you want to drink this over here, where the prisoner can't wrestle your gun away, deputy." Meaning Bear wants to pow-wow.

Red moseys to the bar, sits on a stool and leans in close.

"Here's your problem," Bear whispers. "Molly Mendelbaum. You keep letting her breeze past Doris like she owns you. You stall her now, it only makes her curious. Then she goes around back, looks through the bars to see B.S. Walsh. You think she's gonna believe it's for destruction of municipal property?"

Red sees the problem. "What are you thinking, Bear?"

"Walsh stays right here in The Elk, works as usual."

"You're taking responsibility?"

Bear smiles. "I told him before. If he runs, I'll catch him and kill him. He didn't run last night; just made a little beaver-chase up to Mona's."

"With maybe a side trip to Crazy Daisy," Red whispers.

"Maybe that, too. But my point is where he's gonna go? He goes back to Mona, he gets shot for trespass. He's in jail you got yourself a media circus. Then Augie's got to play ringmaster. You make Augie look like a hick, he'll take away your badge and shove it sideways up your ass."

"Jesus, Bear. You're beginning to think like a white man."

Bear cocks his head. "Right now it pays you to think about the white man's world. Because that's where your halfbreed ass is sticking out."

Breaking a tense silence, The Elk's wall phone starts ringing. Bear pushes off the bar, saunters over and picks up with, "Yeah?" The look on his friend's face troubles Red, who can only hear, "You sure?" then "When?" finally, "Which way?" before he hangs up. Looking over at Red, the big bar-dog says, "That was Jake Laney. Bass Sander's gone missing, along with an Appaloosa."

"Laney say if a Sharps is missing?" Red asks, watching the veiled light fade while he gulps down the last of his coffee.

Bear admits, "Didn't think to ask."

Opening the door, Red feels the keening of the wind, then gives up a bleak smile. Who'd've thought? Bass Sanders.

*   *   *

Red skips the wind suit, adding only riding goggles and warm mitts. They do little good. Moving thirty-five, sometimes forty miles an hour, the passing air slakes him numb. At first that sharpens his mind with the fear of dying. Slow cold; quick bullet. Either way dead. But while he's still breathing and thinking, he at least needs to know why he hadn't thought of Bass Sanders as a suspect.

Maybe because no one would've considered Bass. In a moment of misguided geriatric lust, his parents had conceived a child with big eyes so far down the sides of his face, mouth opening like a fish gasping for air as it went into the creel. Bass fit him fine, but just made other kids laugh. And Bass just laughed along with them. While he never mastered more than third grade reading, a glimmer in his big eyes showed that he finally came to understand he was the butt of playground jokes. And that the kids weren't laughing because he made them happy, but because they saw him as a freak.

From that moment, Bass retreated into his own world, and set about finding a way of getting by. Jeb Holloway gave him a chance. In fact, Jeb once called him, "The near perfect employee. He takes any order, carries it out without complaint, asks for more work when he's done, and never wants a raise or a break. Add to that he doesn't eat much, takes no time off, never oversleeps or get sick, and you've got the kind of man I like: dumb as a post, obedient as a storm trooper, durable as a battering ram and loyal as a dog."

Jeb's own testimonial. But some of what Bass was made to do showed the side of Jeb which made so many folks hate him. Most memorable was the time Bass was asked to move a heap of boise de vache ten yards from where it lay pooled. Quick and responsive, Bass obeyed, fighting the flies as he scooped with his hands and hustled cowshit to the spot Jeb indicated. Jake Laney was there, along with Zack Farnes, Kyle Halloran and Sam Bates, all smiling the way Jeb expected them to.

When he thought he had finished, Bass came running back, asking, "That's what you wanted, Mr. Holloway?"

Jeb studied the relocated dung and said, "About six more inches to the right."

Bass dutifully moved it again, asking, "Okay, now, Sir?"

Jeb had thought about that and said, "You know, Bass, I've never seen a shit castle, the way kids at the beach make sand castles. You think you could make one for me?"

Bass said, "I'll give 'er a try."

They left him at it for six hours. Dark came and Bass still wasn't back. Jake Laney rode out with Bill Smathers and found him sobbing over his efforts. Looking up he told them, "Shit ain't sand. Shit ain't sand. I can't do it the same. You boys want to show me how?"

Enough to make a man want to kill?

Sure, any normal man. But attributing normal motivation to a man whose bubble is that far off plumb is like showing up to watch the Super

Bowl on Crazy Daisy's TV.

Never for a second could Red bring himself to believe the killer was Bass, even now. But he did want the Appaloosa. To see if its shod hooves fit Pete Rollins's computerized measurements as neatly as Cinderella's foot in the glass slipper.

When Red reaches the ranchland, a gusting norther has already erased the horse's track. Ninety frigid minutes of back-and-forth searching pass before he spots the Appaloosa. Greyed by whipped snow, it stands half-melted into the hardening darkness, its rider tall in the saddle, looking east. The mount's tail swishes once and the freezing mist glitters the gathering dusk.

Red strains to see a scabbard and rifle, but can make out nothing. Raising a cupped hand he shouts, "Bass!"

The rider remains motionless.

Throttling up the snowmobile, Red moves slowly in.

The Appaloosa snorts, scrapes a hoof in the snow and rolls its big eyes.

"Easy," he says, slips in to stroke the mount, looking up one last time to say, "Bass?"

The horseman is stone dead, his face blue-white and iced up, staring at nothing. What got him here seems a deeper mystery than who killed Jeb Holloway or Daisy Ramirez.

* * *

Wind rises from the gloaming like a savage beast awakening. Shouldering down against its shrieking bite, Red hitches Bass Sanders across his saddle and reins the horse along beside the snowmobile, back to the Hollow-A.

On the bunkhouse porch Jake Laney stands embraced by a few weary hands. Closer in he recognizes the cavvy, Head Hanley, and the blacksmith, Hugh Marston. Red shuts the snowmobile down and dismounts. His unfeeling lips struggle to make words, "Brought back your dead."

Laney's narrow eyes look anguished. "The ranch ain't no mortuary. Mrs. H says she'll cover the minimum package up to boot hill."

When Red blinks, his eyes hurt. Swallowing with a wind-dried throat he says, "Real white of her. These your slippers on the Appaloosa?" he asks Marston.

Before he responds, the smithy spits, his stream freezing on the ground. "Mrs. H likes her mounts shod slipper."

Red's stare holds the blacksmith like a gaffing hook. "Could you get me a cast of the Appaloosa's shoe. And the other spotted horses with slippers?"

"There's a warrant for this?" Jake demands.

Red regards the men. "Agent Rollins's back soon. When he learns about Bass, he might just impound all your horses. Do the measurements himself. Probably twice."

"Well, shit," Jake says, kicking air with his toe. "No damn need to make no federal case of this."

"Already is," he reminds them. "I'm taking one of your go-devils for my Arctic Cat, to bring this cold fish in. Any of you have enough feeling for your buddy to help me?"

Laney owns to, "I speak for no man in matters of the dyin'. But I'll ask around and call Bear with the takers."

"Do that," Red tells him. "I expect quick answers, even about dead men." But for Jeb Holloway there are no quick answers. And even the one that lay still, frozen in place, seems completely absurd.

* * *

Red Kravitz tells Doris to stonewall the press.

When Doris wants to know, "If Molly asks where you are, is she the press?" he cocks back his hat. "If she calls, tell her I'm on the case."

Then he pushes through the deep white of the last storm. Afternoon winds had raised combers of snow; nightfall has crusted their rills. He studies the sky, feels the sharp air etch his skin. More snow coming.

Into a long box of slotted pine outside the store, Red shoves the bowlegged body of Bass Sanders, stomping away until the whole broken corpse fits.

Puffing with effort and faint with cold, he slides the snowmobile inside and warms up for a few minutes. Then he grabs a snow shovel, goes out again to discover another figure, its breath white with ice. "Figured you could use a strong back," Bear's voice says. "We best get started a'fore somebody has to cram us in there too."

* * *

After packing the dead man in snow, Red padlocks the box and sends Bear back to check on Walsh. Then he marches to the rear of the store and climbs the icy stairs. On the mat inside he stomps ice and snow off his boots, finds a handy chair and heels them off. With numb hands he gathers squaw wood, birch tinder and a few wedges of fat pine. With trembling fingers he puts a match to them and closes the estula door.

Without removing the sheepskin he saunters to the bedroom, slips his legs beneath the covers and begins to read. At first his eyes are so cold that they hurt, and refuse to condense the doubled vision. So he rubs them, letting the warmth ebb through pulses of pain until a sharp focus returns.

Then he plunges into text. Jeb Holloway's family story emerges in previously unknown details. Because there's a rule out here. It says that if a man stays out of trouble, you don't poke your nose in his affairs. Problem is that Jeb Holloway got his head blown off by a very traditional kind of western firearm, and that requires some good explaining.

Simply asserting that it must've been Bass Sanders left a huge gap for questions to howl through forever. Sure, Bass Sanders didn't figure like the rest of us, but this man would build cowshit castles to please the boss. How much more would it have taken to make Bass want to kill Jeb Holloway?

Even if Slo's report doesn't provide the answer, he still needs to read it. And so turns back the cover to page one. The digested history of the clan begins when two Holloway brothers desert the battered Confederate Army during the Civil War, lured by gold to Virginia City, Montana.

There they discover both opportunity and women who breed like flies. By 1880, just four years after Custer's 7th Cavalry was annihilated at

Little Bighorn, the core property of the Hollow-A ranch is fenced, patrolled and secured. The fellows who do the securing are thieves, bushwhackers, claim jumpers, vigilantes, cardsharps, politicians, judges, lawyers and gunslingers. Sometimes serially in different incarnations of the same man. Other times in the same man all at once.

After the idled Union Army become the Federal cavalry, the turncoat Holloways hoot for them with the best, certain that land liberated from the redskins can be better plundered by organized whites with money. Land becomes essential after the panic of 1893, when liquid capital loses fashion to durable wealth. With this revelation, the second generation of Holloways spawn in the third a cast of miners, ranchers, cattle barons, wheat farmers, and engineers.

From scoundrels to landed gentry in two generations is a tough act to follow, but this is what's left to Jeb, the only surviving male heir to the Holloway legacy in the fourth generation. Born in 1949 after all his male cousins had perished in the Second World War, he is also the youngest. Who in addition to growing into a good businessman and rancher, also has a political yen.

Yet even after re-reading the file until the letters begins to blur and double again, nothing points Red Kravitz toward a suspect.

That bothers Kravitz. Because Jeb Holloway isn't the only fatality. Now it's Crazy Daisy Ramirez, butchered like an animal during a raging blizzard by someone willing to risk his life in order to cover his tracks.

Kravitz senses that to recreate those tracks, he will have to determine who the killer is, then rustle up a way to trap him. So he pulls out a sheet of yellow legal paper, and resumes a list that he started earlier:

	JEB	**DAISY**
Gold	Knew?	Knew.
Weapon	Sharps	Knife (check Micky & Mo)
Type	Ambush (distance)	Ambush (close in)
	(by arrangement)	(stealth)
Relation to Killer	Target of	Witness against
Connection(s)	Mona's husband	?
Suspect	B.S. Walsh	B.S. Walsh
Alibi	Mona	Mona
Other suspects	None	None
Killed before?	Walsh (yes)	Walsh (yes)
Motive	Self-protection	Escape detection
Approach	Horseback	? (check Micky & Mo

From the course he took at Quantico, Red knows that the FBI's Behavioral Science Unit wants you to believe their experts can tell the color, age, sex, schooling, employment record, attitude, living situation and addiction history of any perpetrator.

Yet in only one case had they profiled a killer who turned up in Montana: the Unabomber. They had put a hundred agents on it for fifteen years and in the end were totally wrong. Worse, without physical evidence and witness testimony, psychological profiles alone have never produced a conviction.

But supposing something in these notes leads somewhere else? Shouldn't he go over them one line at a time, and ask 'what if?'

Initially it seems a good idea, but in re-examining the list he realizes that it's incomplete. So he picks up the phone and dials.

The answer comes, "Hey, Red. Been wondering what was keeping your call."

"Micky. Hope I'm not interrupting anything."

"Mo and me is at a game of chess, but I can still talk and beat him." In the background Red hears a, "We'll see," then goes on, asking, "What killed her?"

Micky sucks on his pipe, followed by, "Nothin' small as a Barlow knife. What snipped Daisy's stem was a bonafide belduque. Real bulger of a belduque. Ten-inch blade at least. Sharp, too, because there are no rips on the laceration. But as to blade width, it could've been a top-of-the-line chef's knife or a good ole Arkansas toothpick."

"How'd the killer access the scene?"

"Ask the man with the satellites," Micky says, asiding, "Check," to Mo.

"Rollins is getting laid this weekend. It's a Federal holiday," Red explains. "So how do you think the killer got through the storm?"

"What do I know? Whoever got Holloway used a gun, bullet and horseshoe more 'n a hunnert years old, so maybe he came in on a time machine. If you live in the future, you got to think it was maybe an alien in one of them UFOs she's always talkin' about If you think in the past, maybe it was a shape-shifter, something that could sneak up so quiet she wouldn't've heard it coming...Oh, shit!"

"What?" Red asks, coming forward.

"While you were distracting me with your idiot questions, deputy,

Mo snuck up and checkmated me. Didn't even see it coming."

"Now you know how Daisy felt," Red says.

Micky takes exception. "Well, all I can say is you send me another body and maybe there's enough clues that even some Tweedle-Dee forensic twins can solve the sucker."

The line clicks to silence, which only tells Red that Micky is pissed that his brother beat him. Kravitz gently replaces the receiver and returns to the legal pad, hopeful that somewhere in these notes lies a vital clue.

Like many other prosperous settlers in Montana, the Holloways had come up on the backs of mined gold ore. So Jeb understood that float gold in Big Muddy was most likely wash-down from the Blackfoot Reservation. If so, it brings Dave Dooley back into the picture. Because thanks to Ivan Konev's tutoring, Dave Dooley learned the murderous theft whites had practiced on Indians. If Davey had seen the twinkle of gold in the stream, looked up and seen Jeb Holloway's familiar Suburban sitting there, it might have occurred to him to end the problem, then notify the Blackfoot on the res' about the gold passing on his way through to the mountains. Ivan had schooled Davey that the Indians had already lost enough without letting the Great Spirit's water piss away a fortune in natural wealth that was rightfully theirs.

At least that scenario gives teeth to a federal case that is now all gum. Still, in his Indian way of sizing things up, a case against Dave Dooley could sound plausible but still make no sense. Given Jeb Holloway's present worth, float gold was just so much bright yellow chicken feed. After the stock market crash of '29 his grandfather Luther had so much gold and wheat and cattle that they never went hungry. When folks mention the Depression to the Holloways, they look back queerly.

People that rich don't show for secret meetings to hear about a trickle of slickens. But for someone broke, poor and old, who believes the river is rushing with panable gold, it would seem a godsend.

Enter Noisy Noyes, such a stranger to luck that he may just feel entitled to those nuggets. Noisy may have known about the gold, but had no claim, no right, no equipment, no venture capital. Nothing.

Red lets it go. But with a note.

If Noisy knew, he had at least one thing in common with Daisy. And Daisy is dead. Possibly because it leaves one fewer person who knows the actual spot where the gold was fished out. To a man who sees gold as a stake in the future that means something.

And B.S. Walsh is just that kind of man.

THREE DEAD

Out here when autumn greets winter, snow clouds cast shadows so dark the sun seems dead. The clock says shank of the afternoon but there's no light. Soon the sky deepens toward starless black. In this gloom Red hears the door open and sees Molly rattle with chills, "Tell me it doesn't get colder." He folds both hands over the Holloway's history. "Good relationships are built on honesty, Molly. So I won't tell you a lie."

She eyes the report. "So tell me no lies, deputy. What've you got there?"

He smiles. "Honestly I can tell you it's official business. But that's all."

"You had dinner?"

"Only food for thought. And it left me hungry."

"Let's hit The Elk."

"Okay." He gets up, finds his boots, grabs the mule ears and tugs them on. Then unpegs his hat and coat.

Shoulders down, heads lowered, they push into a freak easterly stippled with snow. Her words frosting the air, Molly probes with light chatter.

"You didn't show up at the crime scene."

"Nope," he says.

"Why would anyone want to kill a pathetic old woman?"

"Good question."

"I mean, if it's the same guy – or person – who shot Jeb Holloway, why does he risk leaving his skin under Daisy's nails or her blood on his clothes by getting close enough to cut her throat?"

The Elk is drawing near so he gives her the short version. "With Jeb Holloway, the marskman's got a killshot from up to a mile out. It was the perfect weapon."

"So why not for Daisy, too?"

He holds up at the door and tells her, "In a blizzard the wind is hard enough to blow a long-range shot off target. But if you do kill her in one, you're stuck carrying this massive gun around. If you don't ditch the thing it becomes an anchor to your own grave. But if you do, it's evidence against you in a trial. By convenient contrast, everybody out here has a knife."

He reaches into his pocket and offers his own Barlow. "It's easy to carry, easy to hide. If you lose your way, it helps to burrow down into the snow and wind, wait out the storm."

She folds the Barlow's blade open, then closes it. Handing it back she asks, "What kind of person would be cold enough to ambush a man from a distance then return to kill a sleeping woman with a knife?"

Red stomps the snow off his boots. "Mountain men live close to nature. They've killed, gutted, cleaned and field-dressed everything from whitetail to moose. All mammals bleed the same if you cut them at the throat."

"You're saying that Dave Dooley did this after all?"

They enter The Elk.

Inside, they take the booth farthest from the door and drop their sheepskins onto the benches. Before Kravitz can rise and amble to the juke, Molly lets out a shrill whistle that gets Bear's attention.

Then she taps her watch crystal and says, "Turn on the box."

Bear snaps off a salute, picks up a remote and ignites the tube. Atlanta's anchor is just announcing, "And here is CNN's Molly Mendelbaum."

Molly props her chin on the heel of a hand and studies herself.

The telecast image frames her clutching a mike in a doeskin gloved hand, squinting into the southern sun while Micky and Mo work the scene. Farther back stands the forensic chopper, its rotor juking in gusts that keep Molly sweeping tangled hair from her face. "Ever since Deputy Red Kravitz has been the law in Sanctuary, Montana, there were no murders until senate candidate Jeb Holloway was felled by a sniper's bullet nearly a week ago. Last night another victim appeared, her throat cut while she was sleeping. Eighty-something Daisy Ramirez, an eccentric recluse..."

Red leans in again. "Nobody knows what 'eccentric' or 'recluse' means..."

She shushes him.

"...who lived in a primitive shack about a hundred yards from Poker Bluff..." the camera pans and zooms "...where the sniper who shot Jeb Holloway had waited. From her rustic hut, Daisy Ramirez may have seen the killer pull the trigger. That's the only explanation, authorities believe..."

"Which authorities?" Red whisper.

She pinches his arm hard to get him quiet.

"...which could have made the killer desperate enough to trek on foot through a snow storm..."

"We don't know that either," he insists.

"...then risk getting lost on the way out again, during a blizzard where you couldn't see your hand at the end of your arm."

Red looks up at Bear. "We came down here to eat."

"I'll scare up Walsh," Bear says, going back to fetch his help.

"...Authorities here still have no idea who the killer is, but one thing is certain. He's still in Sanctuary, snowed in with the rest of us. Molly Mendelbaum, CNN news." As the coverage rolls into a two-fur outbreak of cholera and Ebola in the Congo, Walsh appears, tying his slops apron on, asking, "Yeah?"

Molly skims the menu and asks, "Stuffed flounder any good?" Walsh leans in to whisper, "You say it's not good, the man shove it down your throat and ask you to reconsider. So, yeah, it's good. If you catch my drift."

She gives the fare more attention before asking Walsh, "Who do you think killed her?" She bores directly into his eyes, adding, "Daisy, I mean."

"Somebody nuts," he says. "Not catch me out in that cold."

"What about you?" Molly asks as Bear returned. "Who do you think did it?"

Bear picks up a bar towel and dries his hands. "Was me doing the lookin', I'd scope out Caldera Cunningham."

"The woman in the ratfur coat at the funeral?" Molly asks.

"She can shoot, has serious issues with Jeb and regular runs by Daisy's to drop off brochures from her group, the Vengeful Handservants of the Almighty Lord."

She turns to Red, "You think Caldera could do it?" Red refuses her even a blink. But Bear volunteers, "She wouldn't miss the shot, I warrant you that much."

Molly turns from man to man, asking, "Anybody else?"

The big Cheyenne guesses, "A federal servant might slip by an investigation."

Despite his earlier maundering, Red objects. "Come on, Bear! You're not gonna say Luke Brody!"

Back to Walsh, Molly demands, "Who do you like? Brody or Caldera?"

B.S. shakes his head. "I bring you a nice, safe salad."

"I need somebody more talkative than you guys," Molly grumps. "Where's Noisy?"

"Haven't seen him in couple of days," says Walsh. "Guy is all weird. Like Daisy. Half-in, half-out. He keep talkin' but sometime none of it make sense, see? Tha's why, he say gold, I'm like, sure, Pops. And my mamma's Arnold Schwarzenegger."

"Wait. Did I hear gold? I want to talk to Noisy," Molly says. But by this time Red is already on his feet, glaring at Bear. "You should've told me. Old man like that..." Red mutters as he buttons up his sheepskin. "...out in this weather..."

Molly gets up. "I'm going."

Red whirls on her. "You're staying. If you get lost out there, you'll die."

Before she can even say 'be careful,' he opens the door and vanishes in a swirl of white.

*   *   *

Outside The Elk, Red follows the land along a lazy curve that spills down a rocky slope and breaks hard left. Soon it enters a notched draw that slaloms to the flats below, where a kidney-shaped swag gathers runoff. Through wind-shot snow a shallow gully is all he can see. So he uses it to find Noisy's digs.

Like Daisy, the old man refused to go homeless. So he had holed up in a log den, raised enough to let air in and stench out. For nearly two hundred years this kind of put-up was known as a half-faced cabin. It was a quick and dirty shelter for mountain men, and still used by Dave Dooley in winter.

This one sticks downhill puckered outward, so rain washes to either side. A swell of overburden keeps it to lee of winter's wind. After every hard drunk, Noisy would crawl back, pull himself in, grab a salea and sougan donated by Red and a parfleche blanket from Bear, then curl to fetal and snore like a crimped bandsaw. But tonight the den is silent.

Standing an arm's length beyond the darkened slot, Red bellows, "Noisy!" but the stench grows unbearable. "Come on, old timer. It's too cold to..." Now he is close enough to see open eyes staring back. Pinching his nose shut, he feels the old man's carotid artery. No palpitation. Under cause of death Red would recommend, 'stubbornness and stupidity, compounded by alcohol.'

So as to drag the body out before a stray coyote gets to it, Red reaches behind the old man's back. Then feels the hilt of a knife. A belduque, or big one, like the one that killed Daisy Ramirez.

*   *   *

They sit facing one another, Red and Bear, in a booth shielded from Molly and Walsh by the screeching wail of Buffy St. Marie. Bear says, "I'd be concerned about badgers. Hungry critter like that'll claw through pine logs to get at Noisy."

"Could we bring him up here?" Red asks.

"Sure, Red. We lay him right next to Walsh in the store room, so when B.S. wakes up he starts screaming, 'You're dead, you fuck! I killed you!'"

Both glance at Walsh. Red rubs his face in both hands. "After Jeb and Daisy, then Bass Sanders, Noisy sort of dropped off the scope."

"Not your fault, brother."

Red looks at Walsh, jiving and laughing for Molly. "He been out?"

Bear's eyes say yes. "He wanders. Up to Doris's, back to town hall, tries the door. All the time I get this witness protection shit, how they always take care of their own."

"Walsh talks a lot," Red says.

Bear turns as Buffy St. Marie finishes, reaches out his long arm and punches in Lloyd Price, Stagger Lee. The Rockola's lift-yoke runs down the rack, plucks out the 45 and sets it on the turntable. Seconds later it opens

The night was young

And the moon was yellow

And the leaves came tumblin' down..

Standing Bear lets out a hard blow. "What about Molly?"

"I'll keep her at my place. She'll be safe."

"No, I mean about Noisy. You gonna tell her?"

He looks over at her. And at B.S. Walsh. Bear reads the silence and concludes, "I'm not sure you two've got a future if you keep holding out on her."

Red feels a sad warmth. "At one time it was more than I could handle, so I ran. Now I don't even know this woman. So I can't say a thing about the future."

Bear squeezes Red's neck. "Most people who know the future wish they didn't. So count yourself lucky." Or not. But for sure it's high time for Pete Rollins to get back and make a decision. Before someone else gets killed.

* * *

When the snow resumes, each landing flake plants an audible kiss on the window glass. But outside The Elk, the storm soon builds to a demonic terror of windborne ice. Still Molly doesn't leave. As far back as he can remember, she had been social, Red solitary. So she stays on sipping beers while Bear keeps B.S. Walsh in line.

Back at his place, Red throws off his coat, pegs his hat and wiggles free of his boots. In thick wool socks he creeps to the bedside, sits down and dials Moonlight's wireless, waiting three rings, then getting a breathless, "Mom?"

"This is Red, Moonlight. Is Special Agent Rollins handy?"

Moonlight says, "It's Red." Rollins picks up and is breathing hard. "Yeah?" Kravitz eases into, "We got more victims here. Hermit woman named Daisy Ramirez. Somebody cut her throat. Local drunk named Noisy Noyes, knife in the back."

"Where's Walsh?"

"At The Elk. Any chance Glenn Vandrey will spring him if you're not here?"

Rollins seems to understand. "I could chopper in."

"Soon as the weather clears," Red says. Then he clicks off, punches in a Great Falls number. After ten rings a voice answers, "Nobody calls at home. Who is this nobody?"

"Nobody but Red Kravitz."

"Already I don't like this," Micky says.

"You're not the one who found a stinking old town drunk with a fair-sized Bowie knife between his shoulders."

"Was this guy frozen?"

"Like a glacier."

"So maybe the killer took the same knife he used on Daisy and did this fellow a little later, but you just didn't find the body till now. In this cold he could have been dead for more than sixteen hours."

"That's the kind of thing an experienced killer would know," Red concludes.

"Only if he was used to killing in a cold place."

"Detroit cold enough for you?" the deputy asks.

"I suppose you want us to come out and look this guy over."

"And if you're through with Daisy, bring her home for burial."

"Red? From Great Falls is a pretty chancy commute for a chopper with winter gettin' serious. We'd really appreciate it if you could wrap this thing up."

"Workin' on it," is all he can say.

After racking the receiver, he dredges up a clipboard, inserts a paper and picks up a pen. After tapping three times he clicks it open and writes

Gold

On the first line under the header he asks the crucial questions. First, who wins if they know about the gold?

The luckless, the disaffected, the losers, the dreamers. Hit pay dirt, strike the bonanza: that's the fast way up and out. Their net worth goes up from less than nothing to whatever they can squirrel away before someone jumps their claim or kills them for it. More than Manifest Destiny, the rage for discovering a vug was what had really sealed the fate of the American Indian. Sure they were decimated by smallpox. Sure they were hunted like rats. Sure the bison were killed off. Sure they had begun to be herded off to wasteland reservations. Yet only gold can spark the kind of madness that makes men slaughter other men, whether red, yellow, black or white. If someone had killed Jeb Holloway, Daisy Ramirez and old Noisy because they feared the news of float gold in Big Muddy would get out, then that person would be somebody like B.S. Walsh, who is always dreaming up schemes that ride on greed and violence.

But if the motive for these murders was fear of gold, it conjures an entirely different kind of suspect. Because somebody smarter and richer than Walsh would look at the prospects of gold at Poker Bluff quite differently. Kravitz knows this from the history of the west, but gets more clues from an introductory economics course, when they discussed standards of currency.

As his Penn professor put it, "Our economy would be in a lot more trouble if we lost all our sulphuric acid than if we lost all our gold." But to down-and-outers, gold remains the most powerful stimulus to grab a pan and stand in freezing water till you lose your toes to frostbite. So for anyone who values the local status quo, gold is less welcome than an outbreak of plague. Wages are driven up, land rights are ignored or violated. And the people who for generations have legislated and litigated their way to prominence will be reduced to hostages on their own land, confined by fear, threat and abuse. For this kind of person, a gold strike near their property is the worst possible catastrophe.

Especially if it proves wrong. Not wrong in the sense that the recently discovered nuggets are fool's gold. Red can convince himself that Noisy's slickens are probably real. But whatever he fished out might be the last anyone would see for fifty years.

Or not.

Still, you don't go waving a red flag in a field unless you're looking for a good-sized bull to plant its horns a couple of feet up your silly ass. And in the entire course of human history nothing has been more rampagingly bullish than a gold rush.

So who loses most? Who stands to be hurt if it becomes known that gold has been discovered at Sidewinder Twist a few miles north of Sanctuary, Montana?

Mona Holloway, inheritor of the Hollow-A. The ranch would come under siege if prospectors started picking in along Big Muddy, working like an army of gophers, driving unstable galleries and step-sluices under her property line, undermining her fenceposts, letting cattle drift off, destroying two things that most Montanans, red or white, will fight and die for: their privacy and their property.

But after deeper reflection, Red turns over a far more troubling idea. Because when it comes to property, no one has more to lose than the local realtor and mayor, Augie Suder, who has already offered fixed-price rental contracts for prospective merchants looking to cash in on the ski-rush to Bearpaw.

Another casualty, collateral and inevitable, would be the southern border of Timberland Wildlife Preserve, home of seven endangered species and showplace for what Leonard Jarnow's campaign calls, "True proof that Montana's wild country is safe from any possible threat."

This is pretty easy to claim, since the Feds are doing the housekeeping. But the National Park Service is not mandated to defend their borders against a mob of crazed prospectors.

The early historical photographs of Matthew Brady had shown that infestation with gambustos is more devastating to scenery and wildlife than a swarm of termites to a lumberyard. So Leonard Jarnow had something to lose: face. And the loss of face during a hard-fought campaign could be enough to tip the scales against him.

Or once was.

Out here in Cheney country, the Democratic candidate would need a major Jarnow scandal to win. The substance of truth is less important than the suspicion of fault. The fact that gold had been discovered on land that Jarnow had been contesting with Jeb Holloway created an apparent motive for murder, and threatened to topple the Jarnow juggernaut within cheering distance of the finish line.

Then it hits Red so hard that he feels sick. And seems to tie everything together. The complete picture focuses so fast that Red becomes almost dizzy with embarrassment. Because it comes from a world that he knows, but in which he is not a player.

It takes a leap of imagination to understand what a hint of local gold would produce in Bearpaw investors. Montana is sparsely populated and skilled labor is scarce. Already Bearpaw has imported a small army of manpower to hurry-up the construction. Not one of them shapes up as a likely suspect to kill the man who wrote their paycheck.

Another of Bearpaw's advantages is that seasonal work elsewhere hereabouts is hard to come by. Laborers are glad to have it, because it fills pockets and stomachs that would otherwise go empty. But all these workers know that this gig will end even before the bunny slope opens. Like the Hollow-A's summer crew, many will drift south, where there are more jobs, more people, more warmth.

Imagine that just as this imported construction crew, underpaid, anxious to bolt and aching with cold, learns there's gold in Big Muddy. How many will drop their hammers and walk away? And if they do, who would finish the work in time for Bearpaw's first schuss of skiers?

Meaning what?

How does it all fit together?

There is the HIM in Jeb Holloway's computer calendar. Could that be Jarnow? Had he ridden an Appaloosa Indian style past Daisy Ramirez, over to Poker Bluff, the morning that Jeb was killed? Did he pick up the horse at the Hollow-A, with Mona's knowledge?

Certainly he could make a shot like the one that killed Jeb. Maybe Mona had found out that Jeb intended to use Jarnow's infidelity as proof that if Leonard could be seduced by amateurs in Montana, what chance would he have against professionals in Washington?

And fear of Washington looms large enough in Montana to swing an election. This angle is supported by the presence of the blood-spattered copy of the Bozeman Daily Chronicle discovered in the Suburban with Holloway's corpse. On the front page was a report of his opponent's eleven point lead; the meeting, offering Jarnow an opportunity to withdraw or be exposed: Jeb's way of dealing with it. Consistent with that take, Jeb's appointment schedule shows that he had spoken with Jarnow just before the fatal meeting with the mysterious HIM.

Mona certainly would have known.

To better diversify her options, she probably encouraged Jeb. Consistent with her heavy drinking at The Elk that same day, acting in character while drowning her guilt and numbing her jitters. Also explaining her apparent shock when Red revealed her husband's murder that stormy night. It hadn't been in the plans.

He has just about settled on this conspiracy theory when the outer door opens and Molly whirls in on a rush of frigid air. Closing the door behind her, she breathes, "Does it always get like this up here?" Throwing off a hard shiver, she blows warmth into her hands and slowly unbuttons her coat.

"Hasn't even started yet," he tells her, turning the paper over on its pad.

"What you working on?" she asks, eyeing the tablet.

"Just thinking," he says.

"B.S. Walsh is thinking, too. About leaving," she says.

"He tell Bear?" Red wonders aloud.

"Bear was in back. I think that Walsh was just talking out loud, something to say."

Red locks her up in a hard stare. "He come on to you?"

She blinks. "I'm here, right?" Which meant B.S. Walsh is actually dumb enough to be the chief suspect in three murders, and make a pass at the local lawman's woman. Confirming everything Red had heard about the stupidity of the common criminal.

Either that or he really didn't do it.

"How you feeling?" Molly asks, starting to unbutton her sweater.

"Puzzled," he says.

She stops and looks, as if the response has something to do with her plans. It doesn't. But he doesn't know how much rope she is giving him, or when it will jerk back and break his neck. So he just says, "I've got to go downstairs, pull some scrap plywood from the store."

"Now?"

He gets up. "I've got other business tomorrow."

"Can I help?" she asks.

He smiles at her. "Cold out there, remember? And getting colder."

"This time I'll be here when you get back," she says. And the way she says it feels good.

Still he doesn't want to get used to it. Because Molly is still digging for the story, and if she strikes gold, some very powerful people will try to make sure the word doesn't get out.

THREE SUSPECTS

Before Kravitz ratchets the last lag screw into Noisy's half-cabin, the night begins to speak. Not since his vision quest as a Crow brave has this happened, but tonight's voice is different, both sinister and seductive, inviting him to lie down and rest in the endless snow. His Jewish half insists this is pure meshuge. And the Jewish half prevails. But by the time he reaches the store, he hears again sounds that a college education claim to arise from a state of mind, not objective reality. By now those brightly lit classrooms seem as distant as stars lost in a darkness deeper than death.

He closes an outsized double door, shutting out the night, the wind, even — in some measure — the fear. Removing tools from a workman's belt, he replaces them on a pegboard in a neat basement workshop. Then flexes his fingers, feeling the first tingle of sensation returning. The frozen blood from his cracked lips begins to flow, then coagulate. While he's thawing out, Molly's voice reaches out from behind him.

"What happened to the wood?" She tips her head to the scatter of sawdust on the floor. "And what could be so important to risk freezing for?"

He tugs off his gloves and knit watchcap, unzips the Arctic jumpsuit.

"I'm wrecked. I've got to get some rest."

"Someone else was killed." Her inflection betrays a guess.

He tries a half-lie. "Noisy might have frozen. But I need an official cause-of-death."

"Who do you think killed him?" she says.

"He fell into the bottle. It was only a matter of time til he drowned in his own puke."

"Is that how you found him?"

"I found him dead," Red evades. "How he got that way is Micky and Mo's business."

"They phoned here," she says. "The Tweedles, isn't that what they're called? Asked you to call back about the you-know-what. What's you-know-what?"

"I can't reveal official information concerning a suspicious death." The words are right, but their taste in his mouth is wrong. Or maybe it's just the blood from his cracked lips.

"You're beginning to sound like Pete Rollins," she says.

"Maybe you'd get a bit more candor from your new buddy B.S. Walsh."

"What would he..." her eyes flickers, a sign that her mind is outracing the question formed in words.

"I'm going to bed," he says, easing by her.

She touches his cracked lips, kisses them gently, pressing herself against him. "How tired are you?" she whispers.

* * *

Each time that Kravitz had gone into Molly he ended up beyond and outside himself, melted together in some new perspective where he was no longer a man nor she a woman, but fused in an art that few experience. At this moment he wonders if this is a starting point. Or if it is a point beyond which no one can ever go. If so, it would be better never to reach it, but simply to keep trying. Because once you get there, nothing remains but the haunting awareness of a moment that will never be forgotten. Each look back would be a reminder that you can never return, each step forward a reminder that the best is even farther behind you.

That is his preoccupation as the room cools and their sweat evaporates. The split pine in the estula has crumbled to embers. Now the only heat comes from their bodies. Beyond rime-framed panes, blasts of Arctic air whistle and squeal, pushing finely misted ice through unseen cracks.

Fortified by dovetailed beams and delta-joisted walls, the aging wood frame building still creaks with the storm. When air screams by, the joists cry like a trapped animal unable to gnaw off its paw. If the roof collapses, if they freeze to death, if Sanctuary's homicidal maniac breaks in and kills them, they would never feel a thing again.

Evidently Molly is unready to give that up. Because she turns to him, her naked flesh swollen and more eager than before, and whispers, "If you do that again, and again, just like that, until we both pass out, I'll be able to say I've really lived."

They have stopped counting the number of times or positions or sweet music of wordless passion, sounds lovers make but once in all their heartbeats, noises they hear and remember, or hear and forget, but nonetheless are exquisitely aware that their bodies and minds and spirits and hopes have come together exactly when their inhibitions have fallen apart. And that unspeakable all makes proof absolute that experience transcends evaluation. It means you are alive and for once, with no doubt whatever, certain of it.

"Are you okay?" Red asks, caressing her damp hair.

"Never better," she coos, the descending rhythm of her panting a prelude to sleep, her eyelids playing up and down, settling in against his firm body. "You?"

He waits a long while, paralyzed not by doubt, but by the problem of whether some experiences are so uniquely felt they require words never before uttered, words that explode the triviality of lexicons because two lovers venture into sensations and feelings never before shared.

Tonight is unlike all other nights because words fail. And yet it doesn't matter. What matters is what passes between them without words. Here, sheltered from the storm swirling around them, his world finds a new center.

She whispers, "You fill me up, you know that?"

"Go to sleep," he says.

"I'm not empty anymore."

"Go to sleep," he repeats. And before she can respond, she is gently snoring.

Outside, the wind resurrects the world beyond. There is no running from it. Not in this snow. It holds them all in, killer and victims alike, waiting for someone to stop the madness.

He holds her tighter, as much in fear as love, and cannot drop off to sleep without reminding himself that he is the one expected to end the nightmare.

* * *

Come dawn, Kravitz leaves Molly sleeping and trudges through virgin snow to town hall. In his office he takes out a single sheet of yellow legal paper. Onto it he extends the previous table on a new sheet.

	DAISY	NOISY
Gold	Knew	Knew
Weapon	Knife (sharp, 10" blade	
Type	Ambush (close-in) (stealth)	Ambush (close-in) (silence)
Relation to Killer	Witness	Witness?
Connections	?	?
Suspect	B.S. Walsh	B.S. Walsh
Motive	Escape detection	Knew motive
Approach	?	on foot
Alibi	Mona	none
Other suspects	None	None
Killed before?	Walsh	Walsh

Two knifings stuck to B.S. Walsh like rimed hoarfrost on The Elk's windows. Detroit revealed him as a brutal close-in killer. Sanctuary proved he could survive a blizzard. And one powerful motive connected every victim: gold.

Although he couldn't prove that Jeb Holloway knew, people that far up hear about everything any farther down. Daisy saw the glitter of nuggets; Noisy held them in his hand. And B.S. Walsh knew, too. Kill all the knowledgeable parties and go after the gold yourself. With enough gold, Walsh didn't need witness protection.

He could go anywhere in the world.

Plucking up the handset, Red dials. Before a reply comes, he says, "Slo, I need everything you can dig up on Daisy Ramirez."

Slo Lehrner laughs. "I guessed that myself. So I've got DOB, paternity, school and dental records, inoculation and medical stuff, high school diploma, work record as waitress, marriage to Ramon, charges of armed assault on Ramon (dropped), divorce from Ramon, orders of support payments from Ramon, gun licenses, income taxes filed and delinquent, plus the final stuff on the post-mort from Micky and Mo."

"Send it on. And see what you can dig up on Noisy."

"Killed?"

"Sometime yesterday I'd guess. Like Daisy."

"Out near Poker Bluff?"

"How'd you find out about the gold?" Red is curious.

"From Bear. But it was no big secret."

"You figure gold's at the bottom of all this?"

"Doesn't matter," Slo says.

The answer stuns Red. "Why not?"

Slo draws a long breath, then says, ""You remember the New World Mine?"

Red closes his eyes and snaps his fingers until the story started coming back. "What was it, '97?"

"Keep going," Slo eggs him on.

"Gold mining operation on the edge of Yellowstone, right?"

"Almost. The Clinton Administration brokered a sixty-five million dollar buyout if they agreed not to mine."

"Jesus!" Red mutters. The picture finally begins to come together. Land rights in dispute. Senator goes to Washington. National Park Service abandons its claim. New senator wins title to land. New senator files mining plans. New senator is bought out by U.S. government even if there's no gold. It was perfect.

Slo chuckles. "You didn't really think Jeb and Lenny were paying all those wrangling lawyers just so they can put up condos for Bearpaw, did you?"

"What if... somebody challenged the feasibility of a gold mine?" Kravtiz struggles to poke a hole in the scam, believing that Molly, or someone like her, would do just that.

"Again," Slo insists. "Doesn't matter. Poker Bluff is sandstone. Under it is what?"

A geology course from Penn provides Red the answer: "Shale."

"Dig deeper," Slo says.

"Natural gas," Red realizes.

"Deeper still."

"Oil."

"Bingo. A bonanza of natural gas and oil. Now there's the back-up plan. No gold? Doesn't matter. File a drilling plan for natural gas or oil. Result: the same. The government pays you big bucks not to drill."

"But Holloway's dead," Red reminds him.

"And Jarnow's not." It makes too much sense for a rebuttal other than silence. Into that silence Slo Lehrner adds, "I know where to find natural gas and oil. But if I go digging into Noisy's past, I don't know if I'll find anything," then hangs up.

Red replaces the receiver and turns back to his list. Tapping the next line with a pencil eraser, B.S. Walsh still comes up the best suspect.

Maybe Jeb had wanted to bail out of the Bearpaw resort, pour his shares into his campaign fund, defeat Lenny Jarnow. Maybe Mona disagreed, thought politicking was stupid, the mining scam risky, and saw only one way to keep Bearpaw and the Hollow-A spread out of the bank's hands: kill Jeb. Ergo she beds Walsh, sweet talks him, arranges a meeting with Lenny to get Jeb out there, then it's done.

Meaning that Mona is at least an accessory. And her coconspirator B.S. Walsh doesn't need to stand thigh-deep in cold rushing water to get a little rich.

Or maybe Mona called Jarnow, laid it out for him, made him see that if the issue of gold came up during the suit for the land where Crazy Daisy is squatting, Bearpaw would go bust, taking them all down with it. Sometimes, Red knew, the appearance of reasonable compromise is just the path of least resistance to greed.

When everybody wins a little bit, nobody loses a lot. With the expenses of a major campaign beginning to drag him down, Jarnow would have been open to any scheme that limited his outlays. Eliminating his chief opponent would be the most direct one.

In the vast perspective of competing self-interests, Slo Lehrner's dazzling insight still hasn't solved Jeb Holloway's murder. At best it has only increased the complexity of competing interests for post-mortem benefits. So that now there are three suspects. The only one of them he could hope to arrest and hold is Walsh.

But to do that he needs Pete Rollins to keep his linchpin suspect in place. And to do that he needs to scare up Mona Holloway's gynecologist, to see if pregnancy was the reason that Jeb Holloway might ride out to the middle of nowhere with a loaded .357 magnum to meet a man designated on his calendar only as HIM.

By cell phone he reaches Moonlight. She answers, "Pete said you need to get to your speaker phone, the new one in your office. There's something you need to hear. After that he'll be inbound by chopper."

"Thanks," he says, then rings off. Punching through to Slo Lehrner again he continues, "Me again. I need some private information."

Slo laughs. "In the information age there is no privacy. What's the question?"

Red tells him, then dials another number. And gets the answer, "It's all froze just now. Wait till spring, whatever it is."

But Red insists, "Hiram? This is Kravitz. I'll need a backhoe rigged with a jackhammer. One of those big-nozzle blowtorches might help. Picks and shovels, too. Daisy Ramirez is going into the ground. Get Bear to help. Then call around. Let folks know."

* * *

Red sat alone in his office, listening to distant voices. Via the brand-new federally donated speaker phone, Pete Rollins hears out Glenn's Vandrey's shrill objections. Then he pauses and makes his own pitch to Vandrey's boss, the FBI's Assistant Director for Internal Guidance, who is refereeing the conference call from the Bureau's Chicago Field Office.

"For openers," Pete says, "Walsh is not the most important witness to plead down and get farmed. Second, he knows no other witnesses, so he can't compromise them. Third, he knows no other top-downs and doesn't even know Glenn's legal surname. Fourth, against the run-up to the Iraq invasion, this story falls under the radar in a couple of days. But fifth, if we obstruct a state arrest, we set up a duel in the Supreme Court between Montana's AG and the Justice Department, which torches everybody's careers. Sixth and last, the federal witness protection program is not a free-standing invitation for relocated felons to go on killing sprees."

The Assistant Director, a Bureau lifer named Trent Horner, agrees to all of Rollins's points, but asks, "Before we all run bare-ass into a blizzard, does Montana have enough to convict?"

Rollins 'fessed up, "Not forensically. But that's not how we'd present the case. Circumstantially and motivationally, given the attitudinal demographics of jurors in Montana, Walsh is likely to chart the undiscovered country."

From Chicago comes a pause, then, "And if he walks?"

"If he walks, his friends in Detroit will be waiting just outside the jail door."

"We plug them in?" Horner asks.

"Leave it to CNN. Nobody's screening Walsh anymore."

Horner draws a deep breath before saying, "You're the messenger, Rollins. Now get on it before somebody else is killed."

* * *

Alternating with the big nozzle blowtorch, the backhoe's jackhammer punch boot hill's half-frozen ground into a chilly slush. Three men from Hiram's Feed & Grain scrape with shovels and picks, clearing a trough eight feet long and four wide. Over the chugging and puffs of exhaust, the gray sky erupts with thrashing rotors.

Red Kravitz looks up.

Above him circles the state forensics chopper. Between its skids rests a rough pine coffin bearing the recently autopsied remains of Crazy Daisy Ramirez.

* * *

In the snowy nest below Wild Bill on Poker Bluff, B.S. Walsh leaves Mona Holloway in a spew of gore, the Appaloosa pulling at its reigns, rearing high in the air, his eyes wide and terrible. Then Walsh feels the weight of the Sharps in his hand and mutters, "This can't be fucking happening. Hey..."

His mind plays with the idea of chucking the rifle down, wiping it clean. But there will still be snowmobile tracks, and who will believe his story? Feeling the rifle his only friend, B.S. Walsh runs back to Bear's snowmobile and hops on, then heads west toward State 87.

* * *

On the inbound flight Pete Rollins's rides shotgun. The pilot seems to know his stuff, constantly monitoring the dials and gauges that look like a video arcade. Turning to Rollins, the man says, "I've got a bogie on a collision heading. Separation thirty-five miles. Size, speed and movement, I'd guess another chopper. What's your pleasure?"

Rollins doesn't want his life to end in a midair collision, so he suggests, "Come around. Bank North. Follow the river till you see Wild Bill Hickok." The pilot gives him a puzzled look. Pete explains. "You can't miss him. He's sitting upright in sandstone at place called Poker Bluff, surrounded by his partners."

"Aces and eights," the pilot says.

"Aces and eights," Pete Rollins repeats. "Then circle back to town."

* * *

The state chopper sets Micky, Mo and Daisy's body down on the white, windy flats south of boot hill. The engine dies and the rotors coast down. Red Kravitz ducks and clamps his hat with one hand as he approaches, yelling to Mo Morris, "Bear will take you to Noisy. Be nice if you could tell me who put the blade in his back."

Mo blinks but gives no assurances. As he lumbers off, Red's cell phone beeps. He snaps it up. "Rollins here. I'm set down at Poker Bluff. Looks like somebody put a real big bullet through Mona Holloway's head."

"Shit! Any trace of the killer?"

"We've got snowmobile tracks heading Northwest."

"Follow them. Look for a dark object kicking up a roostertail of snow."

"If we locate, you want an intercept?"

"Negative. Stay with him, but wait for back-up."

Rollins says, "We're on it," then signs off. When he does, Molly arrives running, breathless, checks around, sees the pine box under the Montana chopper, the men digging the grave, Micky and Mo slogging through the snow toward The Elk, then Red's shocked expression. His eyes hardly meet hers. In a breathy voice he says, "Follow Micky and Mo. They'll show you the victim."

She shakes her head. "You wouldn't be this rattled about Noisy."

"Find Bear. Tell him to grab a rifle and take the chopper."

"What's going on?" Molly says.

"I really don't know."

"That's a lie, Red."

"No, Molly. That's just a stupid jerkwater cop telling the truth. But hey, I promise you one thing. Before sundown I'll find out." Against two choppers and Red's pursuing snowmobile, the killer is playing out his last hours.

* * *

From his chopper Rollins spots the black Ski Doo shooting across the field, the long rifle strutted on its steering yoke. The driver turns hard and disappears in a whitened arroyo as they drop down to follow.

The FBI agent radios Kravitz, "He's about ten miles northwest of Poker Bluff." The sound of wind whistling through a mike comes back to Rollins. "Keep well clear, you hear?"

Like a vulture to carrion, the pilot swoops down.

After checking around, he spots the upturned barrel of the Sharps' and jerks hard on the joystick, half a second too late. The high-powered slug shreds the fuel pod and Pete Rollins's right lung as the chopper explodes. That's the last sound Red hears before his cell phone hisses static.

"Shit," he says, then radios the Tweedles' chopper. "Bear! The killer's northwest of Poker Bluff, hunkered down in some gully. I think he just shot Pete Rollins out of the sky. Circle west and set down. I'll close the back door."

"Wait... I see a chopper down and burning... There's the ravine. We're gonna do a quick buzz..." Bear's chopper shoots over the cleft in the earth as a single slug whines past the right skid.

"Set 'er down!" Bear shouts. "I'm going in!"

SHARPSHOOTER

Kravitz keeps the Arctic Cat below the crests of low rills. The sky ahead curdles black smoke. As Red speeds in, he sees Bear with a Remington .30-06, weaving along the gully's western rim. Once Bear returns a nod, Red kills the snowmobile's engine and sleds to a stop.

He dismounts and racks a tube cartridge into his Winchester yellow belly. Ducking low, he works north while Bear approaches from the other side. Every ten yards or so, the two braves look across, shake their heads, then move closer. Crouching on one knee, Bear uses Plains sign language: 'He's down low, your side. Wait till I flush him.'

Seconds later, the hidden killer fires a shot that grazes Bear's right arm. Leaning out beyond the edge and aiming down, Red takes a bead on B.S. Walsh, waits out a puzzled moment for the frantic black man to reload, then shouts, "Police! Put your rifle down, now!"

But Walsh reloads, pulls the hammer back and rolls in Red's direction.

"Drop it," Kravitz says.

But Walsh keeps raising the eight-sided barrel. Then his body jerks as one of Bear's bullets tears through him. He spins back toward the big Cheyenne as another of Bear's rounds punctures the man's chest. The Sharps falls and Walsh claws toward the snowmobile, dragging useless legs.

Red shouts to his partner, "We can take him!" but Bear's third shot is lethal, shearing the man's spine just below the skull.

The deputy looks across at his friend. "You okay?"

"Smarts a bit is all. You?"

"Fine," he says.

"The stupid black fuck. It was him all along," Bear says.

Next to arrive is a low-flying CNN chopper. Beside the pilot sits Molly Mendelbaum, recording her impressions into a mike. Behind Molly, her cameraman Al pans the scene below.

* * *

The killings had torn through Sanctuary like a medieval plague, claiming people who never exchanged as much as a distant squint. And yet, all of whom seemed threatening enough for B.S. Walsh to need killing.

Opening with a pan-down shot from the chopper, Molly voices-over the recap of the Apocalyptic scene for the national audience, viewed locally by a group staring at Bear's new flat screen TV. "And still nobody knows what drove a man hidden safely away by the federal witness protection program to go on a murder spree that ended here today in a shootout worthy of the O.K. Corral. This is Molly Mendelbaum, CNN news, outside Sanctuary, Montana."

Bear switches off the set.

Into the resulting silence comes a smattering of applause. Molly turns and smiles, raises a long-neck Lone Star and knocks it back, then signals Bear for another.

The real embarrassment about B.S. Walsh is that the Federal government had authorized his impersonation. Hell is what Walsh brought to Sanctuary. Either he would take his little part of it to the greater theater of the underworld or he would just decompose next to his victims in boot hill.

Earlier, as Red finished up official reports, the good citizens of Sanctuary had planted Crazy Daisy Ramirez. When someone asked for a few words, Luke Brody stepped out of his trademark reticence to offer, "She always had a wonderful smile when I used to bring her check from Ramon. It kind of made my day."

Micky and Mo are burping off beers when Red leans in to ask, "Where's my report on the knife?"

With a mirrored turning of heads, they reflect on the question, then share an identical smile. "It's over. Give it a rest and bend an elbow with the rest of us, Kravitz."

He holds up both hands. "Okay, but where's the knife?"

Mo tells him. "In an evidence envelope on your desk, Deputy. If you like it more than the company down here, why don't you just shove it up your tight Crow ass?"

Micky thinks this is funny enough for a howl, but the sudden relaxation makes Kravitz nervous. Yet even if B.S. Walsh isn't the killer, Red would probably show up for the celebration.

And why not?

The way it's playing out, the Deputy Sheriff of Sanctuary is finally free and clear.

If gold really alloyed these victims, Noisy had been the last chance to find out who knew what. After the old drunk's burial, hands from the Hollow-A began to trickle in, volunteering to help with Bass Sander's grave.

Like a host of others in boot hill, Bass had no living kin.

While others are digging, Luke Brody confiscates plankwood from Red's store and hammers up a simple box, the way things were done when the first Holloways came west. After the graves are tamped down with parched grit, most stagger back to The Elk, wash the dirt from their hands and the dust from their throats, toasting the murderer's death and the end of fear.

At the bar, still streaked with boot hill mud, Bear pours with both hands. Walsh had only nicked him. En route to town, he sashed a bandana around it and kept going, Indian style. His patrons keep drinking, western style, hard and fast and nonstop. Bear is too busy getting his good arm pumped for Red to interfere, so he leans on the bar and scans the packed room.

Molly holds court at a distant table for admirers who may never again come this close to a 'personality.' In the far booth by the silent Rocko-la, a sad-eyed Moonlight gets up to let Doris slip in and sit down. Assisted by chained tires, Slo Lehrner has mushed his way in to join the soiree.

Bear walks a frosty mug of suds to Kravitz. "On the house. You earned it."

Red sips the froth, then asks, "But why'd he do it?"

Bear shrugs. "Walsh does thing for black man's reasons. Not Indian reasons."

"Right now I'll settle for any reason," Red says.

"Well, he's banging the widow of Jeb Holloway good enough to make her want to give him an alibi when he blows out old Jeb's brains."

"But Jeb's going to be a Senator, so Mona's about to step up in the world."

Bear's eyes say no. "Jeb's idea. Not Mona's."

"You're sure on this?"

"Drunks talk. Bardogs listen. And I can tell you, Red, that I can't see her at these Washington parties, getting loaded, lurching around, calling some other senator's wife a 'real slick cunt' or some ambassador a 'fucking towel-head.' Mona liked it here. She's like the queen of some little country, planning to open up Bearpaw for summer rock concerts, set up backpacking and wilderness walks, do Big Muddy on flatboats."

"Looks like she and Jeb were headed different ways."

Bear nods. "But the problem with a smart drunk is that you're half the time smart and half the time drunk. The half of the time Mona's smart she's figuring a way she can come out of the divorce with half the assets plus the ranch. And the other half the time she's drunk, and does whatever she wants to. So Mona's a bit of a whore, which makes her take a fancy to big-dick Walsh. But Mona was careless, got herself pregnant."

"She volunteered this to you?"

"Not while she was sober, no. But drunks get to talking, and Mona was a drunk's drunk. Plus I think she believed in bardog-drunk confidentiality. "

"Which you honored," Red checks.

Bear's eyes glimmer. "Was nobody's business but hers. And that she's telling me, for godsakes, says how damn lonely she really was."

"She went to a doctor?"

Bear shakes his head. "Not as she said it. One of those home pregnancy tests. Plus being real late. Plus barfing a lot. A bigger problem was that she and Jeb slept apart, hadn't been greasing the weenie for more'n a year."

"So Jeb could divorce her for adultery."

Bear stares into Red's glass. "Like we used to joke while I's with the Cowboys, you got to know your players to figure out their program. I think Mona was real drunk when she asked Walsh to kill Jeb. For her it was still a game. Out back, she took taught him how to use the Sharps. But it's Walsh who makes it real when he asks for a down payment. She makes it, maybe a few thousand. Walsh is hooked. But they've got to make the hit so there's no witnesses and a lot of suspects. Walsh threatens to blackmail Holloway about Mona's affair, asks him to meet one-on-one to pay off the first installment. Now he's working both ends against the middle, the Detroit hustle again. Jeb goes along, but has no mind to pay."

Bear tops up Red's beer, before summing up. "You've got this senate candidate who's been like a little god out here finds out this nigger's been rutting his wife. It's too much. Jeb knows damn well he can kill Walsh, a guy's swamping for some piss-ass bar in nowhere. Who cares? So every time Mona stops seeing double, this meeting focuses into a win/win situation. Walsh dies, she cuts a deal, plays the perfect candidate's wife, then walks with half Jeb's worth after Jeb gets to Washington. Or if Jeb is killed, who's gonna believe she would hook up with scum like Walsh? She can just step away and send him off to hell in a hemp necktie."

While it sounds plausible enough, Red isn't all that sure. "What still bothers me is why after he'd splattered Jeb, Walsh didn't look for the payoff money."

Bear rubs his chin. "Put yourself in the Buffalo Soldier's place. You've just boomed off a Big Fifty, can be heard half a mile and more off. So you ask yourself who's around to see you hustle down to the vehicle, or who's gonna show up and see you?"

"Maybe Daisy and Noisy did. But they're dead. Maybe he got spooked and came dirt-biking back later for a second look," Red offers.

"Too risky," Bear says. "Plus he's got around to foolin' himself that Mona's gonna take care of him, set things up here so he don't need witness protection."

Red still isn't convinced. "If Walsh did it, that means Mona was lying. Somebody could have seen her elsewhere when she claimed she was up at the new condo units with Walsh. Best place to start is with María, the maid. My bet is she's running a green card short. And then there's the hands at the Hollow-A, two dozen of them."

"But Jeb is dead. So then Mona's the boss. Who's gonna testify against the boss?"

Red keeps turning the beer mug in his hands, wanting every piece to fit. "But why kill Daisy and Noisy? Neither one would stand up under cross-examination."

"Augie'd know that. Any fucking lawyer'd know that. But Walsh is no lawyer. The man has a Detroit way of solving problems."

"Maybe," Red says. "But still, for Walsh to go out on a night like that, in the wind and snow, after Daisy, and she's got a Sharps, and... well, you see my problem?"

"I think Mona hoped he would freeze. End of problem, solution to murder."

"Meaning that Mona would have to admit to an affair with Walsh as the motivating incident for Jeb's death," Red says.

"Makes no difference. She inherits it all. And it's two bighorns butting heads over rutting rights. Even in Montana we must get — what? — near a hunnert domestic homicides a year."

Bear has the numbers right. But his explanation is a bit too neat. Multiple murder rarely is. So Red wants to know, "How does Bass Sanders fit in?"

Bear admits. "We may never know. Maybe Mona figures that if charged, B.S. is going to open up like a melon under a sledge hammer." He looks over at Molly, then back at Red. "So when things seem a little crazy – somebody killing old Daisy, then Noisy – fixing the blame on somebody a little bit crazy is not such a bad idea. So Mona tells Bass she wants him to mount the Appaloosa, ride out about twenty miles. Wait for her to show so they can ride back together."

"In that weather?" Red asks.

"Bass Sanders don't think weather, he thinks 'yes' when the boss asks him to do something. Mona's the boss. She asks, he does. That way it keeps things simple and Bass don't get confused. If Jeb told him to move the damn cow pie, there must be a reason, even if Bass don't get it. This guy wasn't Einstein, Red."

"So he freezes in his saddle?"

Bear rubs his wounded arm. "That did happen. All we see is some retard together with the killer's horse."

"If so, Mona had to know that the Appaloosa would fill Rollins's computer hoof prints. Meaning she knew who the killer was, and how he got up to Poker Bluff and..." he stops and shakes his head.

"If Mona was still around, you could ask her. But she'd probably lie. She was good at that," Bear says.

"Tell me about it," Red mutters. Three tables away, Molly tosses the hair off her face, laughing, shaking hands, schmoozing.

He looks back at Bear, who asks, "Anything there?"

Red sips his brew. "I don't know who she is anymore. Long ago I knew what I wanted her to be. And in my heart, that's exactly what she was. We're all a bit like B.S. Walsh that way. We learn to fool ourselves pretty good over what we want to believe in."

"I know what you mean," Bear says. "Pour you another?"

"You talked the Jew in me into it," he says. Traditionally, Crows didn't drink. Instead they had traded buffalo robes for rifles and ammunition, and made alliances and learned to outplay the white man at his own game. It was the Cheyenne who drank themselves into extinction. Which is why Bear abstained.

"Still on the house. You're the local hero. Even the mayor's taking credit for you." Hizzoner Augie Suder is holding forth to Molly, draping an arm around Moonlight, pretending as best he can to be sad, wise, reflective and upbeat. Like everybody else, he is brimming for a photo op with a national celebrity. "Walk with me," Bear says. "I've got customers."

Two wranglers lean on the bar. Hands from the Hollow-A, both at the same time yelling, "Buy you a beer, Deputy?"

Bear comes back, "Your money's no good here, boys. What's your poison?" Then fills their glasses with Jack Black or or wormwood willies before they totter back into the crowd. On the Rockola some wag punches in Eric Clapton's

"I shot the sheriff, but I did not shoot the deputy..."

and everybody not laughing sings along.

Red drops his backside on a barstool and turns to the final problem. "You said you were going to keep Walsh locked up."

"You sent me the Tweedles to show'em Noisy," Bear reminds him.

Red scowls. "Walsh had to be gone before that."

"So did I, brother. I can't build a new house at Pine Ridge, run a business, mind a part-time jail and help Hiram start a backhoe at the same time."

"You didn't notice he was gone when you got back?" Red asks.

"Came in the front. Never got around back, so I couldn't see the Ski Doo was gone."

"He knew how to drive it?" Red wonders.

"From Detroit maybe."

"Then why didn't Mona lend him a snowmobile the night he cut Daisy's throat? She must have, what, five or six up there?"

"Closer to ten," Bear claims. "But if you're Mona and give him a snowmobile and he gets caught, somebody like Red Kravitz ends up asking you all kind of questions like, 'Why does he go up to the Hollow-A, the one place the killer doesn't want to get caught, to steal a snowmobile when he can probably find one in town?'"

Red answers, "Because somebody in town might hear a snowmobile start up."

"Exactly what Mona would have said."

"Then why didn't you hear it start before Walsh took off?"

Bear looks wounded. "Red, you know how much racket it makes if you start up a backhoe when it's down-long-cold. How the hell am I supposed to hear the Ski Doo all the way back at The Elk?"

Red raises both hands. "Sorry. It's just, I can't understand why..."

"I think Mona sweetened the deal till he got stuck in the sugar, promised him to be manager at Bearpaw, plus banging rights on the side."

"Guys like Walsh always want a better deal," Red agrees.

"And usually end up dead." Bear refills the mug.

Red raises it. "Here's hoping nobody else gets killed."

Before Bear can second the motion the door flies open, revealing Leonard Jarnow with half a dozen handlers.

Instantly alert, Molly signals Al to focus on the only Republican candidate left standing. He enters with his arms raised and bellows, "Citizens of Sanctuary, I have not come to praise B.S. Walsh, but to bury him. The men I come to praise are the citizens of this great city and this great state, the kind of rugged, independent men who do not need Federal help to solve their own problems. In today's pursuit of a ruthless murderer, your law enforcement exhibited a self-reliance that should make all Montanans proud. And at the same time I come to celebrate justice, I come to grieve the loss of two dear friends, Jeb and Mona Holloway, cut down in the prime of their lives. May they rest in peace. Justice is done."

A sizzle of applause is followed by a few bellowing bravos as Eric Clapton's electronic voice teases

"...but I did not shoot the deputy..."

"I'm standing drinks," Jarnow shouts. "A round in honor of the deputy, Red Kravitz."

This gets a genuine hometown cheer.

But Jarnow isn't finished, "And to Molly Mendelbaum, who focused national attention on this atrocious crime. And, my fellow Montanans, I promise you that when I get to Washington, we will see no more see criminal garbage dumped into our great state."

"Excuse me," Red asks Bear. Shouldering through the rowdy crowd, he finds Slo Lehrner sitting alone, nursing a slivovitz. Slo raises the shot glass, said, "Success?"

Red sits down, stares at it and says, "Something doesn't add up. I can't say what, but I need you to see if you can link together our favorite candidate Len Jarnow with Molly Mendelbaum and/or B.S. Walsh before Jeb Holloway got shot."

"You're serious."

A nod confirms it.

The formula that solves the murders is: killer + motive + weapon +

transport + alibi = victim.

Three prior suspects are now dead. Bass Sanders had no motive other than blind obedience to Mona's sweet requests, but according to Head Hanley, Bass was among the all-night faro players at the bunkhouse. When Jeb was killed, Bass lay snoring, loud and open-mouthed, in the corner. Yet Mona had it all: motive, weapon, an Appaloosa named Dog Soldier and was cross-alibied by B.S. Walsh.

But Mona never needed lift a hand to get her bidding done, and Red felt she hadn't this time either. All suspects but Len Jarnow are conveniently dead. And Jarnow is neatly but unconvincingly alibied by his campaign manager, Sue Slade.

Red downs his beer and squares his hat. "I'm going to see if I can track an order for a Sharps buffalo rifle to each remaining suspect in Montana. Start to whittle it down from there."

"What about Molly?" Slo asks.

Red watches her bask in attention, glow with pride, then smiles. "Molly was always very social. She'll be fine."

* * *

Growling into low gear, the Arctic Cat makes the final climb to Konev's cabin. Even above the lathe's whine, Ivan hears it coming. Because when Red knocks once, the insomniac yells, "It's open."

Inside, the big white-haired man sits with his back turned, pecking at a desktop computer keyboard. "Damn amazing technology. You know you can even order yourself a Russian wife. They advertise, they're beautiful, they're..."

"Greedy, demanding, want to run off to Hollywood and be movie stars."

"Hear Walsh is down permanent. So what's up?" Ivan asks, still ogling Russian babes on their home pages.

"You remember sending The Wild Bunch packing. What was it, four years ago?"

"I don't know what you're talking about," Ivan mutters.

"Okay, let's say, hypothetically, that some small Wyoming town has gone up in flames and there are no survivors. A biker gang is suspected. So everybody should keep a look out. Same gang swings into eastern Montana, turns West, then North."

"This has Hollywood potential," Ivan says.

Red presses on. "The lawman in another town explains the situation, asks for volunteers. He gets a dozen. A friend who's a barkeep, another guy who makes and sells rifles, some hands from up at the local ranch and one woman, the last survivor of a family that came up from Australia through New Zealand, chasing gold fields into California and finally Montana, settled down when the stakes panned out, set up a modest spread, fell for some phony end-of-the-world charlatan, then retired, promising to fight the AntiChrist and his disciples..."

Ivan folds his arms. "You're talking about Caldera Cunningham."

"No, Ivan. I'm just telling you a story. About how this hypothetical town came together. And when the bikers approached, they downthrottled and said they were just passing through. That's when the lawman told them to turn around and ride out."

"Which is when the alpha biker gets off and stalks up in his Nazi helmet," Ivan remembers.

Red continues, "But what they don't know is that they're facing a dozen crack marksmen. Except for some new black guy nobody knows. But they hand him an old Sharps buffalo rifle, only want him to take one shot..."

"When it escalated," Ivan recalls, wiping his lenses, "The new guy missed."

"But Caldera didn't. She put a slug right through alpha's head, then blew a hole through the shoulder of his number two," Red finishes the account.

"Meaning what?" Ivan says.

"Meaning Caldera Cunningham can shoot. She hit a man in the head with a rifle from eight hundred yards. She didn't want her property burned, was willing to protect it."

"So was the rest of us, Red. Use that argument, could've been you or me shot Jeb Holloway, if that's what you're thinking."

"Maybe. But according to Doris, Jeb Holloway promised to build a new house on her land, something more worthy of a kept woman. But Caldera wasn't interested, claimed her place had only one purpose: fighting the forces of darkness, as taught by the Vengeful Handservants of the Almighty Lord."

"That's Caldera," Ivan admits. "But she sticks to herself."

"That's my point. Except for Jeb's funeral, where she drives a couple hundred miles to see a man she hated go into the ground, Caldera's been invisible."

Ivan draws a rattling sigh and scratches his head. "You're a long way out on a dead limb, pardner. You start jumpin' up and down, it just might not hold up."

Red risks it. "The day Jeb was shot, Doris took a phone call from Caldera, complaining of unwanted advances. Maybe she decided to take care of Jeb the way she took off that biker."

Ivan cocks a bushy eyebrow. "Now why'd she call attention to herself if she'd already bushwhacked Jeb? Especially Caldera, who's so alone nobody'd ever alibi her." The gunmaker shakes his head.

Red gets to the crux. "But the last time Walsh tried to make a shot that far he missed by a Montana mile."

* * *

After dismounting the Arctic Cat, Red glances down Front Street to town hall. A light burns in his office. Over crusted refrozen slush, he crosses the street and enters the building. Reflected stairwell lights lead him down. Ancient risers that moan with each step give him away. Slo's voice breaks the silence, "Red?"

Down the pinched corridor he finds the one-thumbed engineer at the computer, tapping keys with his maimed hand, chasing a mouse across a pad with the other. "Cold down here." His fingers dance on keys, reading text, downloading files to the CD burner.

"That's an LEA file," Red observes, entering the office.

Slo nods. "You left your access code on the pull-slab. What I dug up confirms Jarnow as an advisory pretrial assessor with the U.S. Justice Department. That's a fancy name for a legal kibitzer. In this case he was helping bust up some drug-and-pimp operation using anti-racketeering and income tax evasion laws, plus some witnesses allowed to erase themselves if they testified."

"You're saying B.S. Walsh?" Red concludes.

"The relocation files are masked. Otherwise, you risk exposing every protected witness and location in the country in one hack. But the time frame is right for when B.S. Walsh appears in Sanctuary, and when Walter Stanley Addison vanishes from Detroit."

"But nothing about Molly in this?" is Red's next question.

Slo Lehrner looks up with sad eyes, his face half-lit by the monitor. "During this same time Molly covered the arrest and arraignment of the principal figures. She interviewed a few major 'unnamed sources.' One could have been Jarnow."

"What makes you say that?"

Slo pivots away from the screen. "First Jarnow went to Washington. He had no turf to defend, just wanted to see how horses were swapped. Usually in Washington, high level sources don't talk. There's too much to lose. Jarnow didn't have that problem. He was in the know, but was only passing through. Getting to know Molly could have prepared him to..."

Red finishes, "...give her an inside angle for the coverage of this race..."

"...or the murder of Jeb Holloway..."

"...or both," Red whispers.

Slo blinks, just once, but enough to betray his doubt. "Speculation. As an archivist I can tell you that historians use it all the time to create connections that let things make sense. But it's slippery going, like crossing Big Muddy when the ice is just starting to patch and crack. It always looks like you can get to the other side."

He paused, rubbing the bulb of his lost thumb. "But unlike Big Muddy, where you can see the other side, speculation opens up forever on what we don't know, but it's far from proven. It let's you make believe. With a little speculation, the facts never speak for themselves." To emphasize the point, he tips his head at an evidence bag holding a large blood-stained Bowie knife. "Like that belduque there. Fact is, I bet, Micky and Mo pulled it out of Noisy. By the hilt. With gloves."

Red nods.

Slo gets up to look at the weapon. "In tourist turnstiles in Missoula and Bozeman, a toad sticker like that goes eight hundred dollars, the craftsmanship in it, the material." He points at the blood coating the handle. "Maybe you could get some fingerprints from Micky and Mo. Wrap it up that way."

Red closes and rubs his weary eyes. "That's TV stuff, Slo. In real life the more blood you got on an object, the more slipping, blurring, resettling from run-and-pool. Somebody good and lucky might get a partial, but you can't go to trial on a partial."

Slo shrugs. "So you're stuck with Jarnow. And tryin' for some damn reason unknown to me to pull Molly in. What's in it for her, down the road I mean?"

"Hypothetically," Red pursues the point. "Lenny Jarnow promises Molly a Deep Throat view of Washington. At least as much as serves his own agenda."

"Funny, though," Slo offers, "if Lenny promised to keep the witness protection program from dumping in Montana, why did he let B.S. Walsh in here to begin with?"

"Maybe Walsh was a sleeper. Jarnow knew he was a murderer. If Walsh wouldn't kill Jeb Holloway for him, then Lenny could make a little anonymous call to Detroit and..."

Slo holds up both hands. "Next you'll suggest that a nice Jewish girl like Molly keeps the lawman involved from getting too close by fucking his brains out."

They both let a good laugh play out, then fall silent before Red whispers, "Maybe they'll get away with it."

"They, who?" Slo asks, instantly alert.

"The killer. The one who did it," Red answers with what he thinks is so implicit that even a slow learner would get it the first time.

"The word 'they' is plural," Slo reminds him. "Ergo conspiracy."

"Or Freudian slip," Red counters, wanting a break from a chase that has been too long, too hard and too fast.

Slo draws a long sigh, recovers a closed blue file folder from the top drawer and tucks it under his arm. "Maybe so," he says, getting up.

Red raises a chin at the folder. "What's that?"

"Just bullshit," he mutters.

He thinks of Molly and the satellite photo of Poker Bluff, holds out an arm. "Slo, it's a serious matter to walk off with evidence in a Federal homicide case."

Slo's laughter is the painful screech of a collision between pure hysteria and near madness. He holds out the blue folder. "You want it. Knock yourself out. Drive yourself crazy. I did. And still... bupkis."

"Sit down," Red offers. When Slo does, Red pulls up a chair across from him and places the folder, unopened, between them. In a low voice with a sad smile he admits, "It can't be any crazier than my dreams. Why not have a look?"

Slo's voice is as gentle, his smile sadder. "Why not?" he echoes, then answers, "Because the reasoning is suspect."

Red twits him. "So? Some of our best suspects are unreasoning. Like Bass Sanders. I doubt he had a well-reasoned thought in his life."

Slo opens the folder but places his unthumbed hand over the first page. "Jeb Holloway had me make some changes on his computer. Not big things. But, I think, significant things."

"Such as?"

"Jeb had me change Mona's PIN access to the keypad numbers corresponding to the word BITCH."

Right again. But again, so what? "Did he change his own PIN to keep Mona from getting in under his name?"

Slo answers, "He had me transnumerate the letters for JEBHO, but made input on the user name line case specific: lower case je, upper case BH, lower case o. If you didn't use that exact mix of upper and lower case letters, the password wouldn't get you in."

"So you're telling me...what? Jeb wrote 'If I turn up dead, so-and-so did it'?"

Slo shakes his head. "From what I saw of his cool, I don't think Jeb ever believed he was in danger. You'll say, yeah, but what about the Colt Python in the Suburban. He always kept it in the glove compartment. Means nothing."

Slo is too right. In Montana, neither ownership of possession of a firearm constituted the intent to kill. The jury needed a lot more to convict. Usually a body, but at least a good reason Jeb might have killed HIM.

Slo's theory was, "Len is involved in Jeb's plans. The land grab on Daisy's squatter is one link. Bearpaw's ski resort is another. They're partners in both."

Red can't rule it out, but it's only a possibility. So his only response to Slo is a shrug.

Prompting his friend to say, "I checked Len and Jeb's IRS 1040s, public information like everyone else's. Since Bearpaw broke ground, their tax forms show no outlays or deductions, no capital depreciations or other expenses for Bearpaw. They may be on the letterhead and board of directors, but somebody's bankrolling them. I think it's a California bank because the payrolls are drawn on the Bank of America's San Francisco account. But that might just be a pass-through after a wire transfer from a shadow partner. Maybe the same guy he went to meet at Poker Bluff, finalize the details, shake hands, work out any remaining problems, walk away and start drawing profits."

Red could only whisper, "Then...something went wrong?"

Slo's turn to shrug. "If so, it had to be wrong before the other party got there, otherwise... no ambush."

"What about BITCH, Mona's password? In this scheme of total meaning, what does that amount to?"

Slo has an idea. "It's the name on Daisy's Denver Bronco jersey, no? She's the squatter on the property intended for ski condos. At least at first."

Red remembers the architect's model designating the area 'development,' and has to agree. But Slo is relentless. "Until the gold turns up. Then they had to find another off-mountain site for the cheap ski lodgings."

"So... it's about money?" Red ventures.

Slo's eyes are steady. "Both Len and Jeb are out of pocket for campaign costs at the very moment they realize they might be sitting on top of a field of black gold. So with pump gas nearly three dollars a gallon, oil might've been the agenda of the 10-7 meeting. Think about it. Even if the government allows them to drill, they can't. All their bucks are tied up in campaigning and Bearpaw. They're tapped out. That's where a lender comes in, gives them some leverage."

Red barks a simple gruff laugh. "Slo, you are a clever and amusing fellow. But I'll bet with the same facts, somebody else'd come up with a whole different take." He straightens his back and puts a short silence between them, before softening with, "All speculation, no evidence. At least nothing to indict, forget about convicting."

Slo crosses his arms and set his jaw. "Then you can't rule out somebody with a lot of money and not enough oil, like for example, the Chinese."

Even forgetting a Chinese absence in Sanctuary dating back to the railroad days, Red provides more problems with Slo's idea. "I don't think Noisy knew enough to put the killer away, or that Bass was the killer, and to convict for all victims, you've got to explain why these other guys were killed, too."

Maybe because his father had hammered it into him, Slo won't give up. "I locked Mona out at Jeb's request. So she couldn't have set up a hit unless..."

Red sees the wheels turning in Slo's eyes and gives him time. "Unless what?"

"There was no way Walsh could've gotten the time for this meet unless 'HIM' – whoever that is – called Holloway's place directly, got Mona, asked her to pass it on to Jeb. Then she mentioned the call, maybe was drunk, sullen, a little bitchy. He snaps at her, asks, 'What'd he want?' Mona refuses to say. He starts wailing on her, she still doesn't remember, but makes up another date, for another purpose. And that's what gets Jeb out there. Not jealousy, but money. I mean, Red, let's face it. Look at it from Jeb's point of view. You can be indifferent to divorce if you settle on current assets just before you walk into a post-divorce bonanza."

Red lacks Slo's confidence, but is running out of alternatives. The worst part is that maybe Slo's right, but they won't ever be able to prove it. Red knocks a wind-dried knuckle on the desk. "A very big 'maybe.' But sure as the moose is horny, somebody had reason to kill these people."

Slo blinks. "The only other interesting tidbit I got is that Molly has an NRA card. Master marksman. It was a hack to get in. You can't go direct into the list. But if you roll into the gunmakers that the NRA sells member names to, you can crossmatch encoded IDs with mailing lists. But, like you said, it could mean nothing. A lot of women in cities with high crime rates join the NRA. They want a handgun in their purse, want empowerment as much as personal protection." He reaches for his coat. "Oh, by the way, Augie was in his office tonight."

"He left the door open?"

Pinching the fob in his good hand, Slo starts zipping up his parka. "Not a chance. But he was muttering and cursing. Anyway, you've got to admit that bulldogging an ornery computer isn't the way hizzoner likes to spend an evening." Slo grabs a deep yawn, covers it up and concludes, "So if you really want to know what files Augie was dumping, I'd ask Moonlight. She says he talks in his sleep."

"When do you talk to Moonlight?"

Slo touches a finger to his lips. "What? I'm not allowed to be horny?"

* * *

The Elk is packed, elbow-to-elbow. Word of free drinks has spread like a crown fire in a high wind. Rallying for fire water, ranch hands drift in from the Hollow-A, even a few illegals lost in the numbers. In a day or two, half of them will drift south. But for now they join the celebration: the killer has been stopped.

That's what they've come to hear Red announce. After sharing Slo's disturbing suspicions about Jeb Holloway's plotting, Red isn't sure that he can. Cornering Bear after he ferries six frosty brews to a booth, Red asks, "Got a minute?"

"About that." He scans the packed room. "If Bearpaw goes like this, I'll be fucking rich."

Red eases him down the vacant hallway toward the back. Sheltered by the snarling stuffed hulk of Butkus, he tells Bear, "I still can't get it exactly straight in my mind how Walsh got out without your knowing it."

Bear looks offended. "Again: I's down at Hiram's with the backhoe. While I's gone, Walsh busted the hasp on the back door and took off. It's still busted. You wanna see it?"

Red shrugs, a 'no.'

"I said I'd kill him if he ran, and damn if I didn't kept my promise."

"Where'd he get the Sharps?"

"You'd have to ask him."

"And where did Walsh get the knife?" is Red's next question.

Bear shivers. "That gives me the creeps. He used to make steaks, cut to order, with a fancy mirror-finished Bowie. Last one he made was for Mel Keppert couple nights back. He must've used the same knife on Daisy, then Noisy."

Red resists a nod and ends, "I guess that should do it. I'm turning in."

"You better stick around, see your lady doesn't get waltzed off by the soon-to-be U.S. Senator."

Kravitz admits, "The only problem sleeping alone is you notice the empty bed."

"Moonlight's hustling drinks now, but I could send her over later," Bear says.

Red shakes his head. Keeping his back to the wall he skirts the rowdy crowd, tips his hat to Lenny Jarnow, then pauses for a quick glance at Molly enjoying the attention of a full house.

After fifteen years, Molly is the same, and she is different. If you look long enough, you can still see the girl in the woman, the way she laughs or tosses her hair off her face or rolls her eyes, the tapping of one fingernail when she is getting restless or bored, the head turning nonstop, needing to make sure that she hasn't missed a vital connection.

Nonetheless at the bottom of the heap of success lies a hollow insecurity that echoes her own doubts. So she lives to see how far she can go. Yet as hard as he presses his imagination, he can never see her as the next Mrs. Leonard Jarnow.

Sure Jarnow's crumbling marriage would have been a factor in the election. Maybe his pollsters told him as much, and that caused him to kill Jeb Holloway. Except as you acquire real power, you don't need to do your own dirty work. There's always some caged animal like B.S. Walsh scratching at the bars, ready to serve his master's command rather than scrap with wilder dogs.

Molly surveys the crowd, a quick scan.

Her face looks older than he remembers, but no less pretty. Alert eyes, flirtatious even, completing her scan, taking him in with relief or surprise.

Red can't separate the two expressions nor can he penetrate the complexity that lies behind those eyes. And so he smiles — at her, at himself, at them — tips his hat and turns to leave. Blown shut, The Elk's door slams behind him, closing on his past, and maybe his future.

*   *   *

He doesn't bother to light the fire, then reconsiders, unable to shake the cold inside. After charging the estula with punk and fat pine he touches it off, then takes out his cellular. The number buzzes three times, then is answered, "Glenn Vandrey here."

"Kravitz here. Was Leonard Jarnow involved in arranging witness protection for B.S. Walsh?"

A pause, then a sigh. "I'm not at liberty to compromise the security of the program."

"Thanks," Red says. If Jarnow had not been involved, Vandrey could have given a quick, "No." Instead, the line goes silent. Kravitz clicks off the phone just as the door bursts open.

In the frame stands Molly, giggling drunk. She lurches in, slips and laughs harder, then gets up and pushes the door shut. "Well," she says. "You should've stood...stayed, rather... around. They did a couple of rounds to their local hero sheriff... I think 'buscadero' was the word they used...who got the bad guy."

Red gives her a sad smile. "I'd guess Leonard Jarnow wasn't left out."

She brushes stray flecks of melting snow off her hair. "Len, Lenny, Leonard, Leo... he wanted me to call him whatever was comfortable for me..."

"I'd suggest shithead, but you probably wouldn't go along."

She humors him. "Shithead, if you like, is going to host a press conference tomorrow by Poker Bluff..." she hicks, then holds her breath, laughs, then resumes, "He told me all about Walsh's sordid past in Detroit."

"How'd he know about that?"

"Friends in Washington," she whispers, winking.

"I still wonder how he can be so sure."

She drops onto the bed next to him. "I don't know. But if, you know, Walsh was a killer, maybe he just went crazy and started again..."

"Ah. Black man encircled by hostile whites. A sort of Wounded Knee for the urban gangsta. Makes perfect sense to me."

She yokes an arm on his shoulder, leans her head after it. "Anyway it's over."

"Is it?" he asks.

She draws her head away and gives him a strange look. "What are you saying? What do you know that you've been... holding out on me?"

"It just doesn't feel right. I've got the knife that killed Noisy down at town hall. Tomorrow Doris sends it to the lab. Be nice if they at least looked for partials of Walsh's fingerprints."

"I missed you down at The Elk," she says.

"Did you?"

She looks wounded. "Of course. It was supposed to be..."

He cuts her off, "...let me guess. 'The crowning achievement of my career, or maybe the springboard to grander things.' If the Republicans pull out a win in three weeks, Lenny can doff me Chief Yorick of the Bureau of Indian Affairs. A grave digger for a people already in the grave."

She says, "You're upset."

"Did Jarnow want you to spend the night with him?"

"No." She bites her lip. "Well, actually, yes. But I let him think that I thought that he was drunk and I was drunk and I would forget it tomorrow, so that he could pretend I hadn't said 'no.' Does that make sense?"

"Where's he bunking?"

"At Doris's," she says. "She offered. His gophers are burrowing in at The Elk."

"Have Micky and Mo worked the storeroom for evidence yet?"

"I don't know. For a couple of old guys, they were drinking pretty hard, too."

"I'll take that as a 'no.'" Red tells her. "This is all fucked up. Everyone is celebrating and the grand jury hasn't even convened."

"You don't think it was Walsh?" she asks.

In his smile is everything but humor. "What does it matter what I think? Lenny's going to give us the politically correct version." He lies back and shuts his eyelids. "I'm going to sleep."

"Like hell you are," she says, undoing the top button of her blouse.

EULOGIES

Before dawn burnishes the eastern sky, Molly slides across Red, makes sounds like a wounded animal, then whispers, "I can't believe you left me at The Elk and let me drink like that."

Red rolls away.

She massages both temples. "I need coffee. You have any vitamin B-12?"

"Coffee's on the woodstove. Throw some logs on and give 'er a few minutes."

Molly gets up and staggers. "I don't know whether I'd feel better if I puked or not."

"If you've got to, spew in the cold outside. Noisy always used to say that ends a headthrobber real quick."

Molly sets up a make-shift vanity on the kitchen table and squints at her image. "I sleep with a Crow and get crow's feet. I look like I've aged fifteen years overnight."

Red doesn't remind her that she has aged fifteen years since they last connected.

"Nothing a little makeup won't fix," she says, sniffling twice before sneezing.

"What's the rush?"

"Jarnow's press conference."

Red props himself up and yawns. "He'll just remind voters that Jeb's dead. Unlike John Ashcroft, Lenny couldn't endure losing to a dead man."

She ignores him, whisking make-up across her cheeks. "You didn't used to be this cynical."

"Time changes you. It changes everyone."

She turns around to ask him, "How do I look?"

He tries a weak smile. "Like a woman on her way up, Molly."

"Want some coffee?" she says, going for the pot.

"I've got to write condolences to Pete Rollins's folks."

"Jarnow said he'd have some good words for you," Molly coos.

"Tell him I'd rather have a plush job up at Bearpaw."

She shakes him. "Come on."

He shrugs her hand off. Molly sits down beside him. "Red? What if Walsh isn't the killer? Wouldn't you like a shot at Jarnow as he declares the case closed?"

"Now there's an idea."

* * *

Awaiting dawn, Front Street becomes an out-take from The Night of the Living Dead. Through pale purple shadows shuffle last night's drunks, aroused by the slap of cold and a jolt of java from Styrofoam cups. Wind-driven, Sanctuary's hungover voters straggle along like tumbleweeds.

Senatorial shoe-in Jarnow has appropriated Micky and Mo's chopper. While de-icing his rotors, the pilot mutters sound bites CNN could never air. Molly and her cameraman Al hitch a lift with Jarnow, while support crews and retainers pile onto snowmobiles and overpowered 4x4s with off-road axles.

Left behind by the exodus, Red shoulders The Elk's door open.

Inside, Bear is swinging a mop over the floor in ferocious anger.

The deputy says, "You're not going?"

Bear's broad back is turned. "Gotta clean up. Those dickhead's couldn't even piss straight last night."

Red reels at the tang of vomit. "I take it you're not voting for Lenny."

"I'm not voting for any of them," Bear says. "I just wish the buffalo solider was still swamping." When he finally turns and sees the town deputy outfitted in snow boots, leggings, a winter buckskin jacket, and Crow headband.

"What the hell do you think you're doin'?" Bear asks, leaning on the mop handle.

Red gives him a quick wink. "Election comin'. Tryin' to sweep the Native American vote."

"That's just me and Jerry Whitefeather," Bear reminds him.

Red chants through the first few bars of a Crow death dance as a joke, then stops cold when a vision of his mother, battered and bleeding on a Chicago street, flashes into his mind. "Maybe I'll wear my Resistol, to roll in the cowboy vote."

Bear nods. "Be smart, stay alive. That's how the Crows made it."

"Catch you later," Red says.

"Much," Bear is certain.

Clearing the eastern ridge of the Bearpaw range like a blazing eagle, the new sun stretches narrow white talons across undulant snow. Red pull-starts his Arctic Cat and heads out to join the circus. And play wooden Indian. Fierce, truculent, dour.

The ranch hands aren't wrong. This is the best show in town.

What a sad epitaph for Sanctuary.

* * *

Molly's cameraman Al shoots from the south, his light still low in the eastern sky. Everyone but Red is burping off last night's binge with volley's of complimentary coffee in souvenir mugs gilded Jarnow NOW!

Red scans an unclouded sky, then the flanks snowfields, sensing an unseen presence. His focus fixes on Poker Bluff, confected with snow. Then it resettles on the milling men who spat and shat and looked life and death in the eye with equal indifference.

For them there will always be something beyond the Hollow-A. That kind of faith never allows reason to intrude with the ugly question, what? For these guys, asking what or where or when makes no sense. Like old Indians, there is only the moment. Maybe that's why Red Kravitz has been so comfortable here. Outside Sanctuary things run on white time. Out there forces hammer to forge the next moment, the one that flattens your hope and faith and leaves you with a bottle in your hand and a beggar's plea on your lips. Fearing that, he strolls faster, dwelling on this lethal place, and the threads that weave it into a tapestry of puzzling and violent deaths.

Nervous as a waiting bride, Jarnow checks his flashy Movado, and rubs shadows of warmth into his skeletal hands. He wears a blue Alpiner parka, connecting with the economic reality of most voters. In politics, everything is calculated. And no one seems more calculating to Red than Len Jarnow.

"How do I look?" Len asks an aide.

"You're thquinting," an aide lisps, crossing his arms in a huff.

"Maybe I should wear sunglasses."

"That maykth thyou look untrussworthy." The aide keeps arranging so the right image gets through. Moving Molly in next to Jarnow, the lisper says, "Leth do thiss interview thyle, thoh you don't look like you're preaching. Make a perthonal connection with Molly and voters thwill feel it."

Cameraman Al frames the two celebrities. "Three, two, one and... roll."

Molly holds the mike. "We're here with United States senatorial candidate Leonard Jarnow from Montana, on the site where three people, including his rival Jeb Holloway, were slain in the last week. Is this killing spree over?"

Leonard Jarnow's smile looks like a snarl, less gum and more tooth. "Molly, I can promise all Montanans, that this truly shocking tragedy is officially over."

"Some people believe the man calling himself B.S. Walsh may not have committed these killings. What's your response?"

Jarnow raises a boney finger. "Having reviewed all the evidence and files, I have no reason at all to believe..." The next sound explodes in blood, flesh and brain from Leonard Jarnow's lips. A ringing echo follows and dies.

Drenched in gore, Molly screams.

Reflexively, Kravitz knocks her flat. "Stay down!"

Then he turns and watches ranch hands flee. "Everybody! Stay down!"

A second report rings out.

This time they all flatten. But when Red Kravitz looks, no one else seems hit. "Stay down," he repeats to Molly.

Like a sidewinder, Red belly-crawls to the snowmobile and grabs a peek. Over the seat he sees only Wild Bill, staring at his death hand. So he saddles up, pull-starts the engine and flies at the rock formation, schussing ahead, keeping low, drawing no incoming fire.

At the bluff, he spins down from the seat and crawls ahead on his forearms. Rolling to cover, he comes up and ducks back, then rises to check the opposite bank of the river. And seeing there a channel of fleeing footprints in drifted snow.

Working silently into the lee of the sandstone pocket, he inches ahead and removes his Resistol. On one rising finger he exposes only the hat. Chased by a loud echoing crack, it leaps from his finger and lands, spinning on its rim at Wild Bill's stony feet eight feet away. A huge hole is blown through, inches above the feather band.

Shimmying back, he leaves the nest, rolls fast and is swallowed by the nearest gully. Approaching Big Muddy, the gully deepens and switches back twice. Near its outwash the cold sibilant river splashes off scrappy talus. Across the coruscating water he watches the swishing tail of an Appaloosa disappear through a curtain of naked willow on the far bank.

* * *

Red sticks to the gully, scrambling back up through melting ice, re-emerging winded at the snowmobile. He surveys the chaos around Leonard Jarnow, Micky hammering the chest of a corpse topped by only half a head.

Cameraman Al switches from the blood gurgling out of Jarnow's mouth to take in Kravitz as he mounts the snowmobile and roars back to the group, most of the others still prone. He skids in next to Micky, who is on the headset to Great Falls. Breathless but controlled, Red tells him. "I'll need your chopper to track him."

Jake Laney seizes Red's shoulder. "Take it from a Vietnam vet. A single chopper down low's a flying coffin. He's on Federal land. Let the Feds handle it."

"Like they did B.S. Walsh?"

Jake keeps insisting. "Red, think! 'Tween here and Bearpaw, you got nowhere to put down. Except for Wykert's meadow, it's thick forest on rolling land..."

"Damn!" Red screams, then stabs Mo with a finger. "Check that bowie knife!"

Just outside the shouting, Molly is re-framed by a camera, her blood-stippled face reporting, "Here in Sanctuary, Montana, another man is dead by ambush, his brains, as you can see, all over me..."

Red tells Laney. "I need a good night horse with more bottom than a Missouri mule." Laney's shrill whistle brings Head Hanley running. Panting, Hanley says, "We got all sort, Appaloosa to zebra dun. What you need, Red?"

"Yakima cut to Morgan mustang. Good horse sense but low spook. When he smells Grizzly I'd like to see his ears up 'stead of his ass goin' small."

Hanley squints through the rising sun toward the ranch. "Got a blazed claybank might do it, but was me, I'd go with a cayuse canelo: name of Kismet. Best damn mount we got."

Red nods. "Have the lead chopper relay positions to my cell phone. Call them out by features and areas, not coordinates. If they spot him, I want to know where he's headed."

Red turns to Laney. The headtaster reads the look and says, "We got deer rifles, some NATO target guns from Jeb's collection, and Mona's Sharps."

"And you didn't let me know?" Red demands.

The ranny shrugs. "We thought it was B.S. Walsh, his own gun all along."

"You have reloads and a boot for the Sharps?" Red asks. The foreman nods. "Then I'll take it."

* * *

Kravitz heels Kismet along a ridge tracing a steep coulee. For two miles, the shadowy gorge slices into the wildlife preserve on a northeasterly slant. The deep cut forces riders to choose one side. And Red has seen no hoofprints on his. So the killer must be farther west.

With only that much certain, Red answers his cellular. "Yeah."

"Slo here. FBI's crossed Big Muddy. Park Service lined up west. So he can't go that way. Canadians are sealing the border. They don't want him either."

"Your thoughts?" Red asks.

Slo goes silent, then says, "You want to know who you're up against, listen up. You want motive, I've got motive."

"Fire away," Red tells him, letting the roan trot.

"Black Hills, 1874."

"Understood," Red responds. There and then a survey team led by George Armstrong Custer discovered gold.

"Two years later," Slo says.

"Gotcha," Red answers. The same George Armstrong Custer was killed at Little Bighorn as the U.S. government cleared Indians out for the gold rush west. "What's your point?" Red demands, pushing Kismet harder.

"My wife and kids are in Las Vegas; your kin at Reno," Slo insists.

But Kravitz has no kin in Reno. Then it hits him.

Somehow, Slo figured it was all linked not to the town, but the major in Custer's 7th Cavalry, Marcus Reno. Assisted by Crow warriors and separated from the main battle, his detachment survived.

"I understand," says Kravitz, feeling numb beyond the cold. But before he can respond, they are interrupted. "Later. I got a call waiting."

A crackle syncopated the link, then, "This is the Park Service, Kravitz. We've made trail. He's turning Northeast. Where are you now?"

"I'd rather not say," Red informs them. "It's an open channel."

"We just don't want to shoot you by mistake. But if we do, your next of kin are in Reno, Nevada. Right?"

"Yeah," Kravitz lies, understanding this is another war.

A hundred and thirty year later, nothing has changed. Whites vs. Redskins all over again. Front row seats available 24/7, courtesy of Molly Mendelbaum, CNN news.

*   *   *

Even through deep snow and dense stands of pine, the roan makes good time. Red rides below a bladed ridge, mindful of Kismet, his measured pace, his signs of discomfort that humans call intuition.

Horses have more of it. And better, too. Better ability to sense too much stillness, or the vibrations made by distant wolf packs, or faint scents undetectable to humans. But Kismet still keeps moving as the rock converges to an upland cascade where tumbling meltwater crashes through curtains of hanging mist.

The roan canters in shallow feedwater for another half mile before Red decides to cross, easing the jukey horse over slippery bedrock, then coaxing it up hissing pine needles and crumbling soil to the yielding snow beyond. There he stops to look ahead, searching for a lone spotted horse and big rider, seeing neither.

On his mobile phone he punches speed-dial. At the pick-up he says, "Slo? Look, I still can't make trail here. I've seen badger, pronghorn. Snowshoe hare tracks and vole scat near a burrow. You sure he's headed this way?'

"That's the consensus," Slo says. "Where are you?"

"North of the falls above Deep Rocky."

"The Feds have a real hard on. They're airlifting snowmobiles in."

"I'll keep my ears skinned." Red notices the phone's 'battery low' light go on, and turns the unit off. Far to the west, an advancing line of FBI helicopters beats through the thin, cool air. Behind him a pale sun arcs past midday and slices toward night.

He draws a deep sniff and holds it. Northerly breezes carry the fragrant tang of evergreen. An average white's nose can pick up horse scents at fifty yards. An Indian nose might catch trace a mile away, the maximum range of a Sharps buffalo rifle.

* * *

The CNN chopper arrives for Molly Mendelbaum just as Leonard Jarnow's bagged body slides between the skids of the Montana state forensic unit.

Insinuating himself into Al's viewfinder, Jake Laney works his finger over the contour map, telling Molly, "You got a slew of FBI along west Timberline, sweeping east. We got some armed locals picketing Big Muddy, so he can't double back. Our boys at the Hollow-A's secured the ranch perimeters. And Red's working beyond Deep Rocky, this ravine you see here. They figure our shooter's heading Nor'east."

Molly studies the map. "Toward Bearpaw. There's a landing pad up there?"

Laney assures her, "Oh, yeah. It's reckoned to be the ultimate resort.

Indoor shooting range. Even got a herd of trail horses, like the other dude ranches out this way."

"Let's go get 'im," Molly tells the pilot.

SACRED MOUNTAIN

Kravitz reins up his mount behind a line of spruce opening on a vast field. Wykert's Meadow existed for uncounted years before the startled eyes of Samuel Wykert, fugitive, explorer, trailblazer, bushwhacker and thief, spotted its sprawling glory of wildflowers and alpine grass. The Crows still call it the Field of the Moon. It rises northeast toward what the mountain whites call Bearpaw, the Indians, Home of the Great Spirit.

Red dismounts and lets Kismet water. Then he kneels to study the Appaloosa's tracks. The shallow snow under the tree limbs provide a good impression of the slipper.

He looks east. Beyond the Field of the Moon stands a dense wall of lodgepole pines. The sky above the treeline has deepened to an ugly bruise. To the west, breezes fan the fading memory of day into melting bands of gold. Riding high in the saddle, Red's body, backlit by dusk, would etch a perfect silhouette. If the Appaloosa's rider is waiting, it will end here.

The faint beat of rotors crosses the meadow and echoes off the waiting wall of trees. Red switches his cell phone on. Instantly it rings. Kneeling behind a curtain of saplings, he hears a voice from the chopper announce, "This is the FBI. You're on Federal land during a Federal search. If you don't want to become a casualty, hear me out..."

While the man draws his breath, Red cuts in. "I walked this land when no ranger could find me. The guy we're after is that good, maybe better. Now here's your problem..."

"What I don't need is some local yokel telling us our problem!"

Red snaps off a freshly broken branch and smells its sap. "Here's your problem. Don't be fooled by the snow. We had a long dry summer. The meadow's the only place you can set down. And he knows it. If you bring your choppers he'll have a duck shoot. Wind's on the rise. So if you go down, a wildfire is out of control in ten minutes."

A pause fills with the rhythmic throbbing of rotors, then "What do you advise?"

"Stay out of range. If I'm hit, then it's your game."

"And if not?"

"If I live that long, I'll worry about it then." He switches off the phone. Then keens his ears for an Appaloosa's hoofs pawing at snow, urging its rider to keep moving. Because in a few hours the cloudless sky will bleed out the day's remaining heat. The night will bring lethal cold.

Pressing with his knees, Red ducks beneath a spray of low limbs and enters the field Indian fashion, using the roan as a shield. He rides the way the killer did in passing Crazy Daisy on Poker Bluff. He works the horse up the gently rising meadow, keeping it between him and the approaching trees. Far to the west, well out of range, the lead chopper hangs in waning light like an insect in amber. And as the horse takes one crunching step after another, Red Kravitz can hear, loud and drumlike, the pounding of his own heart.

* * *

Crossing Wykert's Meadow, Red imagines the killer watching a horseman backlit by gilded twilight riding into the slot of a Creedmore sight, the long heavy barrel tracking his mount as he approaches, the roan laboring against the sharp cold and rising wind. With the treeline close, Red risks a peek. But snipers are given to stillness and patience, waiting until a killshot is certain. So as expected, he sees nothing, even after Kismet enters the dense lacerating pines.

There he dismounts and makes trail, picking up tracks, long and shallow on entry, steep and abrupt on withdrawal, made as the killer's mount slid down a shallow trough before crossing a pup creek and scrambling up the other side. The killer has taken his mount the only way possible, a perilously narrow pinch in an impenetrable thicket of sappy boles. Yet there is at this very deadly narrows a strange, almost surreal sense of refuge. The dense huddle of pines breaks the rising wind, so the forest floor is calm, while high above, needled crowns sway, hiss and wail.

Flipping out his phone, he powers up and speed-dials. "He's headed toward Bearpaw. Anybody seen Bear?"

Slo answers. "Moonlight's pretty sure he lit out for Bearpaw in the Ski Doo."

"Why?" Red wonders.

"Because Molly Mendelbaum headed up there to shoot the final scene."

"If you reach Bear, tell him to wrestle her down and lock her up, you hear me?" He clicks off, powers down and remounts, heeling the roan ahead, raising his fleece-lined buckskin collar, trying to stay ahead of the feds. From the billowed snow raised by their rotors, it appears that the choppers might be landing.

Maybe that was predictable after Rollins. One of their own taken down, now they're out to show who's boss.

Like the U.S. Army after Little Bighorn.

* * *

Beyond the meadow, fenced boles and tangled branches black out all but the carpet of snowdrift on the narrow trail ahead. Darkness fuses with frigid air, and wind makes ice of tears. The tips of his fingers begin to tingle.

Not a good sign.

He warms them with breath before re-gloving. From the spacing between the hoofprints, the fleeing rider will soon jigger the Appaloosa. A long push without a break does that, no matter how much bottom a mount has. In scant hours the shooter will be needing to push on by foot.

Then what?

Red has no idea.

No visions in his half-Indian mind. No intuition in the Jewish half. Like the halves could never pow-wow. Maybe the man ahead is like any other on the run, waiting only to make some final statement before he gives up. If so, Red wants to find out what was so important that six people had to die.

* * *

The roan stands panting at Timberland's easternmost border, looking across a long field that rises slowly toward Bearpaw Mountain. At the mountain's base stands a well-lit lodge where a skeleton crew of staff and workers has been sequestered. Along the mountain's western foot bleed varicose ski trails.

Their floodlit flux twists and switches back, plummeting then flattening as the ribbons of white slip around narrow islands of pine that vanish at the tree line. At its summit, Bearpaw is rocky and lifeless, punished by cruel winds and brutal chill. Ahead, the Appaloosa's tracks mark the long field before entering a scatter of scrawny spruce near the bunny slope.

Winded, an FBI team scuttles up behind him. After regaining his breath, the leader informs Red, "We'll take over from here."

"I don't think so." Kravitz eases the weary roan onto the ski resort. "Today's shot was taken in my jurisdiction. The victim died in my jurisdiction. And Bearpaw Mountain is my jurisdiction. I do thank you gentlemen for your assistance, but I've got a felon to track."

"But we've got him surrounded!"

Red barks a harsh laugh. "Look, he could've lost us all back there, or holed up in a cave. He could've pulled himself into a tree and run his mount off with a kick on the ass. Or in all the ruckus you folks kicked up, he could even have hooked up with a stowed snowmobile someplace. He had pretty good chances compared to the one he took. But he took it anyway."

"Yeah," says the FBI man. "But why?"

Easing Kismet on, Red Kravitz half-turns to answer, "I'll ask him."

*　　*　　*

The snow now glares with refrozen melt, its crust groaning with every hoof strike. When the Appaloosa passed this way earlier, the surface was softer. Its tracks had punched through. With darkness the cold had come, and with cold the surface had firmed and slickened. If Red's mount it keeps pressing this hard, it will soon be gasping at air.

He sizes up the mountain and wonders if the lead mount would go plug, so weary from the rugged climb and thin air that it can't go another step. That's why he spells the roan, to see if it can make up some ground. But if he passes a riderless Appaloosa, the horseless killer ahead will be more inclined to shoot. And Red will be high in the saddle, a perfect target.

*　　*　　*

Eight hundred feet above the bunny slope, an intermediate-level trail crosses a beginner's before chasing a fall line north. Here the trail widens and levels out. From this position, Kravitz spots the snow-draped summit, where the Appaloosa's tracks lead.

He dismounts and studies the trail. Elliptical distortion in the prints betrays the mount's struggle. Better proof is the pattern change in groups to forging, a clear sign of slippage.

This high up the freeze is deeper than below, the going much slicker. Red feels for the Appaloosa, and for his own roan. But as long as the shooter is riding, Red needs to stay saddled too.

On the next stop, Red's stomach rumbles. And the wind picks up.

In idle luffs, followed by a spell of dead air, then a furious gust. Eyes downturned and misting, he can still make out the forging of the killer's horse.

Every ten or so yards a hoof has punched through. Ankles too narrow for its weight, a big horse might go lame at this. Or not. But deepening cold makes climbing hard and tracking even harder.

Perhaps on FBI orders, the ski resort has left its floodlights on. Even squinting, he is nearly blinded by the glare. Still, unless the killer is a shape-shifter, he can't just fly off the mountain. So Red will follow until the man turns to make his stand.

The roan struggles as they near the intersection of an intermediate trail with a double black diamond run. Red urges his mount on. Seconds later, a shrill chattering noise breaks the light wind; the snow makers have kicked on.

For the first time and without warning, Kismet rears and whinnies. In less than a second, Red realizes that snow makers sound just like rattlesnakes. Enough to spook any horse.

He dismounts and tugs the weary animal's reins, seeking cover by heading into the trees. Leaning on a spindly pine, he is unable to recall being this tired, ever. But this is the first time anyone still alive has seen the killer. He is determined it won't be the last.

Behind him in the night sky, a black FBI chopper flashes by. He ignores it. From where Red stands the mountain embraces the sky and becomes the miracle that the Plains tribes imagined it to be. His mother once said, "A test comes between a boy and a man; the man accepts it; the boy knows he is not yet ready." Red Kravitz smiles at that memory, pulls up his collar and reckons that now is the time.

* * *

Two hours later, Red Kravitz takes in an unobstructed glimpse of the summit. He is standing on a double black diamond trail called Aces & Eights, bounded only by unyielding spruce and open air.

Far below lies the ski chalet, with peaked roofs and cantilevered balconies, its broad windows blackened against sniper fire. A good move. If they know one thing it is this: the man can shoot.

For the tiniest shard of time he wonders if Molly has slipped protective custody and is, even now, whispering coverage for later broadcast about the lone rider coming after the bad guy. Smiling at that, he goes to his phone, powering it back up. "Slo. You got a fix on Molly?"

"Say wh — "

"What about Bear?"

"Moun — Nob — "

"Slo. Speak up. I can't..." He watches the battery icon flicker, then die. He stares at the cell phone and whispers, "Just great." Hunching his shoulders up, he lowers his head and leans into an agonizing climb.

* * *

Thirty minutes later, headed down, the riderless Appaloosa staggers past, its eyes hollow and desperate from a brutal climb in dry thin air. Still saddled with a three-quarter center-fire rig over a salea, its beaded doeskin scabbard is empty.

Red dismounts, strokes Kismet's mane. Then he unboots the buffalo rifle, yokes it in his arms and treks on alone, legs aching, images going in and out of focus. Already the click of Kismet's descending hoofbeats have melted from brittle echoes into the low shrill skift, giving on to a ringing silence, soon followed by ghostly percussion, the rhythmic rising wordless chant of braves readying for battle.

Hallucinations.

Only that.

The real Indians are all dead, even the ancient spirits evaporated. Now it's just breeds and res' drunks. Soon not a trace of either.

He melts into the last trees before Bearpaw turns to stone and snow, then leans on a fir's stout bole to survey the mountain.

He knows its faces and moods, knows it's cold by the way the snow sticks, knows the wind angle by the patterns of spindrift, and can spot a rotten soffit by how it glistens or shadows. When all is considered, he knows Bearpaw better than he knows himself.

On foot and alone, he follows the Appaloosa tracks up until they end. Where its rider dismounted, his footprints puncture the snowcrust. Red studies the tracks, sees no sign of spurs, heel-bands, shanks or rowels. Kneeling down, he traces them with a gloved finger. The heel is broad and shallow, like a mocassin, or Indian snow boot.

Rising up, he continues to make trail. The big drag-tracks, rushing into a long slide with each landing step, veer abruptly left and down, away from the summit. A block of adrenaline ices him up.

His quarry has turned.

All this, feinting, was... for what? To make everyone think that he would start picking off people from a sheltered perch?

And now what?

Red doesn't know.

But it's getting colder. Being a big man, the killer needs a lot of calories to stay warm. Yet there has been no sign all day that he has eaten. Continued flight would leave him hungry, exhausted and outnumbered. When the Appaloosa had passed, it lacked bedroll or pack. No tent, no source of food.

So what does...

The question does not fully form before the air goes still, and Red hears the signature double hammer click of a Sharps.

Spinning away, he ducks and holds his breath.

Inches above him the pine's bole explodes splinters, then chatters and cries as the stress works through it. Not a second later, the report rings and echoes off Bearpaw's granite flanks.

Glancing up, Red stares at the shattered maw of splinters and bark, then rolls down and away, hugging his own Sharps as he tumbles.

* * *

He stops in a deep hollow littered with pine straw and salted with granular snow. Backing up to the nearest lodgepole, he slips off his belt and holds the shiny concha buckle up where it can reflect the shooter.

A distorted image reveals the groundworks of some kind of storage building, its roof incomplete. The dark form of a big man moves, then ducks away, the long octagonal barrel going down last.

Red sizes it up.

The guy has the high ground. He has good cover, concrete breastworks sheltered by thick pine branches and a wide field of fire. He has a weapon lethal at a mile, maybe enough ammunition to mow down a small army.

While the unfinished building will blunt the wind, in time the cold will drive him out. Already the feeling had left Red's ears, the ridge and tip of his nose, and his cheeks seemed like Arctic steel. Without shelter he won't last the night.

He re-loops and buckles his concha belt. The wind turns westerly, carrying a banner of smoke. Looking up he watches its skeins twisting and knotting as they drift by.

Risking a more direct glance, he sees the inner walls of the unfinished bunker limned by a pale glow. With numb, cracking lips, he mutters, "The man has a fire," but the words seem slurred.

To reach the bunker he has to cross a steep icy ski trail, lit up by towering floodlights. Or circle the summit, sneaking up from behind. But that approach puts him in the sharp teeth of a ravenous wind. After all day in the saddle without food, he has no chance of making it.

Squeezing the rifle stock in his right hand, Red grips the dead cell phone in his left, checks for a clearance in the trees above and lofts it in a high arc. It dissolves in night above the black diamond trail. Red reckons its descent and eases his Sharps level, clicking the Creedmore sight up. Seconds later the dead phone scrapes through ice-clad branches and then skitters on the frozen slope.

A silhouette darts up and fires at the unfamiliar sound. Before the figure can duck back, Red squeezes off a good shot.

The man flinches and spins away.

Then it's all echoes. Loud, deafening. And confusing. Because between the shots of the two Sharps' rifles came another sound, another echo or the report of a third rifle.

But no.

They are alone.

It must be, could only be, his mind, again, like the Indian drums earlier. No Indians, no drums. No third rifle, no miraculous help. Just the two of us, pardner. And a long cold night ahead.

He smiles.

The west hasn't changed. It's just gone global.

As the thought leaves his mind, a single tattered cloud rides the wind across the starfield, and a rumble of the U.S. cavalry's artillery shook the slope. Soon the harbinger cloud grows to a curdling monster.

Winter thunderstorm. Lightning and all. Leaving no room for choppers, and no footage for probing cameras. Making what is about to happen as private as an unspoken prayer.

Any last thoughts, Kravitz? the Indian asks the Jew.

The Jew turns it around, asks, didn't Crazy Daisy once say something about ghost dancers avenging the Plains Indians?

The Indian in him laughs. Hey, we have Casino's now. Your relatives in Reno know that.

Red smiles at his two halves.

The first volley of thunder sweeps down the mountain. Followed by echoes, then silence. Minutes pass, every second of each one drains precious heat away, before a voice cries out, "Hey, Red!"

More confusion. Sounds like... "Bear?"

A laugh. "You winged me! Same damn arm as Walsh."

"Bear?"

More laughter. "If they wanted to sneak up on me, they should've sent a Pawnee, not a half-blood Crow. You made more noise than a drunk Kiowa in a Vegas whorehouse."

"Bear?"

"It was me, you dumb watered-down Absaroka!"

Red listens to the tick of fine ice settle on the crusted snow, the pulse of his own rapid breathing, the drumbeat of his heart. "Is there a reason for all this, or you just feelin' ornery?"

"Grievances."

"Grievances?" Red sounds like an echo, because the idea makes no sense.

"You know, when the Germans killed all those Jews, there was a big outrage. We hung those Nazis. When they found them, the Germans hung them, too."

Red can't believe that Bear is avenging the Holocaust. But if there is a better explanation, before he freezes to death Kravitz needs to hear it. "So what is it you want, Bear?"

"Our homeland back, no reservations. The Jews got the country they wanted."

"Not without a fight, they didn't," Red tells him.

"So here I am. You wanna join me?"

Red closes his eyes. "Bear, we'd be Butch and Sundance. And they were white."

"They had the low ground."

"They ran out of ammunition. Like you will."

"Not for a good while," Bear assures him.

"You'll freeze."

"Got a buffalo robe, a sougan, a good Arctic mummy bag and a nice warm fire."

"You'll starve."

"I'm socked in with airtights."

"How?" Red feels dizzy. His teeth begin to chatter. But as long as he is talking, he won't fall asleep.

"Noisy paid off his tab with work. I lent him my wheels till it snowed, then the Ski Doo. Told him to stock this place up."

"But..."

"Shit, Red. There was so much construction and trail groomers and carpenters up here they thought he was one of the crew."

"You trusted a drunk?"

The question whistles off in crimpy winds before Bear let go a chilling high-pitched laugh. "Of course not. What do you think I was doing 'working on my place up at Pine Ridge?' Checking on Noisy's progress, and finishing the job."

"But Noisy knew, so you..."

"He saw me pitching nuggets into Big Muddy. I didn't like killing an old drunk, but he just refused to freeze. I didn't like killing Daisy either, but every now and again she would get real clear, and then with all those Ivy League smarts and that shrewd half-Jew brain of yours, you'd figure it out."

If misplaced trust is going to cost him his life, Red feels entitled to know what set Bear off. "Why Jeb Holloway?"

"He's been here since Custer, making our tribal land a playpen for people who forget that Indians are America's Jews."

"And Jarnow?"

"Cut from the same hide. His kin stood with Marcus Reno at Little Bighorn, and walked away alive."

"Mona?" demands Red, wanting the whole mystery solved, even if no one else will ever know.

"Why you know B.S. Walsh killed Mona, Red. He had to. Or folks hereabout would've lynched him."

Red cradles the Sharps across his arms and stands up. He stares down the bore of Bear's rifle and says, "I already missed the best shot I'll get. I'm coming over."

"Why?" Bear says.

"I'm hopin' to keep from freezing."

"Plant your weapon's muzzle in the snow."

Red obeys. Again he hears Indian drums, loud and clear and rhythmic. The din rises as he nears the eye of death. Overhead, a spark joins two clouds, lighting up warpaint on Bear's face. Black and red across the temple, downward in slashes from the cheeks.

"Get yourself out of the cold. You hungry?"

"Some." Red pulls himself over a cinder block half-wall and in. Bear has some boudins browning on an open fire. In the roofed back of the bunker lie crates of weapons, ammunition, equipment and food. Racked along the back, just visible in the shadow from the half-roof, leans a row of arrows, tipped with pitch. To the far right is a reverse-lashed bow crafted from Osage orange.

Bear offers him a naked concrete floor. "Let's eat. Smoke the pipe. See what the Great Spirit wants us to do."

* * *

Once his marrow thaws, Red lances a fork through the sweet buffalo sausage that sizzles on the fire. The big Cheyenne sucks one off a knife, chews it and sweeps a glance through swaying pines toward sparking clouds. Then asks Red, "You didn't hear the drums?"

"We're real cold. There was a lot of wind. Lots of choppers..."

Bear points a finger. "You heard them." He slaps the deputy on the arm and laughs. "You're a true pure quill Indian after all."

"What's this about, brother?"

Bear glares back. "The Nazis changed the laws to strip the Jews, then marched them off to die. The whites did the same to us." His eyes drift to the mountain's summit. "And like those Jews, we lost everything."

"Sounds like a good case to me."

An ugly smile mars Bear's face. "Even Crows know a white's word is no good."

"All the hippies became born-again hustlers, Bear. Nobody cares anymore."

"That's to find out," he says. "Your belly full?"

"Mostly."

Bear nods. "Thawed out?"

"Mostly."

"Mosey back to your white brothers. Tell them I'm waiting."

"Bear, they got tear gas..." a flash from a small boy's mind crashes through the cold to reveal a huge white man in a blue uniform raising a baton over his mother. He blinks if off, then presses on, "...sleeping gases that puts you out..."

Bear smiles and turns around. "Got gas masks. Even tried one out. I'm ready."

"And the arrows?"

Bear's face lights up. "Cheyenne know the world ends in fire. Old Noisy bought his last drinks by wiring magnesium bundles to lodgepoles..." A memory of bright wire on the storeroom floor flashes through Red's mind. "...then stringing them together with magnesium wire." Bear raises his nose and sniffs. "Wind out of the west. Just right. Should burn up the whole mountain."

"You'll go with it."

Bear laughs so hard his eyes squeeze shut. "Took me a long time, brother, to realize that our kind was dead before we were even born."

The way he says it leaves nothing else to say.

Red gets up. "You gonna crop my head while my back's turned?"

Bear cradles his long tom. "Best make tracks while I'm still confused."

Red scissors over the half-wall and drops down. The barrel of Bear's Sharps comes up as the Cheyenne draws air. "What's that scent?"

Red smells it too, but shakes his head. "Pine sap. From where you blew a big hole right through. That's all."

"You're not a very good liar." Bear scans the slope below.

"It wouldn't be real smart to lie, would it?" Red starts to walk away. Behind him the hammer on the Sharps sets with a hard double click. "Who else's up here?"

Red turns, watches Bear's eye slot in the Creedmore sight as a bright red dot crawls up Bear's arm. "Don't you Jews have some prayer you say before dying?"

"It's called Kaddish," Kravitz tells him.

"Take long?"

"Too long for Nazis to let us finish," he says, playing for time, watching the laser dot settle below Bear's cheekbone.

Bear seems to want it to go on. "Why not try the skookum line, see if you can cut a deal for your sorry Crow life with the dark siders."

Red's smile is pure sadness. "That way I'd be no different from Jeb or Mona or Jarnow..." His eyes refocus on the octagonal eye of death, Bear's finger closing on the trigger. "So long, Crow."

The report echoes off the mountain and Red drops. He feels nothing right away, all sensation lost in the adrenal wash of shock.

But when he looks up, Bear is braced on one trembling hand. Blood washes over his war paint. His eyelids flicker twice before he topples out of the bunker.

From the trees below comes a rush of boots pumping through the snow, then a panting yell, "Kravitz?"

He shouts back, "Molly?"

She comes up, her weapon at the ready. "Are you part of all this?"

He finds himself unwounded, looks up at the sky and smiles. "We were talking over the pipe. That's Indian for seeing if we could work things out without going to war."

"What did you decide?"

He blows out exhaustion. "Like the Middle East. Sometimes you can bring the parties to the table, but they still go on fighting."

"What I can't decide..." Molly begins "...is whether it makes a better story if you killed him, or if you were both killed in a shoot-out."

Red studies what Molly has become, keeping a careful eye on her laser-sighted rifle.

"What do you think?" she asks.

He feels colder than the night.

She shrugs. "Either way, a reporter can't be materially involved in a story she covers..." She looks over at Bear's big body crumpled in the snow. "...which means that if you live, you have to be the one that killed Bear. Okay?"

Roiling clouds stab the nearest light tower with a cracking flash of lightning. The ensuing pulse of air hits them like a collapsing wall. With the floodlights out, images condense into featureless silhouettes on dull white.

Beyond the fading roll of thunder comes the faint sounds of Indian drums. He turns full circle to hear better, then looks back at Molly. When the drumbeat dies, Red dips a shallow nod. "I killed Bear. He didn't give me any choice."

"But a Sharps leaves a bigger hole, so you'll have to shoot him again."

"Okay," Red says, considering this his best choice. Perhaps what he had imagined as drums were just the strange reverberation of thunder off Bearpaw's facets, playing tricks on him. And perhaps the near-miss lightning was the result of being near its highest point, a fact he remembers from college physics. Perhaps the whole world can be explained on terms that make sense to white minds. Eventually. But not tonight. Which is what makes this night different from all other nights.

"You'll be a hero," she says.

"And you'll be a star," he says back.

"Best outcome, overall."

"We better get our story straight," Red tells her.

She nods. "You two disagreed. But he said he couldn't kill another Indian without giving him a fair chance..." This showed how little Molly knows of tribal warfare "...so you picked up your Sharps. He had you in the sights. Then you said something that staggered him."

Red prompts, "And then..."

"Then you leveled your Sharps in one hand..." Only Bear could do that, a gun that heavy. "...shot from the hip and hit him in the head..."

"Billy Dixon would've been proud," he murmurs.

"Who?"

He reminds her of the legend. Maybe she could weave it in. Whatever motivated Bear, it was too complicated to make a punchy story. So when the facts won't sell news, you change the facts.

Molly knows what people want to hear. Possessive lust for a beautiful woman they would buy. The men would feel it and the women believe it. But some latter-day activist Indian rights fanatic, striking out at the white establishment to avenge ancient tribal grievances? Red himself has trouble believing that.

After he blows a bigger hole in Bear's head, the answer does not magically appear in letters of blood and brain along the base of the unfinished building's wall. So he needs to find out the truth another way.

* * *

"In the end, everyone gets religion," Micky is convinced.

Red blinks, too cold even to nod.

He had staggered down the mountain alone, while Molly rode back on the fresh mount that she had stolen from Bearpaw's stables. She is unarmed, having wiped down and stashed her lethal rifle in the arsenal behind where Bear's lifeless body lay, icing up as the temperature falls and the wind sings what to Red sounds like an Indian funeral dirge.

Icicles shaking on swaying branches become ceremonial rattles, and he expects to hear drums and chants again. But there is just Micky's face, the medical examiner doing the after-death play-by-play. Which always included an interview. "He let you get the drop on him?"

Red sticks with the story, "I said I knew he got Mona pregnant."

"I thought it was B.S. Walsh."

He throws off a shrug. "Maybe neither man knew. So I'm going to need a somebody to say if the fetus is half-black or half-Cheyenne."

Micky isn't hopeful. "Depends on how far along she was, Red. Early on, all fetuses look pretty much alike."

Red claps him on the back. "Do your best, Micky. But do let me know."

"With Jeb gone, nobody's pressing for release of Mona's body."

Hitting a wall, Red wiggles toward another way out. "Seen Molly?"

Micky tells him, "She rode up the mountain, tryin' to get close to the killer."

"Surprised she didn't bring her cameraman, Al."

"Somebody put it in Al's head that Native Americans take exception to having their pictures took."

Red looks surprised. "Do tell? So she went it alone, did Molly?"

"Without a blink. Against FBI orders. She is really something."

Red smiles. "We call it chutzpah."

"Whatever it is, she's over there," he points.

Looking more than a little concerned, Molly stands encircled by state policemen and FBI. She waves Red over. On legs numb and weak, he hobbles into a brace of skeptical stares.

*　*　*

A bow-tied FBI lawyer named Simon Holtz plays ringmaster.

Washington had flown him out of Dulles to Great Falls, then by chopper to the ski lodge. A state police detective introduces Holtz, then gets to the problem: FBI recon men on the mountain claim to have heard six shots in an extended exchange. Red's story requires only two.

Molly remains calm, but knows they are departing from a straight Hollywood-style old west shoot-out. Red frowns and scoffs, "Six?"

"Three shots inside a minute, then silence. For maybe fifteen minutes. Then a weaker crack, then a big one," insists Holtz. "Ten minutes later, another loud one."

Red rescripts on the spot. "When a man has a Sharps aimed at you, it kind of gets your full attention."

A few state cops laugh. In a world where you're not quite sure exactly what happened, but fear for your life, you remember what you did and what provoked it. These men had been there. They understand.

Red scratches the back of his neck. "There was a small crack."

"But you said he fired first," Holtz cross-examines. Red forces an unfelt calm and spins the yarn. "I found that queer, too. You know, how little noise it made, the Sharps. We knew from our forensic guys," he nods toward Micky and Mo, "that he was using old ammo. And firearm experts will tell you, Mr. Holtz, that old ammo sometimes gets rotten. When that happens, the cartridge goes off, but the bang is just a sharp wofft sound. And the slug tends to die."

An old Montana trooper is nodding, because he knows guns. The lawyer, on the other hand, is squinting. "So you're saying his gun misfired?"

"You were lucky," says the trooper.

"It comes around," Red admits. "You can never tell when."

The lawyer isn't as easy. "And the second report?"

"Mine, my Sharps, going off."

"What about the other three reports?" hammers Holtz. "And the last one, too loud for anything but — "

Red shrugs. "I didn't hear them. Your guys did. So I can't tell you what it was. But a lot of things on this mountain sound like a gunshot."

"For example," the lawyer presses.

"For example a sheet of water freezing so hard it pops off a hunk of granite. For example the wind blowing the final ice crystal onto a soffit that makes it collapse into an avalanche. For example an old tree, stiff with dying wood, blown so hard by a blizzard that snaps down the bole. For example a lightning bolt so close it cracks before it rumbles. Sounds like that." Red finishes.

If Daisy Ramirez were here, she would have added the sound of spirits cracking birch to kindle campfires in the sky. Or unseen UFOs recharging their batteries in storm clouds. The world is full of sounds that only certain ears can hear. But he chooses not to press the point with Simon Holtz.

"So you're saying..."

"If you want to find out what happened, get up there and have a look."

"But..." the lawyer checks. "...he really is dead?"

"Unless you can resurrect him."

"I'd sure like to hear his side of it," the man says.

"No you wouldn't," Red rebuts. "Washington has never listened to a red man. You're not listening to me now."

It is strange to Red that when logic fails, political rectitude can be so convincing. But then Al has just poked a lens into their group. With its intrusion, all reality dissolves. Red's parting words are, "Gentlemen, I've got paperwork to do and a friend to mourn. Just don't count the flesh wound on his arm. That came a few days ago via B.S. Walsh, or a guy by that name you folks gifted us. I hope you'll excuse me."

Behind him, Molly holds up a mike. "That was Deputy Red Kravitz of Sanctuary, Montana, whose single-handed heroism resulted in the slaying of a serial killer whom locals have dubbed, 'The Sharpshooter,' after the famous old western rifle he used on his victims. Now the killer is dead, his rampage finally over. And the sleepy little town of Sanctuary can return to a way of life little changed from when..."

Red walks into the comforting darkness of night. He feels the sting of the cold, smells the tang of smoke from the fireplace chimney, then grabs a porch rail and throws up. Behind him the creaking door lets an old state trooper out. "First time?" he asks.

"Yeah," Red breathes, closing his eyes. "He was my best friend."

"That's tough," the man says. "You gonna be alright?"

Red answers honestly. "I don't know."

"Takes time," he says. "But you've got it."

"Do I?" Red wonders how the man can be so sure of the future while his own version of the past has just crumbled and blown off in the storm.

"I'm Seth Diehl," the trooper says. He draws his cigartip full red, then curdles the night air with smoke. "When they was passing your file photo around, I saw it in your eyes."

"What?" comes the question. But it's not. Red is just making sounds. His thoughts are far away.

"The look of a survivor."

Red's mind flashes images. Crow warriors standing with Marcus Reno against Sitting Bull's Sioux. A skeletal face with empty eyes, fleshless fingers hooked on barbed wire. His pregnant mother rolling in the street to protect her unborn, a Chicago policeman raising his baton.

Seth Diehl's words crash through a glimpse of the past, dragging him back to the moment. "I told them you'd make it. You won me better'n hundred bucks sashaying in. I mean, after your roan come down, they was all betting if the shooter didn't get you the cold would." The weathered trooper sucks on his cigar. "Yep, you can tell a lot about a man by the way he looks."

Red keeps his doubts unspoken.

He had been looking at Standing Bear all his life, except for the years he was away at Penn. Maybe that was when the man began being haunted by silent silhouettes on the ridge above the Little Bighorn River. Maybe to him those hallucinations were the real world, and everything else an illusion.

If Bear's mind was that far gone, the only way he could reconcile apparent reality with those mirages was to live like a man in a prison whose bars were history. The only way to break out was to destroy the bars, to turn back the clock, arm himself and dab on war paint, to make a stand against his captors. To live free or die.

Or maybe, both more truthful and more disturbing, Bear had a side that not even Red had been able to see, a side that could do the things he had done. All these possibilities. He would sleep on them, dream on them. If he slept or dreamed at all.

Still, some things never seem to change.

Red Kravitz had spent most of the day alone, tracking one man. True to form, Molly Mendelbaum remains long after Red left, chatting up sources, creating her version of the drama.

Tonight, as close to the story as the air, she would give it to the viewers, quick, pithy, provocative. Emmy-award-winning stuff. Opening doors through which she could step and move on. Beyond — what was it she called it? — "... the sleepy little town of Sanctuary..."

MOURNING NEWS

A wise Crow elder once said, "An honest man who sleeps with a lie wakes up a stranger to himself." Maybe that's what keeps Red awake. Or maybe it is just horniness, waiting for Molly to come back.

She never does.

Night drains away, unrelieved by rest, unhaunted by dreams. Exhaustion wrestles with shock, battling forever on the brink of sleep. At sunup he arises feeling older, stiffer, more tired than he imagined possible. Both blinding and enlightening, daybreak illuminates the dark truth that he had never known his best friend. So how can he ever know what a friend is?

Some questions are best unasked, because in truth they have no answer. At least none that stands up to a cold eye and a hot tongue. Despite physical proximity, time can move people apart. With the endless tumble of days, distance increases and fates change.

Sometimes, as with Red Kravitz, people return to their birthplace to sort out what happened to the child they left behind, to listen for echoes of promises that person made, to find the path to fulfillment. But by that time the echoes have faded and the child vanishes.

So Red believes that every person deserved two graves. One for the dreams that die when the kid grows up, another for the dreamless adult aftermath, spent chasing success while searching out a grander reason for being alive.

More frightening than awaiting the killshot of a Sharps, maybe there is no reason for this. Or maybe our reasons get scripted by people like Molly Mendelbaum, whose sound bites digest complex matters into stories not true, but easy to swallow. By day's end, Standing Bear Hatcher would be whatever Molly wanted him to be. The truth is different, but never matters.

The truth doesn't pin viewers to their sets. It's slippery and snakelike and venomous, and far more dangerous. You find its face staring back at you in the mirror after you sleep with a lie.

Because when Red studies his own reflection after his best friend had been killed by a woman he thought he might love, he sees only wind-scoured sunburnt tissue hanging on dying bone, an animal in its small cage about to go out and fill its hungry belly. It is that, and nothing more, that draws him to The Elk.

Bear is dead, but The Elk remains unlocked. So it doesn't surprise Red to find people there, conducting an informal memorial service to its late owner. Not in recollections shared, but in service, the way Bear always had.

Big-headed, burly and shaggy, Ivan Konev works short orders, bitching, "I couldn't sleep last night." Bussing food, Luke Brody answers, "You never sleep." Ivan insisting, "I really didn't sleep last night. Not your routine insomnia."

Jake Laney leans on the Rockola. Next to him in the booth sits the core of the winter crew: Zack Farnes, Pak Randal and Mangey Fuller. Across from them, Moonlight and mother Doris, one cigarette dangling from her lips, another smoldering away in an ashtray. Red pats her shoulder and whispers, "No smoking." She looks up and he says, "For Bear, huh?"

From the Bunn-O-Matic beaker, Mailman Brody pours Red a cup of fierce Texas tar and Doris admits, "Ivan scrapes a mean hash brown." Moonlight breathes, "Eggs not bad, either. A little runny but that's what toast is for."

Micky and Mo waddle in, hang their covers on pegs. "We smelled food," says Mo. "And thought we might have a bite," Micky adds. In this way the Tweedles team up, one starting a thought that the other finishes. In that spirit, they sit down together and flag Luke Brody for coffee.

"My toast is burnt," Laney gripes. But Mangey Fuller counters, "Mine's okay." With each agreeable disagreement, the place feels so close to normal that Red expects to see Bear walk out and throw his arms apart, laughing, "You thought your woman killed me, you silly goddamn Crow!"

Instead Ivan's voice shouts, "Somebody turn on the TV, so's to see what's happening."

Red slips behind the bar, grabs the remote and powers the tube up. On screen Molly faces the morning sun near Daisy's place. Pak Randal speaks through a full mouth, "Damn if she don't look real fresh for a gal's been rode to broke, Red."

The others laugh and Moonlight smiles, but Red spoils it: "Not by me. At least not last night."

On TV, the wind banners Molly's shimmering hair as she speaks, "New developments in the case of the Sharpshooter, as people are calling the killer in Sanctuary, Montana."

A hush blankets the viewers as they sip harsh java.

Molly charges on. "The night after Jeb Holloway was killed, the local deputy made advances on the victim's widow in her own home." Molly walks toward Poker Bluff, tracked by Al's jostling camera. "But if Red Kravitz did kill Jeb Holloway out of jealousy, spurned by Mona, then who killed Leonard Jarnow? It may be that Kravitz, best friend of Standing Bear Hatcher, coaxed him into it. Hatcher, a pure Northern Cheyenne Indian whose ancestors fought at Little Bighorn, may have taken little persuading. Especially knowing that the tracker would be his best friend. During the chase, Kravitz warned Federal helicopters away, claiming they would be easy targets. And once the pursuit left Timberland Wildlife Preserve, Federal officials lacked the authority to pursue.

"So Kravitz followed to the top of the mountain, where he may earlier have offered to make a 'Butch and Sundance' stand in a fort-like structure that Federal officials found laid-in with enough supplies for two months. After the too memorable disasters at the Branch Davidian compound in Waco and the shoot-out at Ruby Ridge, federal officials were taking a more cautious approach. It was during this holding pattern that Kravitz turned and fired a single shot through his best friend's head. Making it look like a shoot-out left one dead, the law triumphant once again. This is Molly Mendelbaum near Sanctuary, Montana."

Like a perfect wooden Indian, Red stands motionless, unable even to swallow.

Ivan Konev, who has been watching Molly while his hash browns blackened on the grill, speaks first. "Now I know why you bunk that bitch,

Kravitz, because she really knows how to screw you."

Everyone laughs because they're so sure he's no killer. So he smiles back and then looks around.

Who is it you know?

Do you know me like I knew Bear?

Is Molly's improv less crazy than what happened?

Approaching Micky and Mo, Red rests his palms on their table. "I sure would be obliged if you find Bear's prints on that knife. I need something to keep me afloat."

Micky and Mo rise as if commanded. But Red pushes them back down. "Finish your breakfast. Whatever happens happens."

* * *

"We're just curious, Kravitz," Seth Diehl says. He's the same officer who said that Red looked like a survivor, that lethal night at Bearpaw. Diehl throws off an awkward shrug. "With the news and all, I had to ask if you can account for your time during the killings."

"On the last one, I was wearing Leonard Jarnow's brains, taking incoming."

Seth Diehl risks a smile. "Other than Jarnow..."

At the moment, Red is disinclined to lay the groundwork for his defense on Molly's alibis. He is still squirming when Doris appears behind him with a cigarette and, "Someone to see you, Red."

"We're busy, Doris."

"Somebody with a confession," she says.

Seth Diehl spins half around, then back at Red, who says, "Send him in."

But it is not a him. It's Caldera Cunningham, eyes as deep and hopeless as hell, her voice as insubstantial as a ghost. She leans on Ivan's Sharps replica with a thin, trembling hand. "I killed Jeb Holloway because he did such dirty things to my body." As wild as her eyes is her hair, a bramble of dry strands. "Then his wife, that Jezebel. Then Leonard Jarnow tried to blackmail me, because Mona told him about me and Jeb."

Red checks the state trooper's rolling eyes, then says, "Doris, take Caldera's statement."

"Aren't you going to lock me up?" Caldera asks.

"No. You're a first offender. So we'll just send you home on your own recognizance, ask that you don't leave the state."

"Why would I leave the state?" she asks. "That's why I killed all the politicians, because they're the devil's disciples. I prayed over it and that's what God said to do."

"Doris, like I said. Take Caldera's statement. And put out the cigarette."

"Yes, sir." Doris coughs, escorting the other woman away.

The balding cop grins. "I guess you're off the hook. Unless there really was something between you and Mona Holloway."

Kravitz confesses, "The night after the killing she was drunk. I drove her to the door and left her inside. That's all. But while I was searching Jeb's bedroom under a legal warrant the next day Mona popped out of a connecting bathroom in the altogether."

"So if anyone came in, she could claim you'd made her take her clothes off?"

"I can't get inside her mind that day. And I sure didn't get into her pants."

Diehl seems to dwell on that, as if not convinced, but moves on. "You're pretty good with a Sharps. The one shot you got off at Standing Bear."

"Maybe I shoot better when I'm scared."

"You see the other gunman out there?"

The question startles him, but he just shrugs. "No. What other..."

"We're trying to make out how Hatcher was standing, guess the two of you were looking through those Creedmore's, each one seeing his best friend. Maybe you heard the crack and figured he'd fired, though you didn't see no muzzle flash. So you fired back."

"Now that you mention it..." He brings one finger up, as if realizing for the first time. "Somebody in cover shot... Bear... first."

"Somebody who liked you a lot is my guess."

"This is the official view?"

"This is something we don't want to rush into and end up with moose scat all over our official snow boots, if you sniff the spoor."

Red nods. "Bear claimed he was on a tear against the whites who'd stole the Indian's land. Bearpaw was a sacred mountain. So that's where he chose to make his stand. Jeb Holloway's family pushed the Indians onto reservations and helped themselves to tribal hunting grounds. One of the early Jarnows was among the bluecoats with Custer. Served with Marcus Reno.

But as B. S. Walsh once forgettably said, 'All that was all a long time ago.'"

"Some grudges don't weary much under the weight of time," Diehl reckons. When the passing silence assures him that Red has nothing more to say, the visitor resumes his questions. "How do Daisy and Noisy fit in?"

"They were witnesses. Plain truth," Red says. "Bear went bad. I don't know when or how or why. He used to be a big football hero on TV, interviewed as the resurrected Cheyenne brave, proof that American Indians survived genocide. After that he becomes a highly-paid joke, a clown strutting in a ring with a war bonnet and robe. Next rung down the ladder he becomes a bardog in the piss-ass town he hoped to leave behind forever. Then Mona Holloway offers him a job bartending at Bearpaw. He'll make at least ten times more money than in Sanctuary. Plus, Mona says, there are rich good-looking women, white women, who want to do the wild thing with a wild man like him. And that, she whispers, is where the big tips come in."

"Don't sound like half-bad work," Diehl interjects with a mischievous smile.

Red smiles back. "To you or me, maybe. But when Bear was with the Dallas Cowboys, gorgeous women came on to him. He had the money. Then he finds he's gone from being a well-paid star where he turned girls away to a well-paid gigolo where he can't say no. And any job where you can't say no is the worst job you'll ever have."

"Just say 'no,' huh?" The big man's smile broadens.

"That's one take on it. He saw himself working for the whites. Now he knew the Crow had a long history of that, but the Cheyenne? Well, the

Northern Cheyenne pretty much played their best hand at Little Bighorn. And nothing they've been dealt since has changed their minds."

"One more question," the visitor says. This is usually the place where the shrewd cop shows he's been onto your grift all along. It's where he points out that Red's version still leaves at least one more shot fired than was reported. But he surprises Red by saying, "You ever give any serious consideration to that opportunity with Mona Holloway?"

Red's eyebrows arch. "If you like women, you can't stop your reflexes when a woman like Mona is naked. But there was no history, no spark, no connection. The time you get in real trouble with beautiful women is when you let your dick overrule your common sense."

"That tends to happen a bit," he says.

"But not this time."

The state trooper rises with a faint grunt of effort and shakes Red's hand. "That's all I have. Anything else that puts a nice bow on this before election day, we'd sure appreciate."

Red walks Seth Diehl to the hallway. "Give Caldera Cunningham a listen."

Diehl's smile grows as large as the mysteries Bear took to his grave. "Why not? It won't be the wildest story I looked into today."

SWEET SORROW

"Am I forgiven?" Molly spoke the words through a swirl of coffee vapor. Like ancient ghosts departing boot hill, The Elk's other patrons rise and drift off. The place feels strange without Bear, stranger talking to his killer after he is dead. Even now the big man seems present, back turned, polishing a glass and checking the two in the mirror. Kravitz breaks the waking dream long enough to respond, "I'm not in the forgiveness business, Molly."

"Strange, no? The last thing you wanted from me was forgiveness for being stupid."

"Being stupid's not a capital offense, Molly."

"I saved your life."

"So you reckoned you're entitled to risk it again? It is no doubt a better story with Deputy Kravitz, now a suspect in the mysterious series of murders out in Wild Ass, Montana, still alive. But did you even think one instant beyond the story?"

For a few seconds she studies her hands. "You came through clean. I knew you would." Too angry for words, his silence hardens. Leaving her to jump start the exchange. "So if you're not in the forgiveness business, what business are you in?"

"As of right now, the arrest business."

"So are you going to arrest me?"

"For saving my life? No. Maybe you thought Bear would kill me. But he could've done that anytime."

"So why did he let you live right up to the end?"

"Like Bear himself once said, Molly. It's one of those answers we may never know." But Red knows that vengeance killings among plains tribes added humiliation to defeat. Each time the deputy had failed to find the killer, the local Northern Cheyenne outwitted the Ivy League Crow.

"Will you tell me if you do?"

He gives his feelings a sad smile. "You got chutzpah, kid. I'll say that."

Molly goes Indian red. "God, Kravitz! I broadcasted a retraction! Everything's fixed."

Red's stares into his cooling java. "Look, if we had a real smart mayor, he'd probably call me in and explain the delicacy of having a suspected killer as your law officer, say it would be better for the town if I just went back to clerking the store."

"You're saying you've been fired? By that... that... putz Augie Suder?"

Red shakes his head. "I said if we had a smart mayor."

"Isn't there anything else you want to do with your... potential, other than..." she sweeps her hand around, the motion sufficient to both define the place and dismiss it. "Stop drinking the coffee long enough to smell it. There's no future here."

"For Indians there's never a future. But there's always a present," he says.

"Red, what? You want to end up like Noisy?"

"You'd like me better rich, is that it?" Red concludes.

"That's a side effect," she says.

"Of what?"

"Of ambition, Kravitz. You're a Jew. What are you doing with that part of you?"

"Well, Molly. Let me tell you a little story about Jews in the west..."

"Spare me, Kravitz. I'm full up with morality tales. They're out of fashion."

"I'm not trying for fashion, Molly. I'm showing you the way things are."

She falls silent, draws a short breath, then lets it out. "Okay."

"His name was Albert Speyer. Came over from Prussia around the time of the Mexican War. Did so well with trading posts, like the little one my folks left me, that he was set. One thing you'd admire about Speyer: he was ambitious. Yes, sir. So like a lot of upstart parvenus, Speyer cashed in his western empire, took his riches to New York City and became a speculative investor."

"Good move," Molly interjects, hoping to get through.

"Well, Speyer joined a conspiracy to corner the gold market. At a time when there was no confidence in government notes. The real thing was gold coins. Whoever owned gold, they figured, was infinitely rich. And so, believing the risk was zero, Speyer and his pals bought gold. Demand went up. Cost followed. His partners took their profits, but Speyer put every cent he had in gold."

"Then cashed out a rich man," Molly concludes.

Then Kravitz comes to the point. "Then came September 24, 1869. Black Friday. The price of gold dropped like a jumper from a Wall Street ledge. In one day, Speyer was a ruined and mocked man. He lost everything."

"He should have sold," Molly says.

"He should have known a good thing. Out here, he had it made. Back in New York, he was tied up by high-rollers who would just as soon stick their hands through his back and pull out his heart before he could drop. The kind of people, Molly, who see friendship as nothing more than a word to manipulate people..." He doesn't finish.

She clears her throat. "...are the most successful people in the country."

"Depends on how you define success."

Molly looks around, checking The Elk's empty booths. "So what happens now?"

Unpredictable as ever, the vintage Rockola jumps to life, the speakers blasting out The Shannon Rover's rendition of Garry Owen, the regimental battle song of the 7th Cavalry. Beneath the blaring bagpipes he can hear Bear laughing, the laughter echoing and echoing before fading out.

"First thing, I've got to get that damn juke box fixed." He sets his coffee down on the bar, walks over and smacks the jukebox the way Bear used to. Then closes his fist and strikes it hard again. When he does, the vision of a four-year-old boy separated from his mother on Chicago's 1968 streets returns.

He is running after her, crying, but the cops are ahead of him. When she falls they are onto her like wild beasts, their batons coming down hard and fast. His father being held by four, still struggling, screaming, "She's pregnant! For godsakes stop!!!" But they don't. And she lost the fetus. Now buried at boot hill, a casualty of shattered idealism. After that, his mother was unable to conceive again.

Red's hand keep smashing the jukebox, unable even to make the needle jump as the words poured out of the speakers

Let bacchus' sons be not dismayed
But join with me each jovial blade
Come booze and sing, and lend your aid...

Richard Daley, the Chicago mayor who had sanctioned his mother's brutal beating, went into the ground to those words, the lyrics of Garry Owen, the last small town that Red and Bear had passed through after entering the Crow reservation to fish together for the last time. Cutthroat trout, three ways.

His whole life spins and turns on that song as it takes him back over a hundred years, his Indian eyes melting into a mental state, watching Libbie Custer as she stands pale and trembling, hearing the regimental drum corp and fifes riff through the same bars briskly, the rearguard of the Seventh Cavalry dissolving into the morning mist, the strains of music fading with the images, until nothing is left but the comforting hand of Bertram Holloway on her shoulder, and "Back in triumph for the Centennial. From there, the White House. For a man like your husband, there are no limits."

With the troopers heading for the Little Bighorn rides a company of soldiers under Major Marcus Reno. These men are more cautious and less hopeful than their younger comrades. They have been warned by a Crow scout, a distant relative of Red Kravitz named Staring Eagle, about the strength of the Northern Cheyenne and Sioux. Reno shares none of Custer's Aryan ideas about the superiority of white troops. His close advisor is a sergeant, a galvanized Yankee named Jeremiah Jarnow, whose poverty makes the army his only hope of getting west, and his subsequent desertion his only means of escaping the army.

But he is desperately loyal under fire, as is Staring Eagle. It becomes the only combat in the Indian wars where Crows fight side-by-side with whites. For the only company that survives the battle that day, the one in which Standing Bear's great-grandfather Elk That Drinks is felled by a single bullet from a rifle by... the records are unclear... two men fire at the same moment: Staring Eagle and Jeremiah Jarnow, just as Elk That Drinks is about to drive Marcus Reno into the spirit world with one savage stroke of the pagamoggon.

"So what now?" Molly repeats. Then he takes her eyes, eyes that could pull any man in, and answers her question, "That's to find out." He recovers his coffee from the bar, finishes it in one gulp. "Gotta go."

She watches him square his hat and pull open the door. "Cold out," he says. "Be sure to button up, hear?"

* * *

Mo's official SUV sloshes through half-thawed snow in the shadow of town hall, then brakes to a halt. Grunting as he steps down, he rubs a yawn off his face before asking, "You got java, Red?"

"We call it that." They drum down brittle risers and fetch cups from beside the urn next to Doris's desk.

Mo plays at the dark viscous surface with a probing finger. Once inside Red's office, he closes the door, risks a sip and winces. "We cut open Mona. It was a baby of color. About four months. She didn't show much for that far along."

"So it was Walsh."

Mo shakes his head. "Nope. Of color. Not black."

"Then what?"

"The unborn showed signs of fetal alcohol syndrome. You see a lot of that on res'. Mostly still-births."

"It wasn't me," Red tells him.

"Red, I heard Bear say that Mona had the hots for you. Then there was that call from Mona to Jarnow about you the night Holloway got shot. I just figured..."

"I didn't do it," he says.

Making it clear why B.S. Walsh asked Red to check out the rumor that Mona was fucking her way through every man in Sanctuary. At last it was all hanging together. Mona pregnant by Bear. Jeb finding out, calling for a meeting. Making Bear HIM on Jeb's calendar.

Crazy Daisy saw Bear riding the Appaloosa Indian-style to Poker

Bluff. While panning for gold at Sidewinder Twist, Noisy heard the report, looked up and saw him. Two witnesses became victims, and the illusive killer might pass into the legends of the modern west. But for one thing: Bear figured Mona out.

With Jeb dead she could claim Bear raped her, then killed her husband. Her call to Jarnow claiming Red had come onto her was really a signal to Bear: Out here in white man's country the tragic widow of a God-fearing Republican candidate would be believed. Especially against a maniacally violent ex-football player known to be a skirt chaser in Dallas, a man violent enough to knock the life out of another player, even without the assistance of the most powerful single-shot killing machine the old west had ever known.

At this point in the investigation Bear had a serious problem. At least until B.S. Walsh became a suspect, and Red unearthed an ugly past that should have been buried by the witness protection program. Enter a much better suspect, a rapist and murderer, a man known to be slipping Mona the evil snake. So Bear played it that way, and, as promised, kills the man in a show of protecting Red. Maybe, if Bear hadn't shot Len Jarnow, they never would have figured it all out.

In fact, up to that point the same arguments and motivation that Red has just pointed at Bear, and the same skills with a horse and Sharps could just as well be turned around and directed at Red himself, as Mo had just figured out.

So why did Bear kill Jarnow?

Then it hit him.

The land where Daisy had squatted, the land that Holloway had planned to use for time-share condominium, would soon be Jarnow's as the sole surviving claimant to the property. As Slo Lehrner revealed, under that land lay shale, natural gas, probably oil. Soon to be claimed by a U.S. Senator with access to back room deals the voters would never suspect.

Maybe before that, it had all been part of Bear's deal with both Holloways: get rid of Daisy, leave no witnesses. We'll trade with Jarnow: the land for Jeb's withdrawal from the Senate race. Then Bear could have the condominium, a job tending bar at Bearpaw and all the white women he could handle.

Had the plan panned out, it would have been a resurrection for a man who tended bar in a dusty little town on a dirt road at the end of nowhere. Molly would have been proud. Bear was ambitious. He had almost learned to play the white man's game.

Did Bear really figure that killing Jarnow would solve his problems? It could have. Disappearing into Timberland created the same jurisdictional hassle that was miring down the Holloway investigation.

Maybe that was Bear's bet when he crossed Big Muddy. Pursuit required a savvy tracker familiar with the terrain. Escape required the same skills. Thus reinstating the FBI's choice, Dave Dooley, as prime suspect.

If Red had stayed put on Poker Bluff and turned things over to the Feds, Bear could easily have ditched the horse and doubled back during the night. Some witnesses believed that during that critical period of time he was at his place on Pine Ridge. Others swore they'd seen him at the Bearpaw lodge. The prosecutor had to prove otherwise. And no local jury hereabouts would let the state tear out the heart, soul and guts of Sanctuary on empty speculation.

Bear had more than rights; he had friends and admirers. He was not required to help chase some maniac killer.

But catching that maniac was Red's obsession. Lacking authority, ignoring the danger of getting shot off his horse, Kravitz had followed. Still, Bear seemed to have planned for that, as if his vision saw straight through the present into the spirit world.

If not, it was sure a good act.

It had even fooled Red. And only when Red showed himself to be too white to cut a deal did Bear consider killing him. Bear might have wanted him to think, jeez, this man I never knew, this man who's killed six people, this man I love, is so scared he's going to shoot me!

Offer a deal!

Any deal!

Because Bear knew that once Red had given his word, he wouldn't go back on it. If a bargain had been struck, Bear would have been left to whatever kind of justice the Great Spirit had in mind.

But that option was shattered by a card-carrying NRA marksman and expert horsewoman. Strange what men don't know about the woman they think they love. They never ask questions. They never seem to be able to get beyond the momentary focus to reflect on who this person is that's literally charming their pants off.

So in truth women cannot be accused as much of being secretive as men can of being unconcerned, of taking aspects presented at face value and never looking deeper. Because with ambitious people, red or white, there's always something deeper.

Red's mind returns to Mo, sitting across from him in the Indian's eternal present. "I need to establish I'm not the father."

"I can't justify DNA analysis when you're not a suspect, Red."

"Can't I pay someone to do it?"

"What's the point? We'd have to necropsy the fetus, too. And that's state's evidence. You'd need a court order to do that. And people would wonder why, unless you're back on the suspect list."

"Wait. You're saying I was on it?"

"Seth Diehl talked to you, right? Unless I push another way, he'll recommend they drop it. The politicos don't want a whiff of scandal till after the election."

"And then?"

Mo puts down his cup. "Red, I did what you asked. Not that I thought we had much hope, but we looked at the belduque was planted in Noisy's back. We lifted prints."

This is the bow that could wrap up the case against Bear.

Mo swallows hard, looks down, then back up, struggling to deliver the news. "They was yours, Red. None but yours."

"From when I reached back behind Noisy to pull his body out that night, never expecting — "

"Well that's what Micky and me already figured, yup. You hang in there, Red. We'll get you through this without a tarnish. You just see." Mo gets up. "Still like to know what in the hell Doris puts in this coffee."

A memory of Bear emerges, almost palpable. Lending him a grim smile. "Some questions we'll never know the answers to."

"And some, if we don't, people will make up their own answers. That's not what we want here," Mo says.

BOOT HILL BLUES

Sanctuary's mayor shows up only if he has a problem. So when Augie Suder drops in with a pained look, it bodes ill. Kravitz braces for it with a smile. "Have a chair, your honor." He grabs the spare, drags it to the desk. "Coffee?"

Augie winces. "Thanks but no. Doctor says I'm off that. And booze if you can believe it. Ulcer."

"When did all this happen?" Red wants to know.

"After the killing started. Specialist says it's bacteria, so I'm on antibiotics."

Red sips at a fresh cup of black death, dwelling on things money can't buy. For those things, you want there to be a God. For those things, you'd like to see the righteous parceled out some compensatory rewards.

"What brings you around?" Red asks.

Hizzoner squirms, produces an envelope and centers it on the ink blotter.

Red draws it in. "Any severance pay?"

A look of puzzlement precedes, "You thinking of quitting?"

"Isn't that what this is about?"

The mayor scratches his head. "No. It's from Bear. His last will and testament."

Kravitz: "Didn't know he had one."

"'Bout three weeks ago he come in. I advised he run it by an estate lawyer but he just asked what it needed to be legal. I told him: of free will and sound mind, dated and signed and witnessed."

In Red's understanding, Montana law requires three witnesses, so he raises the issue.

The mayor gives him the names: "Doris, Moonlight and me."

Bear's timing showed an awareness, as Indians often see in dreams and visions, that he was soon going to die. Red stares at the envelope until Augie erupts, "It's not a goddamn letter bomb, Red. Jesus, you think after Ted Kaczinski and all that's happened lately I wouldn't have Luke Brody check it out down the P.O?"

Kravitz continues to stare at it.

Augie rails, "Look, only reason I rushed in here, deputy, is that when the boys up in Great Falls get around to officially announcing that a renegade Indian was a serial killer, we'll have to deal with the victims' rights issue and..."

"All the victims are dead," Red declares, slitting open the flap with the blade of his knife. "If they've got any rights, they'll need to argue them in a higher court."

The mayor gets huffy, the way he does when he's been out-reasoned by an upstart Ivy-league half-breed. "It's for the survivors of the victims, Red. That's what it's for."

Red lays out the contents on his ink blotter and asks, "Survivors? Who's Daisy got to stand up for her? Or Noisy? Or Bass Sanders? Who ever stood up for people like that? Besides, all Bear had to his name was The Elk and a half-finished dream house."

"Boy, he really kept you in the dark. Maybe it's because you're a Crow."

Red's face heats as if struck. "So you tell me, Mr. Mayor. Was Bear an eccentric millionaire working a piss-ass bar in a dying town, the Howard Hughes of Sanctuary?"

The question makes Augie burst into seal-like laughter. "Bear didn't talk much to anyone but you. Only thing everybody else in Sanctuary could pretty much guess: there's not a lot of white things he put much stock in. But he had white stocks. One of his Dallas teammates, some buzz-cut redneck sort of guy who plugged up the middle of the defensive line...what was his name? From Nebraska? You know who I'm talking about."

Red admits. "Never followed football." A shrug, then, "Sorry."

The mayor scratches his scalp, erupting a plume of dandruff, then continues. "Anyway, he got these investments. Then let them set. Perfect strategy for a long-term hold. Bottom line: your friend Bear liked to play the run-down bedraggled Injun. But in private gave me this old Cheyenne wisdom: 'Where many small streams meet, a mighty river forms.'"

Red smiles at the way native Americans knew more about whites than they knew about themselves.

As the smile faded, Augie flicks a hand through the air and asks, "You gonna look at the check?"

"How'd you know there's a check?"

"I'm the executor of the goddamn will, dummy."

"You read Bear's message, too?"

"Nope. Why?"

"Well, Augie, we all have our secrets. Some might get us in trouble. I suspect there was some of that kind of stuff on your computer when you started dumping files the night Walsh bid his final adieu."

"You got your killer, Red. Sorry it was your best friend. Truly I am. But the case is closed." Red unpins the deputy's badge and lays it on the ink blotter. "I'm asking as a friend. I'd just like to know is all."

Augie stares at the badge, then back at Red. "What the hell. I was destroying all my e mail files that night."

"Why?"

Augie burps, then fights on. "Mona sent me one. Inviting me to deal all-night faro up the bunk house. Lose some money, win some votes. Said she'd bankroll the game. This is the night before Jeb Holloway was shot dead."

Red remembers it, but hadn't put it all together before. "So Mona knew about this game beforehand?"

"Knew?" Augie barks a laugh, punctuated by a weak fart. "She showed up around eight-thirty in the A.M. and played through until say ten-thirty. Fifteen witnesses and the town mayor would swear she couldn't have shot Jeb. So destroying the computer files spared me a summons where I'd have to admit what some fancy climber of a D.A. might make to look like Mona and me conspired to alibi each other while Jeb was gettin' shot."

Which means that she hadn't been with B.S. Walsh, explains the buffalo soldier's urge to split, which might have allowed Mona Holloway to set him as the patsy. But to be sure Red asks, "Any reason you'd've objected to Jeb being dead?"

The mayor massages his stomach and grimaces. "Truth is, or was, that Jeb had promised to take me to Washington with him."

"Jeb went to his damnation with a lot of uncollected markers against him."

Augie rolls on. "And there was e mail 'twixt me and Jeb, about what I might want to do in D.C. other than drugs and women. I dumped that stuff because I figured if I become a big help to Jarnow, Len would show his generosity and take me back east, too."

Red has to try hard to smile. "Jesus, Augie. Then who'd be mayor?"

"Bearpaw may still bounce back. If so, it wouldn't be a bad little place to be. So I figured... you know..." he shrugs "...with your reputation for honesty, maybe..."

Red stares through the mayor so hard it shuts him up.

At least until he asks, "Aren't you gonna read Bear's letter?"

Kravitz walls off the open letter with his arms and and reads in privacy:

You're still alive, Crow.

How'd that happen, against a Sharps and me?

You must've had help.

Whoever it is, you owe them a life. Don't forget that.

Here's something to start over.

Hand the mayor your badge, Red.

When Mona wanted you to fuck her

You should've known.

Don't spend it all in one place you lucky half-blood bastard.

Your brother,

Standing Bear of the Northern Cheyenne

Red shoves his badge across the desktop, and into the mayor's lap.

"What's this about?" Augie demands.

"Honoring a warrior's last request."

"Now who else is gonna do this job?"

"Some questions we'll never know the answers to," Kravitz says, studying the check. On seeing $600,000, the adrenaline burns through him. His eyes go back to the mayor. "This was his idea?"

Augie Suder admits, "Mine. Like I said, Red. He didn't care about money. For some reason he thought you might."

"You're that sure what Bear was thinking?"

The mayor's eyebrows arch. "He was a very complex man for a savage."

Red half-smiles. "As good an epitaph as any."

"Glad you decided, Red, since he wanted to be buried in boot hill."

He wonders why Bear didn't prefer a ceremonial burial ground near the Little Bighorn on tribal land. But Bear was always a shrewd bar-dog, and knew that when they got a hankering for hootch, res' redskins might charge admission.

The only sound reason for Bear's last request seems to be a statement: real native Americans lived and died right beside whites. They weren't villains; they didn't pretend to be heroes. They knew the land, the water, the wind; belonged to them, felt those forces to their core. As much as any people who lived, they belonged here.

But for all that, Kravitz still isn't willing to believe that Bear would rest easy lying next to men who'd shot his unarmed ancestors dead for the raw fun of it. And so he asks Augie, "You're sure on this?"

"I just advised him that he should address all concerns that might arise in the event of his death. You have to admit that burial would be near the top."

"I'll pay for it," Red announces.

"No need. I made him leave a set-aside."

The deputy closes his eyes and squeezes the bridge of his nose. "Buy him a bigger headstone, something special. Bring down the boys from the Hollow-A who used to hole up at The Elk. We'll open it up and raise a glass."

The mayor rises. "He'd've liked that."

Red looks up. "He'll be there."

* * *

A week later on boot hill Kravitz stands admiring the crimson marble headstone on Standing Bear's grave. Its uppers are sculpted like the stuffed silverback Grizzly that guarded the back room at The Elk. If you look hard, you can see Bear laughing through the critter's eyes. On each side of the base runs gold-plated panels. Three remained blank. Red's idea. To symbolize Bear's many facets. Like other men, some aspects were so well hidden they may never be known. In the end, you're left not with what you know, but what you want to believe.

On the front, beneath the snarling marble Bear, Red used Augie's remark:

For a Savage, though, he was a very Complex Man

Do only savages resent the extermination of their kind? How much difference is there between Manifest Destiny and Lebensraum other than a hundred uninstructive years?

As clearly as yesterday, awake or in dreams, he still remembers that terrible Chicago night, down to the ache of teargas in his nose. He remembers being swirled and jostled, knocked to the pavement when he tried to reunite with his mother, down and pummeled by the endless rain of batons, seeing his father's face bloodied and his body bent as he fought to help her. And knows he is wrong.

In America there is room for many kinds. It's new ideas that raise the devil in the too common man. Of that he's certain.

Seven days of warming have melted the snow and ushered in a surreal Indian summer. The sea-blue sky buoyed a drifting armada of ivory clouds. Mercury in the vintage thermometer at town hall passed seventy. A breeze light as a virgin's first kiss caresses sallow pin grass. Yet the passing air bears the sour odor of decay that comes when all life gives up and hunkers down till next spring.

Gliding along a lazy arc, the albino sun stays pale and cool, a ghost of summer's fury. Miles north, Big Muddy narrows and splits, sluicing down braided channels. Hands from the Hollow-A line up on Sidewinder Twist, going knee-deep in icy water searching for float gold. Most likely out of work, they are left with only dreams.

In the aqueous ribbon tying sources in the Rockies to the Gulf of Mexico, not one new fleck of gold appears. Or brass either. Neither riches nor evidence to help solve a puzzle that kept and keeps Red as sleepless as Ivan Konev.

Both Noisy and Walsh had been fools. Fools and dreamers, like most men who galloped west betting their lives on crazy ideas and unfounded hope. What remains is the steady silvery trickle dearer than gold. Without it, mother earth would dry up and blow away. Precious and rare, water is an innocently democratic wealth, for none and all in equal measure.

Kravitz stares at the gravestone, unable to stop wondering.

Maybe Bear was the last wild Indian, the kind that the U.S. government had billed as a scalper of helpless children, raper of white women, a scourge that had to be eliminated in an us-or-them contest. Indian hunter Phil Sheridan was the harbinger voice of Hitler for that campaign, one that left its dazed and shattered tribal survivors to wonder how they could go on.

Kravitz melts in deja vu. With the Righteous Aryan Bundsmen close by, a gathering storm of graffiti waits to usher in a new wave of killings. Political rectitude frowns on all this, for no deeper reason than to harvest votes.

But with the election just two days off, the Republicans have no surviving candidate. Unneedful of the anti-Bush rage now sweeping the country, the Democrats will win because the other players had become latter-day Wild Bill Hickoks, shot dead while holding winning hands.

Into the silence embracing his thoughts intrudes an almost inaudible scraping of gravel. But Red ignores it. The breeze shifts, carrying the unforgettable scent of Forbidden Pleasure to his nostrils. Reflexively he turns, finding Molly's hair bannering in the wind. She rakes it back with delicate fingers. "Doris said you'd be up here."

"Come to bid farewell?"

"Not really." She drops her glance, ambles forward and stares at the grave. "I was thinking. This plot of earth could have been yours."

"Except for you, is what you're saying?"

She blinks. "Can you say for sure he wouldn't have killed you?"

After a long silence he admits, "Nobody could. But I was the first person he was faced with killing that he called brother."

"I'm figuring he slept with Mona a lot," she says.

"You can tell that?" he wonders.

"Every time. A woman picks up on things. Exchanges of glances, the way a body stiffens or relaxes when another person is around, even when they just talk about that other person."

"Sounds a lot like suspicion to me," Red guesses.

"Intuition. It's different."

A long silence draws out while they both fix on Bear's grave. Then Molly asks, "Did you sleep with her?"

He turns back and stares at Bear's grave. "There's nothing she wanted from me just recently that I could've given her. She'd seen the way Bear played football, the raw power and venom when he hit a white man. Then Mona must've said Jeb was out to kill him."

"A set up?"

Red thinks not. "If Bear had come up beside Jeb in that Suburban down by Big Muddy, it would've been Bear's head blown open. It was a genuine wild west shoot-out. Bear just got a weapon to extend the range. Ironic that it was the very weapon Jeb's kin used to kill the bison and seal the Indian's fate."

She inches closer. "You think I came back to hear this?"

He looks away and draws a long breath. "Molly, I don't know what you want. But I'd still trust Bear more than you."

"You're forgetting one thing."

"And that is?"

"You're a Crow. But you're also half-Jewish. Not the best poster child for the resurrection of the Plains Indians."

"What's that got to do with the price of beads in Manhattan?"

"Maybe nothing. But the Jews were the ones who built the supply lines for the settlement of the west." She tips her head toward his trading post. "Like Albert Speyer, the ones who were the merchants and financiers and engineers, the ones who went to unsettled places because in every place that was settled, prejudice chased them out."

He can't dispute it. "There's all of that. But Mormons hereabout reckon that Indians are descendants of the Lost Tribes of Israel. And if Injuns and Jews are related, and Aryan whites wanted us exterminated, there's a nice connection between Sand Creek and Auschwitz."

"This is a theory?"

"I'm all out of theories. I just want to say goodbye to a friend."

"How about the person who saved you from him?"

He stares at her. "Molly? Why are you here, really?"

"Well...you remember that anchor job I was after in Atlanta?"

"They offered it to someone else."

She dips her chin. "Yeah, it seems the appointee was providing the decision-maker with an additional incentive."

"Looks like you were in the wrong bed at the wrong time," he says, kicking frozen dust with the toe of his boot.

"You're still a little too pissed off about that story I made up."

"Kind of blew the center out of my public image."

"So you feel that your job as Sanctuary's deputy is in jeopardy?"

"I'm not deputy anymore. And Sanctuary is just a ghost town just waiting on the ghosts to take over. All the people under this earth, they'll inherit."

"And you?" she asks.

He has no answer, and so asks, "What about you?"

After taking her own deep breath she announces, "They've given me co-anchor for election day coverage."

"Who'd you have to sleep with for that?" he asks.

She smiles and gives him the finger. "It was a consolation prize."

"Are you consoled?"

She ignores the question. "And there's going to be a book, maybe even a movie, about Standing Bear's killings."

He stabs his hands into the rear pockets of his Wranglers. "And you need someone who knew him well."

"Look. What I did. I was desperate. Trying to get on top of something to peek up over the damn run-up to the Iraq invasion. I hoped I could run a tag with enough juice to get me the nod for anchor. I risked everything and still lost."

"Blinded by the glitter, is that it?"

"Something like that."

"Molly, the wind just blows through me. I don't even know if I'm really here."

"You look it, Red. You look lost and staring at a future that doesn't have any shape. You're not old enough to die, but you're still young enough to start over."

"As what?"

"Doctor, lawyer, Indian chief?"

"That's one of the things I always admired about you. You never had one doubt..."

"I was a good actress," she admits, throwing off a shrug.

He hitches his thumbs over his concha belt and cocks his head. "So what happens now?"

"That's the question, isn't it?"

RISING SON

Luke Brody delivered Slo Lehrner's registered package to Red at Bear's dream house on Pine Ridge, encamped within forty acres of country so wondrous that even the Great Spirit must be envious. Red has finished the place, leaving all inside as he'd found it, honoring the Cheyenne's design plans, down to the size and shape of dovetails.

Knowing his best friend's intentions, he placed a single photograph on the east wall. Dressed in fatigues and cradling an M-16, Tom Whitefeather of the Seventh Cavalry looks down from a Huey just hours before he was killed. On the opposite wall hangs Gustav Klimt's haunting portrait of a pregnant woman that Holloway family lawyers catalogued 'missing' after the final inventory of the estate.

While uncertain what drove Bear to murder six people, Kravitz cannot let go until he understands what happened. Not the sound-bite quick-and-easy CNN version that Molly delivered, but the one that wells up from a deeper level, a place he can feel in the timbers and stones of this grand and lonely lodge.

As he opens the envelope's flap, Red feels glad that Molly is on assignment, because she developed the grating habit of reading his mail. And she also proved that ambitious reporters will actually kill for a great story.

Compared to that, reading his mail is a peccadillo. He extracts and unfolds the cover letter inside the package, settling back to read it.

Happy Chanukah, Savage,

Your recent request disturbed me. To ask an old nuclear salt for a low-level waste disposal container smacks of deeply troubled souls like our friends in the Righteous Aryan Bund. But I wasn't alarmed until you sent it back. Even then, I was convinced that you were sufficiently unlike Standing Bear that I could, with confidence, open the metal box without finding body parts. Okay, you promised me a Chanukah bonus for digging up the skinny on Jeb. So here I am with $100,000, still wondering what the hell to do except send it back.

Slo's style is so conversational that Red asks the silence, "Why?"

At this point I ask for your confidence that I did not betray you in taking some part-time work for Pete Rollins while he was chasing this maniac killer, too. We all wanted this schmuck caught, right? But you may be surprised to know this was not Rollins's agenda. The murder was a convenient way to get a federal presence into Sanctuary. Nothing more. Once here, Rollins wanted me to tie Bearpaw in with organized crime. I'll bet $100K they planned to use the ski resort to launder money, selling lift tickets and room charges to phantom skiers.

As if he were reading over Red's shoulder, Pete Rollins's voice leaps out of their past chatter, words spoken which had until now escaped full comprehension, "Washington thinks Holloway's killing is...deliberate and professional... Dave Dooley is under the legal limit for this kind of operation. We've got other fish to fry..."

Red fights through the wave of shock, returns to Slo's words:

But I check this out, and so far, nothing. Dead end.

Is it? Red's mind swirls with new possibilities. Standing Bear was incapable of murder, unless motivated by something deeply personal. Except in fanatical groups, Americans who are ideologically driven killers are extremely rare. Hands trembling, Red returns to Slo's letter.

There was something I ran into during that search to find out if Mona was pregnant. One angle I tried was breaking into medical files of all men who might have been involved with her (yes, even you). Upshot, mostly a big zip. But I turn up something else. Bear visited a clinic in Bozeman. Diagnosis: pancreatic cancer. Stage II or III. Three to six months before the real dying begins. That's it. And so he had to ask what he was going to do with his life. You're a smart Jewish boy, Kravitz. You figure out the rest. I've got cats to feed.

Your grateful fellow tribesman,

Slo

Red walks the folded letter to the fireplace. With a snap of the wrist, he flicks it in. In seconds, golden flames reduce it to ashes. Stepping away from the mantle, he rubs his arms and opens the inner envelope, finding Slo has actually returned the money. All in hundreds, a thousand of them. Two layers of twenty wrapped bundles. Forty neat packages of twenty-five each, just as he had received it via a low-level radioactive water container.

Shooting through the trees just outside Bear's huge glass window, swooping low, an eagle flaps by, distracting Kravitz. Then he looks around. And smiles. Because things finally make sense. All of it.

Stunning as it is, this place that Red has finished to honor his friend's generosity is nothing of Bear. This is where Bear planned for Mona to move once the divorce from Jeb was final, even if she lost everything in court. Maybe it wasn't until Bear saw the bruises that Jeb was putting on the future mother of his child that he got angry enough to kill the man.

Even then, Mona was smart enough to find a chump to take the fall. What did it matter to them? Mona was already pregnant by Bear. She wasn't going to get knocked up by Walsh. But when Jeb asked who the man was, it was Walsh's name that would drive Jeb mad, take him out onto the pebbled banks of Big Muddy to finish it the way that Holloways had for over a hundred years.

Once Bear knew he was dying, killing Jeb Holloway was essential. It had nothing to do with politics or elections or grievances. As often in violence, it was personal and it was passionate. But Bear still wanted Mona. Ached for her in fact.

So he couldn't have any witnesses obstructing the possibility that with Jeb dead, they could live out whatever remained of their love together, a Byronic old west ending. But dying lovers are jealous lovers, so Walsh was a marked man. He must have sensed that. One thing a lawman can see in a man's eye is fear. Red had just misinterpreted it as guilt.

So Bear kept his vow and killed Walsh. From the number of wounds, a couple of times over. For the satisfaction of slaying the man who was sleeping with his lover, the same rage that drew Jeb to Poker Bluff. With women like Mona the best laid plans often lead to murder.

Without ever exposing herself to risk, Mona was at the center of the web connecting all the players. Married to Jeb, manipulator of Augie Suder, partnered with Jarnow at Bearpaw, lover to Bear, user of Walsh, co-claimant to Daisy's squatting ground, imagined rival to Molly, boss to twenty-six reluctant witnesses, temptress even to Red himself. Always at the center of things, never in the gunsights. Until Bear understood from her drinking that she was destroying the only chance he had, the child inside of her.

Only then did he see the hand she was playing, all the cards face up, the ante raised beyond his means and no other response but rage at her betrayal. That's the way it goes with controlling women, the way they keep pushing the edge, betting they'll be left standing while the others take the fall. It's what they live for, and in this case, died for.

So you've got to be careful with that kind of she-critter. Right now that is the only lesson that Red Kravitz is certain he will take away from all this. And so when the phone begins to ring, he stares at it and waits. But the ringer jangles six, seven, eight times. At last he ambles over and picks up, answering with a simple. "Yeah."

"I'm in Mozambique," Molly's voice says. The link is clear and flawless, as if she were standing in the same room. "The floods are back. People are dying."

"Lots of them I guess," Red says.

"Tens of thousands. They ride swollen corpses of cows down raging rivers. The currents sweep some along with their children. They hang onto their kids until the parents start to sink. Then they push their own kids under to stay afloat. It's horrible."

"Except for the ratings," he says.

"The rebels are eating babies. They make the mothers watch, then gang rape them. After the last rebel is through, they slit her throat and eat her, too."

"If you get the recipes, you may find a publisher in New York. And a catchy title: Out of Africa: Manna for a Starving World."

"Don't be so goddamn cynical, Kravitz. People have the right to know. This is a human tragedy of unparalleled proportions. This is really happening."

Free from the confusion of trees, the passing eagle is now free, rising on a gentle thermal, able better to reckon the shape of the forest below.

"Are you going to help them?" Red wants to know.

A long pause ends in, "I couldn't hear you. What?"

"Are you going to help them? Bring medicine, enlist drug companies, recruit doctors, raise money, hire mercenaries, get the U.N. to intervene? At least throw a few life rings out of the choppers?"

"We aren't equipped for a rescue mission."

Red is feeling ornery. "Well, there's a hopeful spin you could put on it, Mol'. Just add a tag line that drowning is quicker and less painful than AIDS, which is what half of them would face if they made it to shore."

Molly injects a twenty-first century perspective. "This is a big story, don't you see that?"

"A career-maker. Will you stick around long enough to learn something from it?"

"You're breaking up again," Molly claims, but there's nothing wrong on his end except the message he's getting. "I've got a refueled plane waiting. And we're taking mortar fire. I've got to go."

This is the woman he once felt that he couldn't live without. Deciding when it ends, plucking at the silky strings of the web, at the patient center of her own plans, checking for trapped men and unobstructed exits.

"Goodbye Molly," he says, realizing at last why Molly had been suspicious of Mona.

"I love you, Red."

In a vomit-like reflex, Red Kravitz starts laughing. It shakes him like a Grizzly, hard and brutal and nonstop, until his ribs hurt. The sound gathers force like a skookum wind. It consumes him, floods his eyes to overflowing with tears, peels from his lungs and rises to the high ceiling, filling his head in crescendoing echoes until he drops the handset, falls to his knees and covers his ears.

And still there is no stopping it.

Until the crack of a large caliber rifle rings off the ridge, shedding echoes that reach until they die, Red is hysterical. Then he is flat, his hands over his neck, horrified that he has been wrong, everyone has been wrong, that the nightmare is not over. But slowly he comes up, realizing it's November 6. Hunting season again. Punctuating this realization, another report again shatters the tranquility.

Not a Sharps, he decides. Probably .30/06.

Having been the Deputy Sheriff of Sanctuary most of his life, his finds this identity too deep to ignore. So he picks himself up off the floor and drifts to the big window intended for the eyes of two dreamers, looks out and checks around.

High and away, like a shape-shifter entering the spirit world of a long-forgotten era, the rising eagle has transited a blind sun and vanished. All that remains, as clear and true as the moment sought in a vision quest, just audible above the static crackling through the dead line from Mozambique, is the steady rustling of the majestic bird's wings, beating through an unseen heaven like the last true Indian's heart.

CPSIA information can be obtained at www.ICGtesting.com
Printed in the USA
BVOW05s1800110916

461474BV00001B/3/P

9 780997 974805